Warbo

WARBOW

Book 9 in the Lord Edward's Archer series

By Griff Hosker

Warbow

Published by Sword Books Ltd 2025

Copyright ©Griff Hosker 2025

The author has asserted their moral right under the Copyright, Designs and Patents Act, 1988, to be identified as the author of this work.

All Rights reserved. No part of this publication may be reproduced, copied, stored in a retrieval system, or transmitted, in any form or by any means, without the prior written consent of the copyright holder, nor be otherwise circulated in any form of binding or cover other than that in which it is published and without a similar condition being imposed on the subsequent purchaser.

A CIP catalogue record for this title is available from the British Library.

No generative artificial intelligence (AI) was used in the writing of this work. The author expressly prohibits any entity from using this publication for purposes of training AI technologies to generate text, including without limitation technologies that are capable of generating works in the same style or genre as this publication. The author reserves all rights to license use of this work for generative AI training and development of machine learning language models.

Warbow

About the Author

Griff Hosker was born in St Helens, Lancashire in 1950. A former teacher, an avid historian and a passionate writer, Griff has penned around 200 novels, which span over 2000 years of history and almost 20 million words, all meticulously researched. Walk with legendary kings, queens and generals across battlefields; picture kingdoms as they rise and fall and experience history as it comes alive. Welcome to an adventure through time with Griff.

For more information, please head over to Griff's website and sign up for his mailing list. Griff loves to engage with his readers and welcomes you to get in touch.

www.griffhosker.com
X: @HoskerGriff
Facebook: Griff Hosker at Sword Books

Contents

Prologue 1
Chapter 1 4
Chapter 2 16
Chapter 3 28
Chapter 4 39
Chapter 5 49
Chapter 6 62
Chapter 7 72
Chapter 8 83
Chapter 9 97
Chapter 10 109
Chapter 11 120
Chapter 12 132
Chapter 13 144
Chapter 14 155
Chapter 15 166
Chapter 16 178
Chapter 17 189
Chapter 18 200
Epilogue 212
Glossary 213
Historical Note 215
Other books by Griff Hosker 217

Warbow

Real characters who are mentioned in the novel.

King Edward II of England
Queen Isabella of England
Queen Margaret of England
Edmund Crouchback - 1st Earl of Lancaster and King Edward's brother
Thomas 2nd Earl of Lancaster - son of Edmund Crouchback
Henry Lacy - Earl of Lincoln and Constable of Chester
William de Beauchamp - 9th Earl of Warwick
Walter Langton - Bishop of Coventry and Lincoln and the King's Treasurer
Robert de Brus - 6th Lord of Annandale and Earl of Carrick and latterly King Robert 1st of Scotland
John Balliol - Lord of Galloway and Barnard Castle and, latterly, King of Scotland
John Comyn - claimant to the Scottish throne, supporter of Balliol and enemy to de Brus
Antony Bek - Bishop of Durham
Sir John de Warenne - 6th Earl of Surrey and John Balliol's father-in-law
Henry Percy - 1st Baron Percy
Henry de Beaumont - French Mercenary
Arnaud de Gabaston - the father of Piers Gaveston
Piers Gaveston - Earl of Cornwall, a favourite of King Edward
Aymer de Valence - Earl of Pembroke
Robert de Clifford - Lord Warden of the Marches
Roger Mortimer, 3rd Baron Mortimer of Wigmore, 1st Earl of March
Roger Mortimer, 1st Baron Mortimer of Chirk, the uncle of Roger Mortimer
Lady Hawise ferch Owain ap Gruffudd ap Gwenwynwyn - heir to Powis and known as Hawise the Hardy
Griffith de la Pole - heir to Powis Wenwynwyn and elder brother of Lady Hawise
John Charleton - later 1st Baron Charleton, Lord of Powis
Thomas Charleton - Sir John's brother, a member of King Edward's retinue and a future Bishop of Hereford
Gruffydd Fychan de la Pole - one of the uncles of Lady Hawise
Gilbert de Clare - Earl of Hereford.
Adam Orleton - Bishop of Hereford.

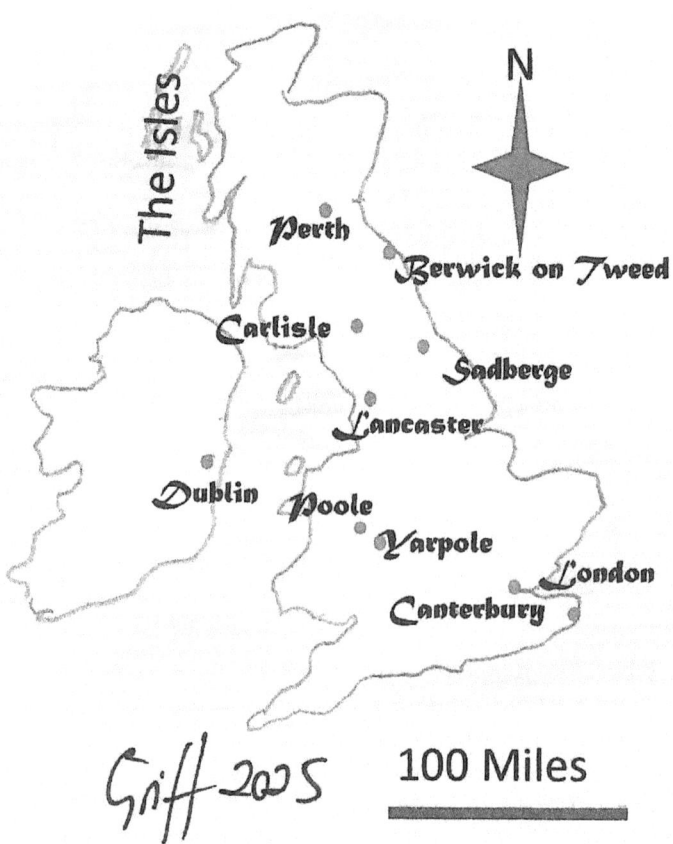

England in 1300

Warbow

Prologue

The Tabard, Southwark January 1308
The innkeeper saw the four men enter his inn and was curious, not to say downright suspicious of their purpose and presence. His inn had a variety of customers, from pilgrims heading to Canterbury and the shrine of St Thomas to merchants travelling to the Cinque Ports. These four were different for whilst they all wore rough and ready cloaks with hoods, their boots marked them as men of substance and they did not look like pilgrims. Their swords and scabbards were the swords of lords and not the usual customers. For that reason he attended to them himself. He had doxies who could serve them but if they were who he thought they were, then he would be the only one to bear the burden of knowledge. He smiled as he asked what they wanted and noticed that none of them showed his face when they answered. They were meeting in secret. They asked for sack, bread and ham. He would ask no questions but he would charge a premium for keeping the men's secret.

The four men kept their faces close together. The hubbub of noise from the room would mask their words but there was little point in courting danger. Had the landlord stayed longer to hear their words he would have heard a Scottish voice, a lilting Welsh one, a Norman French voice and a high-born Englishman. None used names. Names could be overheard. Their servants outside had kept apart but all four of them were discouraging anyone from approaching the horses to identify the mounts and therefore the men.

The Norman spoke first, "So we are agreed." There was silence. His voice became firmer, "If we are not then why have I made the journey from Rouen to risk winter storms and enemies who would love to slit my throat? It was you who contacted me and asked me to bring my men to this damp and dismal land where no one keeps a decent wine."

The Welshman said, "Of course we are agreed. It is merely the manner and the time of the death that are open for discussion."

The Scot said, "Perhaps we need do nothing. When he came north to fight us he did nothing. It was his father who hurt us. This Edward is a shadow of his father."

Warbow

The one who had yet to speak, the Englishman, snapped, "He is ruining England. Does that suit your de Brus? Does he want to take Northumbria and Westmoreland to add to his empire?"

The Welshman sensed the tension and he used his authority to calm the troubled waters. "De Brus has no desire to take anything from England. He chose his side of the bed and my friend is quite right. We cannot simply do nothing. When the king and his," he paused as he sought the right word, "good friend are dead then we will put one on the throne who is more like Longshanks. If that does not suit de Brus then perhaps you should leave."

The Scot paused for a moment and then said, "We are part of this and we will accept whatever king replaces him." He knew why his king wanted Edward dead. It was to create chaos in England so that he could strengthen his position. All of Scotland knew that England would once more seek to take Scotland as a vassal. The next time an English king tried that then they would be ready. The lessons of Falkirk and the wars since then had been learned.

The Welshman spoke again, "We need the king isolated and with few men to defend him. Are your men on hand now?"

The Norman spoke, "They are here in England. They are hidden but I can reach them quickly."

He paused for the landlord brought their wine and food. No one spoke as he placed the beakers and platters on the table. "Would you like your bill now or …"

The Englishman said, "Now."

The landlord scribbled on his wax tablet and showed it to the man. Coins were handed over and the landlord returned to his bar. He would watch. Knowledge might bring him reward. These four men wished to be hidden and if he could discover their identities then there might be a profit.

The four men sipped the wine. The Norman wrinkled his nose at it while the Scotsman downed half of it immediately. They nibbled at their food until they were sure that they were not being observed. The hubbub from the pilgrims would hide their words.

The Norman said, "You have the men for one month and they will need to be paid even if they are not used. That is the way of such killers." He pushed the wine away. "And if the wine here is what you are used to then they will want to do the deed sooner rather than later. They are men who like good wine. They are killing a king and such acts incur the wrath of God."

The Englishman said, "Some acts are necessary for the good of the country." He paused and asked, "Which road will he take?"

Warbow

The Welshman spoke again, "He will be using the Canterbury road but it will be in secret and the timing is in doubt. The horses are being readied and I know some of the men who will be riding as escorts. He will not take many with him in order to enable him to ride in secret. I do not think it will be for a day or so and I will get word to you as soon as I can."

"You are confident in this?" The Scot sounded curious.

The Welshman's voice was low and invited the others to lean in, "Let us say I am privy to the king's arrangements."

Satisfied the Scotsman said, "Very well then all that remains, is the payment."

The three of them each pushed over the bags of coins to the Norman who would not bother to count the silver and gold that they contained. If the three lords tried to cheat him then he and the men he had hired would return to Normandy. He was the broker in these matters and had no direct interest. Of course, when he returned to his home he would profit from the news. He made money no matter what the outcome.

Chapter 1

Westminster

There had been a time when Sir Gerald Warbow had been a confidante of men with power. I was close to the late king and men often tried to use me. This time I had been summoned to London in December like a miscreant. The king and his favourite had two purposes for the high-handed summons. The first was to humiliate me for Piers Gaveston hated me. I had been the one charged by the first King Edward to ensure he left England in exile. He had not forgotten what he perceived as an insult. King Edward was dead but he could punish the man who had escorted him. The two, when Robert, my French priest, and I had reached the palace, had toyed with me much as a cat does with a mouse. They had threatened me and my family. I had endured their taunts for I expected to go to the executioner's block and I knew that no matter what I said they had already made their decision about my fate. The second reason was to enlist my support in the Baron's Parliament. It had been summoned in January and powerful, senior figures would be coming to London and the Palace of Westminster. The new King Edward knew he had enemies amongst the barons and he wanted me to sway some to his side. I had not said I would do it but as I was confined to the court it was a moot point. Robert and I had the run of the palace but guards ensured that we would not leave without the permission of the two men, the Earl of Cornwall and King Edward. Our gaolers were less than happy about this for most of them had fought with me and served under Longshanks. They knew how highly I had been valued before the coronation. This humiliation angered them.

However, even under such circumstances there could be pleasant moments. Queen Isabella, the new Queen of England was twelve years old and had been shunned since the coronation by her husband. Robert and I found her with one of her ladies in waiting in the Great Hall one morning. Most of the court had yet to rise. Why she was not with her husband was clear. He preferred the company of others. She looked sad. I could speak French but I mangled it. Robert, my French priest, had told me that many times. He, on the other hand was a well-educated Frenchman and he spoke it well. After I had introduced myself and asked her if there was anything we could do, Robert spoke. The shy smile on the former French princess was due to my awful French. I did not mind. I had never purported to be a courtier. I had always been Lord Edward's Archer. I was a bluff, some would say common man, but I was what I was and those who knew me best said that I was the same man I had been when I had fled to Gascony to flee the charge of murdering a knight all those many years ago.

Robert was a kind man and, in many ways, the opposite to me. Where I was rough and awkward, he was smooth and confident in his choice of words. He warmed to the young queen and amused her so much that she took to seeking us out each day. I did not want to be in London. I hated the place for Londoners had ever been the opponents of my King Edward. I did not want to attend the Parliament and I hated being coerced into staying there. However, sitting with Robert, Queen Isabella and her lady in waiting helped me to improve my French and also passed the hours each day as we waited for the Parliament. I was able to study the various petitioners and barons who sought an audience with the king and the man who, effectively, ruled England, Piers Gaveston the Earl of Cornwall. I had never seen half of them and that told me much. I had fought for the late King Edward, and the best of the men who had fought for him shunned the court. The ones I saw were some of the old king's enemies. Others were those who were most adept at sitting on a fence to see which way the wind blew. I found no one with whom I wished to speak. The days passed.

The knight who came for me, one cold January morning, was not a young man. He looked to be in his late thirties. That he was one of King Edward's household knights was clear from his livery. However, unlike most of the king's men he was both polite and thoughtful. He waited until there was a lull in the conversation and when he spoke it was in a quiet, gentle voice. There was a Welsh accent I recognised. Living in the borders I could differentiate between the Welsh of the mountains, Pembrokeshire and the Welsh border. He came from the border.

"My lord, the king would speak with you. He and the Earl of Cornwall are alone. If you would follow me." Robert made to rise but the knight said, "The king wishes to speak to the baron alone. I am sorry."

Robert sat. In that moment I began to have the measure of this man and I wondered why such a man served the king. As we made our way from the Great Hall, seemingly every eye upon us, I began to speculate. Kings chose men to be around them for a wide variety of reasons. King Edward, Longshanks, had wanted my skill with a bow. In my youth and when I became a man there was no finer archer in the land. Added to that were my skills at surviving. The king, when Prince of Wales, had sent me and two others to the court of the Mongols to fetch an army. That I had survived and brought an army was testament to my ability to stay alive. In Acre, I had helped to save the life of the king and he had kept me close for those skills. His son, the new King Edward, was more of a political animal. So far as I could tell he had not inherited any of his father's martial skills but he had the ruthless streak his father had sometimes shown. None of that explained the man who led me to the chamber where his master waited.

When we reached the door there were two men at arms on guard. They both recognised me and smiled. The knight opened the door and we entered. Piers Gaveston, the Earl of Cornwall, said, "Thank you, Sir John, you may wait without. Come, Sir Gerald." There was no chair and I would have to stand. The two men were seated and so close that their arms brushed against each other when they moved them.

I stood and waited. Piers Gaveston liked to play games and making men wonder what he would do was one such game. I knew that the king was led by him and very much influenced by the man who was now so powerful and rich that he was treated almost like the king himself.

"Sir Gerald, we are pleased that you have obeyed our commands and made no attempt to communicate with your family and have kept alone." He glanced at the king.

King Edward said, "And it has not escaped our notice that you and your Frenchman have shown kindness to the queen. Thank you, for that. She is young and alone in this court. Perhaps we misjudged you."

His words told me a number of things. We were being watched. Servants brought wine and food constantly. It did not surprise me that some of them reported back to the king. What did surprise me was that he cared what I thought.

He continued, "We have enemies, Sir Gerald. There are men who hate me and wish me removed from the throne." He paused and looked at the earl.

Piers Gaveston said, "The king has to visit with the Archbishop of Canterbury, Robert Winchelsey." He smiled, "We would have you accompany him. I am sure that you would like to be away from the palace for a few days."

So far I had been silent. I needed to have clarification, "You want me, an old man, as a bodyguard?"

"Come, Sir Gerald, you have grey hairs but, as I can attest, there is no one better at surviving than you." It was as close to a compliment from the Earl of Cornwall as I was likely to receive.

"But the king has guards of his own."

King Edward gave me a pleading look and his words reflected his fear, "Sir Gerald, Warbow, you protected my father. He often told me that you were his rock and that while you were close by he never feared for his life. I ask you to do for me, just this once, what you did for my father."

I nodded, "And is this journey necessary? The roads at this time of year are not the most pleasant for travel."

The Earl of Cornwall nodded, "The Archbishop of Canterbury has just returned from exile and the king needs his support in this Parliament. The visit will be in secret, which is another reason for your presence. There will be just ten men with him and all of you will ride in disguise. There will be no liveries."

"And when this is done I can go home?"

Piers Gaveston shook his head, and I noticed that his voice was no longer that of a supplicant. It was the voice of a commander, "You go home, Sir Gerald, when Parliament has assembled and we have what we want. Remember, you are here to support the king as you did his father."

I sighed, "And when do we leave?"

"Tomorrow before dawn. Horses will be ready. Your French priest can stay here. He will serve no purpose on the road and the queen might enjoy his company."

I nodded.

"You are dismissed." As I turned he said, "It goes without saying that this is a matter most secret."

I turned and stared at the man who was everything I hated, "I have been keeping secrets since before the time you were learning to walk, my lord. I know my duty." I held his gaze until his eyes dropped and then I left. As Sir John escorted me back I knew I had enjoyed a small victory. Piers Gaveston feared me but he needed me. Being needed might just keep me alive.

When we reached the hall Sir John said, quietly, "I believe that you will be with us on the morrow. For that I am glad."

I looked at him in surprise, "You will be with the king?"

"I am to lead his escort of men at arms. I chose them and they are good men but you are better than all of us."

I laughed, "I am an old man."

"As William Wallace discovered, you are an old man with teeth, Sir Gerald. We have good horses. I can supply you with mail and a helmet if you wish."

I shook my head, "I have worn armour but I was an archer long before I was given my spurs. If you could find me a war bow and a bag of arrows then I will be happier. I have my own sword."

"I shall find one. I will wake you myself when it is time." He bowed to the queen, turned and left.

I saw the questions in Robert's eyes. I glanced at the queen and gave the slightest of shakes of my head.

Warbow

The queen was trying to improve her English and she said, "A good meeting with the king?" She smiled when she had completed the sentence.

I liked the queen. She was young and deserved better than the man she had married. I think in the king's eyes she was a political necessity and her real purpose was to bear him children and an heir. I spoke slowly and clearly, "It was a good meeting, my Queen. I hope to be of service to him."

She turned to Robert and spoke French that was rapid. I picked up one word in three. Robert said, "She prays that the two of you will be safe."

Her words told me that young as she was she had all her wits about her and knew that something was amiss.

When we dined Robert and I were relegated to our normal low position. I was good enough to be a bodyguard but not to be seated close to the high table. I did not mind. I saw Sir John and he was seated close to the king. I had not really noticed him before but now I did. He was an efficient looking man. He ate and he drank but did so sparingly. He was looking for danger among the gathered throng. His eyes flitted across the room as he looked for movements and actions that might threaten the king. I had been the same with Longshanks. For me the food we ate might be expensive and look wonderful but the food I preferred was that cooked in my home and prepared by my wife, Mary, or the hunter's stews I enjoyed with my men on the road.

It was when we reached our rooms that Robert assailed me with questions. I held up my hands, "All I can say is that tomorrow I will rise early and be gone for some days. I go to serve the king and that is all that I can say."

"You serve the man who threatens you and your family?"

I sighed, "I do what I must to stay alive and to protect my family. Yarpole seems a long way away but the Earl of Cornwall has a long reach and there are treacherous men who would murder for the price of a good horse. You will stay here and gather information while I am gone." I smiled, "And continue to entertain the queen." My one worry was that the earl was not with us. I did not trust the man who had ambitions. I could not see how he might seize power but a handful of men to guard a king seemed, in my view, reckless.

I knew that I was getting old and it had nothing to do with my strength. I could still draw a bow, not as well as my son Hamo, but better than most. It was the need to wake in the night and empty my bladder that told me of my age. The second time I rose in the night I decided to stay awake. I knew that I would soon be awakened and I had never been one to return to bed. I dressed silently so as not to wake

Robert. I slipped from the room and closed the door as quietly as I could. I saw a figure appear at the end of the corridor, lit by the brands in the sconces which were kept burning all night. We had wooden walls at home and a burning brand was a fire hazard.

Sir John smiled as I approached him, "I can see that you are an early riser."

I nodded, "Aye, and like a bear roused from his hibernation until I have food."

"There is food laid out, Sir Gerald. My men have eaten already and are saddling the horses."

"Who chose the horses? You?"

"Yes, my lord. I thought to make the journey in a long day. They will have a day in Canterbury to rest."

"Good." I had been worried that we might have an overnight stop en route. Such rests were dangerous. I thought we should be safe enough in the cathedral.

We were the only two who were dining. There was bread, honey, ham, cheese and porridge. I ate the porridge laced with honey first. It was the wrong season for fruit but I liked my oats with honey and fruit. They seemed to keep me going for longer. The bread was still warm and the butter melted a little when I smeared it. The ale was good and when we had finished I felt replete.

"I am now ready, Sir John."

We stood and he said, "You knew a distant relative of mine, Sir Gerald. I believe he was a good friend of yours."

I was suspicious. I had few men I called friends. The ones I truly regarded as friends were, in the main, dead. "And who would that be?"

"Sir Hamo le Strange."

I could not help but let my face break into the widest of smiles, "Hamo! A good man. I was sorry to hear of his death."

"When I grew up we heard stories about Lord Edward's archer and when it was discovered that you and he had ventured on a delicate task for the king then your name was often mentioned. I have long anticipated meeting with you." We headed to the door that led from the hall, "I was but five when he died, Sir Gerald, yet he has cast a long shadow. He was a distant cousin. My father, Sir Robert, often spoke of him and I was regaled with tales of his service to the king. When we have time I would hear more of his life. He is something of a legend in our part of Wales. He married a queen."

I laughed for Hamo had been the truest friend I had ever had. My son was named in his honour and while I did not begrudge him his marriage, I always regretted that he had not continued to serve the king. I wondered how matters, especially in Scotland, would have turned out had he been alive. "That I will and you shall hear the truth. There were just four of us on that adventure," I stopped myself, "no, five for we brought back my wife from the Mongol court. Only we know the truth. There are many who make up tales and sing songs but all are fantasies for we kept our counsel about that time. We were sworn to secrecy by King Edward and I keep my oaths." I suddenly looked at Sir John with new eyes. "You are not a le Strange then?"

He shook his head, "I am a Charleton. We have land in the borders. Our manor is Wellington in Shropshire." He smiled, "We are lesser nobility, some would call us just yeomen. The le Strange family were the ones who had the power. I believe that one of the last men with a claim to the Welsh crown, Owain de la Pole, was also related to Hamo le Strange."

That made me look up. It meant that Lady Hawise was also related to Hamo le Strange. It had not come up in the conversation with that lady.

"Shropshire, eh?" I shook my head at the coincidence, "Then we are neighbours. My manor is forty miles from yours. I am surprised we have not crossed paths before now."

"The old King Edward had me as a page and I served at court. I saw you many times but you would not have noticed me. Then the king made me a man at arms and asked me to serve his son. It was King Edward himself who dubbed me."

The knight was clearly loyal. I would not test that loyalty by asking how he felt about Piers Gaveston but I now felt an obligation to protect not only the king but also the knight. He was of the blood of a friend.

When we reached the stables the men were waiting. I saw that Sir John had chosen well. They were, in the main, battle-scarred veterans. He would have known whom to choose for he had been a man at arms himself. They wore mail and each had a coif on his head. There were no shields to be seen but they all had good swords. I had been an archer but I recognised well-made blades. They nodded a welcome to me and one handed me a bow in a case and an arrow bag.

"Thank you." I slipped the bow from its case. It was the right length, "Bow strings?"

The man at arms who was younger than the others grinned and took off his coif. He took three strings from the top of his head and handed them to me. I smiled and cocked my head. He said, "I am Richard Davidson, and my father is an archer, my lord. I know where archers keep their strings. It is a good bow. I chose it myself."

The king had not arrived and so, after putting two of the strings beneath my hat I strung the bow. As I had expected it was not as easy as when I had been younger but I managed. To fail to do so would have been humiliating. I drew it back. I could not manage a full draw any longer than a heartbeat but I knew that none of the men at arms could have come close to my draw. I was satisfied and I unstrung the bow and slipped it back into its case.

"Which is my horse?"

Sir John handed me the reins of a grey, "Storm Cloud is a good horse." He suddenly turned to look at me and asked, "You do not think that a grey is unlucky?"

I laughed, "I believe in luck but not when it is determined by the colour of a horse." I rubbed the horse's muzzle. "Gelding or stallion?"

"Gelding."

"Good." I fastened the bow and arrow bag to the saddle. That done, I turned, "And now we await the king?"

He nodded, "We travel in secret so there will be no crown, page or squire."

As we waited and I stroked Storm Cloud's mane I wondered about that. King Edward was many things but being a fool was not one of them. He knew he had enemies but he clearly needed to speak to the prelate and was willing to risk the road in winter in order to do so.

He joined us a few moments later. He was well wrapped against the elements. His oiled cloak was fur lined. When he mounted his horse the lining would not be seen and he would be as anonymous as the rest of us. He did not look at me but said to Sir John, "The guards have been warned?"

"Yes, King Edward. We will not be hindered. Sir Gerald and I will ride in the van and we are our passport across the bridge."

"And from now on do not refer to me as king. We are supposed to be hidden."

I saw Sir John frown, "Then how do we address you, King Edward?"

"My lord will do."

"Then, my lord, let us mount. We have many miles to travel until we can be rid of the saddles and enjoy the comfort of the archbishop's home."

We mounted outside the stable. There was a flurry of sleet in the cold morning wind. As Sir John and I needed to be recognised as we left the palace and crossed the bridge, we did not use our hoods. I was lucky in that I had a good hat. Sir John's coif might protect him from blows but the cold would seep into his skull. The palace guards had been forewarned and we passed through. The ride up to the hill at the Lud Gate had the horses breathing heavily and when we stopped at the gate they were able to recover. Passing through the gate we saw people heading to set up the market at the Chepe. We smelled the bread as we descended to the bridge over the Thames. Once we were on the other side we would, effectively, disappear. We descended towards the bridge across the river that protected London. As our hooves clattered on the cobbles I saw the men emerge from the shelter and take hold of their weapons. Sir John did not slow down and, as we neared them, they saluted with their weapons. Thus far it seemed a well-planned venture. Sir John Charleton and Sir Gerald Warbow would not attract attention. There might be speculation and comments but as the king was known to despise me none would connect the man who rode behind Sir John as the King of England.

Richard Davidson was behind me and as we passed the ***'Tabard Inn'*** in Southwark he said, "A warmed ale would set us up nicely."

Sir John said, "There is an inn in Rochester, Richard, and hopefully they will have good food and a fine ale."

I asked, "And what of the garrison and castellan at Rochester? What will they think of this conroi of armed men riding across the land?"

"You should know, Sir Gerald, that it was damaged in the Baron's war. King Edward did not repair the walls and only the keep remains intact. There may come a time when the castle is deemed important enough to repair but for now…"

King Edward said, "We do not need Rochester yet, Sir John. There are more pressing needs for our coins than a castle that guards the Medway."

The sleet had become hard rain and was in our faces as we passed through the villages that lay south of London. It ensured that we kept hoods over our heads and that few men came from their homes to view us. Those on the road that we met had the same need as we and all we saw were hooded men trying to get where they were going quickly. This was not the time of year to be working in the fields and the only people we spied were those tending to animals. I was not idle as we rode. I looked at places where we might be ambushed or where men could hide. If the king and the earl were right then there could be enemies seeking to take the life of the king. I did not like the man but I would do all that I could to keep the king alive. It was a task I had done for most of my adult life.

Rochester would be the one place where we would see people and as we clattered into the yard of the inn, ***The Sceptre***, I saw that there were many horses in the stables already. Sir John could have used his authority to demand that ours were all stabled but that would have drawn attention to us. As he dismounted he said, affably, to the ostler and his stable boy, "You are busy eh?"

Seeing the spurs we both wore the ostler nodded, "Sorry, my lord, but I can rub them down and feed them." He pointed to the roof, "There is shelter beneath the roof and the rain is ceasing."

Sir John beamed and handed the boy a silver sixpence, "Good fellow and what dish should we choose?"

I sensed King Edward's frustration but Sir John was doing the right thing. We sounded like travellers and not conspirators or men on some clandestine adventure.

"The beef and oyster pie is good, my lord, and any of the ales is to be enjoyed."

"Of course, this is Kent and if we cannot get good ale here then where, eh? Come, gentlemen. Let us shed these cloaks and enjoy the warmth of the inn."

We headed for the entrance to the inn and once inside we all took off our cloaks and shook them. Sir John had clearly spoken to his men about our plan for while Richard followed Sir John, me and the king into the inn the others hung back. Two small groups of men would attract less attention than one larger one.

The inn had a large room and was not as full as the stables had suggested. The landlord, seeing three men with spurs enter, approached, "A table for four, my lords?"

The king kept behind Sir John and me. The room was lit by tallow candles and the orange smoky light hid his features.

"Aye, landlord but with a wall, eh?"

As he led us to a table in the corner I cast my eyes over the men in the room. I saw merchants and their servants. I dismissed them. I also saw men who were not travellers and deduced that they lived and worked in the town. The ones who attracted my eye were the two groups of armed men. They were not together but I saw that they were soldiers. They wore mail and had good swords. I also saw that they were not drinking ale but wine. That marked them for most Englishmen would choose ale. They were foreign, either Norman or French. I did not see them as a threat but if they left before we did then I might re-evaluate the situation.

When we sat the king made sure that his back was to the room. He was clearly uncomfortable with the situation. He liked to be the centre of attention. He knew that to remain hidden he had to be the opposite. I also began to realise just how important Piers Gaveston was to him. They seemed to feed off one another and King Edward here, whilst protected, was without the man who gave him comfort.

We had just ordered the pie and ale when the rest of our men entered. They ignored us but I saw the wine drinkers, both groups, notice them. Our food had arrived when the first group of wine drinkers left. I caught the words of one of them as he spoke to the landlord, "Our bill, landlord. The rain appears to be easing and we will continue to London." He spoke with a Norman accent. I had learned to differentiate between them.

"Your stay here has been satisfactory?"

"The rooms were adequate."

"If you would follow me." He turned, "Will, watch the room while I attend to these gentlemen." As they passed us I saw that none of them had spurs. These were not knights. That confirmed their occupation. They were soldiers and, perhaps, heading to London to seek employment. When spring came, it was said, there would be a muster to deal with the Scots. It was an explanation. When the other wine drinkers did not leave I relaxed a little.

The ostler had been right and the pie was delicious. That it did not meet with King Edward's approval was clear. He left most of it. We three devoured it.

I made innocent conversation as silence would be seen as suspicious, "So, Richard, where does your father serve?"

"He is in the garrison at Skipton in the Honour of Craven. He commands the archers there."

I smiled, "Sir Richard of Craven, the castellan there is a friend of mine."

"My father speaks well of him."

"You did not wish to follow in his footsteps?"

"You know better than any, Sir Gerald, that a man who is to be an archer has to dedicate himself to the art from an early age. I did not. I am the second son and my brother, Dickon, is the archer. I disappointed my father. When he saw that I would not make an archer he had the captain of the men at arms train me to be a man who could wield a sword. I think I was spurred to become the best that I could be as I did not want to disappoint my father a second time. My training as an archer came to my aid and I was stronger than the others. I found myself. I am a man at arms and I am content."

King Edward snapped, irritably, "And now that we have heard your life story, can we leave? Time is pressing and I hope for better fare at our destination."

Sir John sighed, "Yes my lord."

He stood and the man referred to as Will came over, "How much?"

The man looked at the wax tablet and held it for Sir John to read. He paid and we left. We ignored the other men. They would follow. The second group of wine drinkers did not move.

Warbow

The rain had stopped and the ostler ran to saddle our horses. I saw that the first wine drinkers had left. As I mounted Storm Cloud I said to the stable boy, "The men who left did they head to London or to Canterbury?" I smiled, "The company might be pleasant."

He shook his head, "Not those Frenchmen, my lord. They have been here for two days and they have done nothing but complain. They did not give my father even a copper. They took the London Road." He saw my bow case and said, "They had crossbows and my father always says that crossbowmen are the meanest men he knows."

Laughing, I slipped him a couple of silver pennies and, winking said, "English archers know how to pay."

He grinned, "Thank you, my lord."

We four walked our horses from the inn and did not mount until we were beyond the shadow of the castle keep. When we heard the hooves of the others we mounted. The king snapped, "No more delays. We ride hard."

Sir John nodded, "The stop was necessary, my lord. The horses have been fed and they are more rested. Had we not stopped we might not have reached the cathedral." When the others arrived he said, "Well?"

"None followed, Sir John. I wondered about those Normans but they stayed in the inn."

"Ralph, you and Harry ride a mile behind us. You can give a warning if they do follow."

"We ride!" King Edward spurred his horse and it leapt forward. Sir John and I had to ride hard to catch him. The king was reckless.

Chapter 2

The armed men in the inn had made me even more cautious as we left for Canterbury. My vigilance on the road to the meeting with the archbishop was doubled. Every twist and turn in the road was examined and each tree searched for possible killers. It was dark by the time we reached the cathedral. The archbishop had guards but the king was clearly expected and when he had dismounted he simply let his reins drop and strode towards the warmth of the palace. We had done our duty and he left us. Sir John shook his head, "Richard, Sir Gerald and I had better catch up with the impetuous king. See to the horses."

"Yes, my lord."

I handed him my reins and hurried after Sir John. He was right. The king was impetuous. We were here to protect him and just because we were at the cathedral did not mean that the danger was over.

I had never met the archbishop for he had been an enemy of the late king and Longshanks had exiled him three years earlier. King Edward had offered him the chance to return. All that I knew about the archbishop was that he had a fierce temper and there was a story that he had rebuked an abbot so severely that the abbot had suffered a fatal heart attack. I knew why the king was here. He wanted the support of a senior prelate in Parliament.

We reached the refectory to where the king had raced. The archbishop and his senior priests were eating. They stood and bowed their heads. The archbishop's was the merest of movements.

"I was worried, King Edward, when night fell I feared the worst."

"The weather, the road…" the king waved a hand. "We are here now and I hope that we are not too late to be fed."

"Of course, make a space for the king." He saw Sir John and me. He asked, "Do your men need to sit with you?"

The king shook his head, "They are here to guard me and I think that within these walls I am safe."

We were relegated to a table with the ordinary priests. I did not mind but it meant I was not privy to the conversation between the king and the most senior churchman in the land. The rest of the escort arrived and the priests vacated the table so that we could all sit together.

Sir John was a good leader and took his role seriously. When the last two men had entered and were seated he asked, "Ralph, did anyone follow us?"

The man at arms hesitated and then said, "I am not sure. We saw no one but I had the feeling that our footsteps were being dogged. We waited until all had entered before we followed and we saw no one but…"

I nodded, "Your neck prickled."

Ralph smiled, "Yes, Sir Gerald."

I knew then that we had been followed, "Then when we leave, Sir John, I will have my bow strung and young Richard and I will do what Ralph and Harry did in reverse. We will ride ahead of you and the king."

"He will not like that."

I laughed, "He likes little that I do but I would not have him die whilst in my care. If there is a crossbow bolt waiting for us then I am the man to take it." I looked at Richard, "You may ride with the others if you wish. I would not endanger your life too."

He shook his head, "My father holds you in the highest esteem, my lord, for you are an archer who was made a baron. I would be honoured to keep you company."

We could see that the discussion at the top table was not going the way that the king planned. He was growing red in the face. The archbishop, in contrast, seemed totally in control. I knew that the archbishop had hated the first King Edward and done all in his power to oppose him but I had gathered, clearly wrongly, that his son had a better relationship. The new King Edward had not yet said he would tax the clergy. All I wanted to do was to get back home as soon as I could. It now seemed likely that I would be at Westminster until February or March when all the barons would arrive.

The clergy went to bed before we did. There would be services during the night and whilst the archbishop would not attend them all I could tell, when he rose, that he wished the meeting with the king to be ended. When the clergy left there were just some lay brothers to attend to us. The king waved Sir John and me to his table. He downed the wine left in his goblet in one, "I know not why I petitioned the Pope to have the man returned to England. He seems to think that I am my father."

While Sir John was the king's man and obeyed all the orders, I was a baron and I felt that I could talk to the king, not as an equal but, as I had done with his father, a valued advisor. "What is it that you wish him to do, King Edward?"

He turned his head to view me. He said nothing at first and I got the impression he was gauging if he could trust me or not. Eventually, he said, "To support me in the Parliament. He knows I will not tax the clergy and yet…" he shook his head. "There is some plot here but I cannot fathom it."

I said, "King Edward, Rochester Castle belongs to the See of Canterbury. As we saw when we passed it, the castle is not defensible.

Perhaps, if you were to offer to have the work done to repair the defences."

He became agitated, "That would cost more than I wish to take from Parliament."

"I did not say that you would fund it, King Edward. Just make the offer. If it wins his support then when you say that you cannot afford it he cannot reverse his support, can he?"

"And if he does not support me then I can withdraw the offer. You know, Sir Gerald, you do have your uses. And now I suppose we had better retire. The bells for the services will be ringing again soon."

Sir John said, "And tonight, King Edward, I shall be your chamberlain and sleep behind the door."

"Is that necessary?"

He lowered his voice and, seeing that the lay brothers had left us alone, continued, "Ralph and Harry think we may have been followed, King Edward. They do not know for certain but it might be better if, purely as a precaution, I guard your door."

He nodded, "Very well."

The rest of us were in a dormitory used by travellers and so the beds were relatively comfortable and there was a fire to warm the room. I slept well. I did not think that anybody would risk attacking the king in the cathedral. The road would be an easier place.

The bells for the services in the night did not wake me but the other bodyguards complained when we rose. The breakfast we enjoyed was a simple one. Porridge, bread, honey and beer did not please the king but I enjoyed their simplicity. Once the meal was out of the way the king and the prelate went off to the archbishop's inner sanctum where the two of them could negotiate. We waited without and the day passed. It was marked by a constant supply of wine and food sent to the two men. We ate in shifts so that there were always at least three of us on duty.

I learned about the lives of the bodyguards and, more especially, Sir John Charleton. I found many aspects of his life sad. I learned that he was forty years of age. I had married late but even I had married earlier than he. "Do you want a wife?" We were alone. Others were on duty and we were in the refectory enjoying some ale.

"Of course but…" he shook his head, "my father drilled into me the idea of duty. I serve King Edward."

"My friend, kings do not worry about the likes of us. Queen Eleanor did. That lady was truly great and with her hand on King Edward's shoulder and guiding her son, they were both better men. Her death changed the present King Edward. This new king cares for two people, himself and the Earl of Cornwall."

"You should not believe all those stories that are told…"

"I do not. Whilst I was kept waiting in London I spoke with the new queen. She is loyal to her husband, although God alone knows why, but it is clear to me that Piers Gaveston holds the king in his hands. The king does what his friend wishes. The old King Edward knew that. I was the one chosen by the king to take him into exile. Do not waste your life serving a king who will discard you when it is convenient. Take a wife."

He was silent for a moment, "I am too old, now. What woman would have me?"

I smiled, "I thought that but when I was in the most unlikely of places, the court of the Mongol Khans, with your relative, Hamo, I found my wife. I did not seek a bride but I found one. There will be a woman for you, Sir John, and when you find her then cling on to her. Finding Mary was the best thing that ever happened to me and your uncle also found the love of his life in the most unexpected of places."

"You knew her?"

"That I did and if ever a couple were meant to be together it was them. I know he did not have as long with his bride as I have enjoyed and that merely serves to show that when you find a wife then enjoy every day that you have with her."

It was clear, by the end of the day, that an accord between the king and archbishop had been arrived at. The two men smiled and when we dined that night there was laughter and mutual toasts. Perhaps my suggestion had been a good one and I hoped that it would pave the way for my departure from London. Speaking with Sir John had told me just how much I missed my own family. It was easy to rise early in the cathedral. The bells for Lauds woke us and we rose. We ate in an empty refectory for the priests were at their services. It meant we enjoyed bread that was freshly baked and still warm. Although the day promised to be dry it would be cold and I filled up. While the king and Sir John waited for the archbishop, I went with the men to the horses. After Storm Cloud was saddled I took the bow from its case and strung it.

I nodded to Richard, "You chose for me a good war bow, Richard son of Dickon."

He looked pleased that I had noticed, "I may not be able to pull one but I can tell the strength of a bow. When last I was at Skipton, with the king, I noticed that my father was no longer using the bow he had before. His strength is waning. I deemed that you might need an easier bow."

I pulled the string to test the resistance and felt the muscles in my back tighten. When I was a younger archer I had drawn my bow each day. The last time I had drawn a bow had been more than six months earlier. "You are right but I am guessing that while your father practises each day, he is teaching men to be archers."

"He is. In the borders we value archers more than here in the south for the Scots are ever present."

"Aye, and the same is true on the Welsh borders. The Welsh are the masters of their bows." I took out the arrows to examine them. They were workmanlike enough but not as well fletched as those in Yarpole. They were all bodkins and that was good. They would pierce both mail and metal. I paid our fletchers well. I picked out the best three and after hanging the bag from the cantle, jammed the three in my belt.

"Do you fear an ambush, my lord?" It was Harry who spoke.

"You and Ralph have instincts that I would not ignore. A warrior does so at his peril. We have a long ride back to London and if we are alert to danger then, if we are attacked, we can respond more quickly."

Ralph smiled, "And if there is no danger then being alert keeps our minds occupied on the road and not thinking about a celebration in an alehouse."

"Exactly." I liked these men at arms. I was always more comfortable in their company than knights. Sir John had been a man at arms and he was good company. He had made this adventure bearable.

It was not quite dawn when the king and his knight arrived. The king saw my strung bow and he frowned, "You fear danger, Sir Gerald?"

"I am being cautious, King Edward. If I might suggest you wear your coif beneath your hood. Richard and I will ride half a mile ahead of you. If there is an ambush then we would have early warning."

"Ambush?"

"The inn in Rochester had armed men. The ostler told me that they had crossbows and they were Norman."

"Why would Normans seek to harm me? King John lost Normandy to France."

"And there are mercenaries who will happily kill a king so long as he is not their king. Normandy is now a vassal of King Phillip of France."

"He is my father-in-law."

"I did not say that he would want you dead. I doubt that whoever comes to kill you will do so for personal gain. They will try to kill you for gold."

My use of the word kill had an effect. He nodded, "You may be right but I think it is a waste of time."

As I mounted my horse I said, "If you have a guard dog then it is always wise to let him risk the wolf, eh, King Edward?" I slung the bow across the cantle.

Warbow

Richard and I galloped out of the cathedral grounds and took the road to Rochester. Once we had lost sight of the cathedral we slowed and I said to Richard, "You are looking for the glint of metal. The sun is not yet up and it may well be a wintery one but look for reflections. Listen. If there are no birds then ask yourself why. You watch to the left and I will watch to the right. If there is danger then ride back to the king as quickly as you can."

"And you, Sir Gerald?"

"I have a bow and a bag of arrows. When the bag is empty I will join the king."

"I should stay."

"You should obey orders. You are oathsworn to guard the king. His father asked me to watch over his son. I am old and if I am to die then surely the protection of my king is a good death."

My wife and sons would not agree but the promise I had made to King Edward was always there. I had been asked to keep Piers Gaveston from his side and to help him become a better king. It was not in my power to guarantee I could do both but I had to try.

When the sun rose it surprised me. It was a typical winter sun which meant it was low in the sky. It gave little warmth but it sharpened the senses. The problem was when the road turned to the east for then it was in our eyes and blinded us. After the first flash of light had hidden the road I pulled my cap forward so that it afforded me some shade. I did not want to use my hood for I needed my ears to be sharp. Richard had no hat and he was forced to pull his hood forward.

The road was now mercifully heading west. Behind us I could hear the hooves of the rest of the men. I knew they were getting too close. I spurred Storm Cloud and a heartbeat after I moved ahead Richard urged his horse on. There was a long section of the road, I remembered, that had few villages. Between the place we were and Rochester there was just one village, Rainham, comprising a row of houses flanking the road; it lay three miles up the road. When we had travelled to the cathedral we had not even slowed as we passed through it. I worried that at some point in the next twenty miles we would encounter danger. I slowed Storm Cloud as we neared some trees. My movement, after the sudden spurring, took Richard by surprise. He moved half a horse ahead of me before he realised. He must have thought I saw danger for his hand went to his sword. Sometimes such accidents prove fortuitous and so it was. I was slowing and peering at the trees when I saw the unmistakeable shape of a crossbow rise.

I had my bow in my hand and was slipping from the saddle as I shouted, "Ambush! Warn Sir John."

Warbow

The bolt that was sent at Richard struck the space he had occupied a moment earlier. He had obeyed me. I grabbed the arrow bag and moved to my right. I slapped Storm Cloud's rump with my bow. The movement of the horse to the left must have confused the attackers for two more bolts were sent and both missed. One was aimed at my grey and the other at me. It cracked into the tree next to me. I dropped my arrow bag and pulled an arrow from my belt. I nocked it almost without thinking. I had been doing this for most of my life and it was second nature. My position in the trees hid me but also meant I did not have a clear sight of the crossbows. There would be swordsmen too but the crossbows were there to kill at distance. A crossbow takes time to load. Unlike a bow a crossbow needs the man using it to put his foot in the stirrup and look at the machine as he does so. I caught a glimpse, just thirty paces from me, of the man pulling back on the crossbow. He had a coif about his head. I drew back. It was not even a full draw but it would not need to be. The bodkin slammed into the side of his skull, spinning around his body and making him fall into the road. I had a second arrow nocked for in his falling he had revealed another crossbowman who was raising his infernal machine to send a bolt at me. It was a race I was bound to win. My arrow struck him in the middle of his head. The archer in me smiled.

The hooves that galloped down the road were the rest of the king's protectors. I hoped that Sir John and the king were at the back. The ambushers had lost the advantage of surprise but they must have felt confident. The horsemen accompanying the crossbowmen galloped from cover with swords drawn and shields held before them. The king's men were shieldless. I had my third arrow nocked and when the crossbowman stepped from the cover of the trees to aim at Harry, leading the king's men, I slew him. I drew another arrow from the arrow bag. I had no opportunity to see if it was true or not. The leading riders were less than twenty paces from me. There were four of them and at least two intended to end the life of the archer who had spoiled their plans. My arrow plucked one from the saddle. The bodkin tore through his mail and only his cantle held him upright for a heartbeat before he slipped down. His falling made the second warrior have to move to his right and by such margins do men live or die. I was able to draw another arrow and as his sword was raised and he was just six feet from me, I sent the arrow up into his throat. Such was the power that the arrow kept flying once it was through. He was dead in the saddle. I nocked another arrow as the horsemen clashed with Harry, Ralph and Richard. Tom and Walter were close behind. They were outnumbered for the other four ambushers had joined the rest.

Warbow

I stepped back into the cover of the trees and sent my next arrow into the side of a horseman whose shield was protecting his front. I drew another and nocked it. My muscles were aching already. I had not practised enough. The killer who pulled his shield around to protect himself had seen me and his shield guarded his body and his head. What it did not protect were his legs. He wore chausse but as he was just fifteen paces from me the bodkin arrow ripped through the mail and into the horse's side. The man was pinned to his horse as he crashed into the next rider.

When I had spoken to Harry and Ralph about instincts I had been speaking from experience. It was that sense that made me turn at a movement I barely saw. A crossbowman had approached unseen through the woods and was just twenty paces from me. I saw the end raise and knew that his finger was on the release mechanism. As fast as I was the bag of arrows was too far for me to grab one, nock and draw. I did the only thing I could. I reached for an arrow but was ready to move. I was close enough to see the man's eyes and when I saw the look of triumph I stepped to the side. The bolt not only hit the tree but it penetrated and the tip emerged just a handspan from my head. My arrow nocked, I stepped from the tree to see the crossbowman running away. My arrow slammed into his back. I headed into the woods and the swordsman who lunged at me from the side almost took me by surprise. I was saved by two things, the tree which made his swing awkward and the bow that I used to flick at his head, making him jerk away from the tip. I dropped the bow and drew my sword and dagger. I was barely in time for he had adjusted his swing and brought his blade at my side. My dagger held it. I might not be able to send an arrow as far as I once had but my left arm was still stronger than most men's right. I did not make his mistake and swing my sword. Such a blow risked hitting a tree. Instead I lunged up towards his middle. He wore mail but the tip began to split some links. As I had punched with the sword he was also winded and when he stepped back I slashed my dagger across his neck. The blood spurted and showered me. I sheathed the sword and picked up the bow.

I had just four arrows left. I nocked one and ran back to the road. It was over. The assassins who had survived, there looked to be four of them, were galloping back to Rochester. The man who had been hit by the arrow through his leg lay beneath a thrashing horse. I saw that Walter was dead. The savage sword slash had torn half of his face off. I saw that Richard and the others were alive. They had blood spattered on their mail but none appeared to be wounded. I watched the king and Sir John approach. I was pleased to see that both had their swords drawn but they appeared to be unharmed. I walked to the horse. It was dying. After laying down the bow I took my dagger and slit its throat. It was a mercy.

The man was also dying. His back was broken. Blood trickled from his mouth and I took out my dagger, "You are dying." He nodded, "Who paid you?"

He was a tough man, I could see that. He steeled himself and smiled, "Have you heard the joke about the Englishman, the Scotsman and the Welshman?"

Before I could answer I saw his body shake a little and then go still. I closed his eyes, "Go with God. You were brave."

The king was white with shock. "Who did this?"

I took the coif from the man on the dead horse and said, "This is one of those from the inn in Rochester. I think, if you were to inspect the bodies, you would find the others. Someone knew we would be going to Canterbury and that we had to return this way. There were at least four crossbowmen amongst the attackers. I think they were Normans."

The king should have said it but it was left to Sir John to thank me, "And you were right, Sir Gerald, you and Richard saved us. I thank you."

The king nodded, "Yes, I suppose you did save me."

Richard said, "I will fetch Storm Cloud." He galloped off

I went to the nearest dead man and I took his purse. The king sounded shocked, "Robbing the dead, Sir Gerald?"

I sighed as I poured the contents from the purse into my hand, "No, King Edward. The men at arms deserve the coins. I am looking to see who was the paymaster." I examined the coins. Sir John and the king rode close to me. "Interesting," I held my palm flat. "The lesser coins are Norman. That is no surprise but look here is a freshly minted silver piece with your head on it, King Edward, and another with that of the King of Scotland, Robert de Brus."

Sir John said, "Search the other dead." As they went to do so he said, "This is strange."

Harry shouted, "I have Scottish coins and a Welsh one."

Ralph called out, "English and Scottish."

Tom waved a purse, "Scottish, Welsh and English. They are all fresh minted."

"The dying man made a macabre joke about an Englishman, a Scotsman and a Welshman. This seems to confirm it. We have tarried enough. Take the coins. It is time we quit this charnel house."

Sir John said, "Sir Gerald is quite right." He said to the men at arms, "The bounty is yours. Put poor Walter on his horse and fetch the weapons."

Warbow

Richard had brought Storm Cloud and I handed the coins and purse to him and, after putting the bow back in its case, headed into the trees.

The king's voice was higher pitched than it had been. It showed that he was clearly upset, "Where are you going, Sir Gerald? We should quit this place quickly."

I shook my head, "There is no longer haste. We will not be attacked again and I have some crossbows to destroy." I found the last man I had killed and picking up his crossbow smashed it against a tree. I took his purse and his dagger. He had no sword. I found the others and I did the same. I was laden when I reached the others. Two horses had survived the ambush and we loaded them with the weapons. I tossed the purses to Tom, Richard, Harry and Ralph. "Here, you are brave men and your courage should be rewarded."

We rode to Rochester with Richard and I at the fore but we were closer to the others. The men who had ambushed us had been confident and I knew there would not be more. This time we did not stop at the inn but the castle. The king remained in disguise but Sir John told the castellan of the ambush. The bodies would need to be removed. We ate in the castle and the priest was paid to pay for Walter's burial. It was not the king who paid but his shield brothers. The king would not remember his name within a week but they would never forget him.

Once the sun disappeared the evening was icy and promised a frost. We were weary beyond words as we crossed the bridge into London. It was so late that the watch had been set. This time the king identified himself. We rode, not to Westminster but to the Tower. The attempt on his life had clearly shaken the king. As I went to dismount he shook his head, "No, Sir Gerald, ride to Westminster. I have no further need of you as a bodyguard and I need the counsel of the Earl of Cornwall. Report to him."

The looks on the faces of the men with whom I had fought told their own story. None of them thought I had been treated well. Sir John smiled, "When time allows, Sir Gerald, you and I will speak at length. For my part and on behalf of these men I thank you. We owe you much and we," he emphasised the word, "will never forget it." The king had not heard for he had headed into the safety of the fortress.

I rode along Tower Street and passed St Paul's. The gate was closed but I was recognised. As the gates were opened I said, "The Earl of Cornwall will be heading to the Tower." It was a warning and the gatekeepers nodded their thanks.

I handed the reins to the ostler in the stables at Westminster Palace, "He has earned his oats today." I gave him a silver coin. "Treat him well."

He smiled, "That is not necessary, my lord, Storm Cloud is a favourite."

I folded the man's fingers around the coin, "And for that you should be rewarded."

I headed into the palace and the Great Hall. There was a feast and I heard the sound of music. The Earl of Cornwall was playing at being king. When I stepped through the doors every eye swivelled and the musicians, seeing my blood-spattered clothes, stopped playing. I had washed my face in Rochester Castle but my clothes were still covered in the blood of the swordsman. I saw Robert rise. I gave the slightest shake of my head. Piers Gaveston, for the first time in a long time, had a worried look on his face. He came racing over and, grabbing my arm, led me outside.

"The king?" His voice was filled with fear. The door was closed and there was no one in the corridor. We were alone.

"He lives. This blood is that of his enemies. He feared more assassins and he is at the Tower."

I saw the relief and the smile that appeared. Then he frowned, "Who knows of this attack on the king?"

"No one except for the assassins who escaped. We told the castellan at Rochester that it was Sir John who was attacked. No one knows that the king made this journey."

"Good. It must remain so. If I hear a word of this attack becoming common knowledge then you and your family will pay the price."

I glared at the earl, "I grow tired of your threats, Earl. I am a loyal Englishman and I have kept more secrets that you can possibly imagine, so do not threaten me. If you wish to do so then put me on trial and I will have my say in court but I will not endure another threat from you."

I was daring him to order my arrest or to draw his sword but he did neither. He was angry for a moment and then a silky smile came over his face, "Forgive me, Sir Gerald, you have performed a great service and I know of your loyalty. I was merely being careful." He opened the door and gestured for me to enter. He called to the assembled host, "The king has need of me. Enjoy the feast." With that he was gone and every eye was on me.

Robert came over to me and said, "I am glad you have returned. Tell me all."

I shook my head, "When time allows there will be a tale but it will be told to my confessor and not my friend." He nodded and as I took off my cloak I said, "And now food. My stomach thinks that my throat has been cut and I have such a thirst."

He smiled, "Of course, and I have much to tell you."

Warbow

Chapter 3

The sudden departure of the Earl of Cornwall at my arrival had set tongues wagging. Those seated close to Robert and to me were largely silent as they tried to listen to our conversation. I saw Robert frown. He could not be as open with me as he wished. "I know you were gone just three days, my lord, but it seemed longer. The weather was not clement and…" I saw the worry in his eyes.

A servant brought a platter for me and I began to help myself from the plentiful food that lay on the table. A second servant fetched some wine. I would have preferred ale but I nodded my thanks.

Robert frowned and said, "That is strange, my lord."

I took a healthy swig and found it to be good. If I drank wine I liked one with body.

"What is?"

"That Welshman who just left and followed the Earl of Cornwall."

I saw the back of a man as he left, "What of it? He is probably one who seeks a favour."

Robert shook his head, "He has been a constant at court. If I did not know better I would think that he was stalking the earl, but now I see him follow directly it makes it more obvious."

"Perhaps he is one of the earl's men and guards him."

"Perhaps." My clever French healer was clearly not convinced.

"What is his name?"

"Iago ap Daffydd."

I shook my head. I had never heard of him. I handed one of the purses of coins I had taken to Robert, "I took these from the men who ambushed us. They are just coins but something about them has set my mind to wondering. While I eat and drink, put your mind to working out what they mean. I have my own theory but it will be good to hear the views of another."

"I will, my lord." He took them out to examine them. I saw him place them on the table so that he could differentiate them.

I knew he could do two things at once and I asked, "And how did you pass your time?"

He lowered his voice but kept his eyes on the coins, "I spent many hours each day speaking with the queen. If nothing else I improved her English and I was able to furnish her with the differences between England and France. I am well placed to notice such things for I have had to learn what it is like to live in this land." He paused, "She is a clever young woman, my lord, and she is well read. I believe that, given the chance, she could be a good Queen of England. I enjoyed our time together and, I think, that she enjoyed my company too."

Those around us, realising that this was harmless conversation and not juicy gossip that could be repeated, began to talk amongst themselves. That they would be talking about my arrival was clear but it meant their attention was not on Robert's words.

When he heard their words and knew they were no longer listening, Robert lowered his voice even more. I had to lean towards him to hear, "The queen is unhappy with the way that her husband treats her, Sir Gerald, and that the Earl of Cornwall mocks her. She has written to her father, the King of France."

I knew that one reason for the marriage, perhaps the main reason, was to have France as an ally. Such mistreatment might negate the effect of the marriage. "I shall eat first and then we can talk."

The food was rich and I preferred plainer fare but I was so hungry that I just devoured it. I knew that the small quail I ate would be the simplest of dishes and I soon demolished it. The bread was good bread, it was manchet, and with the finest of butter and well-cooked salted ham it was a filling meal. I finished off with cheese and then the dried fruits brought from distant shores. By that time some of those around us had departed and we could speak a little easier.

"So the queen is unhappy?"

"More than unhappy, my lord. With the king away the earl took every opportunity to demean her. I may have angered him for I defended her and he did not like it."

I chuckled, "Upsetting Piers Gaveston seems to me the easiest thing in the world. Merely to exist and not worship at his feet appears to be enough to raise his ire. For one who has yet to do anything of import he has a great deal of self-belief. Perhaps that is what comes of being the king's favourite."

Robert warned, "My lord."

A merchant and his wife were watching us and I had spoken a little louder than I should have. I shrugged, "My opinion of the earl is well known. Such criticism can hardly make me more unpopular but you are quite right and having filled my belly, it is time we retired." I stood and I noticed that a slight hush fell on the room. I waved an arm, "The archer shall leave and afford you all the time to talk about the Warbow." I gathered in the coins from the table and put them back in the purse.

Once outside Robert shook his head, "My lord, Lady Mary would not be happy that you are so outspoken."

I put my arm around his shoulder, "Robert, I have come to realise that it matters not what I say or do. So long as the earl has the ear of the king my life hangs in the balance. Why worry about something that I can not alter? Come, let us go to our chambers. I feel the need to confess."

Robert had long ago told me that he felt ill at ease being my confessor but I liked the fact that I could confess any time I chose. I did not need absolution but if I was to meet my maker then at least I would be shriven and both my age and circumstance meant that I knew I had less time left to me on this earth.

Once in the room I asked him about the Parliament. He had a sharp mind and knew how to listen. "There are more barons here now, my lord, and most are in a belligerent mood. Thomas of Lancaster came the other day and he and the king's favourite had a blazing row. My lord of Lancaster left for his own home. He leads the opposition to the Earl of Cornwall. The king's cousin has many supporters."

"That is no surprise. Gaveston called him the Fiddler. Sir Thomas is a fine knight and he fought with the old king at Falkirk. His father, Lord Edmund, was also a good soldier and went on crusade with us. I would back Sir Thomas against the earl any day."

"And yet, my lord, you have to back the king in Parliament."

I was silent for a moment. Robert was right and had seen into my heart. If I opposed the king in Parliament then I would be held on some trumped-up charge and executed. If I supported the king then many men would feel obliged to side with me and therefore the king but I would lose friends. That seemed to me the choice I had to make. I could lose my honour or lose my life. Honour had always seemed something for others to worry about but now I realised that, despite all that I had done, it had normally been backed by the belief that I was doing the right thing. Supporting Piers Gaveston to please the king did not seem like the right thing to me.

"My lord?"

I had been silent, "Sorry, Robert. Now I shall unburden myself of the last day. I have shed blood and I sent arrows into the backs of men. I need to confess for some might call that murder."

He nodded.

I began and told him all that had happened since leaving the palace. It was a relief to utter the words. It felt as though I had taken a heavy pack from my shoulders. I did not like to send arrows into the backs of men, no matter how much they deserved it. I preferred to face the men I slew. Robert was a priest, at least he had trained in a monastery and ministered to villagers in France, and this was the confessional. I also knew that Robert would die before he betrayed me. He was the most loyal of men and I knew that finding him outside Notre Dame when I had been hunting William Wallace was one of the most fortunate things that had ever happened to me.

When I had finished, Robert gave me absolution and then asked, for he was a clever man, "What are your thoughts about the coins, my lord?"

"The English ones were understandable. There are men who hate the king and would want him dead and replaced with another who was more acceptable. Thomas of Lancaster perhaps. Piers Gaveston might want the king dead, too, but first he would need to be in a position to take power. Queen Isabella is a threat for when she bears the king a child, if it is a son, then Piers Gaveston can never rule. The earl has the means to pay for the ambush but I do not think he was behind it. Thomas of Lancaster is the heir should King Edward die and perhaps he has reason, but I do not think that this is in his nature."

"I think your reasoning is sound, my lord."

"What about Thomas, Earl of Norfolk? He is the king's half-brother."

"And he is eight years old." I shook my head, "Nor, while I think about it, would Thomas of Lancaster hire men to murder the king, however there might be men who support the Earl of Lancaster but act without his authority. It will be a lesser lord but one with money."

"And the Scottish coins?"

"Easy, that would be de Brus. Any man who can murder a rival in a church would not worry about paying for assassins. I think that de Brus does not fear King Edward but he fears England and dissent would suit him. It is another reason to finish what King Edward started."

"And the Welsh?"

"That is harder to fathom. Madog ap Llywelyn was the last Welsh rebel and he is a guest in the tower. I know of none with a claim to the throne and that disturbs me for I should know. Perhaps this Iago ap Daffydd is a follower of the man who paid for the assassins. I do not know. My lands are on the border. When this Parliament is over and if I am free to return home then I would discover who is behind this. The Scots are far enough away for me not to worry about them but rebellious Welsh are a different matter."

"Then it seems, my lord, that this is a conspiracy that brings together people who are not natural allies. The Welsh and the Scottish hate the English but as the old King Edward used Welsh mercenaries in his wars there is little love lost between those Celtic people. The English connection is more disturbing. It seems to me that rebellion is in the air."

"And the Normans?" I had my own theory but Robert had lived on the other side of the Channel and I valued his opinion.

"Easy, since Normandy was lost they have become mercenaries. They are descended from Norsemen and they were, so far as I can recall, pirates and slavers." I smiled. Robert was a Frenchman and they did not like the Normans.

My sleep that night, despite my tiredness, was riddled with dreams. I could not remember them when I woke but they had been disturbing.

The king and the earl did not return to Westminster until the day of the Parliament, the 3rd of March. They arrived with the Archbishop of Canterbury. Robert had been right; there was opposition to the king and his favourite but that opposition was not united. The Earl of Lincoln, Henry Lacy, led much of the opposition but thanks to his daughter being divorced from Thomas of Lancaster, the two men who could have united against the king hated each other. There were a few men who supported the king and there were others who vacillated and would give the king their support if they thought that they could get something out of it.

Robert, of course, was not a baron and would not be attending the Parliament. I felt very much alone as we gathered in the Great Hall. I saw factions gathering. Pointedly, the Earl of Lincoln was seated as far away from the Earl of Lancaster as he could manage. It was laughable really for they both hated the king but for different reasons. I thought back to the meeting at the Tower. I was summoned on the eve of the Parliament. Some might have thought it was to thank me for my efforts on the road but it was not. It had been to make it quite clear that I was to support the king and, by association, the Earl of Cornwall. That done I was dismissed and I noticed that I was kept away from Sir John and the bodyguards. Did Piers Gaveston fear that I might suborn them? The man thought everyone was as treacherous as he was.

When the two of them arrived in the Great Hall the Earl of Cornwall fixed me with his gaze. I knew that by the end of the day I could have lost many friends and my reputation for untarnished honesty would be in tatters. Had it been just my life that was at stake I might have spurned their offer and taken my chances. However, they had made it quite clear when I had been given my final warning that Jack and Hamo would suffer if I did not agree. I stood as far to the back as I could manage and hoped that few would see my capitulation. What I did notice was that the archbishop and the Earl of Lincoln greeted each other warmly. The archbishop had been in exile until recently. Whence came this friendship? I watched with a little more interest.

I had rarely attended Parliament. King Edward 1st had sometimes demanded my attendance but only when it was something that mattered to him and he needed not only my support but the physical presence of the Warbow. There were rituals and words that meant nothing to me.

The king sat on his chair and his face showed that he was pleased with himself. The Earl of Cornwall stood behind and kept a hand on the king's shoulder. Occasionally, while the necessary words were spoken the king would look up and smile at his friend. The king began by demanding that the barons swear allegiance to him. I frowned. Even his father had not done that. What happened next shocked the two men at the centre of our attention and, I confess, surprised me. The smile on the face of the Earl of Lincoln told me that he had been prewarned of the king's demands. When the archbishop handed him some documents I saw a frown appear on the face of Piers Gaveston.

The earl spoke eloquently and calmly at first but gradually his voice increased in power. He argued and provided sources to back him up that we barons owed allegiance to the Crown and not, ad personam, the king. His argument changed a little and I saw the real purpose behind it. He went on to rail against the Earl of Cornwall who, he said, had perverted justice and apportioned coins from the treasury. When he stopped speaking the barons all cheered. There was no support for the Earl of Cornwall. I remained silent but I do not think that the earl and the king were bothered about me.

The king asked the archbishop to speak and it was then I saw the conspiracy come to light. The archbishop took up where the earl had left off. He spoke of the things that Piers Gaveston had done and accused him of disinheriting and impoverishing the Crown. I saw then how clever the two men had been. The acts of the Earl of Cornwall were now, thanks to their legal arguments and the sources they quoted, treasonous. More importantly they were on the records for this was a Parliament and I wondered if Piers Gaveston would be impeached. The archbishop had an even stronger card to play. When he had finished and while a white-faced Piers Gaveston clutched at the back of the king's chair, the Earl of Cornwall was excommunicated. He was given until the 25th of June to leave England. He was also stripped of the title of Earl of Cornwall. He was losing the richest county in England. I saw lords like Gilbert de Clare, the Earl of Hereford and one of the men who had fought the Scots applauding the archbishop's words. There was clear opposition to Piers Gaveston. The Parliament saw the rising up of all that resentment. The old King Edward would have approved. He hated Gaveston.

That was the moment the Parliament ended. There was no vote for no vote was necessary. The king and the earl rose and stood close to one another, their heads in conference. I wondered what would happen next. Could I leave and return home or were the threats the two men had made still in place? I suspected that the two men had more on their mind than Gerald Warbow.

The Earl of Lincoln and the archbishop were surrounded by barons keen to show their approval. It left Thomas, Earl of Lancaster with his handful of supporters. I knew Thomas and had been a friend of his father's. I had known Edmund Crouchback from his days as a crusader. I went to his side. He nodded, "Warbow, you rarely attend these things and I confess that I have not been at one that was so…lively."

"No, my lord and I wondered what happens now?"

"Now?"

"Do we stay or are we free to return to our homes? We were summoned."

"Aah, I see. I for one will be staying for the archbishop has certainly caused a stir and I would speak privately with him when de Lacy is not here. As for you, there is no reason why you should stay." I hesitated and the earl said, "Unless there is more." I glanced at the men with him and he nodded, "My lords, give the baron and I a little space, eh?" They moved away and he said, "Now speak plainly."

I told him of the threats that had been made. I saw anger written on his face and in his eyes, "That is despicable and dishonourable beyond words. You should have come to me and you would have had my support."

"My lord, I do not wish to cause dissension. You are the cousin of the king…"

"Nonetheless, I now know and in the unlikely event that Piers Gaveston remains in England I will defend you and your family."

"Thank you, my lord."

The Parliament dissolved into chaos. The various factions gathered in the hall. The ones supporting the king were noticeable by their absence. The king and the former Earl of Cornwall tried in vain to speak to the archbishop but it was to no avail. The king and the earl left and, at the door, I saw Sir John and the bodyguards as they drew their swords to protect the king and his favourite. I hurried to our chambers where Robert awaited me.

"Well, my lord?" He wondered what was my intention. To be truthful even I did not know exactly what I planned to do.

"Gaveston is exiled and has lost Cornwall and all of its income."

"And us?"

"I do not know. I think that we can leave. Let us wait a day and see what transpires. I think the delay is necessary. We need to prepare our horses in any case. While I go to the stable, wander the palace and see what you can discover. Say little and keep your ears open."

I knew the ostler well for I had often visited our horses and I had rewarded him whenever I did so. I knew that the post was not well paid and London was an expensive city in which to live. "Robert and I may well be leaving in the next day or so. I came to see if our horses were ready to travel."

He beamed, "Yes, my lord. They are fit and raring to open their legs. I have exercised them each day in the yard for they are good horses. I shall be sorry to see you and they leave."

That was my first hurdle passed. He had not been given orders to deny our departure. Now if the same could be said for the guards at the gates…

I headed for the gates. Each time I had tried to leave the captain of the guard, whilst sympathetic to our situation, had denied me permission to leave, even to visit the Chepe. I just stood in the gatehouse and spoke with them, soldier to soldier. After we had discussed harmless and innocent matters he shook his head and said, "Well, here is a pretty pickle, Sir Gerald. The king has told us to stop all the lords from leaving the palace."

"All the lords? The earls of Lincoln and Lancaster? The archbishop?"

"Yes, my lord. It cannot be done, not without bloodshed." He suddenly stared at me, "You do not wish to leave too, do you?" I knew he would obey his orders but he would not be happy about it.

I made light of it, "Not this day but within a few days. I was summoned for the Parliament and now it is over…"

He looked relieved, "Aye, well until we get orders to the contrary we will hold firm. I pray that there will be no bloodshed." He shook his head, "The old king…"

I nodded, "Aye, those days are gone and we live in parlous times, Captain. Good luck." We would not be allowed to leave.

I could not see Thomas Lancaster standing for this indignity and being held against his will. He would dispute the order. I headed back to the Great Hall. I did not see Robert there. The hall was filled with barons and so far none had tried to leave. They were all too busy debating what had happened. It had been a master stroke from the Earl of Lincoln. No one had been expecting it. I had known of his skill as a soldier, I had fought alongside him in the Scottish wars, but it seemed he knew how to use such skills in Parliament. Robert returned not long after a servant had brought me wine and food.

He sat and smiled, "The king and queen are packing. They are quitting London and heading for Windsor."

"And Piers Gaveston?"

"He is leaving it seems with them but I think the king has plans for him." He shrugged, "That was the rumour."

It was late in the afternoon and the gathering of barons had thinned. I think that some had wanted to leave. Those with manors in the south and east of the land would wish to return to their homes. There was a furore at the hall's entrance and I heard raised voices. Henry Lacy and Thomas Lancaster's were clearly discernible. I stayed away from the row and after they had left remained with the handful of other barons who had chosen to stay.

The barons did not return. Instead, while the hall was being prepared for the evening feast, Sir John Charleton entered. He was looking for someone and when his eyes alighted on me he strode over. Eyes followed him for he was known to be the king's man. He reached me and bowed, "Sir Gerald, I have news." He leaned in and lowered his voice, "You and your man have permission to leave Westminster."

"This is not a trick, Sir John? I have your word?" I trusted Sir John but knew that this could be a trap concocted by Piers Gaveston and I could be arrested for disobeying the king's command.

He nodded, "The king's opinion of you has changed, Sir Gerald, and the new Lord Lieutenant of Ireland has other matters on his mind."

I was distracted and did not take the words in immediately, "Lord Lieutenant of Ireland?"

He gave a strange smile, "Sir Piers Gaveston is the new Lord Lieutenant of Ireland with immediate effect. Sir Richard de Burgh, the Earl of Ulster, was supposed to take up the position but the king has made a different appointment."

Robert said, "So exile does not mean exile."

Sir John shrugged, "It is not England, my lord."

This was obfuscation but I cared not. I was free. I was relieved and smiled, "Thank you."

"There is more, my lord. I am appointed the captain of the guards sent to protect the Lord Lieutenant while he commands in Ireland. I shall be abroad too and I fear I will not have the opportunity of visiting you at Yarpole as I had planned." He held out a hand, "This is farewell."

I grasped it, "Watch out for yourself, Sir John. You are a good soldier and deserve a life. Remember our words on the road."

"I will remember them, my lord, and when I have the opportunity I will act upon them. I thank you both for your service and advice. I have learned from your service and I will heed your advice." He turned and left.

When he had gone Robert and I were the centre of attention. It was natural enough. When one of the Earl of Lancaster's men came to tell me that the king had rescinded the order and all could leave I thanked him and turned to Robert, "We have one last feast here and then tomorrow we ride hard for home. Let us see how quickly we can make the journey, eh?"

He grinned, "Aye, my lord. A few saddle sores will be a fair price to pay to get back to Lady Mary and the warmth of Yarpole."

Even though we left as soon as the gates were opened it was still a long journey. Our horses had been rested but there was no way that they could make the one-hundred-and-forty-mile journey in less than three days. The first halt was at Oxford. It was a hard fifty-mile ride but I knew that we could stay at Oxford Castle. There the talk was all about the Parliament and the appointment of Piers Gaveston as Lord Lieutenant of Ireland. Our delay of a day had allowed the news to spread and spread it had for it was momentous. The appointment had angered many barons and the feeling in Oxford was that the king was disobeying not only the wishes of his barons but an order from the highest prelate in the land. His support for Piers Gaveston was costing him dear. We also heard that the king had given Piers Gaveston vast estates in Gascony and England to make up for the loss of revenue incurred by the taking away of Cornwall.

As we rode towards the Welsh border I spoke with Robert, "Piers Gaveston has the king in a web. Until the web is cut and the spider removed we cannot have a king who can rule us well."

"And Queen Isabella, my lord, is most unhappy too."

"A king needs a good wife. Queen Eleanor was the best of wives for King Edward and when she died and it broke his heart, he chose another who was just as good. I know that Isabella will make a good queen but the king has to let her become one."

Gloucester Castle, our last stop before home, showed us that those on the borders were equally unhappy with the king's decision. Gilbert de Clare respected my opinion. He was also not a man to take orders well and he and his retinue had left Westminster as soon as possible after the archbishop had announced the exile. He had not heard of the gift of the lands in Gascony and he spoke openly to me.

"You know, Warbow, that we need the revenue from Gascony to fund the war against the Scots. We left a job unfinished when the king died. De Brus needs his wings clipped. We could do without this distraction."

"And the Welsh Marches, my lord, are they quiet?"

He gave me a strange look, "Aye, why? Have you heard something?"

I could not speak of the attack on the Canterbury road and so I shook my head, "No, my lord, but, as you know my lands lie close to the border and last year the Welsh did have nuisance raids."

"I remember and you dealt with them alone." He looked relieved, "And that is why we need your bow and keen eye watching that land. You served England against the Scots many times. You were the one who caught Wallace." He smiled, "Enjoy your sunset years, Sir Gerald, God knows you have earned them."

When Robert and I left Gloucester Castle for the last few miles home I knew that I had no sunset years ahead of me. I needed to find out which Welsh lord had helped to hire the mercenaries. The Earl of Hereford was quite right, the new King of Scotland, Robert de Brus was still a threat but there was another viper much closer to home.

Chapter 4

Yarpole 1308

There were tears when we arrived at my home. Yarpole is not a large village and word of our return spread like seeds on the wind. I suppose men at the outlying farms saw our horses and my distinctive shape and called across to their neighbours as we wound our way around the hedgerow lined road that led to my hall. We had been away since before Christmas and that was a long time for me to be away without my soldiers. Mary, wrapped against the chill wind, was waiting for us as we clattered into my yard. I dismounted and she hurled herself into my arms and wept. I held her tightly not trusting my voice to utter any words.

My steward appeared in the doorway along with Anna, one of the serving women. John smiled and his voice was thick with emotion, "It is good to have you home, Sir Gerald. Abel, tend to the horses. I will see to your bags, my lord." He smiled at my healer, "Welcome, Robert, we have a good fire to warm you both." Thanks to his skills Robert was one of the most popular men in the manor. He had saved both lives and limbs since he had joined my retinue.

John's words prompted me to put my arm around Mary and guide her into the hall, "It is too cold for you to endure the wind and the elements." The practical nature of my words allowed me to utter them.

She laughed through her tears, "It would be worth enduring a snowstorm to have my arms around you once more." Her voice was husky, "We thought that you were lost forever."

Sarah, the housekeeper said, "I will have the bedding changed on Master Robert's bed, my lord."

The yard of my walled home was not the sort of place to have a conversation about the trials and tribulations of the past months and we hurried inside where the warmth of the hall hit us. Shedding my travelling clothes once we were through the door, Mary led me to the warmth of the fire where Anna and the other servants had already fetched ale and food.

When John came in to see that all was done well he said, "I have sent riders to your son, Hamo and stepson, Jack, to let them know of your return." He added, "They have been most anxious and they need to know that you are safe and home."

Mary nodded, "That was well done, John, I predict that the two will arrive within a short time." She seemed to see Robert for the first time. She held her arms out for him and he hugged her a little self-consciously. He had not enjoyed a cosy family in France but my wife, despite her title, was the warmest of women and she embraced him. "It gave me great comfort knowing that you were with Sir Gerald during his time in London."

"I was happy to be his companion, my lady."

"And is now the time to speak of your incarceration?"

I shook my head, "I would not tell it twice and Jack and Hamo will need to know all." I drank half of the ale I had been given. The ale in Kent had been good but it could not compare with what was brewed in my own manor. I sighed with satisfaction as the amber nectar slipped down my throat, "And I would know all about the manor. How fare my people?"

Mary was a good lady of the manor. She ensured that the poor and the sick were seen to and she attended as many births as she could. As I drank and nibbled the food that had been brought, she told me of the men at arms and archers who had become fathers. Many of them had fought their last battle and were now more farmers than warriors. Others, like Harry, my former sergeant at arms now ran the village inn or had businesses in Yarpole. We were a family and I knew without asking that when my wife had visited my people in my absence they had all asked after me and the Frenchman who had accompanied me.

I ate and drank, as did Robert. Mary just studied me as though I was new to her. Robert remained silent, revelling in the warmth of the house and the welcome. I heard a door slam and footsteps race along the corridor. When Dai entered the hall he looked to have grown a head taller since I had left. We had rescued him and now he was part of the household. He was not a servant and, if anything, acted more like a squire to me but as I had never enjoyed having a squire I saw him as a youth who could fetch and carry when I was at war. Now there was no war and I was greeted by him like a grandfather. I liked the feeling. He raced in with the broadest of smiles on his face, reddened by the wind, "It is good to have you home, my lord." His lilting Welsh accent made me feel that I was truly home.

"And no one is happier than Robert and me. It has been a most interesting time."

"And how was it, my lord?" He was asking about the Parliament. I shook my head, "When Jack and Hamo arrive then it will be time for the telling of stories. There is much to tell." I smiled, "Tell me about Yarpole."

Between the two of them they gave me all the tales of the village. They were not important events but, to me, more worthy of the telling than the stories we had heard in Westminster.

Warbow

I heard the clattering of hooves in the yard and I knew that Jack and Hamo had come from nearby Lucton and Luston. When John came in to tell us Mary said, "John, have rooms prepared."

My steward smiled, "I have already done so and the cook has a suckling pig in the oven. I thought it a propitious meal for my lord's return."

I smiled for I thought I had detected the aroma of roasting pork filling my hall. Part of me had wondered if that was wishful thinking for I yearned for roast pork.

Hamo and Jack burst into the room like whirlwinds and Hamo, now a mighty archer, broad and powerful, almost picked me up in his arms. His voice was that of a young boy when he huskily spoke in my ear, "When we heard nothing from you we feared the worst. I am glad that my fears were unfounded. It is good that you are back."

"I have an interesting tale and it awaited your arrival."

Jack was my stepson. He had been Jack of Malton and we had adopted him. He was no less of a son to me. I thought of both of them as my sons as did the rest of the household and the village. The difference was he was slighter of build than Hamo and could not pick me up. He hugged me just as hard and I felt him shaking. He could not find the words. I said, quietly, "It is good to be back, Jack." I released him and saw the tears in his eyes. I nodded, "Let us sit, drink ale and you can hear of our time in London. If I never see that city again it will be too soon."

When they were all seated I began. I noticed that Anna and John stayed close to see if we needed any more ale or food. They would attend to us if we needed goblets refilling but they were just as interested in the story as any. Whatever I said would be known by those in the hall by the end of the day and in the village by the end of the next day. I told them the truth. I knew that none would exaggerate what I said. I changed the story of the ambush to an attack by bandits. I would tell Jack and Hamo the truth at another time. Mary would hear the rightful tale before we slept. I finished with the news of Gaveston's exile.

Mary was the one who spoke first, "So, we are safe from the wrath of the king?" She knew all of my fears and doubts. I kept no secrets from my wife and when I had left Yarpole all those months ago she had known that I might not return, such was the king's enmity.

I shook my head, "Baby steps, my love. I have been of service to the king and so, at the moment, I am not an enemy but this is not the King Edward that you and I knew. This is his unpredictable son. Even when he is directed by the church to do something he comes up with his own ideas. Piers Gaveston is in Ireland and God help the Irish. Scotland is still a danger but I do not think I will be needed, not for a while anyway. My eyes are to the west and the Welsh. How sits the border, Hamo?" The Welsh coins prayed on my mind.

In my absence I knew that my son would have ridden the land that was until recently Welsh and was now England. He said, "If Gilbert de Clare thinks that the Welsh are cowed he is mistaken. They have no leader yet but there are young hotheads who think that as we have a weak king then the lands Longshanks took from them should be returned. That there is no figurehead is the only good news but when one rises then the borderlands will be aflame again."

Jack smiled, "But when it does we have the men to douse those flames and they will be led by Gerald Warbow. I for one will have my first decent night of rest since the summons to London. Our prayers were answered and I will thank God on Sunday."

There was as much interest in Robert's experiences as mine. He was a popular man because not only was he a well-read man he was also a healer but, most importantly, he knew how to listen. Such skills are often overlooked. He told them of his meetings and conversations with the queen. My wife had been close to Queen Eleanor and she understood, better than most, the problems such ladies faced.

The homecoming feast was like dying and being reborn again. When we had left for London I had convinced myself that I would not be returning. The warmth of my welcome was testament to my family's love for me and I had the joy to come of seeing my grandchildren and my daughters-in-law. I would have a second rebirth. How lucky was I?

Mary shooed everyone to bed despite the fact that they all wished to talk long into the night. She wanted me alone. We cuddled and we kissed and then, as she lay with her head nestled in my arms, I told her the things I had left unsaid. She was particularly interested in the connection with Hamo le Strange. "The old religions believed that such meetings were ordained, husband."

"That sounds like blasphemy."

"Perhaps but you cannot but think about the events that brought us together and Hamo and the Queen of Beirut and now a distant relative has come into your life."

"He is in Ireland and I do not think that we shall meet again."

She laughed, "That is a nonsense and you know it. You can never know what Fate has in store for us." She was silent for a while, "Your news about the Welsh connection was troubling."

"How so?"

"At Christmas we had a message from Lady Hawise ferch Owain. She asked for you. Her messenger said that no one else would do and that she needed to speak to you on an urgent matter. I sent a message back that you were in London and I could not contact you." She sighed, "I was distracted by your absence and I hope the lady was not in any danger…" Shaking her head, "I could have sent Hamo or Jack but…"

Hamo and Jack were good men and kind but they did not have the connection with the young heiress that I did. The king's command might have cost her dear. It would do no good to say so to my wife and I said, instead, "We could have done nothing, could we? I will ride there when time allows. Her home is a day's ride away. Am I being selfish to wish a week with my family?"

"No, of course not, but I know your nature. The plight of this young lady will weigh heavily on you and you will fret. You are doing the same about Queen Isabella, Robert's tale told me that. A man cannot change what he is and I would not have you any other way. If all men were as honest and true as you then the world might not be such a dangerous place."

I was uncomfortable with the flattery. I knew my nature and I knew that my heart could be as black as the next man's. I kissed her, "And now a night of true rest. With you in my arms and my own goose feathers in the mattress I am as happy as the richest lord in the land."

The next day I woke refreshed and bade farewell to Jack and Hamo as they left to return to their manors. I promised that I would ride to both their homes within the next days. I wished to see my daughters-in-law and grandchildren. My sons had their own manors and knew the responsibilities of a lord of the manor. I had people to see. When they had gone I walked around my hall and greeted all those I had not had the chance to speak to on my arrival. I went to the horse master and then the French man at arms, Michel and his son. They were now part of my mesne and as loyal as any natural born Englishman. I then went into the village. Father Michael was in his church and I spoke to him. "I need to give thanks to God for I know he had a hand in my return. What can I do that will show my thanks?"

He nodded to the end of the church, "My lord, we need a better font. Such a dedication would be a monument for all to see and as we have many births in the village it would remind the people of our debt to God."

I nodded, "A splendid idea. I will ride to Shrewsbury and have the masons make one."

My next call was to Harry at his inn. Harry had been the best man at arms who had ever served me. That he had lived long enough to say he wanted to retire was testament to his skill. He was testing a new batch of ale when I entered. He beamed, "I heard you were back, my lord, and I shall brew a special ale in celebration. This one is good enough but your men will want to come here on Sunday after archery and sword training. They will want to give thanks for your return. The ale will be ready by then." He grinned, "And you, my lord, will, I hope, join us. The men would like to hear the stories. I dare say they will not be fit for the ears of ladies but you will be able to regale warriors with them."

I shook my head, "How do you know that I have such tales?"

His face became serious, "Because you are Sir Gerald Warbow and adventures follow you like seagulls with a fishing boat."

"I will drink with my men but do not expect entertainment." My name and my reputation could be a curse. If I had been an ordinary warrior like Harry then my life might be more normal than it was. I was forgotten, for the moment, by the former Earl of Cornwall and the king but I knew that my memory might be dragged to the surface. I also knew that neither the Scots nor the Welsh would have forgotten me. I asked Harry about travellers. His inn was popular. He served good food and many people stopped on their way to Shrewsbury. He was a good listener and picked up pieces of news like a nesting bird picks up twigs. They soon build a nest and by the time I left I had a better picture of the borderlands.

By the time it was noon I had walked the length of my village and greeted everyone I met. They were thankful for my return but each of them spoke of my wife's kindness to them in the harsh days of December and January. Those were the days when the old died but thanks to my wife we had not lost a single villager and that, as they all commented, was rare.

I spent the afternoon with John. He ran the manor for me but what he could not do was deal with the assizes. There were not many cases but there were enough for him to ask if I could hold a session within the next month. I let him arrange the date. What he did not have for me were the accounts of my more distant manors, Coldingham, Sadberge and Balden. I was not concerned about the income but I liked to know how men who had served me, like Dick, Mordaf and Will were faring. We had fought together and I trusted them implicitly but they all had families now and I wanted to know that they were well. Lucton and Luston were close enough for me to have a good idea of their income. The result was that we were well off. The cost of the font I would order to be built would be easily borne. We did not waste coins on what I saw as wasteful luxuries. We grew our own food and my men made our furniture. The extra money went on warriors. My men were well trained and had the best of arms and, where necessary, armour. Thanks to my horse master we had plenty of horses. They were, in the main, neither

Warbow

coursers nor war horses but, like Thunder, my horse, good hackneys. We could ride to war if we had to. For the size of manors we had more men than most but I reasoned that this close to the border that was necessary. Mary did not object and she was my touchstone.

By the time the business was done I could prepare for my evening meal. "Where is Robert, Mary? I have not seen him all day."

She smiled, "He did what you did, husband. He went to speak to the villagers. They missed you but they also missed the kind and clever man you brought from Paris. They will ask him for salves to ease their aching joints and tell him of the small pains they endure. Robert's words can often heal without the need for a salve. He will return, ere long. Whilst it is quiet let you and I enjoy a goblet of sack before we eat. The food is prepared and all know what they are to do."

We sat in companionable silence as we drank the wine from Portugal. I had first drunk it when I had served in Northern Spain with The Lord Edward. Now I could afford the best and not the rough and ready drink that was as good for healing wounds as it was for drinking. When Robert returned it almost felt like an intrusion. It was not and when he made to leave I said, "Come and sit. Enjoy this wine and tell us what you discovered on your walk."

When he finished I noticed a touch of sadness about the Frenchman, "Is everything well, Robert? I know that Westminster was a trial for you but…"

"No, my lord, I was worried, it is true, but being able to help Queen Isabella was a good thing. Now I can help the people of Yarpole once more."

Mary was astute, "Robert, there is something more is there not? What troubles you?" There was the slight hesitation of a man thinking about making up a story and before he did Mary said, "Is it this Welsh lady, Hawise? My husband told me that you fell under her spell."

His face told the truth and he nodded.

I said, "You could try to win her?"

"And what can I offer her, my lord? I am not even a proper priest. I am neither fish nor fowl. She is a lady and an heiress."

My wife shook her head, "She sent a message here for my husband but you were in London. You should visit with her, Gerald and take Robert with you."

I looked at Robert, "And would you come with me?"

He gave a wry laugh, "While I would give my right arm to see her face again such a sight would tear my very heart from my chest. Yet I would go with you. If you could face assassins in the forest I can face my own demons."

Warbow

It was all very well to decide on such a venture but the lady lived in the Welsh lands. Her home was at Poole which was the heart of Powis and as she had sent to me for help I assumed that it was military might that could be required. It was a delicate matter. Too many men might suggest an invasion and too few lead to disaster.

The next morning I went to speak to Michel and his son, Jean Michel. They were tending their small holding. They were not farmers who played at being warriors, both were warriors who enjoyed farming. "I would ride, in the next seven days to Poole."

Michel frowned, "Is that not in Wales, my lord?"

"It is, my friend. I thought to take you two, as well as Hamo's brothers-in-law, James and John. It will be good experience for them."

Michel nodded, "That gives us the chance to put our beans in the ground before we leave. What horses shall we ride?"

"See the horse master. I will take just four archers with me and we have plenty of horses."

That done I went to the hall where my bachelor archers lived. I would not take married men. As we were going to Wales two of them were easy choices. Iago of Ruthin and Gruffydd of Builth were first choices. Gwillim and Hob would be the last two. Gwillim acted as my Vintenar. He was older than the others and, as yet, had not sought a wife. They were all happy for the ride and the ones not chosen looked, to me, to be disappointed.

The last one I would take, if he would go, would be Dai, the Welsh orphan we had rescued from a raid by Griffith de la Pole. If he did not I would understand for he had not only almost lost his own life but everyone he had cared for had died. I also decided to take a war bow once more. The use of the borrowed one had saved men's lives on the Canterbury road. I had only stopped using one because I was no longer as good as I had been. That was pride. Dai would be able to act as a horse holder and to fetch arrows. When I asked him he grew even taller and I could see that my fears were misplaced.

"You would have me go to war with you?"

I shook my head, "This is not war, Dai. We go to visit with Lady Hawise at Poole. The armed men I take are a precaution."

He laughed, "Sir Gerald, your intention may be peaceful but I think the outcome will be more warlike." He so reminded me of young Jack when he had first come. There was a cheerful cheek to him.

That done, I rode with Dai the next day to see Hamo and Jack. Jack's home lay closest to the border and so we went to Hamo first. As with my archers he wanted to come with me after I told him my task. I refused, "Hamo, the lady sent to me. I believe that there will be no danger and if we were to need to go to war then you and your archers will be more use then. I do, however, need James and John." The two men at arms normally lived at my hall but as I had been away they had spent the winter with their sister and my son. After we had been to Wales they would return to my hall.

"And they will be more than happy to come with you."

"Do you need them here?"

"Take them now for you can teach them more than I can. I can train archers but you, Father, have more skills to impart than I do." He smiled, "Besides, they are your men at arms."

I managed to speak to my grandchildren and Hamo's wife Alice while the two men at arms fetched their war gear and horses. The children had grown so much that it made me realise how much I had missed them and as we rode to Lucton I reflected that I might not see them grow up. I determined to spend more time with all of my grandchildren.

Jack had not heard of danger across the border and that was understandable. He kept a watch on the border so that no one suffered in England. Lady Hawise lived in Wales and I knew that Jack could not possibly know what was going on across the River Severn. However the absence of danger on the English side was reassuring. I spent an hour with his wife and children before we rode back to Yarpole to be there before dark.

That night as we lay in bed Mary said, "Back but a short time and then away too soon."

I sighed in the dark. The truth was that I did not want to go. I knew I had to and Lady Hawise had been promised my support but the day spent with my sons and grandchildren showed me what I had missed. I had not even visited my daughter, her husband and those grandchildren who lived within riding distance. Was I doomed to be sent on more and more quests? Was that my purpose in life?

Mary squeezed my arm, "Better you go now and nip in the bud any trouble that there might be and there is something else."

"What?"

"You want to know who was the Welshman who paid for the ambush." My wife was clever and she could unpick my words as easily as a seamstress could take apart a garment.

"We only had coins and a dying man's jest. Even if a Welshman did pay the assassins he could be close to the lands of the Earl of Pembroke or be hiding in the mountains around Snowdon. We do not know."

There was a low chuckle, "Gerald Warbow, you can fool others but I know you. Crossing the desert with you all those years ago gave me a better insight into your mind. You seek to discover if the enemy lies close to your home and you will worry at this like a cat with a thread. Be away as short a time as you must and put your mind to rest."

"You are right and it is good that my enemies do not read me so easily as do you."

I had recently ridden as had Robert but for the rest this was something that they had not done since we had ridden to Kingston more than half a year since. Horses needed to be prepared and tack checked. Weapons were sharpened and blankets and food procured. I was the lord of the manor and others prepared Thunder and what I would need. I sat alone with the maps I had of the lands around Poole. It lay beyond the Severn, that natural border between Wales and England. Mountains rose to the west of it and there was a craggy outcrop to the south. The people there lived just forty miles or more from me but they did not farm the same way. We planted more crops than they did and they raised more sheep. It was a subtle difference between the people. When I had worked out the route I thought again of Lady Hawise and her situation. The death of her father meant that her uncles, her father's younger brothers, sought the valuable lands that had belonged to the Lord of Powis. In times past they had been minor kings. Her father's title had been Prince of Powis. If she had been born a man then there would have been no problem. It was her father's decision to leave her as a subject of the Crown of England in his will. When he had written it King Edward 1st had been on the throne and I think he thought Longshanks would have protected her. When I had met her I had seen how few men she had to protect her. If her uncles chose they could simply take the land from her and divide it up. The one thing that stopped them was the King of England. The new King Edward would not be bothered about the plight of Lady Hawise. The Mortimers might but I knew the Mortimers. They would seek not to ensure that lady Hawise had the land but that they gained another piece of Wales. This was a job for Lord Edward's Archer. My king was dead but I still felt obligated to do that which he would wish. I would go, not to start a war, but to warn the lady's Welsh uncles that they risked the wrath of the Warbow if they challenged the Crown. I knew that I was partly to blame for any problem Lady Hawise might be having for it was I who had caused the death of her brother.

Chapter 5

The eleven of us rode in a column of twos. Until we reached the Severn there was no need to have scouts out. We headed for Lucton and Mortimer's Cross at the crossing of the Lugg. From there we would head north. We had only ridden four miles or so but we stopped at my stepson's manor anyway. Girths could be tightened and I was able to speak to Jack.

"How long will you be away, Father?"

"How long is a piece of string? It could be I get there and see that there is no problem in which case I will pass by this way in two days' time. Equally, there could be a problem that requires Baron Warbow to act for England and Lady Hawise. Remember, all we know for sure is that Lady Hawise asked me to come and that was some time ago." The delay had not been of my making but that did not stop me from feeling guilty. It was strange for I had only met the young lady once and yet the memory of her had remained in my head. Part of it was the effect she had made on Robert.

"If you are not back in a week then I will seek you out." Jack worried about me just as much as Hamo did.

"A fortnight." He looked as though he might object and I emphasised the words, "Fourteen nights." He nodded.

Once we left Lucton I rode flanked by Dai and Robert. The rest rode in pairs. Dai had the smallest horse. He had grown since his rescue and he had been taught to ride by Abel but he was still a youth who might not be able to manage a strong-willed horse. If nothing else this ride would help to train him. I asked him, as we rode, "And what do you see for yourself in the future, Dai?" I gestured with my thumb back towards Lucton, "Jack came to me when he was your age and now he has a manor and is a man at arms. That is one future."

Robert smiled, "Or you could be like me, Dai, and just fill the gaps that others cannot."

I snorted, "Stop feeling sorry for yourself, Robert. You have an honoured place in our home and have skills that Dai does not possess. A man uses what God gives him and makes the best of it. You have talents as a healer as well as one who is clever and can used his mind. He gave me a strong back and the eye of a killer. So, Dai, your future?"

"I like the idea of being a warrior such as James or John, but I am not sure that I have the skills."

James was riding behind and he said, "That is an easy problem to overcome. All it takes is hard work and a willingness to endure the sharp tongue of your captain of warriors. My brother and I are still learning but each day sees us better. It does not come overnight, Dai, but if you spend hours each day you will become stronger. Michel and his son are the best teachers that you could have."

Michel said, "And this ride will show you, I think, little Welshman, what it is that we do. There is more time spent making camps, standing watch and waiting around than fighting."

"They are right, Dai, but if you choose to be like John, my steward, then that is a choice you can make." My steward had looked after Dai and made him welcome. I would always attract soldiers for I paid well and looked after those who no longer served as warriors. Many lords simply abandoned old soldiers. My early days had shown me the parlous nature of the common soldier.

He shook his head and his face looked serious, "My family was slain. Hugh of Kington was butchered. I would learn how to fight for what is right. If an enemy comes for me again then I will defend myself."

We halted at Hopton Castle but the lord there, Sir Walter Hopton, was absent. He and his wife and son had gone on a pilgrimage to Canterbury for Sir Walter was not a well man. The castle lay close to the border. I told the captain of the six men who guarded the castle of my intentions. Captain Edward was an old soldier with scars that bespoke courage, he said, "We would help, my lord, but I am bound to guard this castle and what we could do is debatable. The days when I fought for the old King Edward are long gone."

"And I am the one who is charged with this duty. I just ask you to be vigilant."

"That we will, my lord." He hesitated, "You should know, Sir Gerald, that there have been more armed men across the Severn. They have not crossed over but we have heard from merchants who speak of swords being sharpened and worn, as well as restrictions on English merchants who try to ply an honest trade."

"This part of Wales has its own laws but it has no sovereignty."

He chuckled, "When Old Longshanks was on the throne, my lord, then they lived in fear of his wrath. Since he became diverted by the Scots and following his death..."

He left the rest unsaid. The presence of Dai told the tale of the effect of the death of King Edward. His family had been killed as a result of the lack of an iron fist in the borders. We left but, after we had crossed the border I held up my hand to stop my column. "I wish to arrive in Poole after dark. As I recall there is neither a castle nor a strong wall there and I intend to make our approach to the hall quietly. We will scout it out as though it is held by an enemy. I would rather look foolish than lose any of you." They nodded. "Gruffydd, do you know the place?" I had been there when I had returned the body of Lady Hawise's brother but my mind had been elsewhere. We had approached from the main road and in full view of the village. This time I wanted secrecy.

"Aye, my lord. There is an old, abandoned hillfort to the west of the town but the hall itself is an old one. Men call it Poole Castle but it is like your home, if you remember, my lord. It lies just off the green although the green is not as big as the one at Yarpole."

I nodded and it came back to me. There was a wall but neither towers nor fighting platform. "Then you and Iago can go on foot and scout it out. Can you lead us in by a way that escapes observation?"

He grinned, "Aye, my lord."

I turned to the others, "We ride in peace but we are ready for war. I do not like that there are men sharpening swords and men preparing for war on this side of the border. Archers, string your bows. Men at arms, have your sword hilts to hand. Dai and Robert, ride at the rear."

They both nodded as my archers strung their bows and my men at arms threw the left side of their cloaks over their shoulders to allow them to draw their swords quickly. I had brought a bow in a case but I left it hanging from my saddle. I slid my sword in and out of the scabbard. When we were ready I nodded and Gruffydd and Iago urged their horses on. We headed towards the small town whose woodsmoke we could now smell. The light was fading fast and I would have missed the lane that led to the right. Gruffydd had remembered well. It helped that he had grown up quite close to Poole. Leaving the road meant travelling on sod and that dampened the sound of the hooves of the horses. Almost as soon as we left the main road we found ourselves shaded by trees and that, added to the oncoming of the night, meant that we were hidden in darkness. Gruffydd had served me for some time but he clearly knew the area well. We had not needed his local knowledge when we had brought back the dead Welshman but now it was invaluable.

Night had finally fallen when he held up his hand to stop us. I nudged Thunder next to his horse. He did not speak but pointed and I saw the high wall that clearly marked the rear of the extensive manor. I waved my hand for us to dismount. When we had done so I nodded to Gruffydd who, with me in close attendance, began to walk around the side of the wall. The land was rough and untended. The path we followed looked to be an ancient one. There was a gate but that might be barred and was not the way for a baron of the realm to enter. There was silence all around us. The smell of woodsmoke from the house told us that there were people within and when we had rounded one corner I heard the murmur of voices from our left. There sounded like a few people and they were merrily chattering. I guessed that they were dining and that the hall lay close to this part of the outside wall. We reached the end of the property and Gruffydd stopped and handed his reins to Iago. The green lay before us and the more important homes in the small town were close by. He slipped around the front wall.

When he returned he beckoned me closer, "My lord, there are two men at the gate. They are armed but their weapons are not drawn."

I nodded, "You have done well. Now you and Iago go to the rear." I waved Robert forward. "You and I will go first." He nodded. "Michel, bring the rest of the men when I wave."

"What if there is danger, my lord?"

"Two men, even if they are belligerent, will not cause me a problem." I smiled, "If it does then it is time for me to hang up my sword and begin to drink in **Warbow Tavern** with Harry."

Leaving the protection of the wall, the two of us walked our horses along the road and the hooves attracted the attention of the two guards. There was a brazier and I saw their faces glowing in its light. As I neared them I recognised one as the old sergeant at arms I had met when I had brought the body of Lady Hawise's brother back. He had his hand on the hilt of his sword. He recognised me and, taking his hand from his sword, a smile broke across his face. "Sir Gerald! I feared you might be men come to do harm."

I smiled, "No, but I was sent a message from Lady Hawise before Christmas. Circumstances meant that I could not come earlier. I am here now."

He turned to the other sentry, "Mordaf, stand apart while I speak with the baron." The sentry who looked to be little older than Dai nodded and, picking his nose, wandered off. "My lord, Lady Hawise needed you when she sent the message." I waited for I could tell that the news was not going to be good. He lowered his voice, "Lady Hawise's uncle, Lord Gruffydd Fychan de la Pole came a month before Christmas and said that he and his brothers had decided that, with her brother dead, Lady Hawise had no right to inherit the land of the de la Pole family." I raised my eyebrows and he said, "My lord, I am a common soldier but I know that in Wales women cannot inherit." I nodded, "She is allowed to live here but it is in a small room attached to the main hall. She and her servant, Breffni, live there."

"And you?"

He sighed, "There might have been a time when I would have raised a sword to defend my lady but there were too many of them and I would have died. This way I can ensure that no one molests her."

"And is this Gruffydd Fychan de la Pole in residence?"

"He is. He has his band of friends who live in the house with him. There are five of them." He shook his head, "Nobles they say but Mordaf there has more nobility than they do."

"Soldiers?"

"He has six men who serve him but I would not grace them with the title of soldiers. They are hired swords or bandits more like. They are mercenaries of the worst kind."

I had enough information. I needed to act now. Delay would only warn them of my presence. "The hired swords, where are they?"

"They are in the warrior hall." He pointed and I saw, close to the main hall, a long low building with a single door.

"And servants?"

"Five of them. They will be serving. The new lord likes to eat long meals and drink as much as he can. He spends Lady Hawise's silver as though he had a mine."

I nodded, "I intend to recover this hall for Lady Hawise. She is a ward of the Crown and I am an officer of the Crown."

"Just you two?"

I smiled and said, "No. Robert, leave your horse here and fetch the others."

"Do you need help, my lord?" The old sergeant was both brave and loyal. I could hear it in his voice.

I shook my head, "I want you and Mordaf to ensure that we are not disturbed."

My men arrived, like ghosts. I did not need to explain. They were my men and would obey orders. "Gruffydd, there are six hired swords in the warrior hall, take the archers and secure them. If they resist then bind them."

He grinned, "Yes, my lord." There were only four of them but I knew that my four archers were more than a match for six hired swords who might well be in their cups by now. "Dai and Robert, watch the horses. The rest of you with me." I took off my cloak and laid it on Thunder's back. They all emulated me. I did not draw my sword but its drawing would take only a moment.

A wide-eyed Mordaf stood aside as I led my men to the hall. When we reached the door I could hear the sounds from within. The men were clearly drinking and were very noisy. I reasoned that the door would not be barred and when I tried the latch it lifted easily. The heat from the house hit me as soon as the door opened. The noise of raucous carousing rose in volume. I tried to remember the house from the last time I had been here and I seemed to remember that the dining room was at the bottom of the corridor and was on the left. I moved down towards the door. I heard a wild screech and the door opened. I pressed myself into the side of the hallway. There were lights there, brands burned in the two sconces, but they were closer to the door. I was in the shadows. A woman came out and I saw that she was distressed. She turned and stared at me. It could have been something that happened in the room or the shock of seeing a man but her hand went to her mouth and I feared she would scream. I put my finger to my lips and in that moment saw recognition. It was Breffni, Lady Hawise's servant, and she must have recognised me for she smiled. I pointed to the room and mouthed, "How many?"

She held up six fingers and then pointed to herself and held up two fingers. Two servants. I nodded and waved her further down the corridor. She not only moved further down but opened a door and disappeared from view. I put her from my mind and went to the door. I listened. Someone was telling a story about a female conquest. It was loud and lewd. It showed, if nothing else, that there were only men in the room. I waved my men to wait on either side of the door. When they had done so I opened the door. I did so slowly and my entrance was only observed by the two male servants. Their mouths opened and I smiled. They backed against the wall and it was their movement that made one of the men look first at them and then, as I came into his eyeline, me.

A young, slightly portly man, stood and barked, "Who the devil are you?"

His voice was a little slurred and his cheeks were red showing that he had been drinking heavily. I smiled. My men were still in the corridor and I moved into the room. "My apologies, gentlemen, there was no one at the door. I seek the owner of this manor, Lady Hawise ferch Owain ap Gruffudd ap Gwenwynwyn." I gave the full title for a purpose.

The man at the head of the table was slightly older than the other men around the table, although he was still little more than thirty years of age. He snapped, "This is not her manor." He made the word 'her' sound like a curse. "I am Gruffydd Fychan de la Pole and you are mistaken. Now leave my hall before I have you whipped."

A young man seated opposite Gruffydd Fychan de la Pole stood and grinned, "Let me teach him a lesson, Gruffydd. The man has a sword although he looks like an old man. I shall be gentle with him."

I turned and fixed him with a steely stare, "You are a bold young man that offers to teach me a lesson without knowing my identity. Before you teach me this lesson what is your name?"

"Hywel ap Geraint, and yours, old man?"

The others around the table laughed at the insult. I gave a slight bow, "I am Baron Gerald Warbow, formerly Lord Edward's archer." I saw that Gruffydd Fychan de la Pole recognised the name and all humour left his face.

The portly young man grinned and said, "Never heard of you. Run him through, Hywel, and I can get back to the beef. He is disturbing my digestion."

The man called Hywel drew his sword. "I have heard of an archer who served the old king and you look old enough to be him although, in truth, I thought you dead. Neither your title nor your name upsets me. You are an intruder and this is not England but Wales."

I drew my sword, "True this is Wales. It is the Wales I helped to conquer with King Edward, and, as the last man with any claim to the title of Lord of Powis is now dead, I think your point is somewhat wasted. As I have never heard of your name then I know not if you have any skill but I know that I have. If you wish to risk your life then so be it. Lay on but know this, I finish what I start. I hope that you are shriven for this bout may end with more than a cut from my sword."

Gruffydd Fychan de la Pole had a serious look on his face, "Hywel, there is no need for this. Let us seek the law to challenge this wild man."

I laughed, "Wild? My words are calm and well chosen. I have not shown any anger, Gruffydd Fychan de la Pole. You should know that if I do become angry, it will be over something more important than a gathering of drunks who, it seems, are only fit to make young ladies run from their presence." I smiled again, "In my view a sensible action with men who behave as animals."

I had not taken my eyes off the young man and he suddenly lunged at me with his sword. I had been expecting it. I still wore my gauntlets and I grabbed the blade and punched him in the face with the hilt and pommel of my sword. His nose erupted as my blow, delivered with an archer's arm, broke it. He dropped the sword and put his fingers to his face. The portly young man and another, sat at my side, grabbed their weapons and stood. I smiled, "Really?"

Hywel ap Geraint screamed, "He has broken my nose. Kill him."

"Yarpole!" I did not fear the men but it seemed prudent to reveal that I was not alone.

As the two men clumsily lunged at me with their swords, the door behind was thrown open and my men at arms entered with drawn swords. The two men did not seem to notice the door opening and their lunges were intended to take my life. Had I, indeed, been what they thought I was, an old man who could not defend himself, then I would have been, at the very least, badly wounded. As it was I flicked aside the sword that came from my right and grabbed the sword from the portly man. I pulled it from his grasp and threw it to the ground. My men had their swords at the throats of the two men, as well as the wounded man in a blur of blades. Gruffydd Fychan de la Pole looked shocked as did the last man who pointedly put his hands on the table. The blood was still pouring from Hywel's nose.

Gruffydd Fychan de la Pole recovered just a little of his composure. He stood and shouted, "Guards! Come to our aid." He smiled, "Now you will pay for this. My men will deal with you."

I nodded and sheathed my sword, "The ones in the warrior hall?" He nodded. I turned to Jean Michel, "Go and see if they have been dealt with."

Gruffydd Fychan de la Pole looked deflated. It was as much the calmness of my voice as anything. I said to the servants, "Be so good as to fetch Lady Hawise and I believe the steward who, when last I was here, was called Iago."

One of the men said, "Yes, my lord. Come, Morgan."

The two left and James and John gathered the weapons. I saw that the meal had only just started. I picked a small fowl and smiled, "I am hungry. I take it you do not mind." I tore off a leg and began to eat it. My men were all smiling. They had seen Gerald Warbow deal with three young cockerels in quick succession. The blood that covered the tunic of Hywel ap Geraint told them its own story.

It was Iago the Steward who came in. He took in the blood and the pile of swords and said, "Sir Gerald, you came."

I nodded, "I did and I am sorry that it was late. Do these," I paused to choose the words, "apologies for men squat in this house?"

Iago's voice was stiff, "That they do, my lord, and squat is the right word." I could hear the defiance in his voice. Like the sergeant at arms he must have endured the indignities of these parasites for the sake of Lady Hawise but now he could show his true feelings.

Gruffydd Fychan de la Pole pointed a finger at the steward. He feared me but he could still show his authority over a servant, "Watch your words, Iago, you will be out on the street."

"I think that the ones on the street will be those seated around this table but let us wait until the rightful owner is present eh? It would not do to pre-empt her decision." I put down the bone, "The fowl was delicious, Iago." Just then the door opened and Lady Hawise and a red eyed Breffni appeared. I bowed, "I am sorry, Lady Hawise, that I was delayed. I was with the king and I did not receive your message until a few days ago."

She smiled, "I knew that, if it was in your power, then you would come and save me from this horror." She put her arm around her servant, "Poor Breffni has been much abused by these men."

Gruffydd Fychan de la Pole snapped, "She is a servant!"

Lady Hawise shook her head, "She is a woman and should be treated with respect."

I nodded and said, "This is your property. Do you wish these men to leave?"

Her eyes narrowed, "Yes, Sir Gerald."

"And do you wish them to be punished?"

Hywel ap Geraint stood and his nose bled again, "You have no authority!"

For the first time I shouted and it was for effect, "I have every right. King Edward charged me with keeping order in the borderlands." I turned, "James and John, go with Iago and find these men's belongings. Throw them beyond the walls." I turned to Iago, "Do they have horses in the stables?"

Lady Hawise pointed at her uncle, "He has one, the rest belong to me."

"Then let them have the one horse."

Gruffydd Fychan de la Pole looked defiant, "And if we refuse to leave?"

I leaned forward, "Oh please do, I pray you. My men and I would take great pleasure in making this broken nose seem like a hangnail."

As if to prove the point Jean Michel returned. He said, "The hired swords are bound. Gruffydd took their buskins and they await without."

I nodded, "We have your men and we have you. Now either stand and be prepared to leave or…"

They stood and Gruffydd Fychan de la Pole said, "You have more men than this?"

I laughed, "I do but I am not sure that I need them. Now, before you leave know this, I will ensure that Lady Hawise is protected. She is a ward of the Crown and it matters not what Welsh law states. It is the law of King Edward that affords her protection. Tell your brothers this."

She suddenly said, pointing her finger at him, "And he and his brothers have taken all the lands my brother and I inherited!"

I frowned, "Then when you leave, warn your brothers that I will inform the king and then the men of my mesne will recover all of the lands that belong, rightfully, to Lady Hawise." I stared at her uncle, "I hope I have made myself clear."

He stood, "You have but I promise you that this is not over."

"Then, Gruffydd Fychan de la Pole, the next time we meet make sure that you have confessed for I will not be so merciful the next time you draw a sword in my presence." I let my men escort them out and sat at the table with Lady Hawise.

She smiled, "Iago, bring fresh platters. Breffni, join us. I will enjoy a meal in my own hall for once."

"You have not eaten here?"

She shook her head, "It is Breffni's old room that we share."

"I am so sorry I did not return sooner."

Breffni said, "My lord, are you not afraid that the men will return?"

I laughed as Iago and the servants cleared away the used platters. "Oh they will return, of that I have no doubt and they will come with the intention of retaking this hall but it will not be tonight. I think your uncle will seek his brothers first. I believe we have some days before they come back. They may well await our departure."

Lady Hawise said, "And when you do leave, what is to stop them retaking my home?"

"Firstly, the threat I represent. I do not live far away but you are right. They could return but before I leave I will ensure that you have good men to watch over you." I arrested Iago's arm, "Are there young men who live in Poole who might be willing to be warriors?"

"Of course, my lord, but even those bandits in the warrior hall could quash them."

"The old sergeant at the gate, what of him?"

"David of Abergele?"

"Yes, him. He could train the young men. He was willing to die to defend Lady Hawise but he knew it would be pointless."

Lady Hawise smiled, "He is an old man, my lord. He served my father."

I said, "As I hope I have just demonstrated, my lady, old men are not to be ignored."

Her hand went to her mouth, "Sir Gerald, I am sorry, I…"

Just then the door opened and Robert and Dai came in. I said, "I am not insulted but what you cannot know, my lady, for you are a lady and unused to war, is that old soldiers can be just as good as younger ones. Robert."

"Yes, my lord?"

"How goes it?"

"They have been ejected and the gates barred. Michel has arranged the watch. James and John are cleaning out the warrior hall and we will sleep there."

Lady Hawise said, "My lord, we would be happier with men sleeping in the hall."

"Then we three shall be your chamberlains."

"Very well, my lord, now sit and eat. Iago, have much of this food taken to the warrior hall. There is too much here for we five."

"Of course, my lady."

As he and the servants piled food on platters I said, "And Iago, it is not just David of Abergele and Mordaf who need a sword. Lady Hawise needs as many men as she can get. The ones I saw look like they bluster a great deal and plenty of swords and resolve will discourage them. Every man who serves Lady Hawise should be armed."

He nodded, "And having endured what we have these past months I will make sure it is not as easy the next time."

When the servants had left we ate. Dai looked uncomfortable until Lady Hawise said, "Young man, just eat the way you want. Breffni and I are not precious and we are grateful that you are here."

He smiled, "I will try, my lady."

"And you, Robert, enjoy your food."

"You remembered my name." I heard the surprise in his voice.

"Of course I did. You were a witty and intelligent guest the last time and I have missed your company."

She began to eat a little more heartily and we dined in silence. When we had enjoyed sufficient food she said, "My other lands? What of them?"

"Ah, my lady, not quite as easy a task. I am assuming that they are all as valuable as this manor."

"They are."

"And your uncle will inform his brothers and half-brothers what has happened. That means that it may take either an army or the presence of the king to recover them. I will write to him and let him know what has happened here. If you could petition him too then we could mobilise more men."

"Baron Mortimer, perhaps."

I shook my head, "Baron Mortimer seeks to rule this part of Wales. I do not. There are other knights we might use." I wiped my mouth, "We take it step by step, my lady. We have this hall and I will not leave until I am confident that it can be held. Then I will let the king know what has happened."

I was thinking that if Sir John Charleton had not been sent to Ireland then he and his family would have been able to help. Gilbert de Clare had shown that he was not averse to chastising the Welsh and I hoped that he might send men. That it would take numbers of men to restore all her lands was clear to me.

She smiled, "Well, you are here now and my position is better now than it was before the sun set."

Iago came in, "We have changed all the bedding, my lady. It is not the best bedding. Our," I saw him seeking the word, "visitors made a mess of your best ones. My wife will have the servants spend tomorrow washing."

"Best or second best it matters not, good Iago, just to be in my own bed and bed chamber is something that I have dreamed of." She stood and we all stood too. She held out a hand and I kissed the back of it. "Sir Gerald, you have been the answer to my prayers and this night I will thank God for you and your men, all of them. Iago, when his lordship and his men have finished show them to their rooms."

"Yes, my lady."

When we were left alone Dai's eyes were wide with wonder, "My lord, she is like a princess."

Robert said, "That she is."

I smiled, "You still feel the same, Robert?"

"I do but now I see that she is so far above me. However, I am content that I can still serve her."

"Dai, when Iago returns find out which is my room. I will visit with the men before we retire." I donned my cloak and went out into the chill night.

It was James and John who were on duty at the gate. "We have eaten, my lord. Gwillim and Hob will relieve us at Lauds."

"Good. I do not think that they will return this night but be vigilant."

David of Abergele had joined my men in the warrior hall. When I entered Michel said, "The men who lived here were like pigs, my lord. We will spend tomorrow cleaning. I am assuming that we will be here for some time?"

"We need to train men to help David here."

David smiled, "My lord, you are a true Christian and a noble knight. I swear that I shall do all in my power to keep this home safe. I failed the Lady Hawise once but I will not do so a second time."

I nodded, "I just need your skills and experience, David of Abergele, not your life; we will choose good men to serve you but it will be up to you and Lady Hawise to ensure that you have enough for the future. I am close to hand but the men of Poole will be the first line of defence."

When I retired that night I knew we had done well but I was also acutely aware that I had given myself another monumental task. I had planned on enjoying Yarpole but now, through my own decisions I would not be able to do so.

Chapter 6

I rose early and checked on the sentries. I had not expected trouble the first night but it was as well to be prepared. When I found that there had been neither trouble nor sign of intruders, I went alone into the village. It was Iago and Gruffydd on duty and they counselled caution. "Let one of us come with you, my lord."

I shook my head, "I do not think that those who occupied this manor were popular in this place. I am safe."

I walked into the small town which, like all such places, came to life early. Poole had a communal oven and there were people gathered there waiting for dough to be baked and to collect the bread which had already been baked. There was a wonderfully welcoming smell. It was a place where people would talk and, inevitably, gossip. I went there deliberately to gauge the mood and to use the informal gathering to disseminate information. That I was a lord was clear. I did not wear spurs but the good sword at my side, not to mention the clothes I wore and the ring I bore marked me as a lord and people bowed or curtsied according to their gender. I also knew that some would recognise me from the time I had returned the body of Lady Hawise's feckless brother.

I could see that I was being studied as I approached. The experience, according to Breffni, the people had of nobles was not a good one. I think I was being judged. One ancient gammer must have recognised me from my visit the previous year for she addressed me directly, "Sir Gerald Warbow, have you come bearing bodies this time or are you here at the king's bidding?" She was old enough and bold enough not to care about being reprimanded.

Her words bordered on the insolent but she was old. I saw but two teeth in her mouth when she tempered the words with a smile. I smiled back to show that I was not offended at her words. She was right, I had caused the death of Lady Hawise's brother and that had led directly to the problem I had yet to resolve. "I am here at the request of Lady Hawise. She sent for me. She said that she needed my aid."

In that instant both the attitude and the interest of all the people changed. One of the other women shook her head and said, "About time. Those men were animals. The poor child has been much put upon."

The gammer said, "What of those who came to take over the hall? Where are they?"

Another said, "I heard noises in the night. I thought it was those men having another drunken brawl. Lord Owain would be turning in his grave at the goings on. He was the best of that family."

I smiled. Every eye was on me and each ear listening to my words. I chose them carefully, "We invited them to leave when we came last night. They are now gone. Lady Hawise and her people have their hall back and, for the present, my men and I guard them."

That brought a ripple of smiles and the sounds of approval. The gammer said, "I am sorry for my first words, Sir Gerald. I did not know."

I nodded, "I have often been misjudged but know this, while Lady Hawise has my support, I have a manor across the border and when all is settled here then I will need to return home. Lady Hawise will require the people of Poole to help her to hold on to her home."

A man who looked like a baker and had just taken out a baked loaf, shook his head, "We are not warriors, my lord. The wars that were fought against King Edward took their toll. We get on with our lives as best we can."

"Then all you are doing is growing a plum that, when someone chooses, will be plucked. The people of Poole will suffer. A people who do not defend themselves are doomed to be taken by those who wield weapons. It is the way of the world. It should not be but it is." I knew that if old King Edward was still alive then there would be men patrolling the land and those like the lady's uncle would have been curbed. He had taken a dim view of any who threatened the Crown. I continued, "If there are any young men who wish to become warriors and serve Lady Hawise then they should present themselves at the manor. David of Abergele will be the captain of Lady Hawise's guards."

One of the women smiled sadly and shook her head, "Old David should be able to hang up his sword. He served Lord Owain well."

"And he continues to serve Lady Hawise." I smiled, "Your bread smells good and I pray that it is a sign that the heart of Poole is good too. The men we ejected last night seem to me the kind who would have turned the heart into a black one."

Leaving a buzz of conversation and comment that sounded like a swarm of bees I turned and headed back to the hall. The smell of the bread had made me hungry and I had sown enough seeds amongst the people. The word would spread that Gruffydd Fychan de la Pole and his men were no longer in the hall and that Lady Hawise needed men. I nodded to my archers as I walked through the gates. I knew that I ought to send word back to Yarpole and Lucton but I did not want to risk a single rider. The men who had been evicted would return and, equally, would watch from the hills to see if I sent messengers. I had too few men to risk losing them. My handful of men would have to be as a garrison until we could organise the people of Poole.

Lady Hawise was young but events meant that she had grown into a self-reliant young woman. She seemed older than her years. She threw herself into making her manor what it had been before it had been taken over by her uncle. She ate breakfast with us and then she and Breffni donned working clothes and joined Iago's wife and the servants in restoring the house to the condition before the parasites had descended. My men at arms and archers were already cleaning the warrior hall. Until we left that would be their home.

I waved over James and John and we walked to meet with David of Abergele. He and Mordaf had taken over the duties at the gate. "David, let Mordaf watch the gate alone for a while. We need to plan." Mordaf looked surprised. I said, "You can do this can you not, Mordaf?"

He stood straighter, "Yes, my lord."

"Good, and when we have time then James and John here will show you how to become a better warrior."

"I should like that, my lord." He seemed an eager young man. He was, clearly, a little raw and lacked the real training to be a warrior but his attitude showed that he had potential. I had learned long ago that attitude in a warrior often made up for deficiencies in skill. That said I knew that we had an uphill struggle ahead of us. The best warrior, David of Abergele, was older than I was and leaving the two of them to defend the lady was not something I could contemplate. She needed men who were warriors and could guard her. "Come, we will talk while we walk. When last I came here I did not study the defences and last night I saw only darkness."

David pointed to the wall, "There is no fighting platform, my lord. The manor is defended by a gate. We close and bar it." He pointed to the bar which rested against the wall, "It is a stout gate and well made."

"David, when we came last night we passed by a gate in the rear wall. While that is barred, it is still a point of entry. Had we chosen we could have slipped over the wall and opened it."

His voice was flat, "I know, my lord."

"Is it ever used?"

He shook his head, "I cannot remember the last time anyone passed through it, my lord."

"Then we seal it. Men can still ascend the wall but we can do something about that. I am sure we could allow brambles to ring the manor from that direction. Such things discourage attackers." He nodded. "And there is just you and Mordaf to defend Lady Hawise?"

"There is now. We had more men but when my lady's uncle arrived with his men the two others suffered hurts and fled." I could tell, from his words, that he had not enjoyed seeing his men suffer. It showed that he was loyal to the lady above all things for he had stayed to endure the humiliations heaped upon them.

"I have sown the seeds in the village and I hope that over the next days we can find men to serve my lady. I have not examined the accounts but I am guessing that she could afford to pay more men."

"Lord Owain kept eight men at arms and eight archers, my lord."

That explained the warrior hall.

I pointed to the walls, "An enemy could easily scale those walls. What we need is to make the manor house more defensible." I turned to view the house. As I did so I noticed something that I had not seen before. I pointed, "David, is it my eyes or is there a depression close to the walls of the hall?"

He smiled, "Yes, my lord, that is an ancient ditch. It runs all the way around the walls of the hall. I remember, when I was a boy, that it was kept clear but now…"

I strode over to it. I saw that there were slabs of stone before the door. I took out my dagger and scraped away the soil from the edge. When I had marked it I said, "This is a defensive ditch. I am guessing that this stone is here to cover the ditch. When it rains does the water enter the hall?"

David looked surprised but he nodded, "Aye, my lord, but…"

"Those who built this hall knew their business. The ditch looks to be," I scratched the edge of what I now saw as a bridge, until I found rock, "four paces wide. It is here to protect the hall and, if it rains, to act as a sort of moat. James and John, when the men have cleaned the hall they can dig out the detritus from the ditch."

James nodded, "And the spoil?"

"Lay the stone you find next to the hall and the soil can be taken to the hog bog."

John grimaced, "That is not the work of a day, my lord."

"No it is not and while I have you two here, with David, there is another matter I wish to broach. When I leave I would have you two stay here until the defences are made stronger and David has men to guard Lady Hawise. I would have you paid as sergeants." I looked at David, "Does that suit?"

He nodded, "Aye, it does."

The brothers looked at each other. Suddenly the prospect of hard work faded for they now had the chance to learn to lead others. They both nodded their agreement.

I turned and pointed to the gates, "And there we can build a wooden tower. I hope that there are archers who will choose to serve Lady Hawise and two archers in such a tower can give not only warning but can also keep an attacker at bay."

"You are giving us a great deal of work, my lord."

"I know, David, but until Lady Hawise has a husband who can defend her we shall have to let the manor of Poole do the job for us."

I explained to the others what was needed and Michel divided the men up. Dai and Robert joined those clearing the ditch while I walked with Lady Hawise and her servant to tell them what we were doing. Lady Hawise nodded as I spoke, "My uncle will return and when he does he will bring more men."

"He has to. It seems to me that your uncles divided up your lands like bandits after a cattle raid. He will not let this prize go so easily and he knows the weaknesses of the manor. He will try to exploit them. In a way I hope he comes sooner rather than later for I am confident that my men and I have the beating of him."

"But if you are gone then it will just be an old man and young, untried warriors who have to fight."

"That is true but I will leave you James and John as sergeants for a while. They are good men."

She smiled, "Thank you, my lord, that is reassuring but if I were a man this would not be happening. My brother's foolish action made this come about."

"Perhaps, but all of us have to deal with events beyond our control." I thought back to my father who was killed over a dog and that one event led me to becoming Lord Edward's man. I had not chosen my life but I had made the best of it.

I saw resolution fill her face. She was young but she had an inner strength that reminded me of Mary. My wife had been a slave but had still retained pride in herself. Lady Hawise nodded, "Then let us get on with it."

I waved over Robert, who hurried like a puppy eager to please a new master, "Robert, I would have you and Lady Hawise go over the accounts with Iago. I am guessing that since the arrival of your uncle you have little idea of the value or your assets. I need to know how many men you can afford to pay."

"I know that we were comfortable before he came but he and those men who lived here liked to enjoy expensive food. They slaughtered four cattle since they came." She shook her head, "Before they came we culled one a year and that was for the village feast."

"Then the three of you need a more accurate picture of what this manor can afford."

I had given Robert a job which delighted him and the two left us. I took off my cloak and picked up a mattock, "And you and I, Dai, will sweat a little, eh?"

I quite enjoyed the work and by the time we heard the bell ringing from a distant monastery marking Sext we had cleared some of the ditch. There were stones which must have marked the internal edge of the ditch. They had fallen in and been covered with soil, leaves and other natural things. When they were lifted and placed next to the hall they made the walls stronger. Food was brought out to us and it was while we were eating that Mordaf signalled.

David of Abergele stood and shook his head, "He has a good heart but his head is empty." He headed to the gate.

Michel said, "This is a good manor, my lord, but it needs more than an old man and a young lad to defend it."

Just then David returned with three youths. I had seen one that morning hovering close to the village oven. "Sir Gerald, these three heard that we are hiring guards for the hall."

I stood and wiped my hands on the cloth that lay over my left shoulder. "Are you warriors?"

They looked at each other and I realised that the word was not one that they knew. I said, "Gruffydd, ask them, in Welsh, if they can fight."

He did so and the one I had seen at the ovens grinned and answered in English, "I can fight, my lord."

"With a weapon?"

He frowned, "I can use a bow, my lord, and I can hunt."

"Dai, fetch my bow case and arrow bag." He hurried off, "And your name?"

"Arwen, my lord."

I looked at the other two, "And your names?"

One said, "Rhys ap Brice."

The other said, "Carwyn ap Llewellyn."

"And can either of you use a bow?"

Rhys shook his head, "We can both use slings, my lord, but it is Arwen who is the archer. His father has a flock of sheep and Arwen guards them better than any sheepdog." They were clearly friends and that boded well.

I liked that it was not Arwen who was boasting of his own prowess. When Dai returned I handed the young Welsh archer the bow case. "This is not a hunting bow but a war bow. If you cannot string it then I will do so for you. There is no shame in that."

He took it out of its case and I saw his eyes widen. It was a good bow. At Yarpole we had the best bowyers and fletchers. When I had been at the tower I had seen the bows and the arrows that were stored there. They were good but ours were better. Dai handed him a string. It was as Arwen took the string that I saw he had an archer's build. He was no Hamo but Hamo had trained every day from a young age and it had deformed his body into that of a mighty archer. Arwen looked to be a youth who had hunted with a good bow but he had not practised each day until his muscles and arms burned as though they were on fire. I could see that he was struggling to fit the string and I moved towards him.

He shook his head and said, through clenched teeth, "No, my lord, I can do this." With a mighty effort he fitted the string. I saw him look at the arrow bag. There was a mixture of bodkins and war arrows. They would both look different from the hunting arrows he used.

I took out a bodkin, "Here use this one." I pointed to the pile of spoil that lay just one hundred paces from us. It was a safe target for no one was near to it and while it would have been easy for me to hit, it would be harder for Arwen using a war bow for the first time. I also knew that the spoil would not damage the head. A bodkin was a valuable missile. "Send an arrow into that pile of soil. I would see if you can draw the bow."

I saw my archer, Gruffydd, critically studying the young man as he obeyed me. He would judge him. Arwen nocked the arrow. He then began to pull back. I was close enough to see the look on his face as he failed to pull it as far back as he wished. I smiled, "When you are ready then just release."

The strength of the bow determined the timing of the arrow and it flew straight and true. It buried itself into the soil. Rhys and Carwyn applauded. I saw the critical look on Gruffydd's face, I asked, "Was that where you aimed?" His answer would determine my opinion of him.

He shook his head, "No, my lord. I could not hold the bow for long enough to aim well."

Gruffydd nodded, "That is the difference between a hunting bow and a war bow. While we are here we can teach you." I looked at him and he nodded. My archer confirmed that we had our first recruit.

Arwen looked pleased, "Then I have a place here?"

I smiled, "You have not asked about the pay."

He said, "I do not see many coins when I watch the flock and I do not know how much an archer is paid. I think that you are a fair man."

"But it is Lady Hawise who will be paying. You are right and the pay will be fair but you will need to swear an oath."

"An oath?" The three looked worried.

David of Abergele said, "It is what all warriors do. I swore an oath to Lord Owain. I kept my oath. Mordaf swore one to Lady Hawise. The two men who left did not keep theirs and they are oathsworn. Such men never fare well. If you swear an oath it is binding."

To give them all time to think I said to Rhys and Carwyn, "And you two, what would you do? You cannot use a bow and slings, whilst useful, are not what Lady Hawise and David of Abergele need." They looked confused and I said, "David, fetch me four spears from the hall."

I was aware that the rest of our men were working on the ditch and that we were needed but it seemed important to me that I gave the two volunteers the opportunity to show what they could do. When David returned I took two of the spears and gave them to the two youths. I took a third for me and then said, "Hold them in two hands and try to spear me."

They looked shocked. Rhys said, "We might hurt you, my lord."

I laughed, "And if you do then it will be my fault. Just lunge at me and we shall see."

Carwyn made the first move and he lunged at my head. I flicked the spear away with as much force as I could muster. I was impressed that he managed to hold on to the spear. Rhys lunged at my middle. I pinned his spear to the ground and then used my left hand to push him to the ground. He, too, held on to the spear. I said, "David, show them how it is done."

Aye, my lord." He took a wider stance and feinted with the spear. I flicked the head away and he spun around, showing a remarkably agile step for one who was old, and tried to sweep me from my feet with the haft. I stepped away from it and smacked him on the rump with my own spear. He laughed, "Showing my age, my lord."

I nodded, "Me too." I turned to the two youths, "Now, if you are willing to learn we can teach you how to use a spear and then, when you are ready, James and John will show you how to use swords. Do you wish to take the oath?"

"We do." In that instant we had more than doubled Lady Hawise's garrison. They were raw and untrained and if they had to fight soon they would die but I hoped that we would be allowed the time to make them into soldiers who could defend her. We went to the lady herself who was pleased to have the three young men. She had seen them but did not know them. They swore an oath on the Bible that Robert found.

We had more men to work and the three youths were keen to impress me. They sweated and laboured hard. By the end of the next day we had most of the ditch cleared and another three men had volunteered. One was an older man, Dewi, and he was an archer. I gave him the same test as Arwen and he strung the bow and pulled it well. His frame told me that he had been an archer. He had neither bow nor sword. He was barefoot and I could tell that there was a story but one did not discard such treasure and he was hired. Lady Hawise found him clothes and boots, and he was given a bath. The other two were like Carwyn and Rhys. They were farmer's sons and I knew from my own experience that they had lived a hand to mouth existence. The prospect of food, a bed and pay appealed. Glaw and Ifan would fit in well and we had eight men who could protect Lady Hawise. We now had eight men in the garrison and to work. The ditch was cleared. The edges needed sharpening but it gave the hall a reassuring look. This was how it had been designed. The new men were given just half an hour each day with my archers and men at arms to practise. That they did so after a hard day of labouring boded well for the future. They could have left and returned to their lives but they did not.

Each day that her uncle and his brothers did not return made both us and the hall stronger. It was the third day when we set to building the tower. I had decided that it would be made of wood and hold just two men. As we only had Arwen and Dewi to draw bows that mattered not. Everyone worked hard and Glaw showed that he had skill in woodworking. The hammering and sawing were testament to the effort everyone put in. The frame and ladder were up by the end of the day and that left just the roof to be added.

That evening, as we ate, Robert said, "Your stepson, Jack, will begin to worry soon, my lord. Should we not send a message to him?"

He was right. However, there were inherent dangers in sending away one or two men we would need if we were attacked. "We should but I will not risk sending two experienced men. Between here and England could lie enemies. If we are still safe when two days have passed then I will ride to Lucton with Jean Michel."

Lady Hawise had been listening, "You would not risk your men but you would risk your own life?"

Before I could answer Robert said, "That is Sir Gerald's way, my lady. Part of it is arrogance. He thinks that he can do anything better than any other."

I growled, "Robert, you go too far."

He smiled and continued, "But it is mainly because he feels he has to care for everyone. It is why his men will follow him anywhere."

I allowed Robert licence to speak openly because, alone out of my mesne, he was irreplaceable. I had archers and men at arms but there was just one confessor and healer.

That night, before I retired I walked the outer wall. The gate was barred and Mordaf and Dewi had the night watch in the tower. It had the advantage of good sight lines but without a brazier, it was a cold watch. To compensate I had given them both good, oiled cloaks that not only kept them warmer but with hoods made them, in the tower, almost invisible.

I called up to him, "How goes it Dewi?"

His cheerful voice came down, "I have eaten more in the last two days than in the two weeks before that. I have clothes that do not contain wildlife and I have drunk well brewed ale. All this and I am to be paid too! Why, my lord, it is like I have died and gone to heaven."

"Then let us make this rebirth a good one, eh Dewi? Keep a sharp eye open."

As I made my way back to bed I wondered about his story. In the last couple of days he had worked as hard, if not harder than any and he had a cheerful outlook. How had he come to have fallen on such hard times? I headed back into the hall which was now my temporary home. We had been granted more time than I had expected to make the hall strong but I knew that the men would return. I had spilt blood and even if Lady Hawise's uncle did not relish a return, the young men I had insulted would. They would seek vengeance.

Chapter 7

It was Dai whose hand shook me awake. I realised I must be getting old for there had been a time when just the opening of a door, however silent, would have woken me but I had heard nothing. "My lord, Michel sent me. He says that Dewi saw men approaching the walls. He has awakened the rest of the men."

I was up in a flash. My knees complained when my feet touched the floor. My age sometimes caught up with me. I grabbed my leather jerkin and donned it. "Wake Iago the Steward. Tell him to find weapons and he is to defend Lady Hawise. You and Robert can help him."

"I would be with you, my lord."

As I sat on the bed to don my boots I shook my head. I said, "You have much training ahead of you and besides, if they get through us you might be the only ones left to defend the lady. You are the last line of defence, Dai. Your dirk and your courage will be needed."

He nodded and sped off. I strapped on my sword and stood. I paused only to grab my coif, bow and arrow bag. I saw Iago and Robert when I reached the corridor. They had weapons drawn. That was a good thing and I saw no fear on their faces, just determined resolution. "After I am gone lock and bar the doors. Open them only if I identify myself."

"Yes, my lord."

Robert said, "I should be with you." I shook my head. "You and Dai, help Iago to defend the ladies."

When I left the hall I saw Michel organising my men. Already Iago and Gruffydd were ascending the tower with strung bows in their hands. Dewi and Mordaf were at the bottom. I waved over Dewi, "How many men did you see?"

He shook his head, "The moon came out from behind a cloud and I caught a flash of white. I saw enough to see two men and weapons then the cloud came again and they became shadows. I woke Michel because…"

"You have done well. Arm yourself." He looked at me, "Take my bow and I shall use a sword."

As I handed him the bow case and arrow bag he grinned, "Thank you, my lord."

I joined Michel and the others. The five young men with spears looked terrified and exhilarated in equal measure. None of them had mail but each had a sword and a dagger taken from the archers and the men we had ejected. They had yet to be properly trained but we had taught them how to stand and hold a spear. They each held a spear but they were gripping the haft too tightly. It showed their nerves. This test of their skills was coming too early but there was little point in bemoaning our fate.

Michel said, "We are ready, lord." David hurried towards us. He wore his coif and helmet and he had a sword and buckler.

I said, "If they try to assault the gates then they are fools."

David of Abergele shook his head, "Gruffydd Fychan de la Pole is no hero, my lord, but neither is he a fool. Look for cunning."

I looked around and imagined if I was the one coming to attack, what would I do? The answer came to me. I said, "The back gates." Dewi had strung the bow and stood waiting. I said, "Michel, you and my men stay here. If we fail then you can defend the hall. You have four archers and four men at arms. That should be enough. David, bring our new men and we will investigate the rear gate. Arwen, stand with Dewi and use your bow when he does. This will be a lesson for you." David and Arwen both nodded. I said to Dewi, who had strung my bow, "They will have seen my archers on the walls. You may well prove to be the surprise. Stay close to me."

"Yes, my lord."

"The rest of you, this is not the way I wanted you to use your weapons for the first time. You must heed my orders. I will be in the centre, with David. Dewi and Arwen will stand close to me and the rest of you, led by Mordaf, will be in a line next to me. When you are commanded, you present and thrust your spears as one. What you lack in skill you can make up for in cohesion. If I say fall back then you do so. If that command is given then you head for Michel." I paused and said, heavily, "Any who is hurt stays where they fall. No heroics." I think my words had the desired effect. Three of them made the sign of the cross. Glaw looked around in panic. I knew why. "Make water now. Fighting with piss in your breeks is never comfortable."

My coarse words made them all smile. When they were ready I drew my sword and dagger and led them around the side of the manor house. If nothing else the ditch would come as a shock. It was now a clear deterrent but only we knew its depth. As we slipped around the side, past the hog bog and ovens, still warm to the touch, I realised that if they reached the ditch then it meant I had failed. We had to hold them as close to the back wall as we could. Moving along the cobbles of the yard and avoiding noise was hard. It helped me, however, to focus my mind. We had no idea of their numbers but, equally, they could only guess at the reinforcements we had acquired. What had become clear over the last days was that Gruffydd Fychan de la Pole had no friends in Poole. His cronies had come from further south and north. They were strangers and resented. He would have had little intelligence from the people of Poole. There might be a spy but we had not seen anyone leaving Poole and heading either south or west.

The vegetable garden had been, largely, picked over. The goats had cleared anything that was edible. They were now in their byre. It was as I passed the last of the beans, left in the ground to enrich it, that I heard the sound of the gate being tried. It was a rusty latch and it creaked. We were in time. I heard mumbled voices. That was good for it meant that they thought we were still asleep. I moved slowly until we were within ten paces of the gate. Gruffydd Fychan de la Pole or whoever led these men knew the manor but they would not risk climbing the wall at some imprecise place. They knew the gate and that it had a path through the vegetable plot to the rear of the house. This was the way that they would come. I used my sword and dagger to marshal the men into a line. I waved David of Abergele to the far end with Mordaf. The untrained youths with spears had experienced men flanking them. It made our centre weak but that could not be helped.

Ifan was next to me and I used my dagger to raise his spear so that it was pointed up. The others copied him. I saw that Dewi had loosely nocked a bodkin. Arwen had hunting arrows. His arrows would be more of an annoyance to the enemy but a wound to one warrior would mean one less man to strike at the other youths. We did not know if the men were mailed or not. A bodkin would not be wasted if it killed a man and from his size and the range at which Dewi would loose, I was confident that his arrow would be fatal.

The noise that I could hear told its own story. The men who were coming were not well trained nor well led. My untried youths had not made a single sound. When I heard the sound of scuffling and heavy breathing I knew that they were heaving men over the wall. When I saw the first shadow appear it was confirmed. I hissed, quietly, "Ready Dewi?" The heaving, huffing and puffing from the other side of the wall meant the enemy would not hear.

"Aye."

I waited until I saw four shapes. They had been boosted up but to climb over the wall they had to expose themselves. "Now!"

The crack and snap of the bowstring sounded like thunder. The first arrow flew straight and true. It smacked into the chest of the man who was almost prostrate across the wall. He screamed as he was hit and there was a crash as he fell. Arwen's arrow hit another man but I knew it had only wounded him. Dewi was a good archer and his second arrow was better aimed. It drove into the skull of the next man. At that point the other men dropped.

"Use axes! Break it down!" I heard the sound of axes as, realising that the game was up, they took to brute force to break down the ancient gate. When the horn sounded from the other side of the wall then I knew it was a signal for the men on the Poole side of the hall. The sound of bowstrings snapping from the other side of the manor and the whistle of their fletch told me that they were assaulting the front too. The new men, whilst inexperienced were an unknown quantity. The enemy would think we had just a handful of men at our disposal. Two of theirs had been slain already and, if we could make them bleed they might be discouraged and flee.

The gate did not last long. It was old and the axes made short work of it. At least we would not have to wreck it ourselves before replacing it. When it burst asunder Dewi sent an arrow straight at the first man. Arwen's arrow followed and both hit the first man. A shield appeared and when Dewi's next arrow slammed into it they were able to force the gate.

"Dewi and Arwen, stand behind me."

"Aye, my lord."

"Make your arrows count."

I was an archer and I knew that if we could hold our line then Dewi and Arwen could keep picking them off so long as they had arrows. The bag I had given Dewi contained twenty. Four had been used already. I had no idea how many Arwen had. Both archers might be reduced to using a sword before too long. Once through the shattered gate the enemy raced at us. Some of the men had shields. Dewi began to pick off the ones without shields. One of Arwen's arrows had been wasted on a shield already. I heard Dewi instructing Arwen.

"Aim for flesh. Face, legs, arms, not shields!"

The man with the arrow-struck shield ran at me. The misshapen nose told me that it was Hywel ap Geraint. That suited me for he was angry and out for revenge. He had an axe in his hand and as I had no shield he would be confident in the outcome. He would try to kill me and therefore assure victory.

I shouted encouragement, "Lady Hawise's men, hold firm. You are fighting for a lady's honour and we do what is right. These men are the dregs left by a gong scourer."

My insult made my men cheer and the enemy redoubled their efforts to get to us. The last of the beans tripped one man and Glaw took advantage. He drove his spear into the back of the man. As he tried to pull it out it stuck and the man tried to rise. At that range even a hunting arrow could kill and Arwen killed his first enemy with a hunting arrow driven into the side of the warrior's neck. Hywel ap Geraint swung his axe over his head to smash into my coifed skull. The blow would have succeeded with most men but I was an archer and my right arm was like a young oak. I caught the axe just below the head with my sword and I saw the look of surprise on his face as he failed to force it down. Concentration is everything and although he had his shield before him he was not really using it. I drove my dagger under his right arm and into his shoulder. He wore mail but the end prised open some of the links and penetrated his gambeson and flesh. His scream was feral.

I laughed, "You sound like a girl. Have your balls not yet dropped?"

He spat at me, "I will have your skull, old man, as a trophy for my hall."

He had made the mistake of using words when he should have used his weapon. I forced the axe to the side and then lunged with my sword, not at his middle, protected by his shield, but into his knee. I had never known a man who could stand after such a wound and he was no exception. He dropped to one knee. If I had been fighting alongside my own men then I would have been confident in the outcome of this battle but these were youths. I had to be ruthless. I pulled back my dagger and drove it into his eye. He died silently.

I had come into the fray none too soon. I saw that there were at least twelve men who had broken in. That we had slain four or five was immaterial. The four youths, the new warriors, were poking their spears but some of those that they fought had shields. Sooner or later the swordsmen would get inside the spear heads and the youths would die. Dewi and Arwen were doing their best but I heard, as I pulled back my dagger, Dewi say, "I have just two arrows left, my lord."

"Use them well and then draw your sword."

Fighting in the dark meant that enemies could rise like shadows. Even as I moved to face the warrior with helmet, sword and shield, I saw a man rise from the dark and drive his sword up under Mordaf's arm. David of Abergele screamed out, not in pain but in anger and his ancient sword hacked into the killer's neck. The death angered me too and I brought my sword over to smash down onto the helmet of the man I was fighting. He brought up his shield and almost held my sword but I was forcing him down. I slashed at his right hand with my dagger and it ripped through his flesh. Unlike me he was not wearing gauntlets. I hooked my leg behind his and pushed. He tumbled to the ground. The man had been one of those at Lady Hawise's table. I did not know him but I recognised him. I could have asked him to yield and demand ransom but Mordaf's death drove the blood into my brain and I skewered him.

Warbow

I spied Gruffydd Fychan de la Pole. He was at the gate with two men and all three were mailed with open helmets. David of Abergele had been right, the man was cunning. He had allowed two of his angry friends to try to take me and they had both failed. Now with one of our men down and archers running out of arrows he saw his chance and the three advanced towards me in a small wedge. Those without mail were still trying to penetrate my spear wall. I thought for a moment that Gruffydd Fychan de la Pole would face me but within three steps from the gate he had stepped behind the other two. He would let them wear me down before slaying me. At least that was his plan. I did not mind for it meant that the rest of my men were fighting men without mail.

I did not recognise the two men who came at me. They were not the archers we had thrown out and they were not the other two men from the table. Their mail was good mail but did not bespeak nobility. They were swords for hire. They would not be as highly paid as the ones sent to the Canterbury road to kill a king but they would know their business and would work together to get to me.

Arwen tried to help and sent a hunting arrow at the two men who advanced towards me. It was doomed to failure but luck, perhaps, aided it and it struck the shoulder of one. The arrow spun up and caught the other on the cheek, drawing blood. It would not slow him but it would anger him and make him want to kill Arwen once I was disposed of. This time they would strike at me with two swords at the same time and they would be protected by two shields. With shields before them they both raised their swords at the same time. I heard Gruffydd Fychan de la Pole as he almost screamed with delight, "Kill him! Kill him!"

The screech drowned out the sound of Dewi's last bodkin. He was just behind me and the nearest man was just six feet from him. The arrow drove through the man's head, just above the nose and continued through the skull, crushing bone and brain. The needle like point powered through the back of the skull and then the helmet. The fletch stopped it moving further but Gruffydd Fychan de la Pole was showered with blood and brains and the hired sword fell. It meant I just had one swordsman to face before I got to Lady Hawise's uncle. It should have been two for Gruffydd Fychan de la Pole should have stepped forward, but the shock of the death of one of his hired killers not only made him freeze but recoil, and when Arwen's arrow went towards him he was barely able to raise his shield. All this went on like a blur in the corner of my eye for I was blocking the other mercenary's sword with my own. His strike was a blow as strong as mine and the blades rang together, sparks flying in the night. He had a shield and he punched with it. I took the blow on the gauntlet holding my dagger. It hurt but not enough to numb it. Many men misjudged me because they thought that, as an archer, I could not use a sword. I could. However, this mercenary either knew me or had been told of my skill for he did not underestimate me. He kept a wide stance so that I could not trip him and he did not make obvious blows. He sought for weaknesses. I was doing the same.

Gruffydd Fychan de la Pole saw his chance and he stepped to the side to swing his sword in a long arc aimed at my unprotected left. Once more the young archer, Arwen, came to my aid. He might not have had the strength of a veteran archer or a war bow but he was close enough for neither to matter. When he sent the arrow at Gruffydd Fychan de la Pole, the man flicked up his shield. The hunting arrow drove in and embedded itself. The flight of the arrow made the mercenary glance, unwittingly and briefly to his right and that was enough for me. I lunged down with my dagger and it tore through the mail links covering his thigh. He had not worn chausse and he paid the price. My blade drove through the breeches and into his muscle. It slid through flesh to scrape along the bone. He screamed and I brought over my sword. It struck him on the helmet. I dented it and hurt him. He began to back away.

Gruffydd Fychan de la Pole saw the move and as Arwen drew back his bow shouted, "We are undone! Flee!" They ran.

I needed to catch Lady Hawise's uncle and that meant eliminating the mercenary. The warrior was wounded and he was hurt but he fought to the end. He faced me with a bloody thigh and the blow to his head must have made his sight poor but he stood. I lunged with my dagger and he moved his sword to block it. Had he had all of his senses he would have used his shield. He exposed his upper body and my sword hacked through his neck. "You fought well." I did not know if he heard me. I looked up and saw the last of the attackers that Lady Hawise's men had fought, fleeing and following their leader. As my young charges made to chase them I cried, "Hold!" We had survived but it had been with more luck than skill. While we had just lost Mordaf we had accounted for six men in the exchange but I saw that Ifan and Glaw had wounds. They were not life threatening but if we came to grips with mercenaries who were fleeing then those wounds might return to haunt us.

"Bar the gate and see if any live."

David was kneeling by Mordaf. He shook his head, "I failed him. He was raw clay and needed much work. I should have done more."

I raised him up, "David of Abergele, this was war. I do not think you failed with Mordaf but if you think you did then make up for it with these others. You have time. Make them into good warriors. They showed great courage today. None ran and we were fighting mercenaries. When I leave here I shall be happier because I will know that the men guarding Lady Hawise have a good chance of protecting her."

Dewi said, "We need nails and timber, my lord."

I realised I had not heard fighting from the other side of the manor for some time. I said, "David, take charge here. I will go and find Robert. His skills are needed here."

I saw that Dewi was doing what all good archers did. He was recovering as many arrows as he could. Lady Hawise had an archer. When I reached the other side of the house Michel and my men at arms whirled around, swords drawn. It was only when they recognised me that they relaxed a little. Michel said, "They tried the gate but the arrows from the tower deterred them. We were ready to take them on if they had broken through."

I sheathed my sword and dagger, "They broke through the rear gate. Thanks to Dewi and my war bow we sent them hence." There was relief on their faces. "Mordaf is dead and we have wounded. I will enter the house and then we will open the gates."

Jean Michel said, "Is that not dangerous, my lord?"

"I do not want this rabble to cause mischief in Poole." I went to the door of the hall and banged on it. "It is Sir Gerald, open up."

After a few moments the bar was lifted and the lock turned. Robert and Iago stood there. They had swords in their hands. Behind them I saw Dai with a dagger and Lady Hawise holding a lamp. "Robert, we have wounded at the back gate. Take Dai with you."

He nodded, "Yes, my lord."

As he passed me Lady Hawise said, "Who was it?"

"Your uncle and some of those whom we ejected. Your uncle is fled but they left dead men behind."

I watched as she composed herself and cleared her throat, "And were any of my people hurt?"

There was no easy way to say what I had to say. I had done this many times over the years and I had found that the safest way was just to speak the truth without dressing it up. No death was glorious. No matter how well a man behaved in his last moments he was still dead and left a hole behind him. "Ifan and Glaw have slight wounds but Mordaf is dead."

Her hand went to her mouth, "That poor child."

He was older than Lady Hawise but it showed her compassion. "I must leave, my lady. There are things I must do." She nodded dumbly. I said, "Iago, the men will need food. Until we have searched the village this is not over."

"Yes, my lord." He smiled, "Thank you."

Warbow

Once back outside I saw that the night was almost done. In the east I could see the first traces of daylight. The gates were open and Gwillim shouted down, "I can see no movement outside the walls."

I was on surer ground for it was my men behind me. These were not the raw clay that David had spoken of. James and John flanked me. They were family. I saw that the gate had been hacked by axes. It would need to be repaired but the archers had saved it from real damage. I saw four bodies lying on the ground. They had arrows in them. Knowing that archers were ready with nocked arrows to protect us I headed towards them. I flicked over the bodies of the ones who were face down. They were all dead but, from the pools of blood lying under some of them they had died slowly. Arrows can do that. They strike something vital deep within a body.

James said, "These are poor warriors. Their buskins are worn and they only have short swords."

His brother said, "Fodder for arrows." He pointed his sword at one who had died quickly. The arrow had struck his unprotected skull.

I turned to Michel, "When they fled, did you hear horses?"

"No, my lord."

Almost as though I had initiated it there was the sudden sound of hooves. They came, not from the village ahead, but from the side of the hall. Ten riders galloped at us. I recognised the armour of Lady Hawise's uncle. He had two mailed men flanking him and the rest were the ones we had driven from the rear. The five of us were exposed but these were my men. They formed ranks and we each held our swords in two hands. Had these been the new men then the sight of the horses galloping at us would have made them run and that would have been fatal. What we knew was that a horse will try to avoid men and the riders had no weapons in their hands. It was nerve-wracking but we stood firm as the horses charged the five blades that we held before us. I heard the sound of arrows and saw two men plucked from their saddles. In a flash the horsemen were past and the arrows stopped. My archers were good but the light was not good enough for accuracy when there were their brothers in arms before them. Iago and Hob ran from the hall, nocked arrows at the ready. They did not relax until they ascertained that the men were dead.

I shouted, "Take the loose horses and then close the gates."

I turned and led my men after the horsemen. We heard their hooves as they disappeared into the land to the west. A few heads appeared from the doors as we passed. I said, "Stay indoors until we return."

When we reached the edge of the village I saw that not only were there no more men, I could not see any signs of horses having waited.

The ground was free from horse dung and was not trampled by hooves. I sheathed my sword as the sun cracked the eastern horizon.

"Gruffydd Fychan de la Pole brought plenty of men and his plan was a good one." I turned to Michel and said.

Michel nodded, "Distract us with poor warriors at the front and use his better ones at the rear. Is this over, my lord?"

As we headed back to the hall I nodded, "It was not just the hired mercenaries we slew. Two of his friends died as well. He may well want this manor but he now knows that he cannot simply take it back overnight. He and his brothers will need to plan better and that gives us the opportunity to petition the king."

James said, as we neared the bodies, "Will that do any good, my lord?"

"It may. His friend is in Ireland and this may well be something he can do to show the Welsh that he rules their land." As we passed the bodies I said, "Bring all the bodies within the walls. The sight of them may upset the village."

We closed the gates behind us and the six bodies were laid out in a line. Michel said, "Find something to cover them with. We do not want to upset the ladies."

"And bring the ones from the rear, too."

"Yes my lord."

The door to the hall opened and Lady Hawise and her servant stood there, "Sir Gerald, there is food for you. You should rest."

I shook my head, "First I will see Robert and then we will repair the rear gate."

"You have done too much for us already, my lord. I am the lady of the manor and it is my duty to see to the repairs."

I laughed, "And if my wife learned that I had allowed this to happen then I would suffer her tongue. No, Lady Hawise, all is well. A little labour now will make us secure and then we will eat. After that…" I turned to look at the covered corpses.

She nodded, "They need to be buried. It is the Christian thing to do."

"That it is, my lady."

There was steel in the young woman but there was also humanity. She would make someone a good wife. She reminded me of Mary. Like Queen Eleanor, such women were rare.

By the end of the day the bodies had been buried and the local priest had said words over them. Carrying the bodies to the church was a gruesome task but I joined my men to help them do so. The men who had come to kill us were not buried in the churchyard but the land that lay just outside. It was not hallowed ground. The graveyard was not large and Lady Hawise did not want those who had come with such evil intent to share the ground with her people. Mordaf, in contrast, was buried in the graveyard. His parents and sisters were there along with the whole village. Lady Hawise promised a stone and she spoke of her warrior's devotion to duty. How she held herself together I will never know but she showed an inner strength that I had only seen before in Queen Eleanor and my wife. It was as we headed back to the hall that I knew she would succeed and, with our help, hold on to her father's manor and, eventually, regain her lost lands. That was for the future. First we had to make the manor strong enough to withstand an attack without the aid of my men.

We also began, not to repair the rear gate, but to block it. Lady Hawise and Iago confirmed that it had not been used in the last ten years. We found stones and over the next days began to mortar them in. Brambles were found and layered at the rear wall. It would take time, a year or so, perhaps, but eventually there would be a natural barrier that would yield nature's bounty to the hall.

The wounds to Ifan and Glaw were minor ones. They were the kind of cuts that often resulted from vigorous training. However, when I sat with the new men and David, I offered the new men the chance to reconsider their decision. Both David and I were delighted when all of them were adamant that they wished to serve Lady Hawise. I think their success, against professional and better armoured warriors, had given them confidence. I had feared that Mordaf's death might have affected them more. Two days after the attack two more men arrived at the hall to offer their services. They did not come from Poole but travellers had told them that Lady Hawise was seeking men to serve her and Wyn and Terrwyn were keen to be warriors. Both were archers and whilst younger than Dewi and therefore not as skilled, they had the same attitude as Arwen and David happily accepted their offer. Dewi would be able to train them. They might never reach his standard but they would be better than the men who had left Lady Hawise when her uncle had arrived.

Chapter 8

Robert said, "We ought to be heading back, my lord. It has been more than a week and your sons will worry."

I nodded, for it had been on my mind too. "Michel, you and your son have done all that you can here. We have a little more work to do but I intend to ride home in the next week. Ride to Lucton and tell Jack what has happened and then return to Yarpole and let my wife know when we shall return."

"Are you sure, my lord? If you are leaving John and James here then that will leave just the archers with you."

I laughed, "And what better escorts for Lord Edward's Archer? I am content, Michel. Leave on the morrow."

Lady Hawise made a fuss that night of my two French warriors. She was a naturally kind woman and she showed her appreciation of their efforts. They dined in her hall and she had food cooked that she hoped they would like. She found some wine in the cellar that her uncles had not yet managed to drink and the two Frenchmen were feted. I saw that the evening touched both men. Like Robert they had fallen under the spell of this remarkable woman.

The next day I took David to one side, "The archers and I will be leaving in six days' time. I will try to help you to begin the training of your young warriors in that time. This is just the start. You will have much work to do. My archers will work with your bowmen. If it were me in charge I would happily put Dewi in command of them."

"I agree, my lord. He was the rock that saved us on the night of the attack."

I pointed to the front gate, "And we also need another tower there. Gwillim told me that had we had two towers then the gates could have been defended by just four men."

"A good idea."

He hesitated and I smiled, "David of Abergele, we fought together and there can be no secrets between us. Speak what is on your mind."

He smiled, "The weapons and mail we took from the dead, my lord, what is your intention?"

"You and your men can have the first choice. Your mail is old and that which we took from the young nobles is better."

He looked relieved. The purses from the dead had already been shared by the men but the weapons lay in the warrior hall. We went to tell the men. Dewi approached me with my bow case, "And here is your bow, Sir Gerald. It is a fine one. Thank you for letting me use it."

"And it is now yours. I fear that I have no more arrows but you deserve the bow for your actions that night. You saved my life."

He shook his head, "My lord, that was selfish. Had you fallen we would have all died. My action was an act of self-preservation."

David of Abergele said, "Dewi, Sir Gerald thinks that you should command the archers."

"I would be honoured but…"

"You have the skills, Dewi. I am a master archer and recognise that. Your task will not be easy for Arwen, Wyn and Terrwyn are not yet full grown. We both know that the hard training to make them into archers will have them cursing you."

He smiled, "I am ready and this feels like a home. I have long sought such a place."

David said, "I will go and help the young men choose weapons and helmets that they can use well."

Left alone with the archer I said, "Dewi, you can tell me it is none of my business but I am interested in your tale. Of all those who sought to be Lady Hawise's men your skills speak of experience yet you came here weaponless."

He nodded, "I suppose I should be honest with you, Sir Gerald, for you have given me a new life." He sighed and I saw him steeling himself, "I served in Ireland as an archer. I was part of the company serving the Earl of Ulster. He cared not for archers and we were both treated and paid badly. When he heard that King Edward had appointed another to rule what he considered to be his land we were dismissed without pay. We all sought employment in Ireland but I found none. I took passage on a cog heading to Chester. It was the only way I could afford to come home. We suffered a storm off Anglesey and although the ship survived we had no sail and the deck was swept clear of its cargo. My bow and arrow bag were amongst the things I lost. When we landed I had nothing. The only thing of value I had left was my sword and I sold that to have money to pay for food. I walked from Chester, first to Wrecgsam and then Shrewsbury seeking work. I wore out my shoes." He shook his head, "An archer without a bow does not find work easily. It was there I heard about Poole and knowing that you were here gave me hope." He smiled, "The archer who became a knight is often spoken of by archers."

"Then I am glad you found us, Dewi. You have found a good mistress."

"That we do, my lord. She is young but she has steel for a backbone. If she were a bow it would take a mighty archer to draw her."

Warbow

After talking with him I felt better about leaving. David and Dewi were both good men and I knew that while the men who served Lady Hawise were raw, given time they could become warriors. The question that nagged at me was would Lady Hawise's uncles give her the time?

We had almost finished the tower when the four riders approached the hall. One was a knight; I saw his spurs. A second, from his dress and weapons, was his squire and the other two were men at arms. They had a sumpter with them. It was James who was in command of the gate while the rest of us toiled to finish the tower. The two men in the finished tower had each nocked an arrow but I waved them to lower their weapons. I did not recognise the riders but men intent on mischief would not have approached so openly. They reined in and I approached, "Can we help you, my lord?"

The knight dismounted. I saw that he was about my age and had a beard streaked with grey. His eyes looked sad. His accent was that of someone from North Wales. Coming from the Clwyd I recognised it. "I am Sir Geraint ap Llewellyn and I am here to collect the body of my son, Hywel ap Geraint."

The men around me stiffened. I could feel the tension. I nodded, "He is buried outside the graveyard."

Just then Lady Hawise and Breffni appeared at the door. Seeing the riders they approached. "What is amiss, Sir Gerald?"

I said, "This is Lady Hawise, the lady of Poole. May I introduce Sir Geraint ap Llewellyn, he is Hywel's father. He has come for the body."

Lady Hawise said, "We are sorry for your loss, Sir Geraint, we had the priest bury your son." I saw her chew her lip as she chose her next words carefully, "You should know that he misused my servant here."

He nodded sadly, "I know my son and his weaknesses better than any man but I am his father and he was of my line. I would bury him in his home."

"And where is his home, Sir Geraint?" I was curious for I had thought he was local.

"My manor is on the far side of Wyddfa, Penmaenmawr."

It did not seem right to be talking thus. I said, "James, would you take Sir Geraint's men and show them where his son lies."

Lady Hawise said, "And if you would come within my hall you can have refreshment and we can speak there."

Sir Geraint hesitated. I said, "Let your men and mine fetch the body. We need to speak."

He nodded, "Aye, we do."

I waved over Robert, "Supervise the work, Robert."

"Yes, my lord." As Lady Hawise and the knight moved away, my healer said, quietly, "I do not envy you this task."

We reached the hall and the ever-efficient Iago had already fetched wine and food. We waited until Lady Hawise was seated and then Sir Geraint and I sat as well. There was an awkward silence. Lady Hawise broke it, "And how is your wife taking the news, my lord?"

"His mother died five years since, my lady, and that was when he lost his way. His mother doted on him for he was our only child and she left half of her money to him. It was a mistake. He was profligate and when I counselled him he left. Until six months ago I did not know if he lived or died and then a visitor told me that he was living here with Gruffydd Fychan de la Pole. I had assumed it was his manor. I now know the truth and I can only apologise for any mischief he might have caused."

I saw Lady Hawise's face soften and she gave a sad smile, "I have no children yet, my lord, nor even a suitor but I can imagine the loss. Your son did cause mischief but thanks to Sir Gerald here that is ended."

He turned to me, "And how did my son die?"

I would not, nay I could not lie and I told him the bald bare truth, "He died fighting my lord and I slew him."

He nodded and sipped his wine, thoughtfully, "I have heard of you, Sir Gerald. I fought for the last king of Wales against King Edward. I know that you are an honourable man and I also know my son." He looked me in the eye, "You have children, Sir Gerald?"

"I do."

"And are you proud of them?"

I answered firmly, "As proud as any man can be."

"Then you are lucky and made the right choices. Often we make the wrong choices but know not at the time. My wife indulged our son and I can see now that it was a mistake. I have paid the price. I have lost my wife and my son."

I felt awkward. I said, "Your son's sword..."

He shook his head, "Whichever warrior has it good luck to him for it brought nothing but pain to me and my family."

When they left, the body draped over the sumpter, I felt inordinately sad. I thought of the new King Edward. Longshanks and Sir Geraint had much in common. They had sons whom they hoped would be noble but turned out to be other. I was lucky and I knew it but my country was now ruled by a more powerful version of Hywel ap Geraint.

Over the next days the tower progressed and when Wyn told me that the brambles appeared to have taken for the plants looked healthy, I felt that it was time to leave. I told Lady Hawise of my plans and she invited my archers and men at arms, along with Dai and Robert, to dine with her. After Robert had said Grace and we were seated, she smiled, sadly, "I shall miss each and every one of you. This hall will seem empty when you have departed."

The food was brought in and we ate. Lady Hawise seemed to be picking at her food. I saw her chewing a mouthful but she was studying all my men.

Robert asked, "Is something troubling you, my lady?"

She shook her head, "No, Robert, my gallant French friend. I am just taking in your faces. I know that James and John will be here once you all leave and that, Sir Gerald, is a comfort beyond words, but I was thinking how you all came and risked your lives when I sent to you."

"I am sorry that I was late."

She shook her head, "Sir Gerald, Robert has told me that it was the king who summoned you and that there is some tale there of which he will not speak. You have no reason to apologise. That you came with this handful of men," she shook her head. "You are like a band of brothers. I have never known men so close." She reached over and patted Dai's hand, "Why even Dai here stood with his dirk ready to defend me when those men attacked. I know you men like to give titles to warriors and this one is Dai the Rock. He is brave beyond his years." I saw the orphan blush but swell with pride. "Your French friend, Monsieur Robert, shows his concern and attention to our every whim and you, Sir Gerald, are a knight who, if you do not mind me saying so, should be sat in Yarpole with adoring grandchildren around you and not here in the borderlands fighting for a maid who is nothing to you. All of you came here to help a maid and I thank God for that."

"My lady, that is not true. When I was knighted I was honoured but I took the oath seriously. A true knight defends all. That is his duty. It is true that I want more time with my wife and my grandchildren but when a man takes an oath he keeps it. If he does not then he is not a man."

"Then know, Sir Gerald, that you will ever be a friend and more than welcome in my home. I am determined that we shall defend what is mine and…"

I held up a hand, "I am within a day of you. You now have horses and you have men who can ride. If you have need of me then send one that I will know and I shall return forthwith. I am keen to see if the seeds we planted here can grow."

It was a merry meal and when, the next day, we prepared to leave I saw the sadness on the faces of all. Lady Hawise and the redoubtable Breffni looked close to tears as did Dai. She gave each of us a small, embroidered badge with the mark of Powis sewn upon it, a red Griffin. My men were touched. I kissed the back of her hand and mounted

Warbow

Thunder. I nodded to James and John, "When you deem it safe to leave the service of Lady Hawise then return to my son's hall."

"We shall, my lord."

The seven of us rode out through the gates now flanked by our towers, already named by David of Abergele as Warbow's walls, and passed through the village. The people came out to wave us off and I was touched for they clearly held us in high regard. I hoped that we had done enough to discourage the de la Pole family but I knew that when I reached Yarpole I would send a message to the king. I had done enough for him to expect a favour in return.

My archers were cautious men and Iago and Gruffydd insisted upon riding a dozen paces before us and they all had strung bows. Gwillim pointed out that we could always get more bowstrings but there was just one Sir Gerald Warbow. It meant that I was flanked by Dai and Robert. I let the two of them chatter away across me. I was forming the words for the letter I would write.

"Lady Hawise needs a husband."

"Dai, she is a strong woman."

"But, Robert, as wise as you are, your wisdom comes from France and England. This is Wales. Ladies do not inherit no matter how much they deserve it. Until she has a husband there will be claims upon her land."

Robert said, "For one so young you have a great deal of knowledge."

"I spent a lot of time with Iago the Steward and he seemed to like me. He told me these things. He fears that when a suitable time has elapsed the de la Poles will try to take the land once more and remember, Robert, that there are other lands held by her uncles. She would be the richest woman in Powis but for that."

"I do not think that Lady Hawise cares for gold."

"And I agree but as Iago the Steward told me, gold brings security. Lady Hawise needs more men to guard her lands than we left."

I nodded, "Dai is right, Robert. Lady Hawise needs a husband but I believe she is the kind of lady who will choose her own and not have one chosen for her. He is also right in that the de la Pole family will try to take the manor for Poole is the jewel in the crown. What it needs is a castle."

Robert nodded his agreement, "And I had seen the site for one to the west of the village. It is a piece of land on high ground but it would take money to build and there is not enough in Poole."

"Then we shall have to petition the king to have all of her lands returned to her."

"And, Sir Gerald, is that likely? What is in it for the king?"

"Robert you need to watch your tongue, it is one thing to speak such words here but if the king should hear them…"

"I am sorry, my lord, I forget that you have to obey the king's every whim."

"It is as Sir Geraint said, Robert, when a man's bloodline goes bad there is nothing that can be done. We were lucky to have in the first King Edward, the kind who was strong and did the right thing. His son is not the same but we have to support him."

"And as Queen Isabella is young, it might be many years before we have an heir."

"Then we, the knights of England, have to save the king from himself."

We did not ride hard for I intended to spend the night at Jack's home. We were made most welcome and Susanna, his wife, fussed over me as though I was an invalid. Whilst food was prepared I sat with my stepson in the small room that faced west. He had added the room himself and it was pleasant to sit and peer out on the setting sun. Once it was dark the shutters would be closed and it would become a cosy and secluded place for Jack to use.

"The attack, Father, Michel told us that they outnumbered you, should you have taken more men?"

"Hindsight, Jack, is always perfect. We did not really know the scale of the danger and the men I took were enough."

"And is it over?"

I shook my head, "Not yet. The problem, Jack, is the king. He is so distracted by his barons and earls and how they view his favourite that he has forgotten he is the King of England."

"I think he is a bad king." I made to answer and he held up his hand, "I know, I should not say such things but we are alone and you brought me up to speak my mind. I will support the king but I fear for my country."

"And with that in mind how stands the manor to provide men?"

He frowned, "For what purpose? There is no war."

"Scotland. There is unfinished business there and I fear that King Edward will want to finish what his father started."

"But for that he needs the support of Parliament."

"I know but if the summons comes, could you meet the muster?"

"I could but I would be loath to leave the manor without defence."

"And you will not. I will make funds available to pay for more men."

"You have such silver?"

"I am not a waster of money nor is Lady Mary. I would rather spend the coins I have to protect my family than to waste them on things I do not need. My manors are all productive and I have good stewards. Will, at Balden, has the safest manor and his men have not needed to be mustered. I have the coins."

"Very well then, I will hire another ten men."

We drank in silence for a while. Then he said, "Last Christmas was a hard one. You were held in London and we did not celebrate."

I laughed, "It is not yet spring and you are speaking of Christmas."

He laughed, "When I grew up I never enjoyed Christmas but your home was the most wonderful experience at Christmas. Your family made me welcome and I have come to regard the celebration of Christ's birth as a celebration of my rebirth. When we are all together in your hall it feels like a warm and secure place. I am just saying that this Christmas Hamo and I intend to celebrate with you at Yarpole."

"You have spoken to Hamo?"

"Of course, we speak often." He paused, "I have written to Joan too." My daughter Joan had married Sir Ralph of Wooferton. That manor was just four miles from Yarpole but he had another manor on the borders as well as one in Yorkshire. Longshanks had been generous to him. The manor in Yorkshire was a rich one and they had moved there. Joan had always been close and I missed her but her duty was to her husband.

What was left unsaid concerned my daughter Margaret whose son, Gerald Launceston, had been my first grandson. I was not estranged from her and they lived close to me but her husband was a prosperous merchant and they moved in different circles. I do not think he approved of the rough archer whose daughter he had married. I rarely saw either of my daughters but the reasons were not the same.

"Then I shall endeavour to make the next Christmas the best one yet."

The meal was a happy one. Perhaps meeting Sir Geraint made me realise that I had not done such a bad job with my children. Certainly my sons were the finest a man could wish for and my daughters were both good mothers and dutiful wives. Jack's children, even though he was my stepson, were as cherished by me as those of my blood. When I died they would inherit the same from my estate as my natural grandchildren.

We left in the late morning for we had a short ride home. I had decided not to visit with Hamo until the next day. Seeing Jack and Susanna had made me realise how much I missed Mary. I had spent too long in the service of the king and not enough on serving my family.

As I rode through the village I was greeted by cheers and waves. I suspect that Michel and his son had already told those in **Warbow's Tavern** of the incident in Poole. The story would have spread and, no doubt, been exaggerated. That was the way of the world. One man always sought to give the impression that they knew more than another.

Warbow

The noise alerted my wife and she came to the door, wiping the flour from her hands. My wife was a lady but one who liked to work.

I dismounted and Dai took my reins. I strode over to pick Mary up. She squealed and said, "What are you doing? You will have flour all over you."

I kissed her, "Flour can be cleaned. I have missed you."

She hugged me, "And I you." She put her mouth close to my ear, "Michel told me all. When will you take things a little easier, my love? The Lord Edward is dead and you owe his son nothing."

"And what I did was not for his son. It was for a maiden. Lady Hawise is young and vulnerable. She needs protection."

Linking me she led me into the hall, "And that means that Lord Edward's Archer is honour bound to do so."

"I cannot change my nature."

"And I do not wish you to. I must make the most of every moment we have together. Will you ride on the morrow to see Hamo?"

I laughed, "Are you now one of the sisters who can see into the future? Aye."

"Then I will ride with you. I wish to see him and I do not want you out of my sight…not until you are called away again!"

Having seen the problems that Lady Hawise had suffered I threw myself into making the most of what I had. I knew that I was lucky and soldiers never disparage luck. You helped luck whenever you could. I had been given good people and a good land; I would make the most of those. The first thing I did, however, was not for me but the lady. I wrote a letter to the king. As it was still early summer I sent the letter with Jean Michel who would ride to Balden to receive the annual returns from Will, the man at arms who was steward of my land there. Jean Michel took Dai with him. It was partly for the company but also to keep up his training. The long journey would improve his riding skills and Jean Michel could teach him about weaponry. They would deliver the letter to the Tower. I knew the castellan there and he was a good man. He would ensure that the king received it. I hoped that the king would be in residence and when my men returned there might be a reply. Dai would also be treated, if that is the word, to the sights of London. The Tower would show him a real castle.

Once they had left I felt I had done all that I could for Lady Hawise and I became, once more, Lord of the Manor of Yarpole. Our visit to Hamo resulted in an overnight stay and the reason was simple, my son insisted. He had made many improvements to the manor and he was keen to show them off. I did not mind as Mary and I were able to spend time with our grandchildren. For some reason, despite that I saw them infrequently, they always took to me and seemed to enjoy my company. I did not know why for I was absent more than I was present. The same had been true when my children had been growing up. The king's service had taken me hence too often. Having spoken to the father of Hywel ap Geraint I knew that I had been fortunate. The lines between being a good father and a poor one seemed fine.

Once back in the manor I found that life was good. If I had chosen to sit back and not lift a finger then I would have been accommodated but I was not born that way and I liked to be active. Mary complained because I was still the first one up. She wanted me to enjoy lazier mornings. It did not happen. I developed a routine. The incident on the Canterbury road had shown me that I needed to keep up my practice with the bow. I had the bowyer make me a new bow and thanks to his skill it was perfect for me. He had the bow staves already. They were seasoned and ready to use. He chose a few that were the right length for me and we tested them. We found one that was perfect for me. When I had been younger it might have been a more powerful one but this suited me well. I joined my archers when they practised at the marks. I also went there alone to try to regain some of the strength I knew that I had lost whilst waiting at the king's pleasure in London.

I also took more interest in my manor. My visit to Lady Hawise had shown me dangers that were present at my home. I had more men to defend it and I could not see an enemy like Lady Hawise's uncles threatening me but Parliament had shown me that we had a divided land and there was opposition to the king. If civil disorder filled the land then I would need a manor that could be defended. I walked it alone. I chose the time when Mary was busy with the cooks and in the kitchen.

"I shall take a stroll around the hall and stretch my legs."

She cocked an eye, "Just a walk?"

"It is not the time to pull my bow. A walk will do me good." I was not deceiving Mary. She knew me well enough to know that I was up to something.

The manor had been in need of strong walls when I had come. We had made the ones that already existed higher and, unlike Poole, ours had a fighting platform built into them. We had towers at the front gates but they were an integral part of the walls and not additions. Each could accommodate four men at arms or three archers. The gates themselves were well maintained. We not only had a bar across them but also poles which could be placed in the holes in the ground and secured. A ram might break the gates but an enemy would find it hard to force them. Even my critical eye could see no fault there. Short of building a portcullis or a barbican I could not see how the gatehouse could be improved. There was also the problem of the king. The old king might have sanctioned a barbican but the new one would see it as a threat. The front of the manor was secure.

The hall had a ditch but unlike the one at Poole mine was well maintained. The bridge that led over it could be removed. It had been many years since we had done so. I looked up at the roof. We had made that defensible and archers could ascend through the attic and open the shutters. It was almost as good as a castle. A walk around the hall confirmed that we had built well. It was as I headed for the rear of the property that I began to frown for, like Poole, this was the weak area. The main difference was that my gate at the rear was well travelled. Michel and his son used it to go to their small holdings as did my archers and men at arms. It was also the way to the woods. I allowed my people to collect kindling and to trap rabbits and squirrels for the pot. I knew that often it was not always barred. I could do little about their homes but I could initiate a better system of securing the gate.

Michel was tending the crops that he and Jean Michel grew. They longed to grow grapes and make wine but the land was not suitable for them. Instead they grew beans and kept a small herd of goats. They did eat the meat but it was the milk that they needed. They made cheese. It was so good that they bartered it with other villagers. A vineyard would have made their lives perfect. Along with the animals, I allowed men to hunt in my woods, they had a diet which suited them.

Michel looked up at my approach, alerted by the bleating of the goats. Each of my men used a different form of alarm. Peter kept geese. Richard kept a dog. Some had chickens. All of them would make a noise at the approach of any who was not from the farm.

"My lord, taking the air?"

I shook my head. I could be honest with Michel, "No, Michel, Poole made me think about our deficiencies. What if we were attacked and from the rear or the side?"

Michel did not argue with me for he was a soldier and knew the risks and dangers unknown enemies could pose. He straightened and looked at the gate. His smallholding was the closest to the gate. Peter of Beverley had one on the other side of the path to the woods. He had been crippled fighting for me. Michel knew that, "This is the danger point. An enemy could take the gate."

"Just so. I thought to build two towers here. We managed to make two at Poole with a handful of men. If we choose the next holy day to build them then they could be erected in one day." My captain of sergeants nodded. Sundays were used for weapon training after the services but holy days were days of rest and feasting. I would lay on a feast and the men would build up an appetite whilst working. He nodded his agreement. I did not need it for I was the lord of the manor but I would be a foolish one if I did not consult with the men who guarded it. "We need to be more alert. This gate is often left open."

Michel sighed, "Aye, my lord. Sometimes when men leave your warrior hall to return to their homes and often whilst the gate is shut it is not barred."

I knew that men also used the manor, when the front gate was open, to return to their homes from the tavern. It saved their legs a longer walk. I began to work out how many men now lived in the warrior hall. There were just archers. It had been mainly my men at arms who farmed and had small holdings. Peter Yew Bow had a family and a farm but the others were single men. I said, "I will speak with Gwillim and Hob." They were the senior archers.

I spent a half an hour discussing the farm with my French captain. One day his house would need to be enlarged. Jean Michel had set his cap on winning the hand of one of the maidens in the village. Alice was the daughter of Walter the Archer. Walter was now a farmer and I knew that, at one time, Jean Michel and Alice had planned to live with him. When one of his other daughters had married then the wedding arrangements had been changed. Michel told me that when his son married he would live with his father. We spoke of the enlargements that would be needed. We also spoke of Jean Michel and the wedding. His visit to London would allow him to buy cloth to have made into fine clothes for him. I pointed to the building where there were foundations and the start of a wattle and daub wall, "That is where they will live?"

"Yes, my lord. When children come along we can add another. It is the reason they are not married yet. When Alice's sister became pregnant then we had to delay the wedding. I will have this room finished by the time they return and then Jean Michel will see Father Michael and arrange the wedding." He smiled, "And then my son can give me grandchildren."

I smiled, "And then your life will change a little. If they are to live with you then get used to being woken in the night."

"A small price to pay for the knowledge that my line will continue."

"Just so," I pointed at the gates, "and until we have the towers ensure that the gate is barred. I will tell my archers to secure it from the manor side." He nodded. That done I went back through the gate. I closed it behind me.

My archers were not in the warrior hall but were seated outside in the sun. They were making arrows. Mark the Bowyer was also toiling and fashioning staves. One of the first things I had done when I had come was to plant ash, aspen and birch. Many of them were now mature and my archers chose the wood that they each preferred. I was lucky to have a stand of yew trees already. They were in the graveyard and Mark could harvest the best of woods for his bows. The four men who were in the hall were engaged in different parts of the arrow making. Some were using the shooting boards. Hob was smoothing his arrows with dogfish skin while Iago and Gruffydd were fitting the arrow heads. All of them were busy and did not notice my silent approach such was their concentration.

"How goes it?"

My words made Hob jump. Hob grinned, "My lord, you made me start."

Gwillim laughed, "That is because here we are safe and secure and do not need to keep an ear out for the approach of an assassin." He held up an ash shaft. Gwillim preferred ash. "The trees have matured, my lord, and we have a better choice of shaft. Peter's geese not only feed us and warn us they also have the best of feathers. It is just the heads that are in short supply."

I nodded, "Aye, I must speak to Alf the Smith. We always need ploughshares, mattocks and spades but without bodkins and war arrows we are at risk."

"A glorious day, my lord."

"It is, Hob. I need to speak with you four for there is something on my mind. I trust you, Gwillim, to tell the other archers when they return to the hall." They each laid down the arrow and the tool they were using to give me their attention. They knew, from my tone, that this was important. I pointed to the gate, "That gate is often left open at night." I saw the guilty looks exchanged. "Poole showed me the danger of such laxity. The men who use it normally visit with you and drink here or in the tavern. I will not stop that for there is no harm in it but it is now your responsibility to ensure that when the last one has departed then it is closed and barred. I have spoken to Michel. He will shout if the gate is still open when he retires."

They looked relieved and Gwillim said, "A good idea, my lord, and we have been remiss. It is so peaceful here in Yarpole that we have forgotten how close we are to Wales. We will make sure that the last man to bed checks the gate when he goes to make water."

Iago said, "The uncles of Lady Hawise may choose to avenge themselves at our expense."

I laughed, "They might, Iago of Ruthin, but only if the mad moon touched them for this is not Poole. We had just eight of our men and a handful of raw clay and yet we sent them hence. Yarpole, Lucton and

Luston are too big and dangerous for any but a fool to contemplate taking." They nodded, "And one more thing, on the next holy day, to build up an appetite for the feast we will enjoy, I intend to build two towers at the gate much as we did at Poole."

    I left them to their work knowing that I need not make a formal announcement. Michel would tell those without the walls what was intended and the archers would tell those who were inside.

Chapter 9

As I made my way back to the main hall I spoke with all those who laboured in my manor. We paid our servants well and they were happy. I suppose that it could have been feigned affection but I did not think so. Some of them had been born in the manor and had known no other home but this one. Some were the children of archers and men at arms. They were all connected to me and I found that interesting for I had been brought up alone. My father and the old woman who lived in the woods close to the Clwyd had been my only family and, after a lifetime of serving King Edward and now his son, I had a large family and a host of people who relied on me for their livelihoods. It was almost noon when I entered the hall.

Mary put her hands on her hips, "That was a long walk, my husband. Do you need a lie down now?"

I laughed, "I could do it again and not yet be out of breath. However, it has given me an appetite."

"Sarah, fetch food. His lordship and I will dine in the hall."

When the food and ale had been served and we were alone, Mary said, "So, what changes are to be made?"

My mouth stayed open, the food hovering in my fingers, "Are you prescient?"

She laughed, "You never take exercise for the fun of it and there is always purpose. What changes?"

"Little things. On the next holy day I will have my men make two towers at the back gate and I have asked my archers to ensure that the gate is closed each night." I bit into the bread and ham and chewed. We made good bread in my manor.

It was Mary's turn to pause, "Is there danger?"

Shaking my head and swallowing a mouthful of ale, I said, "No, I do not think so, but Poole made me look again at my home. Gaveston is in Ireland and has not been truly exiled. That will anger the Earls of Lancaster, the Archbishop of Canterbury and the Earl of Lincoln. The king has not done what they wished. Resentment will fester and there may come a time, not soon but one day, when that might be kindled into civil disorder. I would be ready."

"He is the king and does not have to do what they wish. Besides, Ireland is not England. Gaveston has been exiled from England. It is using words as weapons but they have been clever, this king and his favourite, and they have mitigated the punishment."

I smiled, "You use words well, but what I fear is that he will return, and when he does then the barons will rise against him. I do not know our position."

"You would fight against the king?"

I shook my head, "No, but I would not fight against my neighbours."

"You know that you cannot straddle the fence, my love." Her voice was gentle and I knew that whatever I decided would have her support.

"The problem is not just me. I have Hamo and Jack to think about. Joan and Margaret will be looked after by their husbands and I do not think they will be dragged into a civil war, but Hamo and Jack are different. Then there are my manors. Mordaf at Coldingham is the most exposed but Dick and Betty at Sadberge are close to the border. There is just Will at Balden who might escape the fire that would come with civil disorder."

"Let us not make spectres in the night to frighten ourselves. We have peace at the moment. You are right to prepare for danger but let us not make it rule our lives. Robert told me, this morning, that the king's opinion of you has changed."

"It has and while Gaveston is in Ireland that will continue." I wiped my hands on my cloth, "Where is Robert?"

"He went to Father Michael. He said he had things to confess." She frowned, "What has he done that needs the confessional so soon after his return?"

"Lady Hawise. She makes him have thoughts that, for a priest, even one who never took his final vows, are disturbing. You would like the lady. She is young but she is strong."

"And like Robert you are a little under her spell."

I laughed. "I am an old man and there has only ever been one woman for me and she is in this room."

"I know that. Yes, you are right and I would like to meet her."

Robert's visit to the priest reminded me about my promise. "I think you and I, my love, will visit Worcester."

She frowned, "Why?"

"Father Michael needs a font. I had planned on having one carved in Shrewsbury but that is a longer ride and I have heard that the mason who worked on the east end of Worcester Cathedral does fine work."

She nodded, "And they have a good market there. Who will we take?"

"Robert and Dai will be all that I need."

"Then I shall take Alice, Walter's daughter." I must have looked surprised for she shook her head, "Do you not know what goes on in your own manor? She is to marry Jean Michel and there are things that she needs. It should have happened already. If you have visited with Michel then you know that he has built rooms for them."

"It slipped my mind."

She laughed, "It is good that you have me to retrieve such things."

Alice was delighted at the chance to visit Worcester but worried about the ride. Dai promised to watch out for her. Perhaps as he had only recently learned to ride he understood her plight better than most. It was thirty miles to the city. We would only be away for one night. Robert was excited at the prospect of praying in the cathedral which was a fine one. The others were just excited to be visiting somewhere new. I was the only one familiar with it. My visits, however, had been martial in nature. Dai led the sumpter on which we would load whatever we bought in Worcester. I had the gold for the font in a purse. We could have been accommodated in the castle, my rank and title would have allowed it, but I preferred inns. For one thing it was easier to come and go. We reached the city in the mid-morning and I found a tavern I remembered. **The Stag** was on Friar Street and not far from the cathedral but it was far enough from the river to avoid inundations when the Severn flooded. The landlord was delighted to have nobility and we were given good rooms.

While Michel escorted the ladies to the market, Robert and I went to the workshop of Edmund the Mason. He had helped to build the east end of the cathedral when he had been an apprentice. That had been forty years ago and he was now a white beard. I entered a world of dust and the noise of chisels being hammered into stone. Now that the work on the cathedral was finished, masons worked on statues or smaller projects that did not involve huge slabs of stone. I was helped in our meeting by the fact that he not only knew of me, but he also appeared to admire me.

"Sir Gerald, I am honoured that you visit my workshop. I have long wished to meet you."

I was always suspicious of flattery, "Why, Edmund?"

"Evesham, my lord, you and King Edward rid the land of the poison of the de Montforts. Henry de Montfort and Robert Ferrers slaughtered many Jews." He shook his head, "They were good people. One of them, Isaac, was an apprentice like me. It was not right that they were butchered. I prayed for the destruction of that evil family and you helped King Edward to do so."

"They were strange times, Edmund."

"And how can I be of service?"

"My church in Yarpole has no font. I would have one made by you."

He nodded, "That work suits me, my lord. I have built my last church, but now that I am getting close to the end of my life on earth the more I can do for God the better. The design?"

I waved a hand at Robert, "Robert was a priest and he has a better mind than me. He can advise you."

"Good."

"And the price?" He picked up a wax tablet and made some calculations. I did not understand them all but he circled a number at the bottom. I smiled, "You will not be making much profit, Edmund."

"At my age I need little and my sons make money. I shall regard this as my last piece. I shall bring it to Yarpole myself when it is finished." I took out the coins. He shook his head, "You can pay me when I deliver."

"That is not my way, Edmund. Who knows what will happen twixt now and then. Take the coins." He did so.

The ladies had bought cloth and good pots. The sumpter would be laden but luckily the journey home would not be a long one. Alice was overawed by the inn which was, to be truthful, rather plain. It suited me but for a young woman who had never left Yarpole before it was like a visit to an exotic land. Mary had to help her choose the food and I saw Robert smiling at my wife's kindness.

While the ladies chattered away about the items they had bought and the rooms that Michel was building, we spoke of the font and Robert shook his head, "When Edmund spoke of the Jews I was surprised. I know that they were responsible for the crucifixion but surely the men who perpetrated the heinous act realised that Golgotha was more than a thousand years ago."

"The de Montforts were a curse, Robert. Simon de Montfort wanted the crown and he did all in his power to get it. The Jews were a way to get the money to finance his war. Thank God he lost."

My wife glanced over and I saw the look of disapproval. My choice of conversation was not appropriate and I changed the subject.

When we reached Yarpole, Robert and I told Father Michael about the dimensions of the font and when it would be delivered. It pleased him.

We had the towers finished by the time Jean Michel and Dai returned. Both Michel and I had been worried about his extended absence. I was relieved when they appeared to be smiling as they dismounted. Jean Michel shook his head, "I thought that Paris was a mad house, my lord, but it is nothing compared with London."

Perhaps it was my imagination but Dai seemed to have grown and he was now better dressed. "And how did you find it, Dai?" I smiled, "Or, as Lady Hawise dubbed you, Dai the Rock."

He smiled, "Like Jean Michel I found it strange but wondrous, too. St Paul's is a magnificent church and the Tower...it rises so high I cannot conceive how they built it."

"And you come back looking like a different youth to the one who left."

"The clothes, my lord? That is thanks to Lady Mary. She furnished us with coins and told Jean Michel to buy some decent garments in London."

I looked at Mary who shrugged, "I could not expect you to think about such things. You would wear rags so long as they were comfortable."

Laughing in agreement I said, "Come, let us go within. I am anxious for news."

In the hall Jean Michel took two letters from his satchel. One bore no seal and I knew that would come from William of Ware. The other did not bear the king's seal but the seal of the Bishop of London, Roger Baldock. I laid that to one side. William's missive did not take long to read. It was largely a column of figures and it showed that the manor was prosperous. He added more personal information for me. Will had a family and two sons and a daughter. He also told me that my former man at arms could muster eight spearmen and six archers. He would be the only man at arms. It was enough.

I handed the letter to Mary and said, "How was William?" I waved at the letter. "This tells me little about his situation."

"He is happy, my lord, and the land is at peace. We enjoyed our time. His sons are a lively pair and kept poor Dai on his toes."

"They plagued you?"

"I did not mind, my lord. I was taken back to happier times before my home was taken from me." Mary put her hand on Dai's. He smiled, "I am happy, my lady, and I know that dwelling on the past cannot do any good but playing with the boys...it was good for me."

Changing the subject I said, "And the delay, Jean Michel?"

He nodded, "Was because I was just a man at arms. My mail brought me little respect and we were often made to wait for they sought the spurs of a knight. Others were admitted before we were and we spent longer waiting than others."

"Aye, I thought that might be the case but the matter was urgent." I tapped the unopened letter, "And did the bishop give you any idea about what he wrote?"

"No, my lord, I was sent without to wait with Dai and the priest who brought it pointed to the seal." He shook his head, "There was no need and I did not like it."

"Officials are all like that. They enjoy their moment of power so do not take offence. Robert is an exception. He is a former priest who is honourable and honest, not all are like him."

Almost as though he had been waiting the door opened and Robert stood there, "It is good that you think me honest, my lord."

I sniffed, "Although sneaking around doors does not reflect that."

"Gerald!"

"Sorry, Robert, Lady Mary is right. I suppose I have delayed long enough." I took out my dagger and cut the seal. The letter was written in a neat hand. If I wrote anything it looked like the scratchings of a five-legged spider who has fallen in the ink. I read it and then pushed it over to Mary. The others looked expectantly at me. I said, "The king has promised to attend a Parliament at Shrewsbury. That is news to me for I am a baron of the border and should have been invited. It suggests to me that the meeting is not imminent."

"And Lady Hawise?"

"The bishop does add assurances that she is a ward of the Crown and enjoys the protection of King Edward… for what that is worth."

Mary shook her head and put down the letter, "Gerald, the pot is half full and not half empty. The king, through his bishop, promises that the lady will be protected."

"I suppose. At least James and John are there. If there is trouble then they will let me know." I smiled, "Thank you, Jean Michel and Dai. You have done us a great service."

Dai smiled, "And I have been richly rewarded for I am now dressed like a young noble and not an urchin."

"And I have a favour to ask, my lord."

"Ask away."

"I would like to be wed as soon as it can be arranged. As you know I have been courting Walter's daughter, Alice. I now have enough coins to marry her and her father approves but I would have your permission."

Before I could answer Mary said, "And about time too. Poor Alice is getting no younger, Jean Michel. She and I spent some time planning your future on the way to Worcester."

I saw his look of surprise. He blustered, "We had planned on living with Walter, my lady, only his other daughter moved in."

I butted in, "And Michel has asked me for permission to make his home bigger for the two of them so you see, my love, that Jean Michel has acted as quickly as he could."

I saw the grateful smile on Jean Michel's face and the wry one on my wife's, "You are both quick at thinking on your feet, I will give you that. You have, of course, Alice's mother's permission too?" Jean Michel nodded. "Then when you have spoken to your father and Walter then speak to Father Michael. You can be wed within three weeks and the manor can enjoy a feast that does not involve labour and the building of towers!"

My wife was the real power in the manor and we all knew that.

The three weeks flew by. A wedding in the manor was a major event, and as Michel was a man at arms Hamo and Jack would bring their families over for the celebration. That meant expense as an extra bedroom was needed to accommodate everyone. A week before the wedding I went with my archers and men at arms into the woods to hunt. I was not one of those Marcher lords who saw a hunt as sport. For us a hunt was to provide food and to manage our animals. I was judicious in the timing. Robert came along but more as an observer and in case a healer was needed. Hunting wild boars and stags was a potentially dangerous activity.

Peter Yew Bow knew my woods better than anyone and he went out the day before the hunt to find spoor. We would be feeding both the village and my sons who would stay for the celebrations. I had invited Margaret and her family but, as I had expected they declined. They were used to a more sophisticated life. Joan now lived too far away for the journey. We rose before dawn and enjoyed a hunter's breakfast. We would be out all day. Peter had identified an old stag who needed to be culled. He had a badly broken antler and in the rutting season might hurt a younger stag. He had also noticed a lame hind who was getting old. There were also two sows who no longer produced young. Such provender would feed the village and provide salted meat for a month. We would also be able to make a delicacy I loved, blood pudding. Nothing would be wasted in this hunt.

As we ate I said to Dai, "You will have a boar spear, but it will be for your protection only. I do not expect you to hunt. We have enough archers and men at arms to ensure that we kill just that which we need. You may have been willing, Dai the Rock, to defend Lady Hawise from her killers but wild boar or an angry stag are too much for you…yet."

I could see the disappointment on his face. He had enjoyed training to be a warrior but it was early days. His willingness to defend Lady Hawise with his dirk had shown his courage but he needed skills. This was a day, not for fashion but comfort and defence. I wore my trusty buskins and a good leather jack over a rough tunic. My breeches were made of hide. A hunter could not worry about tearing his breeks on brambles when hunting a wild boar. They had thick hides and liked to hide in such places. For the same reason I wore a leather hood. About my waist I had a stout but short sword and a pair of daggers. One was an old dagger with a curved blade. They used to be called a seax and they were now rare. I could not remember the battlefield from which I had taken it but the single bladed weapon was perfect for gutting animals. I also took my new bow and the hunting arrows that Gruffydd had made for me. They were well made and the barbed arrows had been sharpened. I would not choose to use one against a charging boar, that was why we had boar spears, but I knew that I had the skill to hit the eye of a boar and that might save the life of another.

We took no servants. All the men I led, with the exception of Robert and Dai, were warriors. The lords who used servants as beaters were, in my view, poor masters. My warriors knew how to react and do so efficiently. We followed Peter Yew Tree. His days as a warrior archer were now coming to an end, he was the oldest of my warriors and had fought alongside Walter the Archer, Mordaf and David of Wales. He could still, as I could, draw a bow, but he had had his fill of killing men and now he acted as my gamekeeper. He also commanded the archers of the hall when we were away at war. He might be older but he was still stealthy and moved like a cat along the trails he knew so well. I followed him. Dai and Robert were at the rear just in front of Michel and his son. Dai and Robert had the boar spears we would need.

It was a perfect day for hunting. It was not too hot and the sky had scudding clouds. The animals would be grazing. If it was hot they would be sleeping and harder to find. An animal that moved was easier to hear. Peter had told us that we would have to walk a mile or two. We kept a steady pace. I daresay the younger warriors would have gone faster. I did not mind the pace for it allowed me to study the woods much as I had when I had been a young archer. I had an arrow nocked but it was just for speed of release. We were not expecting to find the deer we sought for a while, so when Peter held up his hand he almost took me by surprise. I raised the bow but did not draw it. Peter nocked an arrow and I waved my bow so that the archers filtered silently to our left and right. The men at arms had boar spears. If this was the herd of deer then we needed archers.

My men were skilled at this sort of thing. The men at arms let the silent archers move through the undergrowth barely tickling the leaves and followed in their footsteps. Like me they had already nocked an arrow. They all now raised their bows even though we could not see what Peter had clearly identified, a deer. It was as I raised my bow and nocked arrow that I saw the hind lift its head. Although I was the lord of the manor and it was my right to claim first blood we did not work that way. Peter had identified the deer we would hunt and he could have, if he chose, the first arrow. However, even as he aimed I saw a broken antler rise. It made the stag look ungainly. It had clearly been in a fight in the last rutting season and the victory had come at a price. Half of the right-hand antler had been sheared off halfway down leaving a savage spear waiting to gore an opponent. Nature had rules and a damaged antler broke those rules. I raised my bow. The rest of the archers would wait until Peter and I had loosed before drawing and sending their arrows at the two animals.

   I pulled back. I felt the tension in the bow as I drew back. Aiming was second nature to me. The deer was less than thirty paces away and I was aiming for the neck and chest. I could have risked an arrow at its head but sometimes even the best of arrows could be deflected up and a stag's skull was thick. Mine would be a mortal hit but it might not kill it immediately. I knew when the bow was at full draw and I released. I had, as usual, unknowingly not breathed while I drew but now I did. Peter had waited until he heard my arrow before he released and he was wise to do so. As my string twanged the hind raised her head and even as my arrow hit the stag so Peter's arrow drove into the skull of the hind. It fell as though poleaxed. My arrow struck true and drove deep into the animal. He was a fighter and, dying, he turned to lead his herd to safety. The beast did not know that we had hit all that we intended to. The stag stumbled a little but led his wives and children away from the danger. Peter and my archers went to the hind and began to gut it. Iago cut a stave to drive through her body and to help us to carry the carcass back. I led the men at arms and Hob and Gwillim as we followed the noise of the fleeing herd. They left a clear trail as they careered through my woods. The stag managed to stay alive for a hundred paces before succumbing to the wound. It was a big animal and must have ruled the woods for a long time. The broken antler was his undoing. After gutting the beast I allowed those who wished to enjoy the still warm heart of the animal. It was a ritual. We hung the stag on a stave and then four of my archers headed back to the manor carrying the two animals. The rest of us followed Peter towards our next prey. This would be work, not for archers, but for men at arms.

   We drank some of the ale that Dai and Robert had carried along with the food which we ate. "Where are the wild pigs to be found, Peter?"

   "There is a dell, my lord, about a mile or more deeper in the woods. At this time of year there are the first of the berries that the wild pigs like. It is also close to water. I am confident that they will be there."

   "And how will we know the old ones that we hunt, Peter?"

   He smiled, "They no longer produce young and so they are the fattest two. You will know them, lord, for they will be close to Old Edward, the boar. They rarely leave his side."

"And will he attack when we use our spears?"

"He might, my lord, but if the archers send their arrows at him it might discourage him. If these were young sows he might attack but we shall see." I noticed that Peter did not have a boar spear but he had his bow and a bag full of arrows.

I had sent my bow back with the archers and, as we followed Peter deeper into the woods, I hefted a boar spear. Dai now had less to carry and would be able to carry the other boar spear more easily. The herds of wild pigs we had in our woods were small. There were just two of them. Peter had told me, when we had planned the hunt, that the larger one had more animals and that was the one we should hunt. It was a good choice for we all knew Old Edward. When we had hunted with hawks in the woods he had been the one easiest to see and he kept to a particular part of the wood. I knew the dell. When we rode through the trees it was to be avoided for it was treacherous for horses. Even on foot it might prove difficult. I knew that Michel and Jean Michel would wish to be at the fore and protect me but I was an obstinate old fool and I walked behind Peter. Peter would move away as soon as the herd was spotted because a charging boar would be fatal for an archer. His arrow was loosely nocked in his hand.

Peter sniffed the air as we approached the dell. The wind came from ahead and in it was the pungent mixture of damp earth, rotting leaves and something else. When he paused and sniffed I did so too and immediately I had the distinctive smell of wild boar in my nostrils. I held the spear in two hands. We moved painfully slowly towards the dell. We had to be careful, for the ground, made wet by rain two nights since, was slippery and there was a tangle of undergrowth before us. Creeping ivy added to the danger. When I heard the distinctive snort of a wild boar I readied myself. Wild pigs have poor eyesight but they have good hearing and they have noses that can smell food from deep beneath the earth. The wind in our faces meant that they might not smell us but if we made a noise then they would hear us. Peter held up his hand and then moved forward. He was identifying the herd. He walked backwards after a few moments and turned. He held up two fingers and I nodded. He had identified the two animals. He pointed to my left. They were there. I nodded. I turned and gestured for Michel and Jean Michel to flank me. Richard of Culcheth ghosted up next to my right shoulder. He was my back-up. Even as I readied my arm I wondered if this was my last hunt. I was getting old. Within a couple of years I would have reached three score and ten. I dismissed the maudlin thought. Such thoughts could get a man killed. I moved forward. Peter was to my right but he was there not for defence but as a lookout. The remaining archers were close to him, arrows nocked. Even as we moved I reflected that this was good training for war. Each nerve was stretched. Every sense was working and we all knew that danger, and perhaps death, lay around the corner.

I saw the herd. They were just twenty paces from us. We would be able to get a little closer and remain hidden by the undergrowth but it would only be a foot or so. There were two mothers with piglets around them. I saw a young boar and then I saw the two ancient sows. Unlike the younger others they had scarred hides that bespoke years of living in my woods. Near to them Old Edward snuffled at the ground. I saw that close to him were a pair of adolescent wild pigs. One was a young sow and one an immature boar. I wondered if they were his. We had discussed the hunt and planned it well. Michel and Jean Michel would hurl their spears at the two sows. It was unlikely that just one strike would kill the beasts and that was why we had the archers and spare spears. I bent my knees slightly and took a wider stance.

Father and son needed no words and they both raised and then hurled their spears at the same time. They were well thrown and both struck, cutting through the hide and into the flesh. Neither was mortal. Old Edward reacted to their squeal and sought out the danger. Peter sent an arrow at the beast and when it hit him he gave an almighty roar and then led the herd away. The two sows did not follow him. They were old and they were feisty. They charged at Michel and Jean Michel. The two men turned and ran. Their swords were not the weapon to use against a charging wild pig. Richard and I swung our spears around as the two Frenchmen passed us and the pigs turned their attention to us, the new threat. They were both bleeding heavily but they came on. They had teeth that could tear through hide. I had to time my strike well. I hoped that Richard's spear would be well struck too. My archers sent arrows at the two animals to distract them but this was my fight. I rammed the spear into the throat of the beast. The bar stopped it penetrating too deeply and I twisted. I wanted the beast to die quickly. When I was showered with blood I knew that my strike was mortal. Richard had not been as lucky and he was knocked over. His spear had gone into the chest of the animal and its teeth sought out Richard's throat. It was Dai, the spear carrier, who saved his life. He bravely strode up and rammed the spare spear he carried into the eye of the sow. When the broad bladed spearhead struck the brain of the beast it died.

Robert ran to help Richard who shook his head as he rose. He went to Dai and put his hands on his shoulders, "You are a warrior, Dai the Boar Killer, and you have saved my life."

Warbow

In that dell a soldier was born. Dai had yet to fight a man, although he had put himself in harm's way to save Lady Hawise, but in striking the sow he had shown that he was a warrior. It made the hunt perfect. We had the food for the feast. No one had been hurt and my warriors were all closer thanks to Dai's selfless act.

Chapter 10

The wedding day itself was perfect. How could it be anything else with my wife organising it? Walter and his wife were happy with all the arrangements and looked proudly on at their beautiful daughter. It was a glorious summer day and the whole village was able to eat on the green. The bride and groom were seated beneath a flower covered canopy, with trestle tables and benches ensuring that the whole village was accommodated. The food seemed to be never ending and my cooks had gone out of their way to make it as sumptuous a feast as they could. It might not have been the fare they served at Westminster but it suited us. They had used some of our precious spices to make puddings and to enrich the sausages that they had made. The pies and pastries were baked to golden perfection and oozed flavour. Harry and his ale wives had made a special wedding ale to celebrate the occasion. Michel and Jean Michel, of course, enjoyed the wine I had bought in Worcester. For once Mary and I were not on the high table. As Mary said, it was a day for Michel and Walter's families. It meant I sat with Jack and Hamo. While Mary chattered away to our daughters-in-law, my sons and I spoke about more serious matters. Once we had talked about the hunt and the bride and groom, the three of us naturally spoke about the state of England and the borders.

Sir Richard Craven had been a pursuivant and was now the castellan of Skipton Castle. He had been at a tournament held in Gloucester where he represented the Earl of Lancaster and had stopped on his way home a fortnight earlier. There were many tournaments for it was a way to provide knights with training for war. My family were not knights. We did not bother with such things. It was just an overnight visit but Sir Richard and I had fought together for King Edward. Such bonds run deep and we had no secrets from one another.

"So, what news from Sir Richard?"

"The king wishes reforms and has called a Parliament in Westminster."

Hamo asked, "Have you been invited?"

I shook my head, "But even if I were I should not go. I cannot support the reforms for they would merely pave the way for the return of Piers Gaveston and I do not wish to incur further wrath from the Crown by opposing him."

Jack said, "This is not like you, Sir Gerald. You face danger head on and do not run away from it."

I took a drink of the ale and gave him a sad smile, "If it was just me who would suffer then I would oppose the king in a heartbeat but this is not the old king and while Gaveston lives I must walk on eggshells."

Jack was pensive for a moment and then said, "He threatened us?" I said nothing. Jack said, "Hamo and I wondered why you seemed to acquiesce so easily."

Hamo snapped, "Father, we do not fear this Gaveston."

I said, heavily, "Well, you should. The man has no honour and he is as treacherous as a snake. I am an old man now and pleased that I have lived so long. I want my line to continue and if that means doffing my cap to Gaveston then so be it. While he is in Ireland we are safe. I will fight for England but I will not join those barons and earls who seek to make war against the king. Therein lies disaster for a country that is divided risks ruin for everyone. As we discovered at Poole there is still danger on this border and as for the Scots," I shook my head, "they grow stronger by the day."

Jack said, "Surely de Brus has what he wants. He has the crown of Scotland. He did not play fair to get it but he will not risk war with England."

"King Edward wants to be a greater man that his father. I was there when the old king tore hair from the head of his son and that scarred the young King Edward. He saw that as an insult and the only way to remedy it is to do what his father did not have time to do and conquer Scotland. I fear it will be his undoing. Added to that, de Brus has ambitions in England. Cumbria is seen as Scottish and Northumberland was a bloody ground for many years."

My sons were clever men both and I saw them taking in my words and reflecting upon them.

Hamo said, "And what else did Sir Richard say?"

I lowered my voice, "That the one who leads the opposition is the king's cousin, the Earl of Lancaster." They knew what that meant. Thomas of Lancaster, through his father, Edmund Crouchback, had a legitimate claim to the throne. Queen Isabella was too young yet to bear a child and while King Edward had no heir the crown could be torn from his head. "Say nothing of this for I am sure that Gaveston has spies everywhere. They are not in our manors but loose words spread on the wind might reach his ears and they could hurt us."

After a while Jack said, "And Lady Hawise, how sits the world with her?"

"James and John have still to return. That means that she is not yet secure but as they have not sent for help then she must be safe. The king has promised a Parliament here in the west, at Shrewsbury. We shall see." I smiled, "I will attend that one."

I stopped drinking long before most of my archers and men at arms. Hamo noticed it and asked, "Are you unwell?"

I laughed, "I do not enjoy getting up in the night to make water. I have had a sufficiency and this way I can smile at those who cannot stand."

As the sun set and the tables were cleared, those who could sing a song stood and entertained. We did not hire troubadours for we had all the talent we needed in the manor. Some men sang songs that were bawdy and made my wife shake her head, but still smile, while others sang songs of great deeds. When Walter the Archer, happily merry, though not drunk, sang the song of the archer who found a khan, my wife put her hand on mine. I was always embarrassed by the song but Mary seemed to enjoy it and so I endured it. At the end it brought the greatest of cheers. I wondered then how I would be remembered. When I was laid in the ground what would men say of me? I had done things of which I was proud. The fetching of the Mongols and the saving of my wife were two, as was the capture of Wallace, but there were other deeds that I preferred to remain hidden. I think most men were like me. Their lives were never perfect but I knew, as the cheers rang out, that I had done the best that I could and I did not regret a single action.

Mary came to speak in my ear, "This is your legacy, my love. The whole manor applauds you as they should. Let us hope that your days of adventuring are over, eh?"

Jean Michel and Alice retired soon after the applause had died down. My men at arms and archers made an arch and they passed beneath to head to their new home in Michel's house. When they had gone my family and I returned to our hall. We would continue to celebrate but the lord and lady of Yarpole manor did not want to be a barrier to wild fun and I knew that the younger elements in the village would want such wildness.

Back in the hall I was able to enjoy my grandchildren. Having heard Walter's ballad they wanted to know the story from my lips. They wished to hear the truth and not the ballad. I was reluctant to do so until Mary said, "Gerald, you owe it to them to tell them the truth. The ballad makes it all sound so easy what you did but I know it was not. I know that you will tell them the truth."

I nodded and settled myself to tell the tale. Hamo and Jack were both interested. Jack's lord had been one of the men who rode with me and Hamo had been named after the other. What had not been in the song was the role played by our guide, Ahmed. I knew that without him we would never have succeeded. The other part of the story that made my grandchildren all turn was that their grandmother was referred to as Maria.

She smiled, "That was the name they used for me but I always felt like a Mary. It just shows you, children, that you can change your own destiny. It is in your hands. Your grandfather was a humble archer and now he is a baron who was close to a king. I was a slave and yet I became the friend of a queen. Life is a journey and where you end is in your own hands." There was silence and she smiled, "Carry on, Grandfather Gerald, for the tale is not done. You are yet to come to the assassin."

Their eyes widened as I told of the castle in Acre and the attempted murder of the king. When I had finished I saw that they viewed me differently. The now portly figure that was their grandfather had not always been so. Mary had been right, I was honour bound to tell the story.

The font arrived in August. Edmund brought it on a wagon with his sons and I could tell that he was proud of his work. Robert and my men helped him and his sons to place it in the church. It looked right. He had done a beautiful job of carving for amongst the flowers and the inevitable cross were bows made to look artistic rather than martial. The faces of the four babes carved on each side were particularly beautiful and Robert commented on them.

Edmund looked a little embarrassed, "They are an indulgence, my lord. They are the faces of my grandchildren when they were babes. I hope you do not mind. I thought that this way their faces would live so long as the church stood."

I beamed, "Of course I do not mind and I am honoured." When Mary saw it she was impressed and insisted that he and his sons stay the night.

It was September when we had news of the Parliament. Once more it was a royal rider who stopped to water his horse who brought the information. While such men would not normally divulge their mission, I was known to the man from my time in Westminster and he confided in me. The king had held a Parliament and tried to have his favourite's exile ended. When that had failed he had appealed to the pope and to King Philip of France. He had offered to suppress the Knights Templar in England, and to release Bishop Langton from prison on condition that the exile could be revoked. The word, from the messenger, was that it had been refused and that there would be another Parliament in January. This time it would be in Shrewsbury and that was of interest to me. The king was coming to within travelling distance of my home. Perhaps the position of Lady Hawise would be resolved.

Almost as though someone was spinning a web, James and John returned from Poole a week after the messenger had passed through. They did not go to Luston. I thought they might have wished to visit their sister. They were not alone, they had with them, a woman on a horse. One of my villagers ran the length of the village to tell me of their return, "My lord, James and John, your men at arms, have come home and they have with them a woman on a horse."

My first thought was a fearful one. Was this Lady Hawise and had she been driven from her lands? I headed indoors to warn the steward, housekeeper and, of course, my wife of their arrival. When the three of them clattered into my yard I was somewhat relieved to see that while the woman was young, she was not Lady Hawise. However there was something about her that was familiar. I saw that John led a sumpter that was laden with baggage. As much as I wanted to know the story I was most anxious about Poole.

"Is the lady well and is Poole safe?"

John handed the reins of his horse and the sumpter to Abel. He smiled, "They are, my lord. The men are now warriors and we hired another four. David of Abergele said that they would cope on their own and we were given a gold piece each by Lady Hawise."

"The lady is well?"

"She is a strong lady, my lord. It was a pleasure to serve her."

James dismounted and helped the young woman from the horse. My wife had emerged. This time there were no floured hands to clean. She stood next to me and I looked expectantly at James who held the woman's hand. I shook my head, "Come James, do not keep us waiting. Introduce the young lady whom you have brought along with, I am guessing, her belongings."

He looked embarrassed, "I am sorry, my lord. This is my wife, Rhian." The young woman, I could see now that she was little more than a girl, gave an awkward curtsy as though it was something with which she was unfamiliar. "Sir Gerald."

My wife took charge and she put her arm around the young woman, "Come inside, the yard of Yarpole manor is not the place to hear such tales. Fetch the bags. James, John, let us go within." The force of nature that was my wife led us into my hall. She was still shouting orders. "Sarah, have the guest rooms made up. Anna, food and ale in the dining hall." She seated Rhian on the couch that held two people and gestured for James to sit next to her. We sat on two harder chairs.

Anna scurried in, followed by Meg and they arranged the goblets on the table. They poured beer into them and then Anna said, "Cook is preparing some food, my lady."

"There is no rush for food. We need to hear this story."

We looked at James who held his wife's hand, "This is Rhian and she is Mordaf's sister. When we buried Mordaf we met and John and I often visited the house for Mordaf's parents grieved. I found myself drawn to Rhian and could not get her out of my mind. I frequently went to meet with her and walk by the river. Her father asked me what my intentions were and…we were wed within three weeks."

I said, "Hastily done."

He nodded.

Mary smiled, "Some things are meant to be, my husband, as you of all people should know. However, James, your sister will be unhappy that she was not there."

James looked glum, "I know. It is why we came here first. I did not wish to endure the wrath of Alice's tongue."

"That is for another time. For tonight you shall stay in the hall and then we can give thought to where you shall live. John can return to the warrior hall but it is not right that you two begin your marriage in such a way." She turned to me, "There is a plot of land close by the church is there not?" Nothing in the village escaped my wife's attention.

"There is, my love, but it is not big enough for a smallholding."

Rhian spoke for the first time and she had a lovely, lilting voice. Her Welsh accent made her words sound almost musical. "We do not need a smallholding, my lady, my family planned for me to be a servant in the hall of Lady Hawise. I can cook and make bread. I hoped that the baker in the village might have a place for me. I am a hard worker."

Mary beamed, "Then you shall work here. It is a perfect arrangement. Until your home is built you can live here and we can enjoy your skills. Sarah is a good housekeeper but a baker is always useful." She pointedly looked at me.

I knew when to agree, "Of course, it seems a good idea and John, you should ride to Luston and tell your sister and my son that they have a new member of their family."

"I will do so, my lord, if I might borrow a horse. The one I rode is weary from the ride."

"See the horse master." The food arrived and Mary helped to serve it. I took John to one side, "And the de la Pole family?"

He shook his head, "We have seen no signs of them. James and I rode out regularly to look for signs of scouts. We found none and we heard, through the villagers, that Gruffydd Fychan de la Pole had gone to Ireland to seek men."

"That does not bode well. Gallowglasses are nasty enemies. I wonder where he found the money."

Warbow

"That is an easy question to answer, my lord. After you left Lady Hawise had Iago the Steward go through the accounts one more time and discovered that there was a chest of coins unaccounted for. Her father had kept them hidden for an emergency or, perhaps, as a dowry for his daughter. Her uncle must have known about the chest and stole it."

"Then we can expect him to return."

As John ate and drank I reflected that if Piers Gaveston was in Ireland and, according to Sir Richard Craven, keeping the Irish in check, then the Welshman might find many warriors who were not only looking for a paymaster but also to cause mischief. I decided that, when the king came to Shrewsbury, I would tell him of the theft and its implications. We had defeated the Welsh many times but Irish mercenaries were another matter.

John did not return that night. I knew why and my wife had rooms prepared already for the couple to use as Alice and Hamo would be visiting. The next morning I went with James and my men to inspect the land. Mary had a good eye and I saw that it was a plot big enough for a house. Robert also came with us for he understood architecture and building. As we inspected the land Michel, who had the most recent experience of building, used his dagger to prise up a rock he saw protruding. He held it up, "This will be like our piece of land, my lord. There must have been a building here in the past and there will be stones buried beneath the earth. If we turn over the soil then we can use the stones we find to make good foundations."

I turned to James, "You are happy with a wattle and daub home?"

He smiled, "A roof over our heads will suffice and now I have an incentive to make more coins and provide for my wife and family. One day we shall have a house made of stone but this will do."

My men all knew what he meant. They had an incentive for us to go to war. Ransoms were a good form of income, not to mention the gold and silver that could be found in enemy purses. My men had all done well out of the men we had slain at Poole. Part of me wondered now how much of that was taken from Lady Hawise. We would never know.

Robert said, "I will make a device to ensure that it is level."

Hob said, "We normally use our eye."

He nodded, "The Romans used something called a groma. I have seen illustrations of them. I will make one."

He saw the sceptical looks on the faces of my archers. He smiled, "In the time it takes you to dig out the stone I will make one and lay out where you should dig the ditches for the foundations." He was challenging the archers and they took him up on it.

"Very well, Healer, let us see who is right!"

Robert was confident and whilst he had never made one before he had an agile mind and he enlisted the help of Dai. The two of them had one made by noon of the day the rocks began to be lifted and by the end of the day lengths of old bow strings were being pegged out to show where the walls would be built.

Hob laughed, "It seems that brain overcomes brawn any day of the week, well done."

It was then that Hamo and Alice rode in with John. Poor James looked as though he wanted the earth we had dug to swallow him but Alice was too taken with Rhian for anger. She hugged James and whispered in his ear. They were both smiling when the embrace ended. Mary took the women back to the hall while Hamo and John stripped off to help us to work.

Having laid out the outline Robert consulted James about the layout. As the plot was small then there could only be a few rooms. There would be a kitchen, a bedroom and a room in which to sit and dine. All those were essential but Robert worked out he could add not only a small bedroom but a larder and, if the men were willing to dig, then a cellar to store things. James and John were popular and my men enjoyed working together. They took pleasure in the work which exercised their bodies and gave them the opportunity for banter. Archers and men at arms liked to challenge each other. The result was that a week after the ground had been prepared there were foundations and a low wall that gave the outline of the property. The key elements were the two doors which were offset for Robert did not want what he called a wind tunnel and a ditch running around to take away water. Once the rocks had all been used and the timbers embedded in the walls then it would be the time for the messy part of the building, the wattle and daub. The timber posts were substantial ones. We copsed our woods and always had seasoned timber, Mark the Bowyer was good with wood and he and my archers shaped the timbers to give the frame. My men at arms used their strength to weave the willow slats that would form the external and internal walls. Some were easy to make and were the square panels but others were close studded and horizontal ones, called ledgers. Drilled with an auger they were used to fill awkward sections of the internal walls. For those we used hazel rods to give them strength. It was at this point that the women from my manor came to inspect the work. Ostensibly they came to bring refreshments but the men knew that critical eyes were being cast over the work. I had offered to work but my men refused the offer. I stood with Mary and Rhian to watch the men as they mixed and then slapped the daub onto the willow.

Warbow

Mary smiled, "Your men work hard, husband."

"They are our men and they do this for one of their own." I smiled at Rhian, "You are joining a family, here, Rhian."

"I know, Sir Gerald. It was hard to leave my family but since I have come here I have felt as welcome as though I was back in Poole. I know that I am lucky." She pointed to the house, "I have seen a house like this when it is finished but I have never seen one built. It is hard to imagine the finished dwelling."

Robert had been supervising the mix of clay, mud, sand and straw and he came over. He pointed, "There will be a door with a step and lintel. We get little flooding in Yarpole but a raised step and the ditch will keep it dry within. There will be a small porch just inside the door. That is to keep the wind from whistling through. Your room for dining and sitting will be there. We have enough stones to make a hearth but that will be on the wall that adjoins your kitchen at the rear. Your two bedrooms will be here on the right. The walls for those internal rooms will be the last ones we build. At the back of the kitchen, on the wall opposite the fire and place where you cook will be your larder."

She nodded and pointed to the hole at the rear of the house, "And that is a cellar?"

"Not so much a cellar but more a place where you can store barrels. The roof will have a space below the thatch and that could be used to store things." He shrugged, "I am a solitary man and I know not what families might store."

Mary looked at Robert, "You did not take your vows Robert. You could take a wife."

He glanced at me and shook his head, "I am happy with my celibate life serving this manor. God sent me here and I am more content than you can possibly know, Lady Mary. There are more challenges here than there were in the monastery and it is good to live a life serving others rather than searching into one's soul each day. I have a richer life by living with others."

It took some days to finish the external walls and fit the thinner internal ones. Whilst praying for dry weather we abandoned the building for two days to allow it to dry and to enable Mark, Robert, James, John and Dai to shape the roof timbers. For Dai this was an important process. It made him stronger. He was used as the labourer. John and James pointed out that a man at arms needed great strength. Holding a shield and spear for long hours was as hard as drawing a bow and in battle time spent waiting was often long. I knew that Dai wished for more weapon practice but we had a whole winter to begin to make Dai into a warrior. We had done so with Jack and he had soon shown that he had all the skills required to be a knight. It was as I watched Dai and my men at arms labouring that I realised that no matter how bad a king Edward was, I could never raise a sword or draw my bow against him. I had served his father too long for that and I had sworn an oath to the king to do all that I could for his son. The king had gathered me with others around his deathbed and made us swear an oath. The others were mighty lords: Henry de Lacy, 3rd Earl of Lincoln; Guy de Beauchamp, 10th Earl of Warwick; Aymer de Valence; and Robert de Clifford, 1st Baron de Clifford. As that oath had also mentioned the pernicious influence of Piers Gaveston and asked to keep him from his son then I had no problem with trying to thwart the king's favourite. It would be a fine line I walked. I knew that the others who had sworn the oath might feel less bound now that the old king was dead.

As the harvest was collected in so the house began to take shape. The walls dried and were whitewashed. The roof was the last element and that needed almost the whole of the village men to help. We did so on one Sunday and it replaced the normal weapon training after the service. Father Michael blessed the work. First the timbers were laid and then secured before the skilled thatchers did what they do best and wove the roof. By the end of that Sunday, with food laid on by my wife and cooks, the house was finished and we ate well. James and Rhian were keen to move in but the house was bereft of all that they might need. The next day saw a procession of folk both from my hall and the village. They brought items both large and small to help furnish the dwelling.

Mary and I gave them their bed. It was one which had been in the guest room and was a good one. Mary had ordered a new one to be made for our Christmas celebration. Old Walter and his wife gave a table. When Alice had moved out he had begun to make a larger one for his daughter, husband and family. Others gave chairs. They would not match but they would be functional. Pots, pans, dishes and bedding were also given. It helped that James and John were popular. My son Hamo and Alice came through with a wagon. In the wagon were a crib and a nursing chair as well as a nanny goat for milk. Alice wanted nieces and nephews. The result was that by the end of that week the house was furnished, the walls were dry and James was able to carry his wife over the threshold into their new home. Alice and Hamo stayed the night with us.

"I would have you with me at the Parliament in January, Hamo."

"I am not a baron, Father."

"But you have a manor and one day you will be a baron. I want you and Jack there with me. If nothing else your presence might persuade others to support Lady Hawise and her claims."

My daughter-in-law frowned, "Why would lords not support her claim, Sir Gerald? It is her land."

I nodded, "And if this was England then there would be no problem but it is Wales and in that country women do not inherit. There are others who will be at the Parliament who wish to see disorder on the border."

Hamo said, "Roger Mortimer, 1st Baron Mortimer of Chirk."

I nodded, "His mother and father were cut from a different cloth. Their son is not a pleasant man and if I support Lady Hawise then it is likely that he will oppose her. The lady will need as many voices supporting her as we can find." Until Baron Chirk had been given the title, his parents had been friends of mine. With their deaths we had become almost outcasts.

"Then I will ensure that we are there. It may be we go directly from here for we are coming for the Christmas feast are we not?"

Mary beamed, "That you are. I want this one to make up for the time we lost your father to the king and that man." She would not bring herself to name Piers Gaveston. He was despised.

Chapter 11

Shrewsbury 1309

With the house finished and the couple moved in, we busied ourselves with the preparations for winter. It was not just the collection of the harvest that occupied every waking hour, it was the culling of animals and preserving their bounty. It was the tanning of hides and the copsing of trees. Wood for fuel had to be gathered and fields prepared for the next year. Life in Yarpole had a simple rhythm to it. All those who lived in the manor were involved in it. Even the blacksmith's work was determined by the seasons. He made ploughshares and tools in one season and arrows and weapons in another. He was always kept busy. It would also be the season when babies were born. We had more marriages in Spring and, inevitably, that meant babies born around Christmas and January. The village midwives were kept busy. Sadly, the onset of winter also meant that the old and the sick sometimes succumbed to illnesses that often resulted in death. We had been lucky. My wife and the women of the village watched out for the old and the vulnerable but there were few who did not have younger members of their family to look after them. It meant that many houses were crowded but that was not important, families were. The days were growing shorter but each one was filled with purpose.

I also had duties to attend to. I held the assizes. I knew I was lucky. My people got on but there were always minor disputes. Sometimes they involved people from other manors and they had to be arbitrated by me. I was the lord of three manors all lying close to each other. I could normally make my judgements within one day. While all this was going on we worked and trained so that if war came we would be ready. Dai was the only new warrior and the other men at arms worked hard to train him as well as possible. He was not a man at arms. He acted more as a sort of squire to me. I did not need a squire but it gave order to Dai's life. He grew as the fine food we ate fattened him up. Now that James had moved out he lived in the warrior hall. There my archers and men at arms would teach him about life and the world of war. They would tell him, in the privacy of the hall, of the realities of war. They would let him know how to defeat a man in battle where life and death were separated by the narrowest of margins. It was better that Mary was not privy to that life and to hear those words. I do not think she would have approved. I did and I saw Dai become, day by day, a warrior.

Although I never looked in a mirror I knew that I was getting old. You cannot fight old age no matter how much you wish to do so. After our bone fire and while the house was deep into preparations for winter I was laid low by illness. It came upon me gradually. I sneezed and coughed more. I had pains in my head and I found I could not breathe at night. Those around me who were so normally attentive missed the signs. Robert and my wife were busy visiting the sick in the village and the others within the hall were occupied, so my sneezes were not commented upon. I hid the signs when we dined and it took almost a week for my wife to comment on the noises I made at night. I dismissed them as bad dreams and I determined to hide the symptoms from everyone. I managed to do so for a few more days but they came back to haunt me. I collapsed in the yard one morning when I had decided to take a walk in the first really frosty morning we had enjoyed. I had hoped the cold would heal me. Instead it struck me like the blow from a fellow archer. One moment I was walking and the next there was blackness.

I dreamed and those dreams were more like nightmares filled with images that I did not like. The one that kept haunting me was the look on the face of William Wallace moments before he was hanged, drawn and quartered. His eyes had found mine, the man who had hunted and caught him. There were other unpleasant memories too. I saw Simon de Montfort hacked to pieces by Mortimer and his assassins. I saw the assassin in Acre coming to kill The Lord Edward and I could escape none of them. I wondered if I was in hell and I was being tormented by past sins. Even in my desperate state my mind rationalised that I had not caused any of these deaths but I had been part of them.

What brought me out of the horror of the darkness was a cool hand and a whispered voice in my ear, "Come back to us, Gerald, this is too soon."

I tried to speak but instead coughed and almost choked as phlegm and bile in equal measure filled my mouth. I felt a bowl next to my mouth and I spat. I felt pains in my chest and wondered if this was death but when I heard Robert's voice I felt hope, "A good sign, my lady. There is no blood this time."

"And his head feels cooler." I opened my eyes and looked up into the faces of my wife and healer. Robert was moving the bowl to empty it. Mary's face filled with joy and her eyes welled up with tears as she said, "He lives!"

"God be praised."

I tried to speak but nothing came out.

I saw Robert pour something from a vial and then, after measuring it, he mixed it into a goblet. "My lady, I pray you lift his head." My wife's soft and gentle hands raised me and Robert held the goblet to my lips.

He said, "Drink this, Sir Gerald, it will make you sleep once more but the healing has begun and the corner has been turned. The prayers of Yarpole have been answered and you live."

The taste, as it slipped down was warm and soothing. There was honey and something else in the warmed wine. My veins felt as though they were filled with something rich and soothing and, as much as I wanted to stay awake I could not. Blackness enveloped me again but this was not the nightmare from which I had awoken. I slept a dreamless sleep.

When I woke it was daylight. As I opened my eyes I could see that the open shutters were letting in light. I needed to make water. I felt an urge like I had never felt before and I tried to toss off the covers. I heard Dai's voice and it was urgent and fearful as he called out, "My lady, Master Robert, he wakes." The voice sounded close and urgent, "My lord, you are not to move until the healer says you can."

I turned my head and saw Dai rising from the chair by the door. I growled, "And I am too old to piss the bed, Dai the Rock. Help me up."

Even as he helped me to put my feet on the ground Mary and Robert raced in. Robert put his arm under mine. It was good that he did for I felt unsteady.

Mary looked concerned, "Why do you stand?"

"I need to make water and I did not wish to wet the bed."

She laughed and fetched the pot, "He is getting better, Robert."

They would not let me leave the bedchamber but having emptied my bladder I felt not only more comfortable but hungry. "Bring me fried ham and bread. Perhaps some blood pudding too."

Robert shook his head, "Porridge and honey with warmed ale are your breakfast, Sir Gerald. You have not eaten for three days and we need to build your strength back up. We thought we had lost you."

"It was nothing and I know my own body."

Mary snapped, "No, you do not, and you will obey Robert the Healer or I shall have you bound to the bed!"

There was such determination in her voice that I nodded and said, meekly, "Yes, my love."

She was right, as was Robert. Despite my bravado I felt as weak as a kitten. I was cosseted and tended to over the next days. The potage and bread I had for my meals seemed to make me stronger but it was four more days before I was allowed to leave the bed chamber and go to my hall. There, my men at arms and archers trooped in to pay their respects. I saw in their faces how close I had come to death. I had been in a black hole and oblivious to it. When Michel came in he took my hand in his, "My lord, you need to take better care of yourself."

"I have learned my lesson, Michel. I will try not to be a foolish old man."

He smiled and looked relieved, "While you were ill we had good news. Alice is with child and I am to be a grandfather. I would have Jean Michel's child meet the man who saved us. Do not die."

"Good then the font I bought will be put to good use. I am pleased for you, Michel, and I will do my best not to cross the Styx."

Hamo and Jack came alone to visit and they said almost the same as Michel. Hamo said, "You are no longer a young man, Father. You should be taking it easy. I can shoulder some of your responsibilities."

I was alone with the two of them and I nodded, "You may be right but I have been doing this for fifty years. I cannot change my nature now. If there is something that needs doing then I will do it. A man does not run from his fate. He faces it as a man. I have lived longer than most of my friends and while I do not wish to shake off this mortal coil I know that one day I will die. I am content that the two of you are both fine young men and will look after your mother. I know that the manors will be cared for. I promise that I will try to take life easier from now on but what I cannot determine is what Fate has in store for me."

Perhaps it was my illness or the lack of celebration the year before but whatever the reason the Christmas at Yarpole was the best one I could remember in a long time. My grandchildren were all older and were now able to chatter to me like magpies. They indulged me by hearing my tales of adventures over the years. The newly married couples also seemed to make the celebration more special. The weather added the final inducement to enjoy the feast. A cold and icy wind blew flecks of snow that flurried around the village and rested on the cool corners around the sheltered parts of the hall. It encouraged us to stay indoors and for Jack and Hamo to remain for longer than they had planned. It was my sons and warriors who ensured that the villagers had enough food and fuel to stay warm. No one was lost to illness. When my sons left, the hall felt huge and empty. For my wife and the women it was a time to wash and to clean the rooms that had been used. My men took on the tasks neglected during the shortest days of the year. None let me stir and I was left alone to reflect on my life and its purpose. By the time I was allowed to walk forth, then when the sun shone and the weather abated, I had come to the conclusion that my life had been worthwhile. I had helped a king but that was only the part that others would see. I believed I had done more for the people around me. I had made a difference to many lives and if I had never been born then who knows what their fate might have been? The result was that as we started the new year I was in a positive frame of mind.

Warbow

When I began to prepare for the Parliament in Shrewsbury I had to persuade my wife and my confessor that I was fit enough for the short journey. The last argument I used was the most telling, "If I do not go and plead the case for Lady Hawise then who will?" Neither had an argument for that. I sent a messenger to Poole to tell Lady Hawise what I intended. The rider who returned two days later told me that Lady Hawise would attend on the king. It was a bold move from the heir to Powis. Women did not attend Parliament and I would need to create an opportunity for the lady to speak to the king.

We left two days before the Parliament. I needed to ensure that we had rooms. I knew that I would be able to be housed in the castle but my sons and Lady Hawise would not. I intended to take rooms at an inn and that meant getting there before the mass of nobles arrived. This was not London but rural Shropshire. It would also allow me to speak to other barons and engender support for Lady Hawise. I knew that men respected me and heeded my advice. I would need to use my voice rather than my bow. We left early in the day for the days were still short. Although we wrapped up against the cold I found the journey hard. My illness had taken half a month from me. The last serious exercise I had enjoyed had been the hunt.

Dai and Robert came with us and both Hamo and Jack brought their eldest sons. They would begin to learn what it was to be of the blood of the Warbow. They rode their ponies between our larger horses and were protected a little from the elements. It was forty miles and while that could normally be done easily in a day, my illness and the age of the boys meant it was a long hard ride that took us most of the day. My illness had clearly taken it out of me. We were lucky in that ***The Lamb*** not only had spare rooms but the landlord had been one of my archers, many years earlier. Garth of the Woods insisted that we all stay with him and when I mentioned Lady Hawise he reserved rooms for them too. It made me feel better for I trusted him and knew that we would all be safe there.

I shared a room with Robert and the others had a large but separate room. Dai insisted on being my chamberlain and sleeping behind the door. The next day we saw the barons arriving for the Parliament. Dai watched for Lady Hawise on the road into Shrewsbury and when she arrived he directed her to the inn. David and Dewi, along with Breffni, were with her.

The first words she spoke told me of her fears, "Is the king here? Have you spoken to him?"

I shook my head, "No, my lady. He has yet to arrive but I promise that I will speak to him on your behalf. Have you the petition ready?"

She looked down, "I was not sure how to write it down. I know what I want to say but I do not have the words and phrases that might persuade a king."

"Robert, find quill and parchment. You have the words."

I saw that Robert was torn. He was being given a responsibility but he was also doing something for Lady Hawise. He smiled, "I have parchment and I am sure that an old archer will have good feathers somewhere."

When he had left us she said, "He is a good man. You are lucky to have him serving you, Sir Gerald."

"He is the best of men and I am lucky. He holds you in high esteem."

"Me?" She sounded surprised, "I am just a young girl and dull company compared with a learned man like Robert."

I said nothing. It was clear to me that she admired Robert but I also knew that he would never try to woo her and that was a shame for they would have made a solid couple who would be able to face all that the world threw at her.

The king arrived with great ceremony the next day. When the court moved it was a major event. The young queen was with him and they had servants and bodyguards, not to mention the crown jewels guarded by men I recognised. My men saw them pass and that was our signal to enter the castle. I left Robert with Lady Hawise. My sons and two grandsons, each of us dressed in our finest, headed up to the castle. We did not ride. I knew that the stables would be full and our horses were being well looked after in the inn. I was not precious about walking, like a common citizen, through the gates of the castle. The sentries who snapped to attention as we walked through were surprised. I was recognised. I had spurs but my body was still that of a misshapen archer and my grizzled visage was well known. The merchants who were held back by halberds to allow us to enter were a little discomfited. The captain of the guard snapped, "Do you not recognise Sir Gerald Warbow, Lord Edward's Archer? Welcome Sir Gerald."

I smiled, "Thank you."

The king and his party had quickly dismounted and entered the castle. January was not the time of year to hang around outside. We were admitted but I had to vouch for my sons and their sons. They were not on the list. I was lucky. The pursuivant who checked off the names knew me from my time incarcerated in London. We headed to the Great Hall. I had already warned Hamo and Jack to listen more than they spoke. They were unused to such events. When the Parliament began they would not be allowed to attend but I wanted them to meet the other barons. When I was no longer here the connections they made might ensure an easier life on the borders. Hamo would be the next Baron of Yarpole and it was important that he understood how these things worked.

Sir Richard of Craven was there. He was not present as a baron but he was part of the escort for the Earl of Lancaster and Baron Clifford. He was pleased to see us all. He beamed, "My lord, I hoped that you would be here."

"And you, Richard. I wonder at the presence of the earl. This is Wales and not Lancaster."

He lowered his voice, "News has come from Ireland that Piers Gaveston seeks to return to England. The earl, I think, is here to forestall such a return. As you know, Sir Gerald, the earl felt insulted by the former Earl of Cornwall." I nodded. "I can say that to you for I know that you are discreet."

I gave a wry smile, "Richard, I have been guarding the secrets of those in power for a long time." He nodded. "How did the news come?"

Sir Richard pointed to the door that led to the royal chambers in the castle, "A knight returned from Ireland and went directly to the king. He was waiting in the castle when the king arrived. The Earl of Lancaster spoke with him last night when we dined with the castellan. I think he and the knight must be in conference now."

A young knight in the livery of the Earl of Lancaster hurried over, "Sir Richard, the earl has need of you."

We looked up and saw that we were being scrutinised by Thomas of Lancaster. I bowed my head and the king's cousin waved and smiled.

"I must go. I hope to speak with you again but…"

"I know, old friend, you are tied to Lancaster."

When they had gone Jack asked, "What did you mean, tied to Lancaster?"

Lowering my voice, although the noise from around us made discerning my words difficult, I said, "Until King Edward has an heir then Thomas of Lancaster is the next in line for the crown. There are others who, while they do not like King Edward, would not want Thomas of Lancaster sitting on the throne of England. This is why I want you here. This is the world that you inhabit as a baron. Jack, you are lucky, you just manage a manor for me. Hamo will have to enter this treacherous world where a misplaced word can make an enemy of the men who rule this land."

Jack said, "Then why attend?"

I just sighed and said, "Lady Hawise."

"Ah."

I drank wine, sparingly, and spoke to other barons with whom I felt comfortable. The time was not wasted and I picked up useful information. When the king finally descended, it was almost Nones. He came with Isabella on his arm. She looked frail and lost. He made a grand entrance. I think Piers Gaveston had encouraged his almost theatrical gestures and posing. His father had never used such antics. The usual sycophants hung around the royal couple. They were like sparrows and dunnocks seeking titbits.

Two of those I saw were the two Roger Mortimers, the elder, Roger Mortimer, 1st Baron Mortimer of Chirk and his nephew, the younger, Roger Mortimer, 1st Earl of March. Neither liked me but that did not bother me for they were nothing like the Roger Mortimer and Lady Maud who had guarded the borderlands and fought against Simon de Montfort. It did not surprise me that they were trying to inveigle themselves into the king's company. With Piers Gaveston in Ireland this was the perfect time to do so.

I saw Queen Isabella espy me and she reached up on tiptoe to speak into the king's ear. He nodded and to the clear chagrin of the Mortimers he and the young queen walked over to us. The king smiled and we bowed, "Sir Gerald, I am pleased to see you here. The queen wishes to speak to you."

The queen now spoke English well and with confidence. The smile she gave me was a genuine one and showed that she liked me, "Sir Gerald, your confessor, Robert, is he here with you? I should like to speak to him. He was so kind to me in Westminster."

I nodded, "He is, Queen Isabella. He is with Lady Hawise ferch Owain ap Gruffudd ap Gwenwynwyn in an inn in the town. He will be visiting the castle when the Parliament begins."

I saw the king frown, "That name is familiar."

The elder Mortimer had followed the king and he said, "She is the daughter of Owain de la Pole and claims the lands that her father owned." He said the word *'claims'* in such a way as to make it sound false.

I said, "Her uncles are seeking the land that is hers by right. She has a petition for you, Your Majesty."

Mortimer shook his head, "Under Salic Law, she cannot inherit."

Robert had already explained this to me and in the petition had dismissed it. I said, "Salic Law does not apply in England, Your Majesty."

Thomas Lancaster had also eavesdropped and he said, "Gruffydd Fychan de la Pole claims the land. He would make a good ally, Cousin."

Baron Chirk snapped, "He is a trouble maker and a rebel. His lands should be taken from him."

It was clear that Baron Chirk and Thomas of Lancaster would both oppose the claims of Lady Hawise but for different reasons. I saw a strange smile appear on the king's face. He said, "Sir Gerald, tomorrow is the Parliament. When it is over bring Lady Hawise to my chambers along with your French confessor. That way the queen can enjoy more conversation and I can determine the validity of the lady's case." He smiled at Mortimer and Lancaster, "I can see that there is more at stake here than mere inheritance." With that he turned and led the queen from the hall. The baron and the earl glared at each other and then turned to fix me with their eyes.

I merely bowed and said to Hamo and to Jack, "And let us retire for tomorrow looks to be busy."

I hurried out and did not speak until we had passed through the gate and were heading through the gloom of a January evening to the inn. Jack said, "It looks as though the lady will be disappointed."

Hamo said, "And you, Father, have made two powerful enemies."

"You see why I brought you here, Hamo. This is your future."

"And if I do not want it?"

"You have no choice for you are my son. When I was made a baron by the king it changed all our lives. I could not refuse the honour but I knew the commitment that came with it."

He was silent as we walked the last few paces to the tavern, "Life is simpler for an archer."

I nodded, "And I know that better than any. When I left my home on the Clwyd and fled to Gascony I did not know where my journey would end. No man does. Your life may not be the same as mine and it has barely begun Hamo. When Jack here endured the hard life in Yorkshire, he could never have imagined that he would be the master of a manor. Deal with what comes your way, Hamo, that is all that a man can do."

Garth of the Woods gave us a private dining room in **The Lamb**. It meant that, once the food was served, we could talk openly. I was honest with Lady Hawise and told her what had happened. Her face fell. "So, I have enemies in England as well as Wales. Oh, my foolish brother!"

"Even had he lived, Lady Hawise, Baron Roger Mortimer of Chirk would still have sought your lands and Griffith de la Pole and Thomas of Lancaster would have formed a friendship. We have to rely on the king."

Hamo shook his head, "The old King Edward would have given the matter serious consideration. The new king is a peacock!"

"Hamo, he is your king."

"He kept you a prisoner!"

"He is still my king and all turned out well."

"You are more forgiving than I would have been."

"That is because I am older. I have learned, like my war bow, to bend. It is sometimes hard but a man does what a man must, even if that means bending when he wants to stand erect." I saw that Lady Hawise had been disheartened by the conversation and I smiled to comfort her, "Lady Hawise, do not be downhearted. We support you as do the people of Poole." I gestured with my eating knife at Robert, "And there is an ally who might well win your lands for you."

Robert was both surprised and pleased that I identified him as the saviour of the lady he had placed on a pedestal, "Me, my lord?"

"Queen Isabella is much taken with you. When you speak with her tomorrow, win her over to support Lady Hawise."

Hamo said, "From what you have said, Father, the king does not seem to value her or her opinion."

"While we were in the hall I kept my ears open. I heard a morsel of news that was interesting. The queen wrote to her father, the King of France, who has since written to King Edward. I knew that already but I did not know the result of the missive. He is not pleased with the way the king treats his daughter. I think it is why the king brought her with him. Perhaps the young queen will begin to pull on the strings of the bow that she uses. Like the ones your sons use it may not yet be powerful but, as you know, Hamo, you need to pull a small hunting bow before you attempt a war bow. I have not yet given up hope. In any case we have nothing to lose with the petition."

I saw Lady Hawise nod, firmly, "And we come to the castle after the Parliament, Sir Gerald?"

I knew that the longer Robert was with the queen and Lady Hawise the better would be our chances, "No, come with us when we go. I know it means you, Robert and your lady will have to wait around but you never know who will be present. As Robert discovered at Westminster those who are on the periphery of power often have their uses. You need allies and there may be those who are not at the Parliament who can offer aid. This is a war, my lady, and we need to muster as many troops as we can to win the king to our cause." I sat back and wiped my mouth with my cloth, "And Hamo and Jack, wander the castle and seek information. There may be those who serve the Baron Chirk and the Earl of Lancaster who can give more information. Their involvement is, in the earl's case, unexpected. What has he to do with Wales? It would be as well to gather as much information as we can. Regard it as a scouting expedition and this time tomorrow we can share what we have gleaned."

Warbow

That night, as I prepared for bed and Dai laid his blanket behind the door, I reflected that the rest of my party were in lower spirits than I was. I realised there were two reasons. I had survived my incarceration which I thought would have resulted in a cell in the tower and then the block. The other was my recent illness. I had felt as though I was dying. I had not and I had enjoyed two rebirths. It was a sign and it made me more hopeful.

We dressed in our finest and made our way, after an early breakfast, to the castle. Hamo and Jack's sons were dressed as pages. Their grandmother had employed good seamstresses in the village and they both looked smart and, in their own way, grand. Hamo and Jack wore my livery. Men would know whence we came. Shrewsbury Castle was a well-made building and had many antechambers and chambers. There were corners, nooks and crannies where my scouts could discover intelligence that might help the lady. I left Hamo and Lady Hawise with the others and made my way to the Great Hall. As at Westminster the factions were gathering. I looked around for my son-in-law, for Wooferton was close to Shrewsbury. He was not present and that disappointed me. He would have been an ally. I stood with another couple of minor barons from the borders and we spoke, as barons do, of taxes and harvests. It was only those with great power who could afford to fret over politics.

The king entered and sat on the throne that stood on a raised dais. There were bishops flanking him as well as the Earl of Gloucester, Gilbert de Clare. His huge tracts of land meant that he was almost a ruler in his own right. While he had no claim to the throne he would have an influence on any contender for the crown. When he spoke it became clear that he aligned himself with the king which was good for England. As soon as he spoke it became clear that the king had come with a clear strategy and plans to make the Parliament do as he wished. He wanted the exile and excommunication of his friend lifted. There was vocal opposition which was led by Thomas of Lancaster. The Earl of Lincoln was not present and as Thomas of Lancaster had a claim to the throne it made the opposition more serious. The king offered all sorts of inducements for the support of his request but the opposition grew. Even Baron Mortimer of Chirk sided with Thomas of Lancaster. He had wanted land or power in return for support. However the king had little money to spare and even less land to give. Baron Mortimer had been given nothing, not even a promise. By the end of the day nothing had changed and I could see that the king was angry. That did not bode well for the claim of Lady Hawise but I believed we still had to go along with the plan that we had devised.

I followed the king who strode with just his squire, out of the Great Hall. I wondered if the petition would be dismissed in a fit of pique. When we reached the small chamber he was using to receive petitions he said to his squire, "Go and find this Lady Hawise." He gave a thin smile, "You might find her with the queen and the baron's confessor."

"Yes, King Edward."

Nodding to the two guards who flanked the room, I recognised them as men who had protected him in Westminster, he said, "Come, Warbow. I have a decent wine for us to enjoy."

Once inside the two servants held a chair for him to use and then poured two goblets of wine. He did not invite me to sit. At my age I liked a chair but I endured the standing. He waved the servants away and they scurried to the rear wall.

His voice was almost petulant when he spoke, "Why will the barons not support my request? I was more than generous in the titles that I offered."

It was not a rhetorical question and he needed an answer. Mindful that I had a request of my own I was diplomatic, "Perhaps, my lord, as the excommunication came from the Archbishop of Canterbury, it might be that they think their support is of little use if the church does not support it."

He angrily swallowed some wine, "That snake! That ingrate! I made a plea for his return after my father sent him hence. I should have left the man to rot in Italy!"

Just then there was a knock on the door. His squire opened it, "I have found the lady, King Edward."

"Is she alone?"

"The confessor and the baron's party are with the queen, Lady Hawise is in conference with the captain of your guard."

"Then let them in and leave us."

The door opened and Lady Hawise came in. The captain of the guard was with her and I recognised him, it was Sir John Charleton. More than that he had the same look on his face that Robert had when he had met the lady. He followed her more like a puppy that was eager to please rather than a captain of the king's guard. What was going on?

Chapter 12

The king looked at me, "So this is the lady?"

"It is, King Edward."

I saw him study her and frown, "She is little more than a child and you wish her to be given Powis, an ancient Welsh kingdom?" I heard the disbelief in his voice. I also saw the look on the face of Sir John Charleton. He did not like her being called a child.

The meeting had not begun well.

Lady Hawise looked at me and I smiled to give her confidence. She bobbed her head and handed the parchment to him, "King Edward, here is my petition. I hope that you will give it a fair consideration for your father made me a ward of the Crown." He took the document written by Robert.

I saw the look on his face at the mention of his father. The scales were being weighted against her. He did not read it immediately but dropped it on the table next to his chair. He drank some wine and looked at me, "And you, Warbow, what is your interest in all this? Do you wish a manor in Wales? Is this to increase your power?"

I was being baited. This was the influence of Piers Gaveston. The time I had spent at Westminster had taught me how to deal with such situations. I was honourable but I knew others who were treacherous. King Edward always thought the worst of people and I used that to back my argument and to persuade the king to support the case of Lady Hawise.

Shaking my head I said, "King Edward, I have never asked for a manor. Your father was the one who gave me my manors for which I was always grateful but I never sought more land. I am happy with what I have for my needs are not great." I waited until he nodded and then continued. "Poole was occupied illegally by Lady Hawise's uncle. I had to eject the occupiers and it was they who used violence to try to retake it. The other lands inherited by the lady are also in the hands of her uncles. The Earl of Lancaster supports the eldest uncle, Gruffydd Fychan de la Pole who is opposed by Baron Mortimer of Chirk. I am not sure that Your Majesty would appreciate having a war fought between two supporters on land in Wales. Such a war might ignite the Welsh and encourage them to rebel. Lady Hawise is the rightful owner and she supports the English crown."

I knew that my words, when they were repeated to the two men, and that would happen, would result in two more enemies. In the case of Roger Mortimer he was already opposed to me but Thomas Lancaster was a different matter. My words worked. I saw anger flare in the eyes of the king. He snatched up the petition and said, "Wait without while I read this. Sir John, see that they are secure."

"Your Majesty."

We left the room and the door was closed. Sir John said to the two guards, "Stand at the ends of the corridor."

"Yes Sir John."

Lady Hawise looked at the knight, "Does the king think that we will plot?"

I was going to answer for Sir John when I noticed the gentle look in his eyes. I had seen that look before. Both James and Jean Michel had displayed the doe eyes and half smile when they had spoken to the ladies in their lives. "My lady, the king does not often come into the presence of such innocence. Apart from the queen the people who greet him often have daggers in their eyes. He cannot help but be suspicious. It is his nature." He looked at me, "He still craves the company of the Lord Lieutenant of Ireland, Sir Gerald, it affects his judgement."

"And you, Sir John, how did you fare in Ireland?"

He smiled, "This is not the place for those tales but suffice it to say that in the time I was with you I learned much and turned that to my advantage when I served the Lord Lieutenant." He turned his attention back to Lady Hawise. "My lady, you do not know me well but Sir Gerald does. Will you trust me when we return to the company of the king?"

She looked at me and I nodded, "Sir John is an honourable knight and while I know not what he has planned I trust him and we are perilously short of allies."

"Then Sir John, as Sir Gerald has been the knight who has championed my cause I will trust you."

"And that is good for I intend to be your new champion."

I had no time to reflect on his choice of words for the door opened and we were admitted. I saw that the goblet had been refilled. King Edward took a long drink and waved a hand towards the petition, "A well argued case but Sir Gerald's words have made me realise that these lands in Powis are of value. Can a child such as you hold on to them?"

Before she could answer Sir John stepped forward, "King Edward, I have served you since you were the Prince of Wales." The king looked puzzled but he nodded. "When I returned from Ireland you said I could choose my own manor as a reward for my service to England, yourself and the Lord Lieutenant."

The king had a quick mind but it was a suspicious one and he always looked for motives that were similar to his. "You would have the manors of Owain de la Pole?" Had I not heard the words uttered in the hallway I would have suspected treachery. The king's half smile told me that he thought that too.

Sir John shook his head, "As you know, King Edward, my father's manor is close to the border. In due course I will be the lord of the manor. I have spent many years serving you and rather than being given a manor, I would learn to be the lord of the manor. If you would allow it I would watch over the Lady Hawise and guard her rights to Poole and, in the fullness of time, the lands of Powis of which she is the rightful owner. I would be Lady Hawise's champion and protect her from her enemies."

Sir John's words had surprised the king and I saw him drink more of the wine and consider the words. The atmosphere was so tense that I believe it could have been cut by a sword. Eventually, the king said, "It is an intriguing proposition that you make, Sir John. If I did not know you I would believe that you sought the land for yourself. I will not make a decision now. I need to have food and a night of sleep to help me evaluate the matter. Return in the morning and you, Lady Hawise and you, Sir John, shall have my judgement."

"And me, King Edward?"

"You, Sir Gerald?" I knew from his tone that I was to be dismissed. "You are no longer needed in this matter. You have done your duty and for that we thank you but now King Edward's knight, Sir John Charleton, shall be the one I consult in the matter of Lady Hawise and her claim to Powis." We all nodded.

If he thought he was humiliating me he was wrong. By the same token I would not simply walk away from Lady Hawise no matter what the judgement was. I would be at the meeting too. I also realised that Sir John had given the king the means to hold on to the land. It might be that Lady Hawise would lose the land despite our efforts. We backed out of the room.

Lady Hawise said, "We should speak with the others."

"Aye, that would be for the best." We headed for the small room where they waited. I heard the queen's tinkling laughter as we approached. I had thought she would have left when Lady Hawise had done so. When we entered I saw that Dai was doing a comic impression. It was of me and the way I walked. I knew it was supposed to be me when Hamo hissed, "Dai, my father."

I made a mock frowning face and said, "Dai, was that me you were imitating?"

"My lord I..."

I smiled and nodded, "It was a good one and the queen thinks so for I heard her laughter as we came down the corridor."

The tension I had created evaporated like morning mist. The queen asked, "And what is the king's judgement?"

Lady Hawise had regained some of her composure and she smiled, "The king will consider my petition. Thank you, Master Robert, for the king said that it was a well written and well-argued petition."

Robert said, "But he was not swayed."

She shook her head, "I think he was going to dismiss the claim but Sir John here came up with a solution that he is now considering."

Every eye swivelled to look at the man who was a stranger to all but me and, perhaps, the queen. He seemed ill at ease with the scrutiny. He shuffled his feet and began, "When I was with Sir Gerald on his service to the king I learned much about Yarpole, Luston and Lucton. I saw how he managed his lands and let others run his manors for him. I merely told the king that as I would one day be inheriting my father's manor some experience in running a manor would be useful. I asked him to allow me to be a sort of castellan for Poole. That would stop Lady Hawise's uncles from retaking it. I said that I would be her champion."

Robert frowned, "But it would not have her other lands returned to her."

Sir John shook his head, "No, Master Robert, but it secures one manor for her and I believe that until I spoke he was considering finding for Lady Hawise's uncles. What say you, Sir Gerald?"

I poured myself some wine, "Sir John is right. This is not a perfect solution but a better one than we might have expected. There are politics at work." I smiled at Lady Hawise, "You once told me that if you were a man then there would not be a problem. You are a beautiful young lady and what you need is a husband for then the king would have to let you have your lands, even under Salic Law."

The queen snorted, "That is not fair. Just because she is a woman…"

Robert said, "Queen Isabella, you, more than any, know how unfairly women are treated."

He said it in French and she nodded. She then spoke in her accented English, "Lady Hawise, as Master Robert says, I know your situation as well as any. When I speak to my husband tonight I will add my support to your cause. It may not persuade him for I think he does not hold me in as high a regard as others but you shall have my voice."

"Thank you, Queen Isabella, thank you all. I do not feel so helpless knowing that I have the support of so many kind and noble people." She put her hand on Dai's, "And with Dai the Rock and his dirk then we can do anything!"

The queen, not understanding the allusion frowned but the rest of us, Sir John excepted, laughed. In explanation Robert then told the story of the Welsh boy who protected Lady Hawise. Sir John and the queen laughed. The story was halted when the door opened and a liveried servant entered, "Queen Isabella, the feast is about to start. The king demands your presence."

The frown reappeared but she sighed and stood. I could see her making a decision, "And all those in this room Edgar, are invited to dine at the feast." She suddenly sounded like a queen, "All of them, even the pages, do you understand?"

"But Queen Isabella…"

He got no further for she snapped, imperiously, "Am I the queen or a piece of jewellery to be displayed at the king's whim. Make it so!"

The man visibly recoiled, "Yes, Your Majesty."

She had a look of triumph on her face as she left.

Robert smiled and I said, "The kitten we met at Westminster has grown claws, Robert, and I think that is your handiwork."

He smiled, "She has the potential to be a strong queen, Sir Gerald, and as I am her countryman I felt obliged to help."

I turned to Sir John, "And you, Sir John, have changed." I was inviting him to speak but he looked around the room. "If you trust me, and I think you do, Sir John, then trust these people for there is not one of them who would betray me."

He nodded and sat, "As I said when we awaited the king's judgement, my lord, I used much of what I learned from you when I served the Lord Lieutenant of Ireland. I prevented his death by spotting an ambush. He was grateful and when we had subdued the rebels he rewarded me with a return to England and a letter for the king. The king was pleased and offered me a choice of manors." He sighed, "I am not an ambitious man and, when I heard of it, I was touched by the plight of Lady Hawise. Perhaps I can use what little influence I have to help this lady hold on to her land."

Lady Hawise went to the knight and, picking up his hand, kissed the back of it, "You are like Sir Gerald, you are a true knight. I pray that the king heeds your words for with a protector like you then the people of Poole will be safe from the privations of the predatory de la Poles."

I think that only Robert and I saw the connection that was made in that moment between Sir John and the maid. I watched as their eyes met and felt the warmth that oozed between them.

Before more could be said the door opened and a harassed looking Edgar re-entered, "I have obeyed the queen's wishes my lords, my lady, but you must come quickly for the king is impatient for provender."

I smiled, "Thank you and let us hasten for we must do all in our power to make a good impression on this king. It is for Lady Hawise."

The table we were allocated was at the lower end of the hall. Those like Mortimer and Lancaster were on the high table but I cared not. Lady Hawise's two champions, Robert and Sir John, flanked her and Hamo and Jack sat by me with their wide-eyed sons next to them. Grace said, the food was brought in and the hubbub of noise grew. It meant I could not hear the conversation between Hawise and the others however my sons and I could not only talk, but as we faced the high table we were able to observe all that went on. Jack was highly observant. It had been one of the skills that had enabled him to survive when he had been mistreated in Yorkshire.

"See how the Earl of Lancaster tries to have the ear of the bishop who is seated next to the king." I nodded, "And the knight who is seated next to Queen Isabella, is not that the younger Baron Mortimer?"

"Aye, it is."

"Perhaps he is trying to influence the queen."

"He might be, Hamo, or he could be trying to inveigle himself into her confidence. She is young and she is impressionable."

"When you were with the king we spoke with her. Robert is right, she has grown and I do not think that she would be taken in by flattery from such a man."

I said nothing but I knew that both Queen Eleanor and King Edward's second wife, Queen Margaret, had been assailed with knights trying to get the ear of the king through them. It would be the same for Queen Isabella.

The food was good and I was hungry. While I ate I watched the factions as they devoured the food and wine and jockeyed for position. Eyes were cast in our direction and I knew that similar judgements would be made about us. In their eyes the fly in the ointment was Sir John Charleton. I knew his motives but to the likes of Lancaster and the Mortimers he was an unknown quantity. He had been a mere protector of the king and had been absent for some time. Why was he sitting with us? They knew me and understood me but a former King's Knight was something that they did not.

As I turned my attention to Sir John I saw hope. He was honourable and our time riding to Canterbury and back had given me an insight into the knight's character. His offer had surprised me but the more I thought about it the more I realised that it might work. If Lady Hawise could hang on to Poole then the king might be persuaded to let her have the other manors once she married.

When the king rose the feast was over. Sir John escorted Lady Hawise and Breffni to the gate. I saw resignation on Robert's face. I know that he had long ago given up any hope of winning the lady's hand but Sir John had now taken on the mantle of protector. We left the castle and headed to the inn.

As we entered Lady Hawise said, "It has been a busy day. We are tired. We will retire and see you on the morrow. Thank you for all that you have done. Your words, Robert, were well written and I will be forever in your debt. You, Sir Gerald have been the sort of knight that lives in the songs of troubadours. I am grateful that you came into my life. All of you."

We stood in silence while she left; Garth of the Woods had been serving customers and he smiled as he approached, "You have eaten, my lord?"

"We have but I think we will talk a while."

"Hywel, kindle the fire in the small dining room."

"Yes, Master Garth."

"Sack, my lord? I have a good one and I daresay you will be heading back to Yarpole soon."

"On the morrow I think. We have to visit the castle and then we shall leave."

"Then a good jug of sack will give you all pleasant slumbers."

Once in the room and with the fire fed with fresh logs and flaring well we sat and drank what was a good wine. Dai and my grandsons had theirs watered; Dai less than my two grandsons. I decided that things should not be hidden. Thoughts that were not given air often festered and turned malignant.

"So, Robert, we are alone now. What is your opinion of this plan?"

He took a deep swallow, "May I speak openly, my lord?"

"If you have to ask then I am hurt."

"I am sorry, my lord, it is the poisonous air of the Parliament that makes me so. You know Sir John better than I do. I believe that he is an honourable knight but I cannot see why he takes this on. What motivates him? That is what I cannot understand."

I sipped the wine. I did not want to drink too much as I did not wish to be up and down in the night. "Sir John is not a young man."

I saw the frowns on all their faces. Hamo said, "Nor is he old; what has that to do with it?"

"When we were on the road to Canterbury, he confided in me that he had served the king since he was Prince of Wales. He had been a page and then a squire before being given his spurs. What he yearned for was a family."

Hamo snorted, "Surely he cannot think to be Lady Hawise's father or brother."

"No, Hamo," I paused, "I think he seeks to win her hand."

It was as though a thunderclap had sounded. My grandsons apart, they were dozing under the influence of the wine, the mouths of the others dropped open. Surprisingly it was Robert who first smiled and then spoke, "I saw the looks they exchanged. Lady Hawise is not averse to his company."

Jack said, "But they have just met."

"And Sir John has wanted a wife for some time. His position meant he did not come into contact with suitable brides and Lady Hawise, well, she is in these dire straits because she has no husband. If the king decides in her favour then time will do the rest but this all hinges on the judgement of a king whom I do not know well." I knew that Longshanks would decide in the lady's favour but this king… "I am just surprised by the effect she had on Sir John."

Robert said, "Dai and I were in the room when Sir John entered. He was enchanted from the moment he saw her. I saw the spell her beauty wove and his heart was lost." He looked at me and I nodded. I knew he was also talking about his own experiences. "When he spoke to Lady Hawise I saw her look at him not as she did with the rest of us but as a man. I believe that this was meant to be, Sir Gerald, and I am happy."

I know that my sons were confused. Robert had left unsaid much that I understood but they did not. Now that I had heard of their meeting it made more sense to me.

We paid our bill and left before the sun had barely peered over the eastern horizon. Garth of the Woods had not even wanted to accept payment but I pressed the two golden coins in his hand, "My lord, this is too much."

"It is not for we were safe and looked after. It is also in remembrance of your service and those who served me and did not live to enjoy retirement, eh?"

"Yes, my lord, you were always the fairest of captains."

I leaned in, "And if you hear gossip or news that is of interest to me…"

"You will hear within the day, my lord."

Lady Hawise and Sir John were already waiting outside the chamber the king was using. Hamo and the rest of our party remained in the outer bailey with the horses and it was just Robert and I who joined them. I saw, as we approached, that they were easy in the company of one another. It boded well.

Sir John said, "The king leaves this day. He is less than happy with the support he received and I fear that his humour may make him decide against this lady."

Robert said, "I observed the high table when we dined last night. Baron Mortimer of Chirk spoke for a long time in the king's ear."

I said, firmly, "And I noticed, Robert, that when he left his cousin the Earl of Lancaster leaned over the bishop to engage him. Let us not make the king's decision for him. Speculation is useless. He will do that which he wishes. It is true of all monarchs. As much as I respected King Edward the old he sometimes did things that made no sense to me."

When the king appeared he had with him the Bishop of Chester and the Bishop of Hereford as well as Roger Mortimer of Chirk and Thomas of Lancaster. There were two clerks with them. When they had entered we were commanded to follow. Robert, of course, waited without. The king sat on the throne and the bishop held the parchment in his hand. I saw that it was not yet sealed and that gave me hope. Perhaps we could, if he decided against the Lady Hawise, persuade him yet.

"We have deliberated upon this most contentious of matters long and hard. Cogent arguments have been made by Baron Mortimer of Chirk as well as our noble cousin, the Earl of Lancaster. Lady Hawise ferch Owain ap Gruffudd ap Gwenwynwyn has also made a strong case." He was enjoying the power. I knew that in reality it mattered not to him who ruled in Powis. We had defeated the Welsh in battle and if it was a problem then he would send in an army commanded by Sir Gilbert, and probably me, to take it again. However, his decision now might serve to show his barons and earls who ruled. "We have decided. Sir John Charleton of Wrockwardine, Wellington and Apley Castle is hereby appointed to act on behalf of Lady Hawise ferch Owain ap Gruffudd ap Gwenwynwyn as the champion of her rights. Until she marries then the ownership of the lands other than Poole will be held in abeyance. We shall have to take more advice on the matter. I will make another judgement in the fullness of time and at my own leisure."

I saw the faces of Mortimer and Lancaster. They felt that they had lost. That Lady Hawise had not won entirely was a moot point. Sir John was her champion. It was an old-fashioned title but one that carried with it the idea of fighting for the lady. I had been an unofficial champion. Now the king had made it official.

"Sir John, do you accept the position?"

His answer surprised even the king for Sir John, whom the king had seen as a dull soldier, spoke with passion, "With all my heart, King Edward. I swear to be the champion of Lady Hawise ferch Owain ap

Gruffudd ap Gwenwynwyn against all enemies, no matter their rank, title or position."

Even I was taken aback and Thomas Lancaster coloured as he realised that he was included in the threat.

The clerk had already melted the wax and when the bishop nodded, a blob was dropped onto the parchment and King Edward used his seal to give it authority. "Then it is done. There being no further business for me here I dissolve the Parliament." Sir John, as champion, took the document.

The Earl of Lancaster said, "King Edward, there is still the matter of the Scots! We have yet to muster the army."

"I will hold another Parliament in Stamford in June. Let us hope that my barons can make the correct decision then for I will not go to war while my friend is in exile."

I caught the eye of Sir John and we bowed and backed out of the room. Lady Hawise curtsied and backed out also. We left the earl and the baron arguing for the continuation of the Parliament. Once outside Robert looked at the document and his eyes widened. I said, "Sir John is appointed the champion of the lady. It is not all that we sought but I think it is more than we hoped, eh, my lady?"

She nodded, "It is but I am determined to regain my lands, all of them."

Her new champion sounded determined as he spoke, "And you now have my sword and my men to aid you."

"Your men, Sir John?"

He nodded, "Aye, Sir Gerald, when I went to Ireland I increased my mesne. I have a squire and ten men at arms. It is not an army but it is a start and I will emulate you, Sir Gerald. Lady Hawise has told me how you hired good archers. It is a fool who does not use the best that there are and Powis has good archers."

I nodded.

Lady Hawise took my right hand in hers, "But, my lord, do not be a stranger. You are a neighbour and I know that I would not have my manor but for you. I will still need your war bow."

Robert laughed, "My lady, he is the Warbow!"

I shook my head in irritation at Robert's attempt at humour, "My lady, send word and I will bring the might of Yarpole, Luston and Lucton to your aid. I have unfinished business with your uncles."

Sir John held out his hand, "And Sir Gerald, I thank God that you were sent to escort the king. Had I not met you then this meeting may never have happened. I was ever your friend but now I am beholden to you. If you need me then send to me."

I could not think of a time when that would happen but the offer was a generous one. We turned and headed for the outer bailey. Once we were out of earshot I said, "Robert, I know you have feelings for the lady, how does this touch you?"

His voice was calm as he spoke, "I will always have feelings for the lady, until the day I die, but I cannot be her champion. From what you told me Sir John is not only an honourable knight he is a good warrior. He is also, my lord, younger than you. He will protect her and I am satisfied."

"Do not write me off yet, Robert the Healer, but I am pleased that you are reconciled. I would not have you harbour bad feelings."

"No, my lord, my heart is still filled with love. I am content."

Robert, Hamo's son and John, Jack's were with their fathers and holding the reins of Thunder and my healer's mount. Their fathers looked at me expectantly, "Well?"

I nodded, "It was all that we might have expected. Lady Hawise is under the protection of Sir John Charleton and while that did not please Thomas of Lancaster it gives the lady the support of the king."

Hamo looked relieved, "Good, then we can go home with a clear conscience."

As I mounted Thunder I said, "I always have a clear conscience. That does not always keep me from trouble but I am content."

As the boys mounted I said to Hamo's son, "So, Robert, do you still wish to be an archer or has the sight of so many knights made you wish for a different path?"

He shook his head and said, cheerily, "I am happy to be an archer and I have done the hard part of the training already."

His father laughed, "You think that but believe me there will come a time when you wish to incinerate your bow for making your muscles burn."

He was right. "And you, John?"

"I know that I have yet to put the hours in to be an archer. My father says that I have skill with a sword. Who knows, I may grow up to a life of peace."

His father and my son exchanged a look. That was unlikely to happen. We were on the open road when Jack said, "This means that if we wish to support Lady Hawise we have to back the king and that may be hard."

I had seen that dilemma coming. So long as the king's favourite was in Ireland then there were few problems and the king would rule in a slightly more reasonable manner. Once Piers Gaveston returned then who knew what might happen. That he would return was obvious to me. I just knew that we had another Parliament in Stamford and there both sides would try to manipulate the earls and barons to get the result they wanted. I would stay away.

It was dark when we reached my home. My sons had taken their families directly to their manors and it was just Robert, Dai and myself who clattered through the gates. Abel took the horses and he and Dai took the bags from their backs. That done they led them to the stables.

Mary came to the door, "It is settled?"

I shrugged, "We have achieved all that we can. I have much to tell you but let us do it while we eat."

It was when we lay in our bed that I was able to tell her all that I hoped and feared. When I told her about Sir John and their mutual attraction she almost squealed with delight, "Good. Robert might have made a good husband but he would never have kept the lady's lands safe. He can now put her from his mind and we can begin a new chapter of our lives without the threat of the king's judgement hanging over us."

I hoped that she was right.

Chapter 13

I slept better that night for Mary was right. It was a more optimistic time for us. However, while we were no longer the sole protectors of Lady Hawise, we still had manors to run and nature conspired against us. We had snow in February that made, for a short time, travelling to even Luston and Lucton impossible. We had to look to our own people. After two weeks the snow melted and brought with it the inevitable flooding. The plots and plans of others became immaterial as we looked within our borders and saved all that we could. The fishpond I had put in saved the hall from the worst of the flooding as did the well-maintained ditch around the hall itself. James' new home also remained dry and I saw the look of satisfaction on Robert's face. He had designed well.

As soon as the roads were passable, I rode with Dai and Robert to visit my two sons. I had taught them well and they had not suffered too badly. If anything the inundations would improve the fields once they dried out as they deposited silt and earth on our land. When I spoke with Jack, who lived the closest to the Welsh border, he told me that the Severn had burst its banks and that the border had been closed. There had been no danger of raids from the Welsh or mischief from the de la Poles. Nature had come to our aid.

"I wonder how Sir John and Lady Hawise coped. This event is beyond the experience of both of them." I could not help but worry about the knight, for protecting against blades was one thing but nature was something entirely different.

Jack smiled, "I know that we were lucky and were shown what to do by example but they have good people there. Iago and David of Abergele know their business. If you wish, when the crossings are open I can visit with them."

I shook my head, "Kind of you, Jack, but you have your own manor to run and they need to learn for themselves."

"You say they as though they are a couple, Father."

I realised then that Jack and Hamo had not seen what Robert and I had, "They will grow closer, Jack, and this was meant to be."

I saw that I had intrigued him but he voiced no more thoughts.

As I mounted Thunder to ride home once more I said, "The king holds a Parliament in Stamford soon. I think he will ask for more money and begin, if the barons and earls have their way, to raise armies. Make sure you have all that is needed for the muster and yet leave men to guard your manor. We helped Lady Hawise but made enemies of the de la Pole family. The Welsh will not be involved in a war with Scotland and I fear mischief."

It was at the start of May that I heard more disturbing news. It came, not from Wales but Westminster. A rider, wrapped in a travelling cloak, clattered into my yard. He had a sword, a shield and led a sumpter. My archers and men at arms stopped their practice to study him. He was hooded and I did not recognise him but when the hood was lowered I did. It was Richard Davidson, the archer's son who had served the king. I smiled, "John, Sarah, prepare a room, we have a guest. Abel, take the horses."

The man at arms said, "I would not impose on you, Sir Gerald. I can stay at the inn. I hear it is a good one."

"It is but you are a friend and we fought enemies together. There is a bond, Richard, I pray you enter." Mary appeared, "This is my wife, Lady Mary. This, my love, is Richard Davidson. He is one of the king's guards and was with me on the Canterbury road."

The short introduction was enough for Mary and she beamed, as he stepped into the hallway. "Then you are welcome. Iago will take and dry your cloak. I will fetch wine." Mary did not stand on ceremony and I saw that she had taken the man at arms by surprise.

The man at arms shook his head and smiled, "Lady Mary is not what I expected of a baron's wife, my lord."

I laughed as we entered the warmth of my dining hall, "You are used to the wives of the popinjays who flock around the king at court. I married a good lady. Come and sit."

"And I should correct you, Sir Gerald, for I no longer serve as a king's guard."

"Then there is a tale here."

Just then Mary and Susanna came in with refreshments. My wife said, "I will see you later, Richard Davidson. You are welcome in our home and if you desire anything then let me know."

When we were alone he said, "A gracious lady."

"That she is and now, your tale."

"The king has ennobled some men at arms and made them knights. He has also knighted the sons of many of his supporters; I was not one of them." He shrugged, "I am the son of an archer and good enough to be a piece of metal to save him in battle but not enough to be knighted." I heard the bitterness in his voice. "Luckily, Sir John wrote to me just at the same time as I was relieved of my position. He offered me a place in Poole. I am to be captain of the guard and I accepted. He said the old warrior, a man called David of Abergele, had been ill over the winter and while he had recovered he needed a younger man. I am honoured and, I have to say, relieved."

There was more beneath his words and I said, "Why do you say that?"

He took a deep drink and said, "There was a Parliament at Westminster."

I frowned for I had thought the king had said the next one was to be at Stamford and in June. "The king called a Parliament?"

"No, the Earl of Lincoln. They called themselves The Community of the Realm. They drew up a list of eighty-one new barons."

I was shocked at his words, "They cannot do that. The creation of a barony is the king's decision."

"Aye, my lord, and that is why the king began to knight his own supporters."

"If the king was not there then the baronies cannot be ratified."

Richard nodded, "And now you can see why I was pleased to leave. There is a dispute between the king and his barons."

"There are always disputes between monarch and barons."

"Aye, my lord, but this is threatening to become martial. There has yet to be the rattling of swords but that day will come. The border with Wales seemed a safer place."

"I am pleased that Sir John has asked for you. He has some good archers and you are one who recognises the value of archers. I can see why he chose you." He sipped his wine and put his hand to the fire for warmth. "When did Sir John send his message to you?

"Before the floods, thank goodness. I was able to settle my affairs and buy what I needed from London. I do not like the place but the Chepe is a good place to buy that which I cannot get in Wales." It explained the laden sumpter. Richard was leaving one life to begin another.

As we ate that evening, Robert was most interested in the politics of Westminster and spoke to me at length. He had lived with me there and being an intelligent man had observed the manoeuvrings of the lords as they vied for power. He disagreed with me about the prospect of civil war, "The king, it seems to me, needs Piers Gaveston at his side. He will not risk a war without the man he thinks is a talisman. If he has any sense he will win over the most powerful of lords and with those on his side, win over the wavering barons. The two factions who oppose the king, the earls of Lincoln and Lancaster, hate each other. That is an advantage the king holds."

Richard had also lived in Westminster but he had not seen what Robert, a Frenchman, had, "And who is there powerful enough to support the king?"

"Gilbert de Clare springs to mind. He is rich enough and has the power to back the king. De Clare would increase his power in the west. The king then needs to turn one of the other of his enemies to his side and he can win. The young Earl of Surrey, although he hates Gaveston, was knighted, I believe, along with Edward, at the Feast of the Swans. If he could be turned then who knows what might happen. I think that before swords are unsheathed there will be plots and conspiracies that do not involve daggers but words."

I laughed, "And there you have it, Richard Davidson, a French priest who was not born in this land has a greater insight than we do."

"Do you mock me, Sir Gerald?" I could see that my laughter had offended Robert and I shook my head, "No, for I think you are right and it shows the difference between a thinker and a warrior. Richard and I are used to dealing with threats through martial arms. You think of ways with words that will achieve the same end."

When Richard left the next day I gave messages for both Sir John and Lady Hawise. I wanted them to know that they had my support.

Despite Robert's words I still feared that war might come sooner rather than later and I began to take on young men to serve with me. My archers, men at arms and the men of the village had sired, since I had come to the manor, many sons. There were limited opportunities for employment in the village. We only needed one or two carpenters and one blacksmith would suffice. Some farmers' sons needed the chance of a life outside the farm. The eldest normally inherited and so the second son had the choice of working without the hope of land at the end of it or taking up a sword or bow. The sons of archers had all been trained by their fathers. Farmers' sons and the children of men at arms were naturally strong. A week after Mayday I had it announced at services by Father Michael that I sought archers and men at arms. The next day saw twenty young men arrive in my yard. I was pleased with their enthusiasm but I knew that was too many. Michel and Peter Yew Tree sat with me and eliminated those who were too young or, quite simply, not ready yet. I asked the ones we rejected to return the next year at the same time. The six archers and six soldiers we hired were told to return the next day. They would live in the warrior hall. Whilst it would be crowded it still afforded them more room than they had in their own homes. They would all have a last night with their families. For all of them it meant pay. Like the men hired in Poole some had never seen coins and when payday came I knew they would hasten to the tavern to spend their first coins. It was a rite of passage.

When they arrived they had a rude but necessary welcome. The archers thought that they were trained already. They were not. The

Sunday morning training was nothing compared with the life of an archer of Gerald Warbow. By the end of the first day some were ruing their decision. For the soldiers, they were not yet ready to be called men at arms, it was even worse. They might have seen a sword or a spear but none had ever handled them. Michel and son, along with John and James, would teach them to use a spear first. It was not glamorous but it was necessary. First they used a spear haft and learned that even without a spear head they could still be hurt, especially when it was wielded by someone as skilled as John. Their training would take all summer. Once they had mastered a spear they would learn how to use a spear and a shield. Only then would they progress to a sword. The issuing of helmets and pieces of mail would not take place until September.

The training made May pass quickly. When Richard Davidson and Ifan rode into my yard in the hours before dusk at the start of June, I feared the worst. Even as the thought flitted through my mind I dismissed it. Sir John would not have sent his right-hand man if there was danger. "Welcome. Enter my hall."

Ifan shook his head, "My lord, I am not worthy to enter the hall. The warrior hall will do."

"All are welcome in my home, Ifan."

"I know but having worked with James and John, I should like to meet with your men at arms and spearmen."

"Very well. Dai, take Ifan and his gear to the warrior hall. Richard, you will stay the night?"

"Of course, my lord."

I knew that he brought news but I was patient and waited until the five of us were sat at the table and we had finished our food before I asked the reason for his visit. He smiled, "Sir John and Lady Hawise are to be married on the 26th of July and they both wish you and all of your family to attend. Lady Hawise knows that she would have lost all but for your family and in the absence of her family she would not only have you there but she wishes you, Sir Gerald, to act in stead of her father."

I was touched beyond words, "I would be honoured." I hesitated for this appeared a little hasty, "This seems sudden, Richard. Do not get me wrong I am happy but just a couple of months ago they had not met."

My wife shook her head, "Gerald! We were wed within a short time. They are in love."

Richard nodded, "Your good lady is right, my lord. When I arrived at Poole I was amazed at the changes wrought in Sir John. He was always a good warrior and a great leader but Lady Hawise seemed to have brought out another side to him. It feels right and the disparity in their ages seems as nothing."

"Was some comment made about that?"

"I believe that some in the village think that he is too old. I do not."

"Nor me," I said, "And I am pleased for both of them. This means that Lady Hawise has, not only the manor of Poole, but now the right to claim the other lands."

His face became serious, "Already there are legal papers presented arguing against that, my lord. The uncles of Lady Hawise are gathering allies."

"War?"

"They are trying words but when that fails I think that they will seek force. They have let it be known that they have the support of the Earl of Lancaster, the king's cousin."

"Then we have taken on more men at just the right time."

I took a drink of wine and Robert used the silence to ask, "And Lady Hawise is happy?"

Neither Dai nor Richard knew what my wife and I did, that Robert had lost his heart to the maid. Richard beamed, "She cannot wait for the wedding! The date has been set so that Sir John's family can attend. Sir John's brother has an important role in King Edward's household. They had to seek the king's permission." He smiled, "He gave it readily. If she had had her way then they would be married already."

Mary raised her goblet, "To Lady Hawise and Sir John Charleton. God has made this happen and nothing but good can come from it."

Richard and I spoke after my wife had gone to ensure that his chamber was ready for him, "The men who will fight for him, they are ready? You have sufficient weapons?"

"We are ready but Sir John only has fifteen archers."

"Not enough."

"He knows that, my lord, he has Dewi visiting the villages close to the manor but he dare not travel too far without an escort. We have seen scouts watching the land and that does not bode well."

"When I come for the wedding I will bring a couple of local men. They might succeed where Dewi has failed. And Sir John's brother, what is it that he does for the king?"

"You know that he is a priest?"

I shook my head, "I did not know that."

"You might have seen him in Westminster. He has inky fingers for he does much of the clerical work for the king. He is trusted with confidential matters and I believe that someday he will hold high office. He is like Sir John. Their father has raised good sons. Neither has become tainted by the Westminster diseases, politicking and treachery."

Warbow

I liked Richard Davidson for his father, an archer, had also raised a good son. Richard might never win his spurs but, as I knew from bitter experience, the winning of spurs did not always make for a good knight.

The two men left the next morning. I sent sheafs of arrows back with them. We could always make more and it seemed to me that they might need them. I rode to visit with my sons to tell them. Their wives, of course, were delighted. The wedding of such an important lady necessitated a whole new wardrobe. For my sons it was the news of imminent action that provoked their preparations.

Jack said, when I spoke to him, "Will her uncles try to disrupt the marriage ceremony? Such mischief seems a likely outcome."

"I think that such a thing might cause outrage. Sir John's brother is one of King Edward's household. It would be deemed as an attack on the king. I do not think his enemies are ready yet for such a confrontation. The Parliament at Stamford is imminent. The outcome of that meeting will determine the opposition. We will travel to Poole with a small escort but choose good men."

Jack's mouth dropped open, "They might attack us? Even though we have women and girls with us?"

"I think it is possible but unlikely. I do not know how desperate they are. We will gather here and stay overnight. We might do the journey to Poole in one easy day but with women…it will be a long day in a carriage."

He laughed, "Carriage! That is a fine word for a wagon!"

Of course, Mary wanted me to look splendid too and I was made a new set of clothes. I did not need such things but I accepted that as the most senior of the guests at the wedding I would need to be appropriately attired.

Even as we prepared for the wedding news arrived which overshadowed it. Edward had petitioned the Pope and, somehow, had managed to have Gaveston's excommunication annulled. That meant the king's favourite was free to return to England. By the time the news reached us Piers Gaveston was already back in England and attending the Parliament in Stamford. I began to wonder if events would conspire to prevent the wedding. For one thing I doubted that Sir John's brother, Thomas, would be allowed to be at his brother's wedding.

It was early July when a messenger, on his way to Chester, stopped to water his horse. I knew the man and when I offered him refreshment he accepted. I was not subtle when I spoke to him, "The Parliament, what did it decide?"

He nodded, "You served the old king well, my lord, and I know that you are an honourable man. I will tell you." He sighed, "The Earl of

Warbow

Cornwall has had his earldom and the income returned to him and the manors in England and Gascony revert to the Crown." I said nothing but I knew there must have been a great deal of negotiation and compromise. "The Earl of Gloucester and the king pushed the ordinance through. The Earl of Lincoln persuaded the Earl of Surrey to accept the return of the Earl of Cornwall."

I said nothing for I was wondering why the Earl of Lincoln, an avowed enemy of Piers Gaveston, would accept the return of the king's favourite. Perhaps it was to spite Thomas of Lancaster. That he could persuade the young Earl of Surrey was not a surprise. For once I wished I had been present. If I had been I might have a better idea of why the Earl of Cornwall had won. That was what it was, a victory. The barons and earls had supported the Archbishop of Canterbury, the Earl of Lincoln and the Earl of Lancaster to have him exiled. He had not suffered during his exile. Sir John had told me, in confidence, that when Piers Gaveston had been the Lord Lieutenant of Ireland he had increased his personal coffers. Old King Edward would be turning in his grave. As the next Parliament was called for October, the king and his favourite had a short time to show the barons that the Earl of Cornwall was a changed man and would not be as profligate with the treasury. The messenger said that the king wished to punish the Scots. There would be a war and the men of Yarpole, Lucton and Luston, would be marching north to the killing grounds of the borders.

I did not sour the mood of the preparations for the upcoming wedding. My news, depressing though it was, did not suggest a sudden change in our circumstances. I would tell no one until I was in Poole. Sir John and his brother might have more information.

We left three days before the wedding. As I was acting as the bride's father, Mary and I would be housed in the hall. The rest of my family would be accommodated in the village. The messenger with the invitations had said that there were two merchants in wool who had offered to put up Hamo and Jack, along with their families. Hamo and his family arrived the night before we were due to leave. The ladies and my granddaughters would travel in a wagon that had been fitted with seats and cushions to make for a comfortable ride. Michel and John would be the men at arms who accompanied us and I was taking Gruffydd and Iago as archers for they had shown that they knew the area and would be useful as scouts. We were not going to war but it paid to be cautious. We left early and reached Lucton within the hour. Had we ridden on the backs of horses then the journey would have been halved. It was good that it was high summer and the days were still long. We would still reach Poole before it was dark.

Warbow

Once we left Lucton there was a gay atmosphere in the wagon. Peter of Beverley, my crippled ex archer, drove the wagon. The wound that had stopped him being a warrior was a crippled knee. He could drive the wagon and it gave us, if we needed it, another archer. I hoped we would not. In any case Peter had asked if he could be of service. He knew that he could never go to war again but he was one of my men. My archers rode at the fore, as scouts, and my men at arms at the rear. My sons, grandsons, Robert, Dai, and I flanked the wagon. One advantage of having the wagon was that we did not need to bring sumpters. Clothes, food and, of course, weapons, were in the rear of the wagon. My grandsons were enjoying riding with their fathers and grandfather. My granddaughters were just revelling in the pleasure of riding in a wagon while my wife and our daughters-in-law were just pleased not to have to ride and were able to chatter as they travelled.

Our long stop was at Hopton Castle. There we learned that Sir Walter had died and his heir was but a boy who was about to become a youth. Lady Hopton offered to have food prepared for us but I knew we could not afford the time. We ate, instead, in the outer bailey for it was a sunny day. Lady Hopton enjoyed speaking with my wife and the young Walter Hopton, who was of an age with my grandson, Robert son of Hamo, was able to chat about horses, weapons and his future as a knight.

While the others ate I went to speak to the Captain of the Guard. Until young Walter was of an age to run the castle then Captain Edward was, effectively, the castellan. "How many men do you have, Captain?"

"Not enough, my lord. I have seen more than forty summers and I should hand over my duties to a younger man but..." he waved a hand. "I have six archers and four spearmen. I would not even grace them with the title of men at arms. They are keen enough and if we had to defend the walls then they might be of service but if we were to go to war then they would be fodder for the Scots. Sir Walter was ill for a long time. He died by inches and that is not the way for a man to die. He was pale and shrivelled when God took him. His mind was not on the defence of the castle but his soul."

"When last I came through he was not here."

"No, my lord, he could still ride and he and the family were escorted to Canterbury to visit the shrine of St Thomas."

It had clearly not resulted in a cure. "You will train young Walter?"

"I will, my lord. I know this will be my last duty for his father but I will endeavour to mould him."

"And my stepson, Jack, lives the closest to you. Do not be shy about sending to him for help."

"The Welsh have been quiet of late, my lord, and that is a mercy. Our position here means that when they do become belligerent we are seen as an easy target. The last time they came we had a good garrison but, even so, ten good men fell in the failed assault." He smiled, "When the Severn flooded, it was a blessing for it did us no harm and meant we were safe from bandits and poachers."

I had fought in the war that Captain Edward had mentioned. We had defeated the Welsh and, I had thought, ended the threat but Captain Edward's words were a warning that we no longer had a ring of steel around Wales. The north, along the Clwyd and the coast were ringed with castles and the south was fortified against rebellion but here…

When we neared Poole I was pleased with the way the walled manor now looked. The towers were no longer raw and new. They looked to be an integral part of the defences. The men who stood on each side of the gates wore livery and it was a sign that there was a warrior's hand at the helm. I knew that at my manor of Balden, Will would not need guards on his gates. My son-in-law at Wooferton would not have such sentries but here at Poole and at my hall we did.

The towers had given Sir John and Lady Hawise warning that we were on our way and when the wagon creaked to a halt in the yard they were waiting. Iago had servants ready and after the ladies and my granddaughters had been helped from the wagon, then it was unloaded.

Until they married this was still the hall of Lady Hawise and it was she who spoke, "Carwen and Rhys will take your sons to the merchants with whom they will be staying. It will only be at night for we have food for you here. You are our honoured guests."

Mary knew the problems of hosting so many and she said, "I hope we will not inconvenience you. Sir John's family will require rooms."

Sir John spoke, "It is just my father and youngest brother Alan who will be attending. There is not a problem."

Mary asked, "Your mother?"

"She died last year, and my father still grieves. We hope that this wedding will lighten his heart." He put his arm around Lady Hawise, "He has yet to meet this lovely lady."

Aware that we were standing in the open Lady Hawise said, "Come, let us go within. Carwen and Rhys, wait with Master Hamo and Master Jack, escort them back here when they are settled into their rooms." The young girl had blossomed into a woman in the months since Shrewsbury Castle. I had known that she and Sir John were meant for each other and now I saw the evidence with my own eyes.

As we entered the hall Mary, who was seeing it for the first time, saw the defensive ditch and the solid door. She squeezed my arm, "I can see your hand here, husband."

"Aye, but Sir John has made a good start. I am content."

"As you should be. King Edward, old Longshanks, would have approved. His son may not care one way or another but you are a man with a conscience."

"Perhaps such a good deed might make up for things I regret in my past."

"I know little of your life before you met me in the desert but from what I have been told, your life has been a good one."

I said nothing for while I did not regret a single thing that I had done I knew that I had sinned, and when the final reckoning came God would weigh the good against the bad. In the years I had left I was determined to do as much as I could to tip the scales in my favour.

Chapter 14

Sir John and Lady Hawise were keen to thank me for what I had done for them. The dining table was laden with food that should have graced the wedding feast. I felt humbled for I was toasted, along with my sons and men, so many times that I found myself flushing with embarrassment. They praised me and I was not used to such words. When I had served the old king he had just taken it for granted that I would do what I had done. It was a joyous feast but the fact that my sons and their families had to leave to sleep elsewhere meant that, as the sun set and before the gates were closed and barred, the party ended for them. Sir John and Lady Hawise, however, did not want the night to end. Breffni helped Iago and his wife to clear the table. Robert and Dai excused themselves and there were just the four of us sat before a cheery fire. We did not need the heat from the fire but there is something about an empty grate and hearth that looks and feels sad. The fire was there for reassurance that all was well.

The two ladies sat on a comfortable settle and chatted. Lady Hawise's mother had died when she was young and I think that Mary was just what she needed. That the two got on as well as they did, did not surprise me but they looked more like mother and daughter than two ladies who had just met for the first time. Their heads bobbed closely together making them look like two caged songbirds chattering away. It allowed Sir John and I to speak. We were relaxed and open with one another.

"How do you like your new home, Sir John?"

"You made some sound improvements, Sir Gerald, and for that I thank you."

I nodded but saw beneath the words, "But it is not enough, is it? You need a castle."

He looked relieved, "Aye, there you have it. Hawise's father had permission from King Edward and there is no legal bar to build. When I came here I saw that there is nothing to stop the Welsh, should they grow belligerent, from taking this manor." He glanced over to his wife to be and then lowered his voice, "Her uncles are recruiting men. The return of Piers Gaveston has emboldened them for they know that the eyes of the king will not be on this border. Gilbert de Clare and the Mortimers are at court. Each side seeks to gain favour with the king. Gaveston does that. I know the man well for I was with the king a long time. He is a malignant influence on our ruler."

"War will come then?" Sir John had information to which I was not privy and it was to be heeded.

"It will."

I nodded and sipped the heavy dessert wine he had served, "And a castle takes time to build, not to mention money."

"That it does but I have gold both in my own right and from my father who has promised to help fund my new castle. Lady Hawise has gold too but until we recover all of her lands it may not be enough."

I was thinking beyond the mere decision to build, "And once you begin to build then Lady Hawise's uncles will know. They will seek to destroy you before you are secure."

He nodded and smiled, "I can talk to you, Sir Gerald. I do not feel that I can burden my bride with such talk."

"Lady Hawise is stronger than you know, Sir John. She is like my Mary and I share my fears with her."

"Perhaps." He gave a sad smile as he glanced lovingly at his young wife to be, "I wake each day and wonder if this is a dream. That such a beauty as Hawise should wish to be my wife seems fantastical to me. Why did she choose me?"

"Because you are a good man and you deserve this. Sometimes, oft times in my view, Fate determines such things."

He gave me a steady stare, "Is that not blasphemous?"

"Robert my healer was a priest and he thinks not."

We drank in silence and I saw Sir John studying Hawise. He went to refill our goblets. I waited until he returned and said, "You need to take the war to the uncles."

"Begin the war? Do I have the right?"

"As soon as you are married then Lady Hawise has the legal right to all of her lands and properties. Once you are the lord of the manor then write to the uncles and ask them to quit the lands that rightfully belong to Lady Hawise. When you do that the law is on your side. You can begin to build the castle and to ensure you have the means to defend it."

"I do not have the army to do so."

"You have more men than you know for my three manors will go to war with you."

I saw his eyes widen, "There is no need, Sir Gerald, you have done more than enough already."

I knew that when Lady Hawise's brother had been slain, in line of duty, it had set in place events that could not be undone. They were leading me to war. It was not a war of my choosing but nor was it a war from which I could walk away. I had started this and I needed to finish it. "I began this journey and it is a poor knight who quits before it is done."

He drank again and then said, "My brother, Thomas, is not here but he let me know that the king plans to go to war against the Scots. It may be after the next Parliament. You may need your men for that conflict."

"And that is not until the end of October. By the time a decision is made it will be a new year and you do not make war in Scotland until May at the earliest. I have fought there and know that precipitous aggression ends in disaster. We have ten months to secure this land and to begin work on your castle." He nodded. I asked, "Do you have a site picked out? This is not a good place for a castle."

"Aye, Sir Gerald, tomorrow the women will be busy with the last of the preparations. They do not need a nervous bridegroom worrying about tiny details. What say we ride abroad and I can show you the site? I would appreciate the advice both of you and your sons."

"Of course, and do not forget Robert. He may have been a priest but I have never known a mind as sharp as his."

He smiled, "He is a good man and he seems to dote on my future wife."

Was there the hint of suspicion in his voice and eyes? I shook my head, "Robert is a kind man and, to all intents and purposes, a priest. He will do all in his power to ensure that Lady Hawise is happy. He shows affection for all strong women." I saw the relief on his face and knew that I had said the right thing. When we had ridden back from Canterbury I realised that Sir John was unused to the ways of love. That he and the lady had planned a wedding so quickly showed me that higher powers were involved.

After we retired and Mary and I lay in bed, she said, "I can see why Robert and Sir John fell in love with Hawise. She would enchant any man. She has the face of an angel but within her is the spirit of a warrior."

"I knew that you would get on." I heard her contented breathing. "I should tell you that I think her family will fight to destroy her." She said nothing but I knew that she had heard me, "I advised Sir John to make war first. If we strike then we might be able to save this manor from suffering."

She was silent for a moment and then she said, "You said we and that means our sons and you will be going to war."

"Do you not think that this is a better quest than the Great Cause?"

I heard her sigh in the dark, "It is but you are no longer a young man. Our sons can do this, for Sir John seems to me a leader."

Warbow

I laughed a dry laugh, "I may be old but this war bow is not yet broken." She laughed in the dark, "Besides, Sir John is a leader but he is not the Warbow. This grey flecked hair knows how to win and I want to win for this couple deserve nothing less."

The next morning Sir John and I summoned our men. His squire, Hugh of Gainsborough, had been the son of an old friend of Sir John's. A youth still, he looked to have the potential to be trained as a knight's squire. Sir John had acquired him whilst Hugh was still young and he had yet to learn bad habits. Our two archers and men at arms came with us along with Dewi and Ifan. The choice of Ifan was only because he was the better rider although the hill pony he rode made him seem almost dwarf like next to us. Even my grandsons rode bigger horses. We went armed but the reason was because we were riding to the west and that was the heartland of Lady Hawise's uncles.

Dai said, as we rode, "But, my lord, as it is less than two miles to our destination surely we are safe from harm?"

Dewi said, "Dai the Rock, you may be right but Arwen and I have scouted this part of the manor with Sir John and we saw the prints of shod horses. They were not ours." He left it at that but my experienced men knew what he meant. If there were hoofprints and they could be seen then it meant men had ridden over open ground. It suggested danger.

Sir John rode next to his men and my sons and their sons were just behind. The three archers had strung bows and they were watchful. It gave me the chance, as we approached the site, to inspect the ground in terms of a castle. A small river ran east to west and it was to the north of the rising ground that was the castle site. The Severn ran north to south and it was to the east of the ground. The natural features gave protection on two sides. I liked that. The ground, although it rose, looked as though it would not present too many difficulties in terms of building the castle and there was plenty of rock close to hand. It would save both on the cost and the transportation of the blocks needed for the building of the castle.

"King Edward the 1st gave my wife's late father permission to rebuild the castle in stone." I think he said that for the benefit of Robert who had a wax tablet hanging from his saddle. He was here as one who would give architectural advice. It was one thing to build in wood but a stone castle involved far more.

That was important. The Anarchy had made English kings cautious about allowing castles to be built. I nodded, "I remember now. There was a wooden castle here but Llywelyn ap Gruffudd destroyed it." I turned in the saddle to look back towards Poole, "Do you intend to use the same site?"

"It makes sense. The first castle was built by the Prince of Powis, Owain Cyfeiliog. That was more than a hundred years ago but he would have chosen the best place. We may be able to use the foundations." I saw the hesitation and he went on, "I would appreciate your advice on the matter, Sir Gerald."

"I have never built a castle, although I have attacked them enough times. What I would say is that while I can advise about the defence it is the comfort that will be most important for Lady Hawise. There will be children and they need to be safe."

Hamo piped up, "We were attacked at Yarpole, Sir John, as well as Luston. It cost us good men to learn how to build something we could defend and which was comfortable."

We reined in and looked up at the site. It ran northeast to southwest and I could see that it was steep sided.

He began to dismount, "It is better if we leave our horses here, Sir John."

I nodded, "Archers, watch our horses and keep an eye on the road."

"Yes, Sir Gerald."

The road that ran along the Severn lay just a short distance from us. Lady Hawise's uncles lived further west but the road led to their homes.

I said, "Dewi, was this where you found the hoofprints?"

"Yes, my lord."

My grandsons scampered up the slope like spring lambs but I took it steadily. That was not just age, I wanted to spy out the land. Rock peered out from beneath rough grazing. Scrubby bushes and weeds proliferated but there were no trees. I viewed the site as I would a castle to be assaulted. The natural obstacle was the steep slope. It would make it hard for a ram. While the rock would make the digging of foundations hard it would also make the digging of a mine equally difficult. When we reached the top I saw the blackened remains of the wooden castle. They helped me to see what Owain Cyfeiliog had in mind when he had built it. He had used the natural contours to build an oval outer wall. The keep had been at the western end.

It was Robert who, after scampering around the burnt out remains of the wooden castle, made the first suggestion, "I can see what was intended with the first wooden castle but if you are to have a home that could protect your family and also give shelter to your people, you need to make one which is much bigger." He looked at Sir John, "That would be the intention, would it not, Sir John?"

Warbow

The knight smiled, "I confess that I had only thought of my family but Poole is more of a town than a village and its people might need to be defended. Yes, Robert the Healer, it should have a bailey that is big enough to house the people of Poole."

"Then, my lord, let us use nature." As he spoke he pointed, "Straight walls might look all well and good but a curved wall that follows the contours of the land can be just as easy to build. We do as the first builder did but make it bigger. The well is at the western end and that needs the keep. We make the outer wall a long oval. We put a good gatehouse at the eastern end and the keep on the western end. We can use this relatively flat piece of ground for the outer bailey. See how the land rises, there," he pointed, "that is where you build the gatehouse to the inner bailey. This would, perforce, be much smaller but if you just used it for your accommodation, the kitchens and barracks then it would suffice."

I said, "And the horses?"

"In the outer bailey. Their stalls would give strength to the walls and it is large enough for all the buildings necessary to help a strong castle function."

I saw Sir John visualising what he had been told. I said, "Prudhoe Castle in Northumberland also uses a linear plan, Sir John, but it does not enjoy a piece of rising ground as large as this one. Windsor, too, uses an oval site."

Hamo was a practical man and he said, "And that is where your problem lies. The building of such a magnificent castle would take time, not to mention money."

Sir John said, "This is going to be a legacy. I want this to be a refuge for our descendants. We cannot know what the future holds but if Sir Gerald and his men had not come to the aid of Lady Hawise then the hall in Poole would have fallen. We cannot risk another disaster of that magnitude. As for cost? It is only money and when we have recovered all Lady Hawise's lands then we shall have enough income to build two such castles."

We spent an hour making plans and Robert used his wax tablet to make notes and to sketch the site. I said, "There must be masons who reside in Poole. Better to pay local men to build the castle than pay for men from England who might charge a fortune and not produce such a good job."

"There are such men and I had already planned to do so." He smiled, "Come, let us go back. The ladies will be fretting over us. This has given me an appetite. Thank you, Robert, your suggestions were good ones."

"So long as Lady Hawise and yourself are comfortable and safe then I am happy."

I knew the significance of his words but Sir John merely beamed and put his arm around my confessor. "You are the best of fellows."

When we reached the three archers who had moved the horses to the side of the road where there was some decent grazing, we mounted. Jack pointed at the stand of trees that lay next to the road some two hundred paces from us, "The timber from those trees could be used in the building and the removal of them makes men travelling on the road easier to see."

It might have been Jack's words, I know not, but as we all looked towards the trees Iago shouted, "I see men there, my lord!"

We were already mounted and I said, "Hugh, Dai and Robert, watch the boys!"

We galloped. That it could be something innocent never crossed our minds. If it proved to be men gathering firewood then we would have merely had some exercise for us and our mounts. That was unlikely if they had horses. When we spied the horses and men mounting them then we knew that there was danger here. The men did not ride along the road. Instead they took off through the woods. It meant we could not truly ascertain their numbers and made identification of them all but impossible. I might have been the oldest rider but I had the best horse and Thunder began to outstrip the others. Even Sir John's hackney was struggling to keep up with me. I knew that most archers could stay on a horse and that was, probably, the limit to their skill but I had ridden a horse across the Persian desert. I had evaded Turkish horsemen and I knew how to ride. I had realised that to be a good rider you had to be fearless and to trust your horse. The men we were following probably expected me to slow when we entered the woods but I did not. The momentum I had built up swept me through the thin branches. My hands guided Thunder as though they belonged to another. I did so instinctively. I kept his head fixed on the tail I could see occasionally flicking through the undergrowth. When I saw the man's back then I knew that I was gaining. I counted three more horses ahead and I assumed that each one had a rider. The riders were all lying as flat as they could to gain speed. It meant it was hard to identify the men.

The wood proved not to be as long as I had expected for I saw it thinning and one of the men turned to look behind him. I spied a bearded man and I recognised that he had a leather jack. He was a soldier. I guessed that he was an archer for as I closed with him I saw that he had a broad back and a leather bow case slung from his saddle. It explained why I was catching him. It was a combination of inferior horse, a bow case which unbalanced the man and poor riding skills. He was dropping back and the others were getting away. They headed for the road and I knew that we had just one chance to catch one of them and that was the archer at the back. The thunder of my horse's hooves as we struck the stone of the road made the man turn in fear. I drew my sword as he did so. I was just forty paces from him. I have a good sword. Some men call it a bastard sword or a hand and a half sword. It was not. The sword had been made specifically for me by my blacksmith and both the weight and feel suited me well. It must have looked enormous to the man who tried to urge his horse to go faster. The hoof went into a depression and as the horse's shoulder dropped the rider lost his stirrups and sailed over the horse's head and neck. I heard the crack as his head hit the stones. I began to rein in. The other men were too far away to catch now.

I dismounted and walked over but I could see that his skull had been crushed like an egg. Bone, brains and blood oozed slowly from it. Jack reached me first and I pointed, "Get his horse."

I handed my reins to Hamo and searched the man. His purse had few coins in it. His dagger was that of an archer. It was a bodkin that would be perfect for slipping through the eyehole of a helmet. His sword was a short one. I took the bow from its case. It was a war bow. His arrow bag, however, only contained war arrows. There were no bodkins.

Sir John dismounted, "Sir Gerald, you put us to shame."

"I have a good horse and I can ride."

When Dewi reined in he looked down at the body and said, "I know that archer. He was a nasty little man, Madog of Harlech."

As Jack led the horse back I said, "Where did you know him from?"

"Before I went to Ireland he came to seek work with our company of archers. The captain of archers did not like him. I believe he went to serve another."

"Not in Ireland."

"No, when Captain James rejected him, for he knew him of old, the others refused to take him on. That is why I remember him so well. Other archers said, as we crossed to Ireland, that he was an assassin and killer of men. We all kill men in war. That is our trade but Madog was paid to kill men by sending arrows into their backs."

Hamo said, "I have heard of such men. I cannot understand it. There is honest work for archers who seek it."

I said, "The question is, who hired him?"

Sir John said, "I think, Sir Gerald, that there is an obvious answer, the de la Poles and their presence here, close to my land with my wedding day imminent, means that we have to take precautions."

Dewi said, "My lord, your men can watch this road. I will have four men watching here. We will relieve them every day. I will tell David of Abergele and we will be doubly vigilant at the hall."

After draping the body over the horse we rode slowly back on the road. There was no point in exhausting our horses. Sir John said, "This has decided me, Sir Gerald. When September comes we will hunt the de la Poles and put an end to this. We cannot live our lives looking over our shoulders."

"You are right and I shall bring men to aid you."

We could not hide the body and the ladies waited for us in the Great Hall after we had taken it to be buried with the other killers outside the walls of Poole graveyard. As we walked through the doors Sir John said, "You are the married man, how do we tell the ladies what happened?"

"Simple, we tell the truth. I know that they are all strong women. They will not faint or take fright."

It was Sir John's task to tell the others of the danger. I stood back and it was as I did so that I realised I would soon be allowing the people like Hamo and Jack, the ones I normally commanded, to make decisions for themselves. The time of the Warbow was almost over. When I brought my men to fight for Sir John and Lady Hawise I would have to allow Hamo and Jack to make more decisions. I had a duty to train them so that when I was gone they could continue as I had done. When I had been a solitary archer, Lord Edward's Archer, my life had been simple. I fought for the king. The ride across the sands and the meeting with Mary had changed my life. I was now a different person.

I was proved right. There were no tears. The four women all stiffened slightly and then Hawise smiled, "If my uncles think that they can take what is rightfully mine they will learn that the lamb now has a sheepdog to guard her." She smiled and held Sir John's hand. Mary looked at me and nodded.

The rest of Sir John's family, his father and brother, arrived that evening. We all dined in the hall but this time it was Sir John's father and brother who were the centre of attention as they got to know the young woman who had stolen Sir John's heart.

The wedding was a splendid one. That there were neither kings nor bishops did not detract from the ceremony for the people who mattered, Sir John's father and brother, Lady Hawise's people and my family were there and all had dressed as though the king himself was being wed. David of Abergele and the guards were the only ones absent. They would be rewarded with a feast of their own but that would have to wait until the day after when my men would take over. My archers also watched for they understood the danger better than anyone.

For my part I was nervous, for I was standing in for the Prince of Powis but I was also proud that I had been chosen and with Lady Hawise on my arm, it felt like I was standing next to one of my daughters. Perhaps I was prouder of Lady Hawise than my daughters. Both my daughters had enjoyed relatively easy lives whereas Lady Hawise had been incarcerated and abused by her own family. When I handed her over to Sir John I felt as though I was truly giving away a great gift, a precious jewel, but I knew that Sir John would cherish and polish that jewel. All that we had to do was to prevent Hawise's uncles and the other vultures that they would gather to feast on the treasure that was Lady Hawise and her people.

Lady Hawise had hired musicians for she wanted a celebration. There were too many people to be housed in the hall and as the weather was clement the feast was held outside the hall in the courtyard, swept clean and well decorated by Iago and his people. There was dancing and there were songs. Dai amused the guests with some of his jokes and impressions. He did not repeat his impression of me but the one he did of the old man walking home, with a stick, drunk from the tavern, was a little too close to reality for my liking. I did not dance. It was nothing to do with my status it was just that I had never learned. Hamo was like me but Jack did dance and Robert surprised us all, for when my wife complained about my reluctance to dance he offered to take my place, and he enchanted her and everyone else with his skills. I later learned that when he had lived at home his father had insisted that he learn all the skills necessary for a squire.

While Robert and Jack danced I sat with Hamo. It was a party but we were both practical men. There was danger and we had to be prepared. I waved my hand at the guests who were seated at the benches enjoying the ale and the wine. "You know, Hamo, that there must be people there who support Lady Hawise's uncles."

He studied the faces, "Then they are good at dissembling, Father. I have seen nothing but love and affection since we arrived."

"As have I but I know people. The odds on everyone in Poole being a supporter of Lady Hawise and her new husband are not good. It is likely that there will be one or two who will report to Gruffydd Fychan de la Pole, his brothers and his half-brothers, perhaps in the hopes of a reward if they should take over. They may not be spies as such but they may report on the progress of the building of the castle. Those men we found were too far away to be able to report about the defences of Poole." I saw his face as he realised that what I said was true. I nodded, "The archer was an assassin. Dewi told us that. He was there to kill Sir John."

Hamo shook his head, "That is a guess."

"But a good one. Sir John told us that he had visited the site before. They would be expecting him to return and they could wait. I have seen, first hand, the patience of assassins. The one who tried to kill The Lord Edward in Acre was like a spider. He climbed a high wall and entered a guarded chamber through the narrowest of openings. I cannot imagine how long it took him. The men who ambushed the king on the Canterbury road waited in a cold wood in the depths of winter to try to kill him. The four men we saw had summer evenings and the protection of the wood. If we had not been with him who would have gone to inspect the site?"

"Probably David and Dewi."

"The killer would have slain Sir John and the other three would have eliminated Dewi and David. This day and this marriage mean that Lady Hawise's uncles have lost. There is now a lord of the manor here. I daresay that sometime in the next couple of days someone will leave Poole and report to the de la Poles." I supped some wine, "Or it may be that a traveller passes through and while they water their horse then information will be exchanged." I let the words sink in. "When we travel home we will be in more danger than when we rode here. This is the second time I have thwarted them. They see me as an old man, a dangerous old man but an old one, nonetheless. If they can get rid of me and my sons then Sir John will be alone."

"That could not happen but, even if it did, then our men would have vengeance."

I emptied my goblet, "And that is the difference between me and Lady Hawise's uncles. They have to hire mercenaries. We have men who are brothers in arms. I know we are expected to stay here for some days after the wedding but believe me I would rather leave tomorrow. Each day we remain gives our enemies more chance to plan and to plot."

Chapter 15

Sir John's father and brother left for their home the next day. I had found both of them to be pleasant men but I had spoken at length to them, and neither was what one might call a warrior. I had never seen Sir John's father in the various campaigns. They watched over their people but did not go to war. If Sir John was going to have aid it would have to come from Poole itself and my men. After they had departed we rode, once more, to the site of the new castle. Sir John's sentries had seen no one while we had feasted. Perhaps the death of the killer had upset their plans. While the ladies helped Lady Hawise's people put the hall back into some semblance of order, we began to lay out the markers for the foundations. It was another reason for us to stay. Robert made a groma and made sure that the foundations would be laid in the right place. He had spent, in the days before the wedding, some time drawing the plan that Sir John would follow when he and his people built the castle that would protect Poole and become the fortress of Powis.

Sir John was in unknown territory. He had never built a castle and while we had never built a castle we had built walls and defences to protect our homes. We knew what was needed and we knew how to build. We understood the need for deep and wide foundations so that the keep, especially, could be built on solid foundations. We knew how to make outer and inner walls with good blocks and filled with infill. Such work did not need masons. Their skill would come when the foundations had been dug and filled with rough stones. They would be needed to carve the better blocks of stone and the placing of doorways, lintels and hearths. That would not be until after the winter.

While Robert, aided by Dai, laid out the foundations I sat, on the high point of what would be the castle, with Sir John and my sons. "This will cost you and your wife gold, Sir John." I saw the smile when I used the word wife. "You can use it to your advantage. The people who build the castle for you will be paid and that is like an investment. They will feel part of the castle and part of the manor. No man likes to see his handiwork torn down. The blood and sweat of you and your builders will be in the very foundations of the castle. That is a good thing. If you use local men then you are doubly rewarded."

Hamo said, "But you will need men here watching while you build for your enemies may cause mischief."

He nodded, "And how do I reconcile this building with your advice to take the war to my enemies?"

"Now it is high summer. Your farmers will be busy until September. Use the long days for those who are not farmers, your masons and carpenters, to do as much as they can. This is Powis, Sir John. Once the winter comes there will be no building. Mortar needs heat and not cold. The work will have to cease once November comes. That gives your people October to complete as much of the work as they can. I will return in September with my warriors. Until we go to war then the men I bring can help the people of Poole." I pointed to Robert, "We leave Robert here to supervise your people and we attack the de la Poles. We need to bring them to battle."

"You want a battle?" I heard the surprise in his voice at my choice of words.

I smiled, "In my experience if we can win one battle then the war will be over before it began. We had the Battle of Lewes won until Prince Edward tried to chase the enemy from the battlefield. We learned our lesson and at Evesham the king ensured that de Montfort was taken. He cut the head of the snake. If we have a battle and win then we can make terms and force your enemies to give up the lands that they have taken. We do what King Edward did and we take the enemy leaders, your wife's uncles."

"You think that you can win?"

Hamo answered for me, "My father will win but men will die, Sir John. They will be your men and they will be ours. War is not the place for the faint hearted."

I said, "Nor am I arrogant enough to think that just because Warbow goes to war that he will win. Before we return you will need to have men find out where your foes are to be found. Just as they have spies watching us so you will have spies watching them."

He looked around as though there were men close by, "Spies?"

I said, "Remember the tavern at Rochester, Sir John."

He nodded, "Then I need to make sure that I have enough men to fight for Poole."

Jack said, "Sir Gerald makes a point of speaking to the warriors who will fight. You have your men at arms and they, along with your archers, will be the cutting edge of your retinue but you need stout men with spear and shield who can stand resolutely and defend your standard. They will not be warriors, at least not yet, but, in my experience, they can be made into men who can fight. You will need a shield wall of determined men. We have found that such men can defeat enemies who come to steal and take."

My stepson made a good point and I reinforced his words, "And remember, Sir John, your enemies have already shown their reliance on mercenaries and what I would call bandits. Such men will desert the cause once we have taken their leaders."

Sir John shook his head, "And you have planned this already? You have a battle plan?"

I smiled, "When Gruffydd Fychan de la Pole attacked this hall the last time he kept himself out of harm's way. It is that weakness that gives me hope. No matter how many men we face, their Achilles heel is the lack of steel in men like Gruffydd Fychan de la Pole. I have not yet met his brothers and half-brothers but if they hire men like Madog of Harlech, then I have their measure. Your task is to get as much work done on this castle as you can and train your men. I will have my people here by the end of the first week in September."

He nodded, "Then I am resolved and I will do all in my power not to let you down."

I smiled, "It is Poole and Lady Hawise who need your resolve, my lord. I am just here to help."

That we stayed a week longer than I intended was not the fault of Sir John or the needs of the castle survey, it was the ladies who had got on so well that my family did not wish to leave. My granddaughters had also fallen under the spell of Lady Hawise. I was forced to be assertive and commanded them. It did not go down well and you would have thought that I was an ogre.

Our parting saw tears from the ladies. That my family had been popular was evident from the parting. There were smiles and waves as my wagon passed through Poole on its way back to England. My daughters-in-law were unhappy to be leaving. Lady Hawise and her ladies were good people and I understood their sadness. The two assiduously avoided speaking with me. If they thought their silence punished me then they did not know me. I did not mind for I had much to discuss with my sons. "I know I have committed us to a course of action which may well result in suffering. Men who fight cannot tend fields and men who go to war can be hurt or killed. If either of you …"

I got no further. Hamo said, "Father this is the right thing to do. Our wives are close to Lady Hawise and her people. If we did nothing then it would hang over us like a spectre at the feast. This is not like fighting for a piece of land in Scotland because a king wishes it, this is defending the right of a young woman who has been betrayed by her family. We are both happy to go to war with you for this is a just cause." He smiled, "It is not the Great Cause but, to my mind, a better one."

"Good, then have your men at arms and archers help the people to gather in the harvest. It will mean long hours. When we muster I want only warriors. Sir John can summon his fyrd. It is their land that they defend and they can provide the numbers but we will be the edge of the sword that cleaves the enemy in twain. You, Hamo, will lead the archers."

"And will you be using a bow?"

I shook my head, "I could but I think that God has selected me for this task because of my mind and military experience. I shall be helmed and mailed. Jack, you will command the men at arms, I suspect that Sir John's retinue will be our mounted element. I want our men at arms to fight on foot. This may well come down to a bloody slog for I suspect that, even though we begin this war before they are fully prepared, as they have at least four leaders each with a retinue, not to mention mercenaries, then we will be outnumbered. Until we know where we fight I can do no more planning. You both need to have the men fight as a shield wall. I will have Michel do the same. Our block of sergeants may well surprise the enemy. I am Warbow and they will expect archers but well-trained sergeants at arms might come as a shock."

We made what was intended to be a brief stay at Hopton Castle. Lady Hopton insisted upon feeding my ladies. Before I could join them Captain Edward took me to one side, "My lord, a word."

His demeanour suggested something serious and I went with him. Robert made to follow but I waved him away. The Captain of Hopton Castle led me to the top of the gatehouse. He pointed to the road which we would be taking. It ran south from the castle. There was a small stream which the road crossed and it went south too. "That is the road you will be taking, my lord."

I nodded, "It is the road to Yarpole, aye." I knew he had more to say and I waited for his words.

He moved his arm to point at the thick wood which lay just half a mile south. He said, "Hopton Forest, there is good hunting in there for the forest extends from that stream five miles or more to the west. Yesterday, about dusk, one of my lads, Stephen, heard horses coming down the road. Lady Hopton had warned the men that you might be returning and that she wanted to be informed so the lads were keeping a good watch. It was after dark and James, the sentry, said to Stephen that he did not think that you would arrive in the dark. They said that riders, hooded and cloaked, ten of them, passed by. They heard the sound of their hooves as they clattered over Hopton Bridge. He said he thought he saw crossbows hanging from the saddles but, in the dark, he could not be sure. The riders did not stop."

"And you think that they might represent a danger?"

"My lord, you asked me to watch for strangers. These were strangers and men with nothing to hide do not ride cloaked in August. The days are long enough so that men need not travel at night. These men chose to ride in the dark." He smiled, "Call me a suspicious old curmudgeon, if you like, but if I rode from here after a fine meal and with ale in my belly, I might be relaxed and not fear what lay in those trees. You were seen entering the castle. It may be I am wrong, my lord, and the men carried on but…"

"You are right and let us act as though there are killers waiting along the road." I liked Captain Edward and I put my arm around his shoulder. "Captain, I have a plan but I need your help."

He grinned, "Whatever you wish, my lord."

"First I should like to meet your archers."

My wife was surprised not only that I did not join her for food but also that I allowed them to eat for so long. "Did you not want food, husband?"

"I was not hungry and Captain Edward found something of interest." As we loaded the wagon I said, "I shall not be with you, my love, Morgan the archer here will ride Thunder. I have explained all to Hamo."

Morgan looked at my wife. He gave a smile and said, "I am honoured to serve Sir Gerald Warbow, my lady."

Her eyes widened, "Sir Gerald Warbow, you are an old fool. What is it that you do?"

"Mayhap, nothing. It could well be that I am just going to enjoy a stretching of the legs to no good purpose, but I would rather that than risk my family coming to harm." I turned to Hamo, "You know what to do?"

He nodded, "Aye, Father, but I would rather Morgan was pretending to be me."

"The men who wait must believe that I am still with the wagon and, besides, I have to be the one who orders arrows to be sent into the backs of men, not you." I knew that if Captain Edward was right, and I believed he was, then that would be what it would come to; ambush the killers and send arrows into their backs.

Hamo and Jack would make a grand show of leaving. It would allow Captain Edward and I to lead the six men at arms and three archers out of the small sally port in the outer wall. From there it was a mere two hundred paces to the edge of the wood. I had my bow strung. My archers had wanted to come with me but I told them that if these were enemies waiting in ambush then they would know our numbers. They had to see the same number leaving Hopton as arrived. We hurried down the track that led to the trees. Captain Edward led and I followed. It was a hunter's trail and well worn. I had a pair of arrows ready in my hand. As

Warbow

I had given my cloak to Morgan I was unencumbered. He had been the archer whose size most resembled mine. With my hat upon his head and riding Thunder, he would only be identified when it was too late. I hoped that the killers would be dead before they saw that it was not Sir Gerald Warbow riding Thunder. I was relying on Captain Edward's local knowledge to find these would-be assassins before the wagon passed the killers. I believed him and his instincts. It made sense to me. We were now in England and anyone expecting to be ambushed would relax for we were no longer in Wales. We moved down the trail in silence. His men were keen for some action and this seemed like an adventure. Stephen had been confident of the numbers but not the weaponry.

In the distance we heard our wagon as it clattered over Hopton Bridge. That meant it had left the castle. We could not see it but as we had heard it I assumed that if anyone was waiting they would have heard it and their attention would be on the road and not the woods behind them. One of the younger spearmen, Alwyn, grabbed my arm and pointed. I looked through the trees at where he indicated and saw the swish of a tail. I touched Captain Edward's shoulder and pointed. He gestured at Alwyn and Stephen to go to the horses. I waved the men into a line. If the horses were close then the riders would be too. Captain Edward drew his sword and the three archers and I each nocked an arrow. I chose a bodkin. We had to leave the trail and that meant watching our feet. The last thing we needed was to step on a branch and break it. I could hear the wagon trundling down the road. They would be going as slowly as they could. My two archers would be twitching nervously for they would be twenty paces ahead of the wagon and it would be they who would trigger the ambush.

It was Captain James who spotted the men. I saw the devil's machine, the crossbow, in the hands of four of them. That told me they were mercenaries and not Welshmen. The archers and I would target them. We moved until they were just forty paces from us and did so stealthily. Captain Edward looked at me. What we were doing was almost murder. We would be loosing arrows into the backs of men. In answer to the look from the old sergeant at arms I raised my bow and the other three emulated me. I took a breath and drew back. I would be the first to loose and an archer did not hold at the full draw for more than a heartbeat. I drew and released. The other three did so too. To my horror, although I struck one of the crossbowmen, two of Captain Edward's archers had aimed at the same man. It meant one man was free to release his weapon. Even as I nocked another arrow and Captain Edward led the men at arms to charge I heard the crack of the last crossbow. My arrow ended the life of the man who had sent his bolt at my family. It smacked into the skull of the crossbowman. Dropping my war bow I drew my sword and I ran. This was sword work now.

I heard an English voice shout, "Warbow is dead! Our work is done. Flee."

The men ran. I heard hooves as my archers and men at arms charged up the road. I heard the clash of steel from the woods behind me and shouts of pain as Captain Edward's men dealt with the horse holders. A figure ran towards me and almost blindly I slashed my sword at the man wearing the leather jack with an old-fashioned helmet and nasal who tried to hack at my head with his sword. I still held an arrow in my left hand and as I blocked his sword with my own weapon, sending sparks into the air, I rammed the arrow up into his skull. When I heard horses behind me I knew that some of the attackers had escaped and I was angry.

The man with mail who ran towards me was clearly the leader and had to be the one who had thought me dead. He had an open-faced helmet and I saw the surprise on his face when he saw me, "You!"

I wanted him alive so that I could have confirmation of his employers. He drew his dagger and I drew mine. He was intent on killing me and had more skill than the man I had slain. His sword came down and I blocked it with mine. They rang together. I sensed, rather than saw, the dagger which came at my unprotected middle. He wore mail and I did not. I blocked it and instead of sending another blow at him I used my arm to force his sword arm down.

"Yield."

He had a look of incredulity on his face, "You are an archer!"

My pride had brought us to this moment and his pride led to what happened next. He tried to push up and his feet were clearly not correctly placed, nor was he balanced. He thought he could beat me because he was a trained swordsman. He lost his footing and fell. I, too, lost my balance. As I fell my sword landed across his throat. I tried to stop the sword's descent but I failed. The blood spurted and he was dead. I had failed. I began to pull myself up. Hamo, Jack, Jean Michel and John galloped up through the trees. I pointed behind me, "They had horses." The four chased after them.

I hurried to the horse lines and found Stephen and Alwyn had both been wounded. Stephen said, "Sorry, my lord, we failed you." Their wounds were not serious but they had allowed some of those who might have given us vital information to escape.

"Robert!" I needed my healer. I looked at the young man, "I let you all down. This is hubris. I thought I was being cleverer than my enemies and you have suffered hurts."

Robert, Dai and, to my surprise, Mary also ran towards us.

I shouted, "What are you thinking, Mary, get back to the wagon!"

She said, sadly, "The man who was you, Morgan, is dead. I wanted no more men of Hopton to die because my husband thinks he is immortal."

She was right. It was all my fault.

My horsemen rode in and Hamo shook his head, "They have escaped."

I helped the others to search the bodies for clues. They were clearly mercenaries. They had a variety of coins in their purses as well as weapons and clothes that were not English. None of them had a fortune in their purses but they had more than any of my warriors would carry. Their leader, however, had been English. His dress, his clothes, his weapons and his coins were all English.

We spent the night at the castle. Stephen and Alwyn would recover but the archer who had the misfortune to be the same size as me had paid the price and he had died. As we had headed back to the castle Captain Edward had said, "Old Morgan knew what he was doing. He could barely pull a bow any longer and he was drinking more than is good for a man. The other archers told me he had blood in his piss. He died a warrior and he died quickly." He shook his head, "His wife had warned him about his drinking but he liked his ale. By, but the man could drink."

I shook my head, "A man died for me and that is not right."

Everyone tried to make me feel better but six men had escaped and the only good news was that they thought they had killed Warbow. Eventually, they would discover their error but by then we would be back in Yarpole. I gave coins to have a stone carved for Morgan and paid for a good coffin. He had left a wife and a son. I promised that when we returned to Poole I would pay my respects at his grave.

Captain James and his men insisted on travelling with us as far as the hamlet of Bedstone. The journey was sombre, especially when we passed the place where the crossbow bolt, intended for me, killed Morgan the Archer. We left Jack and his family at Lucton and rode in silence to Yarpole. Hamo, aware of the time he had been away from his home, took the wagon and continued to Luston. I felt angry but I also felt guilty. Someone had died not only because of me but instead of me. Although it made me more determined than ever to rid Poole of the threat of the de la Poles, I also knew that men would die in the conflict. Could I live with that?

I was largely silent as we ate and both Dai and Robert left as soon as the food was finished.

Mary took my hand and led me to the settle where we could sit together. "Do you remember when I was a slave?"

"A lifetime ago."

"And yet in my head it is like yesterday. The Mongols treated me well but I was still a slave. I knew that my life could end on the whim of a khan or one of his wives. I accepted that and lived each day as though it was my last." She shook her head, "That is not easy when you are a slave. Once I came to England and we were married, I have tried to do the same. One worry I have endured for my whole married life was the thought of living without you. As much as I am sad that Morgan died, in the grand scheme of things, it is more important that you live. Lady Hopton told me about Morgan's illness. She said it was similar to the disease that took Sir Walter. That was a wasting disease that killed from within and made him shrivel. She had tears in her eyes when she spoke of him in the days before her husband died. His face turned to a colour that made him look not like a man but a misshapen creature. His eyes sank into his head and he was asleep more than when he was awake. The times he was awake he was in such pain that she wanted to make his suffering disappear by giving him poison to drink but she did not. She said that Morgan was spared all of that. She was not happy that he was dead but she was pleased that he was spared a painful and horrible end."

I stared at the flickering flames in the fire.

"Does that make you feel better?"

"No. I am pleased that he was spared a wasting disease but I know that others will die because of me."

"They will not die because of you!" She was assertive and her voice commanding. She softened her words and stroked my rough archer's hand with the delicate velvet touch of her fingers, "Men will die when you fight the de la Poles but if you are not there then more of Sir John's men will die. They are Lady Hawise's people and I know, better than any, that only you can stop more of them dying. If you want to blame anyone then blame the de la Poles, a vacillating king, a preening peacock of a favourite but do not blame yourself. Now let us retire and on the morrow plan for the harvest and what, I hope, will be a swift and successful campaign to secure the lands for Lady Hawise and Sir John."

My wife's words and a good night asleep in my own bed made me feel better. A man does not bemoan his fate. I would do what I had to do.

Warbow

I first spoke to my steward. "I need every person in the manor to help gather the harvest. In the last week of September I will take my archers and men at arms across the border to fight."

I saw John chew his lip, "Do you need the fyrd too, my lord?"

"No, but they will have to defend the manor. We both know, only too well, how those with malice in their hearts can prey on the ones they consider weak."

His eyes narrowed and there was steel in his voice, "Those days are many men's lifetimes ago. The manor and its people will be defended. You have my word."

"Good."

I then went to the smith. I took with me a bag of silver. "We need a thousand arrow heads, ten swords and twenty spearheads."

"You go to war, my lord."

"I go to war."

He nodded, "When do you need them?"

"By the last day in August."

"It shall be done, my lord."

I knew that my men at arms would have told others all that had happened and that Iago and Gruffydd would have done the same in the warrior hall. When I sent for them it was a much easier conversation for they were already prepared. What surprised me was the anger all my men felt. A crossbowman, that most hated of warriors to an archer and my men at arms, had tried to kill me. They would have left for war that day.

I shook my head when they asked to return immediately, "September is when we shall travel. Remember this, it will be the men of Yarpole, Lucton and Luston who will be at the fore. One day Sir John may have a retinue to rival mine but it is not yet. Let the men know that if any do not wish to fight for Sir John and Lady Hawise they can stay here."

Gwillim gave a snort of derision, "I know our men, my lord, not a one will choose that path. They will tread the way to war."

I was satisfied. "Michel, how stand we for horses?"

He shook his head, "Not enough to mount all the men and I doubt that your sons will have enough either."

Jean Michel said, "Then use the wagon." We all looked at him. "Sir Gerald, the archers only need the horses to get to the battle. They fight with the earth beneath their feet. They can travel in the wagon which can also be used on the battlefield. It protects as well as a shield and can give height for archers."

I looked at my archers who nodded their approval of the idea.

By the end of the day the strategy for departure was complete and each man knew what he had to do. Those like James and Jean Michel who had recently married would also find the leaving harder than the rest but were no less determined.

As I walked back to my hall, flanked by Michel and John, John asked, "What of Baron Mortimer? Will he fight alongside us? He hates the de la Pole family."

I shook my head, "He does not like me and I do not think he would help us but more, he seeks the land of Powis. He would try to not only defeat the de la Pole family but find some way to take the land from Lady Hawise. He is an ally we can do without."

Michel said, quietly, "And should you tell the king?"

"For once that is not a problem. Sir John served the king. Thomas, his brother, has high office at court. We fight with Sir John and his banner will lead."

Michel stopped, "But it is you who will decide how we fight, my lord."

I smiled, "Of course."

Warbow

- Poole
- Shrewsbury
- Dolforwyn Castle
- Caersws

N

- Hopton Castle
- Lueton
- Yarpole
- Luston

Griff 2025

6 miles

Chapter 16

August was the start of the harvest and all my people worked long hours. The days lasted far longer than they had in spring but once September came they would begin to grow much shorter. We gathered, we harvested and we stored. Animals were loosed onto freshly cleared fields to graze on what was left and to fertilise the fields. The crops that would be stored were placed where they would be dry. The dogs and the cats would prowl and protect them from the rodents who sought to feast on our bounty. Preparations were made to cull the animals. It would not take place until the end of September or, if the weather remained clement, October. Farmers identified the animals that were unlikely to survive the winter or those who would no longer produce either milk or young. All the time that my men were labouring at these tasks they were also preparing for war. Each day they would find some time to train or to make more arrows or simply to talk about war.

Dai was my charge. I had rarely employed a squire and it was satisfying to see how Dai had grown in the time he had been with us. He was now a youth and, if nothing else, could be my shield bearer. It was an old-fashioned term but, in Dai's case, a good choice. He would carry my shield and spare weapons into battle. He could plant my standard, if that was needed, and he was given a short sword with which to defend both me and the flag. I knew that if he had to fight to protect the standard then my strategy had gone awry. I hoped that my plans would go perfectly but as Lewes had shown, it often took one slip to turn a victory into a defeat. I quite enjoyed moulding the youth into a warrior. It took me back to the days on the Clwyd before I had joined the band of archers. That was when my father had shown me how to use a bow and then, because he was wise, how to use a sword. It had saved my life. It had also made me an outlaw but such things are not determined by mere mortals.

I spent an hour a day with Dai in weapon training. It was as much for me as him. The hot days of August meant I wore just a cambric shirt and breeches. Dai had his buckler and short sword. Few men used bucklers these days. The one I had given him was taken at Falkirk when William Wallace's dream of an independent Scotland had ended. The spearman who had used it to protect his hand while holding the long pike had died well. It seemed fitting that the small shield would be used again. While I wore just a cambric shirt Dai had a leather jack and helmet. The reason was not that I thought I might hurt him but he needed to become used to fighting with the restrictions of a helmet that would limit his vision and a jack that impaired his movements. I used just a blunted training sword and an old short sword. I did wear my gauntlets. I had found them to be invaluable. An archer who lost his fingers in a fight was no longer an archer.

"Balance yourself, Dai. Fighting with a sword is like a dance. You need to be light on your feet. I know that I am bigger than I once was and that I chose not to dance at the wedding but I dance like a prancing pony when I fight with a sword. It is as much about avoiding blows as striking your own. Swinging a sword tires a man." I chuckled, "I think that much of my success as a swordsman was because I am an archer and my arms do not tire as quickly as most men. Tire an opponent out and look for a weakness."

Dai looked puzzled, "A weakness, Sir Gerald?"

"Every man has one. There is no such thing as a perfect warrior. Often it is a weakness of nature. The height or shortness of a man can determine the outcome. Some men are arrogant or overconfident. Others will underestimate a youth like you. There will be warriors who have a weakness such as using the same blow and movement. My father did not train me as a swordsman but as a fighter. Even I do not know what blows I will use until I begin fighting. Men cannot predict how the Warbow will fight. Enough talk, let me see you hit me." I saw the hesitation and snapped, "Come, you will not hurt me and if you do then it is time I hung up my sword." To encourage him I smacked the short sword hard against the buckler. It hurt him.

He swung his sword in what we call a swashing blow. I flicked it away easily with the short sword and then hit his buckler with my sword. He reeled.

"Feet! Use your feet. I am a lumbering bear and you are a snapping terrier. Use your speed."

It took time but he learned, through dint of bruised arms and hands, to move faster. He never came close to hitting me but over that hour or so we sparred I hit him less and that was my intention. I was sweating when I decided to call a halt. "You did well, Dai."

He took off his helmet and shook his head, "I did not once land a blow of any moment, my lord."

I sat on the stump we used to split logs for kindling and wiped my head with a cloth, "Dai, I hope you survive the battle and to that end merely avoiding blows is all that matters. Besides, they will be coming for me. They will try to break the Warbow. That may be your chance to dart your sword and strike men who are trying to get to me."

He dipped his coistrel in the water trough and drew some water. He said, "Is that honourable?" He drank.

"Let me tell you now, Dai, that you should put all thoughts of honour from your mind. Nobles have that luxury, we do not. They can spare an opponent or yield themselves knowing that they will be ransomed. For most of my life I was an archer and the best I could have hoped from capture was being maimed. You hurt your enemy any way that you can and if you are able to kill then do so."

He nodded and reflected for a moment or two, "Is that not a sin?"

I sighed, "You are asking the wrong man. If you want moral or religious answers then speak to Robert. I confess before each battle but when arrows fall they will kill. Is that murder or is it war? Soldiers do not have the luxury to pick and choose who they kill. They fight to survive. Each man who fights for me hopes that they will be alive at the end of each battle and will have all their limbs intact."

He stood for Robert had emerged from the hall, "But if they are hurt you have a healer and if they are maimed you will care for them."

"Of course."

"Then I am lucky to serve a lord like you. With your permission, my lord, I will speak with Robert." He smiled, "He does not seem to mind my constant questions."

As he headed to speak to Robert I knew I had been lucky with the men who served me. I paid them but they were not mercenaries. If we fell on hard times and they could not be paid they would still fight and I knew that when we faced the de la Poles and their mercenaries, that might be the edge that would win the day.

When I entered the hall through the kitchen my wife shook her head, "My love you stink like a horse that has galloped too far."

"And you, my love, smell of rosemary and summer roses, yet you will still hold me."

Laughing she shook her head and said, "Not until you have bathed." She turned, "Anna, have a bath filled with hot water. Put some herbs in it."

I shook my head, "I will be training with Dai each day."

"Then, my husband, you will bathe each day!"

August raced by but every Sunday, when the men of the village and my soldiers trained together, I saw an improvement. The men of the village would not be going to war but they knew that when we left for Wales they would be the ones who would have to defend our homes. I think it made my soldiers happier. James and Jean Michel were leaving their wives in Yarpole. Both were with child and I knew that both men at arms would be thinking of their families as we rode to war.

I spoke with Robert, my Vintenar and my captain of sergeants on the village green as we supped Harry's ale and let the toil of training drip from us. "We have enough arrows?" Dai acted as a servant fetching us fresh drinks from the tavern.

Gwillim nodded, "We have four hundred made up but we have shafts and arrow heads for a thousand more. The wagon will be used to carry them."

"Spears and lances?"

Michel downed the wine he drank in lieu of ale. Harry kept a barrel just for Michel and his son. "Most of the men at arms prefer a spear. They are easier to use when we fight on foot and your plan, Sir Gerald, is for us to do just that."

"Aye, if men have to charge on horses then that will be Sir John and his retinue. When we were at Poole I met them and they all aspire to be knights."

Michel smiled, "There was a time when I wished so too. Now I am content to serve you, Sir Gerald."

I nodded my agreement, "I know that I was dubbed but I never asked for it." I turned to Robert, "You have all that you need?"

"I have. My salves are prepared. I have jugs of vinegar as well as many pots of honey. They will travel in the wagon. I have plenty of bandages and the animals you hunted gave me enough catgut. I will produce more when we cull the cattle. I have enough bone needles."

"Good then we are prepared."

"Yet, my lord, we do not know where our enemies are to be found."

"No, Dai, but Sir John will not be idle. He has a good archer in Dewi. Sir John knows not the land but his archers do. They will have scouted. I am confident that when we get to Poole they will have an idea of where our enemies are to be found."

Michel nodded and held out his goblet for Dai to refill, "And, my lord, you have a battle plan?"

I smiled, "That will largely depend upon the terrain. If we are lucky then I will choose the ground but wherever we fight, Michel, your men will be the front two ranks and my archers will be behind. There will be archers and men at arms with Jack and Hamo. We will have more than double the men with whom you train. Add to that Sir John's men and we have men who can hold our enemies at bay."

Dai had refilled the goblet and he said, "That is it, Sir Gerald? You merely hold."

"Dai, my archers can send a thousand arrows before you have counted to two hundred. They will winnow the enemy. They may not be the ones who decide the battle but they will give me the edge so that I know when to take the head of the enemy."

I let them take that in, Dai refilled my beaker, and I saw them thinking. In the case of Michel and Gwillim it was visualising the battles they had seen before and in the case of Robert and Dai it was trying to picture the scene.

Eventually, Robert said, "That wins the battle and, perhaps the war, but how will you win the peace? How will it ensure that Lady Hawise and Sir John win back all their lands?"

"We use the law. Just as de la Pole held Poole and the Lady Hawise to ensure he had that which he wanted we take the de la Poles as prisoner." I nodded at Dai, "Remember how I said that nobles were different from common men?" He looked at me. "That is how we win her lands back. We hold the de la Poles and their ransom shall be the agreement that Lady Hawise and Sir John have the right to rule Powis. There will also be ransom to compensate us for the efforts and expense of fighting this war. I am not a mercenary but our manors deserve reward."

My two soldiers understood such things but I saw scales falling from the eyes of Dai and Robert as they realised that I had thought beyond the lowering of the standards.

Knowing that I would be standing with my men at arms made me look at my hauberk and shield. The hauberk was well made but I took it and my coif to my blacksmith. I had ordered the spears, swords and arrow heads already but I needed a repair to my mail. There was a hole where the bolt had killed Morgan. It needed to be whole once more. "Check over every rivet and joint. I need this and my coif to protect me."

He smiled, "I will do so, my lord, but Lady Mary has paid for this for you." He went to a corner of his workshop and picked up a heavy sack. He carefully took out a brand-new mail hauberk. It was well made and the links were closer together than the one I had brought for repair.

"She paid for this?"

He nodded, "When you were delayed over the winter in Westminster," from his words I knew he understood what had gone on, "she told me that when you returned you would need a new hauberk."

I could not help but smile. My wife was a Christian but she believed in superstition too. The making of the new shirt was to ensure my return, a sort of sacrifice to the gods of war. She was paying for a hauberk so that they would free me from my gaol and I would be able to wear it.

"I will still need you to repair my old one. There will be times when I do not wish to dazzle my enemies with my new mail shirt."

"I will make it perfect, my lord. Do you wish me to make it shine?"

I laughed, "Vanity is not one of my sins." I nodded to the shield, "It is some time since I used the shield. It will need to have metal studs added and the leather replaced."

"Yes, my lord, my daughter Matilda has a good hand. I will have her paint your sign upon it." I took out some coins but he shook his head, "I do not go to war with you, my lord, nor do my sons. This is the least that we can do."

"No, Alf, that would be bad luck. A warrior pays for his weapons." He understood that and he nodded.

I returned to my hall, carrying the hauberk. I placed it on the table, "And what is this?"

She stood defiantly, "I know that you are a stubborn old man who will go to war no matter what I say. This is just to keep safe." She smiled, "Do you like it?"

"I love it but I pray that it stays in the sack!" I knew it would not.

I visited Hamo and Jack to see that their preparations were moving well and that they had all their tasks completed. Time was passing.

The horse master also had a surprise for me. It seemed that my time in Westminster had affected the whole village. While most prayed and hoped, others like my smith and horse master had been planning for my return. My horse master had bred a new horse for me. It was a courser and he had already schooled the animal. He had bred well and the horse had a greyish hue to its black coat. He had used the young animal to sire foals before gelding him. As he told me when he brought him out, I no longer needed an aggressive horse. "He is called Hope, my lord, for when you were away and all hope seemed lost this animal became a symbol of your return. I bred him five years since but I did not know his nature and so I kept him a secret while you were away with the king. I knew that Thunder would stand you in good stead but he is getting old and Hope is the future."

"And I thank you." I was genuinely touched by the affection my people had for me. I stroked his head and ear. I had always done that with the horses I had ridden. When he snorted and inclined his head towards me I knew we had a bond already. As soon as I mounted him I could tell that he and I were meant to be together. He responded to every movement that I made. I believed I could have ridden him with just my knees. When I urged him to gallop around my training ring he flew like an arrow from my war bow. His speed almost took my breath away. He would be able to outstrip even Thunder.

I dismounted and took the horse master's hand, "You have done a fine job and I am grateful."

"Yes, my lord, and we pray he keeps you safe. Already there are mares carrying his seed. When your grandsons are ready to ride then they will have his offspring."

Mary seemed more concerned with these preparations than any I could remember. When I had hunted Wallace she had not seemed as worried. One night I asked her about her fears. "Gerald, you are not a young man. Those white hairs on your face and thinning hair are testament to that. Your illness was a warning. What did not worry you when you were a young man are now dangers to be judged and considered. I know it is foolish to say so for you will ignore me but I pray that you take care. You have a wife, children and grandchildren that would see you grow even whiter and your belly fatter."

"And I intend to be there when they grow into men and women but I cannot change either my nature or my fate. If I do not lead the men to fight the de la Pole family then, I fear, that Lady Hawise will lose."

"Vanity is a sin, my husband."

"It is not vanity, Mary, I am good at what I do. God gave me gifts and I use them to the best of my ability. Do you think I am a good warrior?"

"I know that you are a good warrior but you are an old one."

"And that is why I shall use my mind more than my arms."

By the second week of September we had the fields cleared, the spring and winter crops sown and the animals were being culled. While we were away their meat would be salted, their hides tanned and their bones sorted into those we would use as tools and the ones we would burn on the bone fire to feed the soil. Animals were being trapped before they hibernated and both squirrel and rabbit, not to mention doves and pigeons would be eaten for the next month or so. Berries were collected. While some would be eaten most would be boiled and, using honey, preserved to enliven the duller diet of winter. Trees had been copsed and the wood stored for firewood. Rooves had been repaired in preparation for autumn and winter rains. Ditches were cleared to avoid flooding and both men and women worked just as hard as they had at harvest time. The difference was that the manor knew that the warriors, their lord and their healer would be going to war. As we walked through the village, visited the tavern or prayed in the church we were watched, for people knew that this might be the last time that they saw us. My men were not considered, as they were in many manors, as oppressors, they were friends. While no words were spoken, eyes said their goodbyes. Prayers would be said both in church and in bed chambers for our safe return and those thoughts gave me a warm feeling within. The young archer who lived for the moment was long dead and he had been reborn as Warbow, lord of the manor.

Warbow

We left Yarpole on the autumn equinox. We were not like those who consulted astrologers for propitious dates, it was just that it was the right time. My steward, my Vintenar, my healer and my Captain of Sergeants all told me that the manor was ready and so we left for Poole and the Welsh border on a bright autumn morning. The air was crisp and there was a slight breeze. I had Dai ride behind me with my banner in the stirrup holster and it fluttered in the breeze. My men at arms wore my livery. The hose, tunics and surcoats were freshly laundered and bright. My archers wore their hose and hats that marked them as Warbow's men and the people cheered as we passed. Harry raised a goblet of ale as a toast and Father Michael blessed us. There were tears. Some of my men at arms and archers were courting maidens in the village and it was they who wept. The road felt empty once the cheers and waving arms disappeared. We kept the flag flying but we rode in silence. There was just the steady clip clop of the horses and the creak of the wagon as we headed to Lucton. Hamo was also going directly to Lucton and we would leave for Wales from there. The reason was simple, it gave Hamo more time with his family before he left. As his son and Jack's would be coming with us, for their mothers this would be a tearful time.

We paused only to allow Jack and Hamo's men to fall in with ours before we headed for Hopton Castle. Some of the archers brought by Jack and Hamo walked. They walked quickly but it would necessitate an overnight stop at Hopton. The men camped in the outer bailey but my sons and I were given chambers.

It was while we ate that Lady Hopton asked a question that I had not expected, "Sir Gerald, I would ask a favour of you."

"Whatever you wish, my lady. We are in your debt as it is."

"My son Walter was to be my husband's squire." She shook her head and made the sign of the cross, "God took him too soon. As much as I do not wish my son to suffer wounds, one day he may have to defend this manor. He is not trained and cannot fight but I would, if you will allow, have him accompany you, with Captain Edward, so that he can see what a lord of the manor has to do."

Her question made me study the youth. He was about the same age as Dai had been when I had rescued him. He had more meat on his bones but I could see that his hands were soft. He had not been trained at all.

"My lady, war is a dangerous business. I would happily take him but I cannot guarantee that, in the heat and press of battle, he does not suffer some hurt."

She looked at her son who spoke, "Sir Gerald, I should have begun training two years since and I have not. Captain Edward has promised to begin my training. I have a sword, a helm and a metal studded jack. My horse is a good hackney and whilst I am not yet a warrior I can ride. Captain Edward suggested this and he has promised my mother that he will do all in his power to keep me safe. He and I will take care of my safety. I will be there to observe you, your sons and the Welsh youth you keep at your side."

"Then if you will accept my lack of guarantee then I accept. We ride on the morrow." I rose, "And I will speak with Captain Edward. If this was his idea I should like to know what was behind it." I did not care if they thought I was being rude. I did not want to take a callow youth to war for I wanted no more deaths on my conscience. I saw Hamo and Jack smile for Lady Hopton was taken aback.

"Of course, Sir Gerald, he will be in the kitchen dining with the servants."

I headed for the kitchen and heard the laughter as I approached. When I opened the door I was hit by a wave of heat from the fires and all talk ceased. I took in that the cook or housekeeper was seated next to Captain Edward. The food looked to be the same as we had eaten but was on wooden platters and the spoons were wooden too. There was ale on the table and they drank from beakers. It was the same in my kitchen. He stood, "Sir Gerald, is anything amiss?"

I shook my head, "No, Captain Edward, but you and I need to speak."

I saw realisation dawn, he rose and nodded, wiping his hands on the cloth over his shoulder, "My lady spoke to you."

"She did."

He squeezed the hand of the cook and dropped his cloth on his platter, "I will finish this later, Jane."

"I will keep it warm, Ned."

Captain Edward said, "Let us go to the gatehouse, my lord."

We said nothing until we were at the gatehouse. With my men in the castle there was no need for sentries and it was deserted. I said, calmly, "Is this wisely done, Captain Edward?"

He sighed, "I should have asked you myself, my lord, warrior to warrior. For that I apologise but young Walter needs to see what war is like. His father was ill for a long time and I was remiss. I should have begun his training. Since we hunted the assassins I have put that to rights and he has been given sword and spear work. It is a journey that will take time. I believe it will be a speedier one if he watches you and your men."

"I cannot watch out for him…or you. Neither can my men."

"I know, my lord, and I would not have any of you risk your lives for us. I believe that you will win. The day we hunted those killers was the first time I saw you fight. I confess that I had seen an old man before you drew first bow and then sword. You are a warrior. Sir Walter was not a real one. However, if fate is against you and I think you are losing then I will take young Walter and flee. You have my word on that."

"You swear?"

He nodded, took out his sword and kissed the crosspiece, "I swear."

I smiled, "Then you can both come." I put my arm around his shoulders, "And now let me take you back to Jane, Ned. I think she is more than just another servant of Hopton Castle?"

"Her husband was Morgan. She and I are close for Morgan was my friend. I am too old to be wed but..."

I nodded, "In the Danish manner."

He said, "Just so, my lord. This night is a sort of goodbye."

"Then I wish you well."

I was a little happier after our talk but I still fretted that night as I slept in Hopton Castle. It might have been the strange bed but I did not sleep well. The result was that I rose long before dawn. I went to the kitchens and found Jane there. She smiled and curtsied, "You are up early, my lord."

"I did not sleep well." I held her gaze, "I do not wish your Ned to suffer the fate of your husband. I am sorry for your loss. He was a good man."

She made the sign of the cross, "God has taken my husband. I now have Alwyn only."

"And Ned."

"And Ned." She cut me a slice of freshly baked bread and began to smear butter on it as she spoke, "How does Lady Warbow feel about you going to war, my lord, if you do not mind the impertinence?" She took some of the ham she was frying and placed it on the bread.

I smiled, "So long as you feed me with such delicious looking food, be as impertinent as you like." She smiled and poured me some ale. I bit into the ham and bread. The butter had melted a little and, mixed with the fat from the ham, dripped down my chin. I did not care. It was just the kind of food I loved. "My wife does not want me to go to war but she knows that I must. Lady Hawise deserves my sword."

"And she knows that you are a warrior and you want to do that which you are good at." I had just taken another mouthful and I just nodded. "It is the same with Ned. He has been a warrior for years but until you came to seek out the killers he had not drawn a sword. I know he grieved over the death of Morgan but he was a different man when he returned to the kitchen. He spoke of you and your deeds. If this is one last chance for him to be the man he should have been then who am I to stop him?"

Warbow

I had finished the food and after washing it down with dark beer I nodded, "You are a good woman and I now know that this was meant to be. I will do all that I can to make sure you do not have to bury another man. Two is two too many."

She impulsively kissed my greasy hands, "My lord, you are noble. I pray that God watches over you."

"As do I."

We left with three more men than we had planned for Stephen came to watch their horses. They would not fight, or at least I hoped that they would not fight but wearing the Hopton livery they might give my enemies pause for thought. At a distance it would look like three more men at arms. Any doubt I could put in the mind of the de la Pole family could only help us to win.

Chapter 17

I rode Thunder into the town while one of my archers led Hope. My new war horse would not be used until we battled, if and when we battled. I looked at the small town as we rode through. The settlement of Poole had not changed materially. The hall and its walls were still the same. The towers had weathered that was all but there was an air, as we rode through the town, of purpose. The people waved as we passed their farms and homes but quickly resumed their work. Sir John had made a difference. He, his squire and Richard Davidson rode out to meet us. His men kept a good watch for they had been forewarned and had the time to saddle and mount their horses.

"Sir Gerald, I thought your men might use the site of the new castle as your camp. My hall is too small for this mighty retinue and I have had my men preparing it for you. We have made a bread oven and there is plenty of grazing."

I know many lords would have been offended at having to camp but I applauded Sir John's practicality. "I am more than happy." I turned in my saddle to introduce the three men that Sir John did not know, "and this young lordling is the heir to Hopton Castle, Master Walter Hopton and his captain of the guard Edward, with a man at arms, Stephen."

"You are all welcome and we are grateful for any aid." He leaned over and said, "While your men settle in you and I need to talk, Sir Gerald."

"Of course, Sir John."

I waved my arm to signal the move and we rode in silence towards the rising ground that would, one day far in the future, be Powis Castle. To a stranger who had never visited it then there would be little apparent difference from the site we had inspected the last time we were here but I saw the changes. I spied the beginnings of the walls. They rose from the rocks although at the moment they almost blended into the rocks that naturally lay there. I saw the stone oven that lay close to where the keep would be. It stood out for it was man made. I also saw the men toiling over the digging of foundations. There were soldiers and the people of Poole.

"It moves on apace, Sir John."

"It is slow work and had I not had to send my scouts out to find the enemy then we might have built more. As it is, this looks like the most we can do before winter. We can dig out the lines of the foundations and then leave the masons to work on the blocks when the weather allows."

Warbow

I knew that a Welsh winter would limit those number of days. "My men can work until it is time to take the de la Pole family to task." We stopped and I said, "Hamo, Jack, make camp." That was all I needed to say. They were both experienced campaigners as were my men.

We dismounted and while Robert went to inspect the work in progress and my men began to make their camp, Dai took the reins of Thunder and I walked with Sir John to stand where the keep would be, looking west. I saw Walter Hopton watching all that went on. He was being given a master class by my sons in the arranging of a camp.

"Now we are alone, Sir John, speak openly." There was just his squire with him.

"I now command two hundred men." I raised my eyebrows in surprise. He smiled, "If you take away my oathsworn and the men who guard my hall then it is just one hundred and fifty local men who are keen and eager to defend our land but little more."

"And I bring small numbers but they are soldiers of quality. Thirty-eight archers and twenty men at arms are my retinue." I smiled and pointed to Robert, "And a healer."

"That means almost eighty archers. However, Dewi and Arwen apart they are Sunday afternoon archers."

"No matter. We have forty archers who can send five arrows before a man can count to ten. That will thin out an enemy."

He pointed to Walter Hopton who was standing and watching the busy men I had brought working as one, "And what is his story? I do not recognise the livery."

"He is the heir to Hopton Castle. His mother wishes him to observe war. He will merely be here to confuse our enemies." Although I feared a little for the young man I knew that the strange livery would confuse the de la Pole family. Confusion and doubt were two good weapons to use.

"Ah."

"So where are our enemies to be found?"

"Dolforwyn Castle is less than twenty miles from here and they have garrisoned it."

I had known that there were small castles close by and I knew that they might be seized. Castles needed only small garrisons and yet they could control larger areas. "How many men?"

"Not enough to trouble a determined attacker. We would need to build rams and the like but it is not well maintained." He smiled, "It is bait, for the bulk of the men of the de la Pole faction are at Caersws to the southwest." I waited, "He has, we think, at least five hundred men at Dolforwyn Castle and Caersws. As you predicted most are mercenaries.

They have many Irish. The brothers themselves share, according to Dewi, just forty in their retinues."

"You say bait? Why?"

"They have made no secret of the garrison there. They flaunt their flags and have men riding openly almost as far as here. We have chased them back enough times to almost know their identities. That is how we know they have many Irish. They have cursed us in their language; I came to know it when I served with the Lord Lieutenant. So far no blood has been shed. When we near their walls they taunt us. They want us to attack."

I finished his sentence, "And when we do they will spring the trap."

"Just so."

"I take it there are spies?"

He pointed to the north of the woods where we had scouted, "They have men there. You cannot see them now and if we rode close they would flee. We let them think we cannot see them for they just watch."

"So they will report my banner."

"Almost certainly."

"Let us make them think we are complacent. I will have my men labour with yours to get as much done as we can. You say they often ride to taunt you?" He nodded. "Then when my presence is reported here they will, I expect, send men. I will chase them back and then, when I return, we will raise our banners together here. It will trumpet our intention to attack."

"You will attack Dolforwyn Castle?"

"We will make them think we attack it." I pointed to Walter Hopton, "And he will help us with our deception. This is my plan." I made my plan up as I spoke to Sir John although, in truth, I had been nurturing it in my head on the way to Poole as I ran through all the choices that were open to me. The news given to me by Sir John had refined the plan in my head. I preferred to be in command for then all the decisions rested on my shoulders and I would not have to suffer the incompetence of another. If we lost then it would be my fault. I had no intention of losing. He offered suggestions and by the time Hamo and Jack strode up to ask us what the men ought to do we had it. I refined it whilst telling it to them. Their smiles told me that they thought it a good plan. "We keep the plan to ourselves until I deem it is right to tell the others. I trust our men but as we know, Sir John, there are spies in Poole."

That decided, I was given a tour of the building work. Robert estimated that it would take three years to completely finish the castle but that it could be made defensive in a little over a year. "When spring comes I would suggest, Sir John, that you begin the donjon. You can keep masons working over winter cutting the stone for the building work. That way it will not take long to build the inner bailey and curtain wall for much of the stone will be ready and on site. The outer wall and outer bailey will take more time especially as there are more buildings to fit in."

Jack shook his head, "You are a healer and yet you could have been an architect. Is there nothing you cannot turn your hand to, Robert?"

He smiled, "I cannot fight."

"You fight for us with a most powerful weapon, Robert, your mind." I put my arms around my sons, "And with these two you need not fight. The blood of Warbow is belligerent enough for any man."

We set sentries from our men. There was a practical reason for that. We needed them to be familiar with the layout of the future castle. It would be their home while they were here. I thought it unlikely but there was a possibility that we might have to defend the building site from enemies. Sir John and my sons insisted that I sleep in Poole Hall. I went reluctantly with Robert and Dai but as we rode back to Poole, Robert said, "This is better, my lord. Your sons are now the leaders. When you are there they walk in your shadow. You have often told me that one day you will hand over the reins to your sons. This gives them the chance to lead the horse, albeit at a walk."

Sir John said, "And a wordsmith too!"

When I left the hall I did not do so before dawn as was my wont normally but I waited until people were about. I also took the time to dress in my old mail. I had worn it when I had first come and I wanted the people of Poole and their spy to be able to identify it. I needed spies and scouts to see me and when I reached the camp I made sure that Hamo warned my men so that I could be welcomed. It was not for vanity but to let the enemy know that I was here and I had brought my men. I strode around the camp, ostensibly studying the building work but, in reality making it quite clear to the watching enemy scouts that Warbow was here and in command.

Walter Hopton was here to learn and he was a curious youth, "My lord, what is the purpose of these perambulations? I am a callow youth but, as far as I can tell, there is no real purpose to them."

Dai was also with us acting as a sort of unofficial bodyguard for the young noble. His eyes darted around for danger but I could see that he was curious too. I smiled, "The men I brought are reinforcements but our enemies will not know if I come to fight, build or simply defend. Their scouts will have counted the campfires my men lit last night. De la Pole and his brothers are half a day away and by now they will know our numbers. We know theirs but they do not know that. By strolling around

I am familiarising myself with this land and giving them a good view of me. I believe that within the next day or two they will make one of their forays to draw us to their walls."

I was silent until Walter said, "And you will go?"

"I will go and we will rattle our swords and, perhaps, send a few arrows at them to make them believe that we are angry and intend to attack them."

"And will you?"

I tapped the side of my nose, "Master Walter you are learning but let us take baby steps, eh?"

Captain Edward, who never left the young heir to Hopton's side chuckled, "Sir Gerald is a clever man, young Master Walter. These lessons will stand you in good stead when you inherit."

"Captain Edward, I have a handful of men and Sir Gerald has a large retinue. It is not the same."

"And my retinue has been built up over the years, Master Walter. When I first came to Yarpole, before my sons were born, I had a man at arms and half a dozen archers. The wars I fought against the Scots and the Welsh necessitated increasing the numbers and we did that by being more successful than our enemies and using the gold and silver that we won to increase numbers. You have more men than I began with. Your journey as their leader begins now. When you inherit the title and the land you need to decide how best to spend your income."

I saw his mind taking that in.

To the surprise of Walter I joined Sir John and our men to help build the walls. I had Dai help me to shed the hauberk and I worked in cambric shirt and breeches. There would be no Lady Mary to complain about the stink of sweat. There was a simple crane that lifted the large blocks of stone into position. While three or four of Sir John's spearmen were needed to hoist a block, Hamo and I did it alone, easily. I enjoyed the physical labour. For September it was relatively warm. I also saw Walter watching me as I ate and drank the same food as my men. When he went to make water, accompanied by his shadow, Dai, Captain Edward came over to me, "My lord, in one day I can see a change in the young master. It is as though the scales have fallen from his eyes. I think he thought a lord of the manor hunted, hawked and took part in tourneys. You have shown him a more workmanlike lord."

I nodded, "There are many who do hunt, hawk and joust, Edward."

"Yes, my lord, but they are not border knights." He paused, "There will be fighting, will there not?"

"Oh, yes, Edward," I tapped the side of my head, "the fight is already here in my mind. Within the next days I will know where the battle is to take place."

"A battle, my lord?"

I nodded, "We need to return to Yarpole and the last thing we need is a winter wasted watching each other. That is like a boil that festers. I will burst the boil before that can happen. Blood will be spilt but the land will be healthier because of it. You and the youth will be back in Hopton by Christmas."

It was the next day, not long after we heard the bell for sext, that the riders came. I still had my mail hauberk on. Our archers acted as sentries and their horns warned us of the approach. As soon as we heard them I shouted, "To horse!"

The men at arms ran to their waiting horses and mounted. Dai raced ahead to hold Thunder's reins as I climbed into the saddle. With Sir John at my side and Jack behind we led the men at arms to chase the riders who had halted, in plain view but beyond arrow range. That they were waiting for us to chase them was clear. Captain Edward had arrested the motion of Walter. They would stay with Hamo and Robert at the building site but Dai rode behind me, the furled standard in his hand almost like a weapon. We did not ride hard but merely kept the men in sight. They were close enough to count; there were twenty of them and half were mailed and rode coursers.

I turned to talk to Sir John as we rode, "This is what normally happens?"

"It is but we usually turn back about now."

"Then they will see our pursuit as intent on my part. Dai, when I give the command then unfurl the banner."

I had given Sir John an outline of what I planned but not the detail. I was the only one who knew exactly what I would do when we reached Dolforwyn Castle. I knew that it had belonged, after its capture from the Welsh, to the Mortimers. How the de la Poles had got hold of it I did not know but it explained the enmity of the Mortimers towards the de la Poles. I knew when we neared the castle for it rose above the surrounding land, built upon a platform of rock. The horsemen galloped through the gates which slammed shut and I saw the de la Pole standard fluttering above the ramparts.

We reined in and I held up my hand for the men who were following me to spread out in a line. We were out of the range of all but the best archers. I was curious as to what they would do and I took the time to study the walls and defences. I had no intention of attacking them but for my plan to work they had to believe I would. I had to appear to be studying their defences. It was not a large castle but one designed to control the river and the land around it. There was a rectangular keep at the southwest end of the castle and a circular tower at the opposite end. The two defensive structures were connected by ramparts, to make a rectangular enclosure with a D-shaped tower on the northern wall. The main gateway into the castle was in the west wall.

I turned to Sir John. "They have a sally port?"

"There is a small gate in the south wall. I believe that they have a ditch in the middle of the castle to protect the keep." He smiled, "They have no well and that is why they cannot afford a siege."

"Good, then it is time." I rolled down my coif and said, "Dai, the banner."

As he unfurled it I rode forty paces closer to the walls. I held my right hand with the palm showing to let them know I intended to speak and I came in peace. I knew that I was taking a risk but I had to know what sort of defence they would offer. When I was stopped I pulled back on the reins and stood in the stirrups to make Thunder rear. His black coat glistened in the September sunlight and his teeth flashed white against it. They would remember the war horse. It was a deliberate gesture to make them think that I was being arrogant. I was not, I was playing a part and that part would help in my deception.

I shouted, "I am Baron Gerald Warbow of Yarpole. I am Lord Edward's Archer and I am here as the representative of King Edward II, the master of these lands." My words were carefully chosen. I waited a moment and then said, "And who commands here?"

A bare headed man appeared on the walls and shouted, "I am Gwilym de la Pole and we do not recognise the authority of your king and we are certainly not afraid of a fat old man who can no longer draw a bow." The men on the wall laughed and jeered. The man was younger than Gruffydd and he had said the words for the benefit of his men; he was making himself look and sound superior to me. I feigned anger at his words, "You dare to insult me and my king! I will wreak such a vengeance on you that the land will run with blood and I will tear down the walls of Dolforwyn Castle stone by stone."

I almost laughed at my own words but they worked for he shouted, "You will bleed your last here in Powis, the land of the de la Pole family."

He lowered his hand and I saw the crossbowman rise and level his crossbow. The worst thing I could do was what he expected and turn and run. If I did so then my back would be a good target and I would be hit. I waited until I heard the snap and then jerked Thunder's reins to the right. I saw the blur of the bolt as it came at me but my movement meant that it would pass to my left. I flicked up my gauntleted hand as though I was swatting a fly. Luck was with me and when I fortuitously struck the flight and it veered away the men behind me cheered.

"Treacherous curs! We will return and I will take back the lands stolen from Lady Hawise ferch Owain ap Gruffudd ap Gwenwynwyn." I then turned my back and rode back to the waiting riders.

Jack shook his head, "Father, that was a risk you did not need to take."

"I was in no danger. I knew where he aimed and I assumed he was the best of their crossbowmen. I was at the extreme range and I trust my mail. As soon as I heard the snap then I could move but what it does tell me is that they do not have good archers. If they had then I would be a dead man. Let us return home. We give them two days to stew and then we return." I smiled, "Or the besieging army will return."

That night I had Sir John invite Hamo, John and Walter Hopton to dine in Poole. It was time to give them my plans. Robert and Dai were already staying in the hall and I used them, along with Captain Edward, to watch the doors. I trusted Iago and his people but I wanted no spy to secretly enter the hall and hear my words. Lady Hawise watched me as I spoke. I waited until the food had been finished and every eye was upon me.

"My plan is a simple one but it involves trickery. I would rather be a trickster than waste men's lives." I saw Lady Hawise nod. "Master Walter, you will be the one who leads the men of Poole to the walls of Dolforwyn Castle." I saw his eyes widen. I wagged a finger at him, "You are not there to be in any danger. As well as Captain Edward and Stephen, Jean Michel and James will be with you to ensure that you do not get within crossbow range of the walls. You will ride out of range of any crossbows. What you will do is ride around as though you are commanding the men who pretend to besiege the castle."

"Pretend, my lord?"

"Pretend, Walter of Hopton. I do not intend to fall into their trap. They want me to besiege their castle so that they can then launch their real attack on our camp. None of the men I send to the castle will have to do any fighting. They are there to draw the eyes of the enemy to us there."

Lady Hawise said, "You are using the people of Poole as bait?" I heard the anger and surprise in her voice.

"There will be no danger to the people for once the riders have ridden to Caersws with the news I will put my army, my real army, in their line of march and we will bring them to battle. I will not risk an ambush where they might evade us. I will draw them onto our swords and we will end this tyranny once and for all."

She smiled when she realised that the danger would not be to her people but her warriors and mine.

After we had left the walls I had ridden with Sir John and four good men towards Caersws. I had found a place, just under four miles from Caersws where the Severn was close to the main road and there was a wood which afforded protection. It was as good a place to fight as any. I had scouted but, unlike the enemy, done so unseen.

Jack said, "But, Father, if you are not with the army then they will suspect something."

I smiled, "But I will be there, or at least Captain Edward will be there wearing my armour, riding Thunder and Stephen will carry my banner. When we fight, we fight under the banner of Sir John Charleton and his family, the rightful rulers of Powis."

Walter said, "But the last time someone did that, he died."

I had spoken to Captain Edward already and he was happy at the deception. "And Ned, Captain Edward, knows that. Your captain will not be in danger. He and Morgan were friends. He and Morgan's wife, Jane, are together now. It is meant to be." I saw that he had no idea about the liaison. I understood it. "He will keep his helmet on and will not get close to the walls. I do not think that there will be any within the castle of rank. The de la Pole who spoke to us will leave another in command." I sighed, "Young Walter, this is another lesson for you. A man has to weigh up risks and make his decision. Vacillation is disastrous. Sir John and I are happy. You, Hamo and you, Jack, what do you think?"

Hamo smiled, "It will work. When Gruffydd Fychan de la Pole brings his army to destroy us he will have such a shock that no matter how few men we have he will be defeated."

The next day, when I visited the camp, I took aside James and Jean Michel to explain my plan, "You two will not be with the rest of my men at arms. You will aid the illusion that I am with the fyrd. You will wear your livery and guard Walter and Captain Edward."

They were both clever men and deduced my reason. James said, "This is because we are recently married! You do not wish to risk our lives."

"James, no one is safe from harm for the men at the castle could be hurt, but you are right. I need two men to tell the enemy that my men at arms are at the castle and you two suit. I am Warbow and I make the plans." My voice had enough steel in it for them to nod. They were not happy and they would grumble. They might even curse my name but I had promised Mary I would do all that I could to ensure that their wives did not become widows before they were mothers.

It took two days to muster the fyrd. We had plenty of arms for them. Sir John and his horsemen were at their fore. Captain Edward looked splendid in my old mail hauberk. He had learned to ride Thunder and, from a distance looked to be me for the cloak added to the bulk. The defenders would see what they expected to see; the same black horse that had reared ridden by the man with the same mail and the same helmet. He was flanked by Hamo and Sir John. When the time came the two of them would slip away and join us. I wore an old cloak to cover my new mail and was hidden amongst my mounted men at arms that were led by Jack. We waited within the walls of Poole Hall. The people of Poole all turned out to cheer away their men as they marched to war. It would take them most of the day to march the ten or so miles to the castle. The rest of the men and I would have plenty of time to make our way, through hidden paths and tracks, to the place I had selected. All eyes would be on the marching men and their spy would have left as soon as they did to send the news ahead. Lady Hawise played her part, waving tearfully at her husband.

We did not leave by the main gate. That was barred and servants, wearing warrior's livery, played the part of guards. We went, instead, to the gate we had boarded up. We tore down the boards and, after removing the newly mortared stones, we walked our horses through the narrow gateway into the wild land behind. We used the little stream as our guide and headed past the ridge with the building work and worked our way to the small road that led south and east. We would have a longer journey but we were mounted. My mounted archers acted as scouts. Their noses would sniff out danger. When we crossed the main road that had been used by Sir John, Captain Edward and the rag tag army that he led, we saw no one. We skirted the road that led to the castle and only when we were south of it did we leave it to head across country to the place I had chosen to give battle. Robert and Dai flanked me. I knew that Robert would be making a mental map in his head. He always did.

The scouts reported that a rider had ridden south on the road ahead from the direction of the castle. They had taken the bait.

We reached my battle site before dark but not much before. I had my scouts dismount and then check that the road was empty. It was. There would be no fires and it would be a cold camp. Our army was laughably small but we had confidence. While my archers cut saplings to make stakes to embed before us we watered our horses and cut brambles to make a night camp.

Hamo and Sir John rode in an hour after darkness had fallen. Sir John had his mesne with him. He dismounted and I asked, anxiously, "Well?"

Hamo laughed as he dismounted, "Sir John has missed his vocation, Father. He could have been a travelling actor giving shows in inns. He stormed up and down our lines berating an unfortunate called Captain Ralph. It is good that there is no one of that name in the army. He said that the fool had left the wagons with the siege equipment back in Poole and he would have to return for it. He even apologised to Captain Edward, as though it was you. He rode north in a flurry of hooves with his men and, while those on the walls watched them, I slipped south and waited for him."

"It was your plan, my lord, and a good one. I was determined to do the best that I could. Will they believe it?"

"No one passed us from the direction of the castle and so it matters not. The ploy was, perhaps, unnecessary but better to plan than merely to hope. Now we wait. My archers say the road is clear. Iago and Gruffydd are half a mile from Caersws and they will give us warning of an enemy. Until then Robert will shrive any who need it and we can rest, for tomorrow, I hope, we shall see the battle that wins your wife's inheritance back."

Chapter 18

The sentries reported nothing in the night. We had a good watch on the camp but I deduced that the de la Pole family must have thought we had fallen for their trap. Their spies, not to mention the men in the castle, would have reported a large army led by Warbow and Sir John Charleton heading for Castle Dorfwyn and would spring the trap at their leisure. We had not raced to get to the site I had chosen for the battle and the snake of mailed men heading for their castle would have been clearly seen. The scouts' report told me that all was going to plan. We ate cold food but drank fresh ale provided by the good people of Poole. The night had been one for reflection. I had sat with my sons, Sir John, and his closest men and squires. They were more nervous than we were for this would be the first time that Sir John had fought under his own banner. He had fought, as had his men, in Ireland but they had not been battles. This would be a battle albeit a small one. My plan was to make our enemies think that we had even fewer men than they expected. Half of my archers would be hidden in the trees. I had foregone the original plan to use the wagon. I wanted mobility and we had mounted all my archers. That they rode the diminutive Welsh hill ponies was immaterial. The animals had brought them close to the enemy and that was enough. We had carried our arrows in bags and sacks. My wagon was at Dolforwyn Castle. My banner was atop the wagon bed and, should a disaster strike, then Jean Michel and James could defend Captain Edward and Walter.

"Sir Gerald."

"Yes, Richard?"

Richard of Davidson felt that he could speak to me. He had been with us on the Canterbury road and as his father was an archer then there was a connection. "You think that the bulk of the enemy army will be mercenaries?"

I nodded, "When he tried to retake Poole, he used such men. He can use the promise of the gold that they will loot and he has the lands of Powis that he has taken to lure them too. He is gambling that he wins this encounter and then takes Poole."

"Is that a good thing, my lord?"

"I prefer to fight alongside men who fight for a cause. Men who fight for money always make me suspicious. Most will have been paid before we begin to fight. What is to stop them from running?"

One of the men at arms, Wilfred said, "We seem to have a small number of men, my lord."

"That we do but in my experience it is not the numbers that determine the outcome of battles but the quality of men. We have quality."

Sir John said, "I know you have told us but, for me, let me know again the plan."

"We array my men at arms and those of my sons before our archers. Half of our archers will be in the trees and hidden. You and your men will be ready and mounted on your horses."

He shook his head, "I know we have increased our number but there are just twenty of us and that includes my squire. Will that be enough?"

"There will be twenty-one for I will join you."

Hamo and Jack snapped their heads around. Jack said, "I thought the plan was for you to draw the enemy to you."

"And it will. Once the arrows have winnowed them and you and our men at arms have halted their progress, Dai will sound the horn and I will leave the front line."

Hamo said, "You want them to think that you are fleeing."

I nodded, "It is what Gruffydd Fychan de la Pole did when his attack on the hall failed. Men who know me know I would never flee but I want the leader of our enemies to think I am made of the same base metal as he. When I run I will mount Hope and then turn to lead Sir John's men and charge." I nodded at Jack, "You and the men at arms will follow my flight back and shelter before the trees. The trees become our castle and our sally will seek to take the head of the Hydra."

Robert said, "A fine plan but, as one who will not have to fight or draw sword, I can see many places where it could go awry."

"As can I, Robert the Healer. I will have to hope that God does not want me yet."

Those words had ended the discussion and, I hoped, dispelled the doubts. I had faced Gruffydd Fychan de la Pole before. I did not know his brothers and half-brothers but I knew the leader and I believed that I had his measure. He had bullied Lady Hawise and there was just one way to deal with a bully, stand up to them. I would use our apparent weakness and ally it to his arrogance.

Before I had retired I had walked to the Severn with Robert. It was an ancient river and revered by the people who had lived here before the Romans. It was a good place to be shriven. I took off my boots and rolled up my breeches. I walked into the water which despite the time of year felt icy. I bent my head and told Robert of my sins. I included vanity amongst them for I knew that I had such self-belief that it amounted to vanity. I did not think we would lose. Later, with dried feet and a lightness in my step, we had walked back to the camp. The shriving and the icy water of the ancient river made me feel happier.

Warbow

Men had fought by this river since the time before the Romans. The ancient people believed that it was a living thing. Such beliefs might appear blasphemous but I had seen more of the earth than most priests. God worked in mysterious ways and I felt his power in the river. I was not a religious man but it felt as though I had been baptised again.

The last thing Robert said, as I rolled into my blanket was, "I will pray for an hour, my lord, for more hangs on the outcome of this battle than your apparent vanity. I would not have Lady Hawise lose all so close to the victory for which you hope." I slept well knowing that my priest was speaking to God on my behalf.

I was up before dawn. It was not nerves, it was the need to make water.

Iago and Gruffydd rode in during the midmorning. Throwing himself from the saddle, Iago said, "They are coming, my lord. They march with fifty crossbowmen at the fore, on foot." He spat and I smiled. "They have forty mounted men at arms and it looks like more than three hundred spearmen. There are a mixture of men and weapons. There were some gallowglasses from Ireland and low life Welsh and Englishmen; the mounted men at arms apart, they are little more than bandits in my view."

"And their leaders?"

"There are six men wearing fine mail and with full helms on their head who follow the crossbows. They lead their army. The six are riding war horses but we saw no spurs."

I turned, "Then it is time. Trust to God and the right that is our cause."

I took my helmet from Dai as well as my shield and my spear. I walked with Jack and the other men at arms to stand between the stakes. We had not embedded them in the road. For one thing it would have been too hard and for another we wanted to draw them to me. The road narrowed and it would negate, somewhat, their numbers. I stood next to Jack and John. Michel was on the other side of Jack. We filled the road and the four men at arms on each side of our line had the protection of the stakes we had embedded. In my shadow stood Dai with a short sword and a horn. His buckler was strapped to his back. He had the bulk that was Gerald Warbow as a shield. Behind us were Hamo and my archers.

We heard the enemy before we saw them. The road was not Roman and it twisted and turned. They were still some miles from the castle and they were confident. There was laughter and chatter as well as the noise of hooves. We were stonily silent. I knew that the sight of us would shock and surprise them. It was a weapon I could use.

Warbow

It was the enemy crossbowmen who saw us first. They were mercenaries, although as the man who led them rode a horse, I guessed that they were one company of hired crossbows. They were just five hundred paces from us, where the road bent around some trees. They immediately halted and I heard shouts. Horns sounded and hooves clattered up towards us. I had chosen the place for the battle as best I could. We had the narrow choke point. The river to our right prevented us from being outflanked there and the trees and rising ground to our left allied to the embedded stakes meant the only place they could use their horsemen was with a frontal attack. They had room to deploy on a wide front but I had deliberately made our lack of horses look to be a weakness. That the ground was not totally flat also helped us rather than them.

Their leaders emerged and stood peering over the top of a double line of crossbowmen. They were not using pavise. That was a mistake. They had loaded their weapons already. The conference took longer than it would had I been in command but that reflected their leader. The plans made, the rest of the army was brought up. They began to form up their lines. The spearmen, gallowglasses and dismounted men at arms formed three ranks. I saw the forty-six horsemen form two lines behind the infantry. I think that the mercenaries had been drinking for the Irish gallowglasses screamed and shouted insults at us. They waved their fierce two-handed weapons in the air. Two of them pulled down their breeks and bared their buttocks. We were impassive and stood in silence. Those men in their army armed with a spear and a shield banged the hafts of their spears on their shields to make a cacophony of noise. It was as much to give themselves courage as it was to try to frighten us.

Jack said, quietly so that only I could hear, "Those Irish men have terrifying weapons."

"Aye, they do, Jack, but they wear neither armour nor helmets and they are wild men. Trust to the skill of our men and the accuracy of our arrows."

They were eager to get to grips with us but the crossbowmen looked to be reluctant. The leader of the army, I recognised his livery, it was Gruffydd Fychan de la Pole, turned his back on us to address them. His voice was lost on the wind but I guessed he was exhorting them to deeds of valour and, from the reaction of the mercenaries, promising them loot. He turned and, raising his sword, tried to rear his horse as he waved his men forward. He almost over balanced but he kept his saddle. The line advanced.

The crossbows would release their bolts first. Jack said, "Ready shields."

Warbow

I heard Hamo say to our archers, "I want the field before the Warbow littered with their dead. I care not if we use every arrow we have. They will die!"

The crossbowmen needed to be within two hundred and fifty paces of us to ensure that they hit us. That was well within the range of my archers. The best archers were behind me and led by Hamo. Those would be the ones who would do the most damage. The others, hidden in the trees, were there to hit the men on foot when they closed with us and they would be the surprise. As soon as the crossbowmen stopped and knelt then we knew what they were about to do. They had wide brimmed kettle helmets that would give some protection to their heads and their necks but their shoulders and chests were unprotected.

"Draw!" As the bows creaked back I heard, "Loose!" The next command of 'Nock' was lost as the strings twanged and the arrows whistled over our heads. There were no more orders needed. Men would draw and release as fast as their arms and skills would allow them. I did not hear the answering crack from the crossbows. I was peering over the top of my shield at the enemy and I saw the blur of bolts. A number of crossbows never got to send a bolt as the arrows crashed into the men operating them and when the second and third showers struck them they were defeated and even as a few crossbow bolts cracked into shields I knew they had lost the short duel. I saw the survivors of the arrow storm, with just helmets for protection, take their weapons and try to flee. The gallowglasses did not wait for an order. They knew that they had to cover the three hundred paces as fast as they could. I daresay they had estimated the arrows and gambled that most of them would reach our thin line and crash through it losing just a handful of men in the process. They had not reckoned on archers in the eaves of the trees. They ran, screaming ancient curses and battle cries. The fleeing crossbowmen disrupted their line and even without my archers, I knew that they would not reach us in a cohesive manner. However, such was the ferocity of their charge that I was glad that I was surrounded by my oathsworn for they were strong enough to withstand the charge and not flinch. This was not the measured attack of enemy knights and men at arms such as I had witnessed at Lewes and Evesham, this was a primitive warband intent on butchering us.

Hamo and his archers thinned them but it was when Hob, commanding the archers in the trees, shouted, "Loose!" that the destruction began in earnest. The extra arrows made a hailstorm of goose feather fletched ash and poplar. The war arrows tore into bodies and wreaked horrific damage there. These were brave men and the strongest element of the de la Pole army. Some came on with two and in one case three arrows in their bodies. They were mortally wounded but some primitive instinct made them come on. However, when they neared the stakes then they were all funnelled into a narrower front. Men fell as they were struck in the side by the warriors seeking a more direct route to us. As men fell they were trampled. Some, wounded by arrows, died at the feet of their brothers in arms. The other mercenaries had more mail and were behind the gallowglasses for they were slower and more measured in their approach. It was they who did for the wounded and the prone as they trampled over them.

Twenty or thirty of the gallowglasses made our line but by then they were no longer a mass of men. They were individuals and they were running into a hedgehog of spears. We would normally have collided together as lines of men but these twenty or thirty were spread out. I rammed my spear into the neck of the screaming warrior whose bare chest was spattered with the blood of others. He had raised his two-handed sword when he was twenty paces from me and while his chest was an inviting target I had seen his fellows still ready to fight when stuck with arrows. I wanted a quick kill. It was almost as though he did not see the shining spearpoint for his eyes widened in anticipation of slicing my skull in two. I thrust hard, with all the power of an archer who could draw a mighty war bow. His head jerked back and I saw the light leave his eyes. The sword fell behind him. I twisted the head and retrieved my spear, aware that I now had a barrier before me.

I prepared for the next man and saw that there was a line of ten men coming purposefully for me. They had shields, helmets and leather jacks but they were armed with swords and not spears.

Jack took command. I could have given the order but I had entrusted the command to my stepson. When I fled it would be he who marshalled the retreat. "Spears, ready!"

We each pulled our spears back as the line came at us. The new mercenaries were forced to come carefully, negotiating the bodies before them. They had endured the arrow storm on their approach and the survivors were huddled together with shields now held before them. This was all a matter of timing and Jack, standing next to me, was a clever man who had been taught well by my captains of arms and he understood the timing of an order. As the mercenaries clambered up on the prostrate bodies bleeding before us he shouted, "Thrust." Our spears moved as one. That was their strength. A man can avoid one spear. He can move his head or raise his shield but many spears coming at your face and body is a disconcerting event. Some men reacted correctly and managed to block or even partially block the spears but many did not. My spear smacked hard into the shield of the man before me and although he blocked it by angling his shield, that action ended the life of the man next to him for the spear slid into his side. John had even more success. His spear went into the mouth and skull of a Norman wearing a nasal helmet. The nose piece afforded him little protection from the spear that entered his brain and made him die quickly. The man in the second rank who had a spear himself saw his chance as John tried to withdraw the spear head. It caught on the nasal and the spear came at my son's brother-in-law. The arrow that was sent from behind was on a horizontal trajectory and was a bodkin. It slammed into the helmet and skull of the spearman. Hamo and my archers were just twenty or thirty paces from the enemy. When their arrows struck, they were fatal.

Then the bulk of the attackers struck. They had seen the funnelling effect of the stakes and someone had ordered them to raise shields and form a wall to protect them from the arrows. They could not move quickly but they would be able to push us back. Even as I surveyed the advancing men I saw a man at arms on the end of our line fall. Two archers pulled his body back. It was almost time for my command. I said, over my shoulder, "Are you ready, Dai?"

"Yes, my lord, three blasts and then run for the trees."

"Aye," I growled, "and do not let his old man catch you!" I heard him chuckle, "Hamo, are you ready?"

"Aye, Father. We wait on your command."

The enemy struck our line and we buckled a little but thanks to the stakes and the armour my men wore we held. As more men pushed into the backs of the wall of men so would the pressure increase and, eventually, we would break. I had planned on breaking the line myself.

I heard Hamo shout, "Archers, hold."

The arrow storm stopped and the enemy would think that we had run out of arrows. It was not an uncommon occurrence in battle. However, this was a trick for we had plenty.

"Dai!"

The horn sounded and, naturally enough the men who were pushing to get at us slowed for they knew that the horn told them some order had been given. We all thrust with our spears as the last note sounded and then turned. Dai, Hamo and my archers were already running to the trees that were forty paces away. It was a risk turning our backs but Hob was ready. On Hamo's order he had ordered his archers to stop sending arrows. I knew what these archers would be feeling. Their muscles would be burning but the brief pause would have a dramatic effect. I heard him shout, "Draw!" Hamo and the other archers were almost at the trees. I headed for the horsemen waiting, almost unseen by the enemy. Dai was already there and holding Hope's reins. "Loose!"

The men who had suddenly found their enemy gone had been given, they thought, an opportunity to win and they ran. Their cohesion was gone. Shields slipped down as they raced to get at the prize that lay ahead. We had bare backs. The arrows that slammed into them were like a wall of steel. Men fell and I heard a voice shout, "Lock shields and hold." It was a Welsh voice and told me that someone still maintained control.

Sir John was visored and his mail gleamed. His lance had a gonfanon streaming from it and the horses of his retinue stamped and snorted in anticipation of battle. These were warhorses. Dai took my spear and shield as I mounted Hope. He handed them back to me and I nodded, "Ready, Sir John!"

He shouted, "Dai, sound the charge!"

There were only twenty-one of us and that was a pitifully small number for a charge. We were aided by a number of things. One was that our horses were fresh, the second was that they were not expecting it, but the most important thing was that Hamo and my archers were in position and, with arrows already nocked, Hamo shouted, "Loose!" Their arrows were sent at such a close range that shields and helmets afforded no protection. They tore through metal as though it was parchment. They ripped into bodies and they demolished the men who were blocking the path we would take. I was next to Sir John and Richard Davidson flanked me, and Sir John's squire, Hugh of Gainsborough, was the only one in what might be termed a second rank.

This was the first time I had ridden my new warhorse into battle and he did not disappoint. He began to edge ahead of Sir John. Lady Hawise's husband had a full-face helmet and did not notice but my open helm gave me a good view. Hamo's arrows had ceased but they had done their job. The men who stood before us were leaderless. The Welshman who had tried to stabilise the line must have been dead and while there were still more men left to face us than were in our entire army, their leaders still waited behind them. Men do not like to face horses at the best of times but waiting to be struck by charging warhorses needs nerves of steel. These were mercenaries and were the ones who had not been reckless and charged us. They tried to get out of the way and my spear plunged into their backs and bodies. I thrust and pulled as Hope galloped on. War horses are trained to trample. It goes against a horse's nature but Hope had been schooled well. I reined him back a little for it was important that we kept a solid line.

I found myself laughing. We had twenty men at arms and a squire. More than ten times that number were facing us and yet none opposed us. I shouted, "Sir John, make for the standards."

"Aye, Sir Gerald."

I did not want the joy of our charge to go to his head. My plan only worked if we took the head of the hydra. They had forty horsemen yet and that was twice our number. Would they form a line and protect their six leaders? As we closed with them I saw the men on foot before them evaporate and move to the sides. That may have been ordered by the horsemen, I could not hear but it was then that they made a cardinal error. They waited. Had they begun their charge then it might have ended differently, but they did not. I saw the horsemen turn and, I guessed, ask for orders. When their horn sounded and the forty men began their charge it was too late. Our twenty horses were at full gallop. My reining in of Hope had brought cohesion to our line. We had lances and spears couched and our shields were held close to our bodies. Crossbow bolts might have succeeded but the men with those weapons were long fled. Their horsemen began to move faster but they were trying to do a number of things at once. They were spurring their horses, trying to keep one line and they were moving shields, spears and lances into position. Crucially, their leaders were not joining the charge.

Behind me I heard Dai's horn sound as Jack and Hamo ordered the charge. My men at arms and archers would fall upon the disrupted enemy. Men would be relieved that they had been neither trampled nor speared. They would not expect men on foot to attack them. We were twenty-one men charging greater numbers but soon we would have support.

I concentrated on making a good strike at the man I was charging. He had a full-face helmet and wore a hauberk with a red surcoat. His heater shield also had a plain red coat. He was a mercenary. His horse was not a warhorse. It was one bred from a courser and a hackney. It was a workmanlike horse but it was no Hope. While Hope wore a leather shaffron on his head, his horse had no protection. Hope stood at least three hands higher and, as we closed and the horse was urged to go faster, I knew that while Hope would not deviate from his line the mercenary's mount would veer. The question was which way? I moved my reins slightly so that I would be spear to spear with him. I hoped that would encourage his horse to move away. Hope was now a head ahead of Sir John's warhorse and that decided me to continue with my plan. I pulled my arm back as we closed. Hope was at full tilt and the mercenary was at a canter. Hope opened his mouth to snap at the mercenary's mount and, as we closed the horse did what I anticipated, he moved to his left and as I thrust, my spear went beneath the mercenary's spear, into his mail and sank into his body. His spear scraped along my upper right arm. Alf had made a good hauberk and the spear slid along the mailed links and did no harm. He fell from his horse.

I barely had time to pull back my arm to strike at the next rider. He had seen his companion fall and turned his horse so that we would meet shield to shield. I scarcely had the time to switch my spear and thrust. If I had not had an archer's arm the result might have been different. As it was I had enough power to smash into his shield and make him lose balance causing him fall to the ground. Richard Davidson, on my left had the easiest of kills. The mercenary never saw the lance drive into his chest. My success was almost my undoing for even as I looked for my next opponent a mercenary saw his chance and rode at my right-hand side. My spear was facing the wrong way and his broad headed spear came at my unprotected right side. I swung my spear around and almost managed to block the blow but the strikes I had made and the sharpness of his spearhead broke my spear just behind the head. His spear came at my side but I had deflected it enough to minimise the effect. It punched into my side. I would be bruised but Alf had done a good job. I hurled the broken haft at the man and Sir John drove his lance into the man's chest. I drew my sword and spurred Hope. There were no more mercenaries between me and their leaders. The six of them stood waiting, they were almost impotently observing the destruction of their army. I saw the face of one, I did not recognise him, and I saw the incredulity on his face. Even as my sword came from my scabbard and I galloped towards them I saw the man turn his horse and flee.

I knew then that we had won but a simple victory was not enough. We needed the leaders of the de la Pole family in our hands. I recognised Gruffydd Fychan de la Pole and as I hurtled towards him I roared out a challenge, "Fight me, you cur, and let us end this now."

In answer he and two of the men with him wheeled their horses and fled. The other three did not move. I wanted Gruffydd Fychan de la Pole but to get at him I had to pass the three men before me. As I spurred Hope I saw their livery: Or, a lion Gules armed and langed Azure. As I had explained to Dai that meant a red lion with a blue tongue on a gold background. The other symbols told me that they were his brothers. Gruffydd Fychan de la Pole was the elder. The red crescent, mullet and martlet told me they were his younger brothers and half-brothers.

I pulled my sword back and swung it at the warrior with the red star on his shield. He did not have a lance and he brought his sword around to sweep at me. Our swords crashed into the shield of the other almost at the same instant. I felt his arm reel. I barely felt his blow. That was partly the well-made shield I held and also the weakness of his strike. His reeling allowed me to swing again. This time there was no responding blow as he was trying to control his horse which was attempting to avoid Hope's teeth. I stood in my stirrups and brought my sword down on his helmet. He managed to bring his shield up to partly block the blow. If he had not done so then he would have been a dead man.

"I yield. I yield."

Hugh of Gainsborough was behind me with drawn sword. I said, "Hold this prisoner for me, Hugh of Gainsborough."

I saw that Sir John had unhorsed the warrior with the martlet on his shield. Sir John said, "And this one also, Hugh."

The warrior with the mullet had fled to follow his brother and Sir John and I, with Richard Davidson in close pursuit, hurtled after him. He was clearly terrified and constantly looked over his shoulder. It was a mistake and when his horse put a hoof into a hole in the road and dipped its shoulder he was thrown to the ground. He rose groggily and the three of us surrounded him.

"I yield."

"And you yield all claims to the land of your niece?"

"My brother left those to me!"

Sir John put his sword to touch the nose of Llewellyn de la Pole, "That is a lie. He left his lands to his children and if you wish to dispute that we can put it to God and have a trial by combat."

He shook his head, "I yield my claim."

"Richard, bring this man and his horse back to our lines."

"Yes, my lord."

We both wheeled our horses. The flight of the de la Poles and the ferocity of our attack had won the day. Those who could had fled while the rest laid down their weapons and threw themselves on the mercy of our men. They would enjoy a better fate than my men if they had won.

We reined in next to the other two brothers. They were seated on the ground looking most unhappy. Sir John had taken off his helmet so that his words would be clearly heard, "Do you yield your claim to the lands of my wife Lady Hawise ferch Owain ap Gruffudd ap Gwenwynwyn?"

The two were surrounded by the lances and spears of Sir John's men and they both nodded. "I want to hear the words!"

They chorused, "We yield our claim."

He pointed his sword at the warrior with the red mullet on his surcoat, "And you will pay ransom to Sir Gerald Warbow?"

The warrior nodded, "I will."

It was only then that Sir John raised his sword, "Victory! God has shown whom he favours and we have the right!"

Warbow

Our men all cheered. It was a fine victory. The flight of Gruffydd Fychan de la Pole had taken some of the gloss from the victory but we had recovered three quarters of Lady Hawise's lands and I was sure we would be able to restore the rest. I was content.

Epilogue

It was the twelfth of October when we eventually rode through the gates of Yarpole. For once we returned from war without losing a man. We had men who had been wounded but thanks to the presence of my healer they were not maimed and he was confident that by the time it was spring they would be fully healed. Dolforwyn Castle had surrendered the day after the battle when we displayed our captured three de la Poles. Walter of Hopton had enjoyed his first victory without unsheathing his sword. We spent some time at Poole while the ransoms were paid and the three brothers signed and sealed their acceptance of the status quo. The Bishop of Hereford, Adam Orleton, was sent for so that they could swear allegiance to the new Lord of Powis, Sir John Charleton and also witness the documents. Sir John knew how to manage things.

Walter Hopton, Stephen and Captain Edward left first. I had made a lifelong ally and friend of the man who would, one day, inherit the vital border castle. I could see a difference in his body as he rode with his two men to head for Hopton Castle. My sons and their men followed a day later. They had done their duty and they had taken purses and weapons from the battlefield. They were content. I stayed longer but that was at the request of Lady Hawise. She was keen to show how grateful she was to me and my men. Robert was happy at the delay. He was able to help Sir John with the building of the new castle. It was the torrential rain that made us leave. We could no longer work and we did not want the Severn to burst its banks and become a barrier. This time as we left the people of Poole, despite the weather, all turned out to cheer the handful of men who had defended them against an oppressor.

Dai had ridden ahead to warn my wife and, as we entered the yard, our people were there to greet us. We had done our duty and Warbow and the men who had followed him had shown the border that he was not yet ready to put his sword above the fireplace.

The End

Glossary

Banneret - the rank of knight below that of earl but above a bachelor knight
Bachelor knight - a knight who had his own banner but fought under the banner of another
Cannons - metal armour for arms
Caparison or trapper - a cloth covering for a horse
Carter's Bread - dark brown or black bread eaten by the poorest people
Catgut - the natural fibre made from the intestines of animals
Chepe - the market in London
Chevauchée - a mounted raid
Centenar - commander of one hundred men (archers)
Familia - household knights of a great lord
Gardyvyan - a bag containing an archer's equipment
Hogbog - a place on a farm occupied by pigs and fowl
Liberty - a unit of men which was independent of the regalian right
Mainward - the main body of an army (vanguard- mainward- rearguard)
Manchet - the best bread made with wheat flour and a little added bran
Martlet - in heraldry, a bird
Mêlée - in battle, a confused fight or a combat between knights at a tourney
Mullet - in heraldry, a star
Othenesberg - Roseberry Topping, North Yorkshire
Poole - Welsh Poole
Raveled or yeoman's bread - coarse bread made with wholemeal flour with bran
Shaffron - a metal plate to protect a horse's head
The Danish manner - a marriage without a priest (living together)
Tithe - a tenth
Vintenar - a commander of twenty men (archers)
Wallintun - Warrington
Wapentake - a Saxon term for the fyrd or local muster
Westhalton - Westhoughton (Greater Manchester)
Wrecgsam - Wrexham

Canonical Hours

Matins (nighttime)
Lauds (early morning)
Prime (first hour of daylight)
Terce (third hour)
Sext (noon)
Nones (ninth hour)
Vespers (sunset evening)
Compline (end of the day)

Classes of hawk

This is the list of the hunting birds and the class of people who could fly them. It is taken from the 15th-century Book of St Albans.
Emperor: eagle, vulture, merlin
King: gyrfalcon

Warbow

Prince: gentle falcon: a female peregrine falcon
Duke: falcon of the loch
Earl: peregrine falcon
Baron: buzzard
Knight: Saker Falcon
Squire: Lanner Falcon
Lady: merlin
Young man: hobby
Yeoman: goshawk
Knave: kestrel
Poor man: male falcon
Priest: sparrowhawk
Holy water clerk: sparrowhawk

Historical Note

This novel concentrates on the interaction my fictional Warbow had with the life of the very real Hawise the Hardy and I make no apologies for that. Her story is a remarkable one and it deserves the telling. The occupation of her lands by her uncles is true. It is also true that she met the king twice at Shrewsbury and petitioned him there. It was she and not the king who nominated Sir John Charleton as her champion. I have changed the facts to suit the story. They did marry in July 1309 and as Sir John served the king in Ireland until spring 1309, then my story, incredible as it might seem, is the only one that fits the facts. She cannot have met him before 1309 as he was serving the king and was in France for a time when the king married his French queen. He was a slightly older knight and I used my imagination to have them falling in love and marrying. Her uncles had planned on sending her to a nunnery and perhaps the life with a man she barely knew seemed preferable. They married on the 26th of July 1309 and had a son, John, and a daughter, Isabella. It took until 1320 for all of her lands to be recovered. Sir John became Lord of Powis. He had to fight Hawise's uncles to stop them from retaking her manor. That the king did not interfere might be explained by his preoccupation with Piers Gaveston. It was not until Gaveston's death in 1312 that the preoccupation was brought to an abrupt conclusion. It was Sir John Charleton who began the building of Powis Castle. Little remains of his castle. There is a gatehouse and the range near the stables are the only parts. It became a bastion against incursions from the west. It remained Welsh but with an English knight in command it meant England had a toehold in Powis.

When I finished '*The Prince and the Archer*' I planned on this being the last book in the series. Sir Gerald was not quite ready to hang up his bow. The story of Lady Hawise and Sir John intrigued me so much that what might have been a chapter became a novel. I make no apologies for that. I think that the story of Hawise the Hardy needed telling. That story is not yet ended. It will not be until 1320 that her lands are all restored. There was a battle between Sir John Charleton and the de la Pole family. Gruffydd Fychan de la Pole was the only one of Lady Hawise's uncles to avoid capture.

Books used in the research:
Edward 1st and the Forging of England - Marc Morris
The Normans - David Nicolle
The Knight in History - Francis Gies

Warbow

The Longbow - Mike Loades
The Norman Achievement - Richard F Cassady
Knights - Constance Brittain Bouchard
The Tower of London - Lapper and Parnell
Feudal England: Historical Studies on the Eleventh and Twelfth Centuries - J. H. Round
Peveril Castle - English Heritage
Norman Knight AD 950-1204 - Christopher Gravett
English Medieval Knight 1200-1300 - Christopher Gravett
English Medieval Knight 1300-1400 - Christopher Gravett
The Scottish and Welsh Wars 1250-1400 - Christopher Rothero
Lewes and Evesham 1264-65 - Richard Brooks
Cassini Historical Map 1840-43, Liver Poole

Griff Hosker
March 2025

Warbow

Other books by Griff Hosker

If you enjoyed reading this book, then why not read another one by the author?

Ancient History

Roman Rebellion
(The Roman Republic 100 BC-60 BC)
Legionary

The Sword of Cartimandua Series
(Germania and Britannia 50 A.D. – 128 A.D.)
Ulpius Felix- Roman Warrior (prequel)
The Sword of Cartimandua
The Horse Warriors
Invasion Caledonia
Roman Retreat
Revolt of the Red Witch
Druid's Gold
Trajan's Hunters
The Last Frontier
Hero of Rome
Roman Hawk
Roman Treachery
Roman Wall
Roman Courage

The Wolf Brethren series
(Britain in the late 6th Century)
Saxon Dawn
Saxon Revenge
Saxon England
Saxon Blood
Saxon Slayer
Saxon Slaughter
Saxon Bane
Saxon Fall: Rise of the Warlord
Saxon Throne
Saxon Sword

Medieval History

The Dragon Heart Series
Viking Slave *
Viking Warrior *
Viking Jarl *
Viking Kingdom *
Viking Wolf *
Viking War*
Viking Sword
Viking Wrath
Viking Raid
Viking Legend
Viking Vengeance
Viking Dragon
Viking Treasure
Viking Enemy
Viking Witch
Viking Blood
Viking Weregeld
Viking Storm
Viking Warband
Viking Shadow
Viking Legacy
Viking Clan
Viking Bravery

Norseman
Norse Warrior*
The Dragon Rock

The Norman Genesis Series
Hrolf the Viking *
Horseman *
The Battle for a Home *
Revenge of the Franks *
The Land of the Northmen
Ragnvald Hrolfsson
Brothers in Blood
Lord of Rouen

Warbow
Drekar in the Seine
Duke of Normandy
The Duke and the King

Danelaw
(England and Denmark in the 11th Century)
Dragon Sword *
Oathsword *
Bloodsword *
Danish Sword*
The Sword of Cnut*

New World Series
Blood on the Blade *
Across the Seas *
The Savage Wilderness *
The Bear and the Wolf *
Erik The Navigator *
Erik's Clan *
The Last Viking*
The Vengeance Trail *

The Aelfraed Series
(Britain and Byzantium 1050 A.D. - 1085 A.D.)
Housecarl *
Outlaw *
Varangian *

The Conquest Series
(Normandy and England 1050-1100)
Hastings*
Conquest*
Rebellion*

The Reconquista Chronicles
(Spain in the 11th Century)
Castilian Knight *
El Campeador *
The Lord of Valencia *

The Anarchy Series
(England 1120-1180)

Warbow

English Knight *
Knight of the Empress *
Northern Knight *
Baron of the North *
Earl *
King Henry's Champion *
The King is Dead *
Warlord of the North*
Enemy at the Gate*
The Fallen Crown*
Warlord's War*
Kingmaker*
Henry II
Crusader
The Welsh Marches
Irish War
Poisonous Plots
The Princes' Revolt
Earl Marshal
The Perfect Knight

Border Knight
(1182-1300)
Sword for Hire *
Return of the Knight *
Baron's War *
Magna Carta *
Welsh Wars *
Henry III *
The Bloody Border *
Baron's Crusade*
Sentinel of the North*
War in the West*
Debt of Honour*
The Blood of the Warlord
The Fettered King
de Montfort's Crown
The Ripples of Rebellion

Sir John Hawkwood Series
(France and Italy 1339- 1387)
Crécy: The Age of the Archer *

Warbow
Man At Arms *
The White Company *
Leader of Men *
Tuscan Warlord *
Condottiere*
Legacy

Lord Edward's Archer
(England in the thirteenth century)
Lord Edward's Archer *
King in Waiting *
An Archer's Crusade *
Targets of Treachery *
The Great Cause *
Wallace's War *
The Hunt*
The Prince and the Archer*
Warbow

Struggle for a Crown
(1360- 1485)
Blood on the Crown *
To Murder a King *
The Throne *
King Henry IV *
The Road to Agincourt *
St Crispin's Day *
The Battle for France *
The Last Knight *
Queen's Knight *
The Knight's Tale *

Tales from the Sword I
(Short stories from the Medieval period)

Tudor Warrior series
(England and Scotland in the late 15th and early 16th century)
Tudor Warrior *
Tudor Spy *
Flodden*

Conquistador

Warbow

(England and America in the 16th Century)
Conquistador *
The English Adventurer *

English Mercenary
(The 30 Years War and the English Civil War)
Horse and Pistol*
Captain of Horse*

Modern History

East Indiaman Saga
East Indiaman*
The Tiger and the Thief

The Napoleonic Horseman Series
Chasseur à Cheval
Napoleon's Guard
British Light Dragoon
Soldier Spy
1808: The Road to Coruña
Talavera
The Lines of Torres Vedras
Bloody Badajoz
The Road to France
Waterloo

The Lucky Jack American Civil War series
Rebel Raiders
Confederate Rangers
The Road to Gettysburg

Soldier of the Queen series
(1876-)
Soldier of the Queen*
Redcoat's Rifle*
Omdurman*
Desert War*
An Officer and a Gentleman

The British Ace Series

Warbow

(World War 1)
1914
1915 Fokker Scourge
1916 Angels over the Somme
1917 Eagles Fall
1918 We will remember them
From Arctic Snow to Desert Sand
Wings over Persia

Combined Operations series
(1940-1951)
Commando *
Raider *
Behind Enemy Lines*
Dieppe
Toehold in Europe
Sword Beach
Breakout
The Battle for Antwerp
King Tiger
Beyond the Rhine
Korea
Korean Winter

Rifleman Series
(WW2 1940-45)
Conscript's Call*

Tales from the Sword II
(Short stories from the Modern period)

Books marked thus *, are also available in the audio format. For more information on all of the books then please visit the author's website at www.griffhosker.com where there is a link to contact him or visit his Facebook page: Griff Hosker at Sword Books or follow him on Twitter: @HoskerGriff or Sword @swordbooksltd
If you wish to be on the mailing list then contact the author through his website: www.griffhosker.com

www.ingramcontent.com/pod-product-compliance
Ingram Content Group UK Ltd.
Pitfield, Milton Keynes, MK11 3LW, UK
UKHW021322270825
7605UKWH00014B/146